Duets

**Two brand-new stories in every volume...
twice a month!**

Duets Vol. #93

Wendy Etherington is back with a fun, fiery
Double Duets about the crazy Kimballs of Baxter,
Georgia. These characters create sparks—and
trouble—wherever they go! This author made
"an impressive debut with *My Place or Yours?*,
a beautifully written story featuring a scrumptious
hero," says *Romantic Times*. Enjoy!

Duets Vol. #94

Dorien Kelly kicks off the month with
The Girl Least Likely To..., a quirky story about a
heroine nicknamed Horrible Hallie, who's
determined to change her reputation. Look for
Dorien's linked Temptation novel in April 2003—
#922 *The Girl Most Likely To...* Sharing the volume
this month is Intrigue author Delores Fossen and the
delightful *The Deputy Gets Her Man*. Heroine
Rayanne will do anything to get her Aunt Evie out of
jail—but could she really date the *arresting* sheriff?

Be sure to pick up both Duets volumes today!

The Girl Least Likely To...

"You're making me nervous," Hallie stammered.

Steve grinned at her grudging admission. The preppy Polo shirt she'd smirked at earlier was lying on the floor. There was nothing to smirk at now. Not that broad, tan chest with just the slightest dusting of golden hair. Definitely not the six-pack abs.

"Now, I think we should carry this a little further, don't you?"

"No, really, I..." His hand was closing over the button at the top of his jeans and she was babbling. Her gaze was riveted to the button coming open, but as his hand moved to the zipper below, she squeezed her eyes shut.

Temptation whispered to her. *So what do you think, is it boxers or briefs? Or maybe nothing at all...*

"Now we're a little closer."

Hallie forced herself to open her eyes, but couldn't look beyond his face.

"I dare you," he joked.

She sent her gaze on a journey south.

My, oh my...

For more, turn to page 9

The Deputy Gets Her Man

"At least we agree on something!" Rayanne exclaimed.

"You bet we do," Rios concurred. "That's why I've thought about us just making love and getting it over with." He continued before she could make her outraged mouth produce a response. "But having carnal knowledge of you won't make anything go away. Well, it might temporarily, but I don't think we're talking more than a half hour or so at the most. So, the way I see it, this is something we'll have to learn to deal with."

"Deal with? What the heck does that—"

"I have to go. Evie will be up by now."

Rayanne's gaze fired to her watch. "Heavens, you're right." Intent for the jailhouse, she grabbed her bag, but stopped. "I trust you won't be around when I get back."

"Never can tell. The world's chock-full of surprises."

"I've already had my surprise quota for the day. The year," she quickly corrected.

Rios begged to differ. The surprises were just beginning.

For more, turn to page 197

HARLEQUIN DUETS

ISBN 0-373-44160-6

Copyright in the collection:
Copyright © 2003 by Harlequin Books S.A.

The publisher acknowledges the copyright holders
of the individual works as follows:

THE GIRL LEAST LIKELY TO...
Copyright © 2003 by Dorien Kelly

THE DEPUTY GETS HER MAN
Copyright © 2003 by Delores Fossen

This edition published by arrangement with Harlequin Books S.A.

® and TM are trademarks of the publisher. Trademarks indicated with ® are registered in the United States Patent and Trademark Office, the Canadian Trade Marks Office and in other countries.

Visit us at www.eHarlequin.com

Printed in U.S.A.

The Girl Least Likely To...
Dorien Kelly

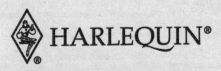

HARLEQUIN®

TORONTO • NEW YORK • LONDON
AMSTERDAM • PARIS • SYDNEY • HAMBURG
STOCKHOLM • ATHENS • TOKYO • MILAN • MADRID
PRAGUE • WARSAW • BUDAPEST • AUCKLAND

Dear Reader,

America is blessed with so many things, including small towns that embrace some of the most wonderful and unusual people you'll ever meet. I'm lucky enough to spend my weekends in such a place.

Hallie's Sandy Bend isn't real, but I'm hoping it gives you some flavor of my favorite no-stoplight, everybody-knows-everybody-else's-business paradise. If you enjoy your visit, be sure to return in April 2003, when Dana's story, *The Girl Most Likely To...* appears on the shelves as a Harlequin Temptation novel.

And, yes, I'm keeping the name of my town cloaked in mystery. After all, I'd hate for us to grow so big we'd have to get a stoplight! But if you're ever on the shores of Lake Michigan, look around and you might see a little bit of Sandy Bend.

If you think you've found my haven, drop me a line. I love hearing from my readers! Fellow e-mail addicts can write to me at Dorien@DorienKelly.com and check out my Web site at www.dorienkelly.com, too! My regular mail address is P.O. Box 767, Royal Oak, Michigan 48068-0767.

Wishing you Sandy Bend sunshine!

Dorien Kelly

Books by Dorien Kelly

HARLEQUIN DUETS
86—DESIGNS ON JAKE

For Kathi Kolosieki, Jaclyn DiBona and Sonja Baker—
writers, friends and guides through the craziness!

1

HALLIE BREWER liked to think of herself as a sophisticated woman—calm, cool and collected. Of course, she also liked to think the freckles marching across the bridge of her nose weren't very noticeable, and that her hair didn't go haywire in humid weather. One glance in the rearview mirror told her none of this was true.

It didn't help that her car's air-conditioning had given up the ghost in Nevada, and that she'd lost her courage somewhere around Chicago. Hallie shifted uncomfortably, trying to unstick her legs from the vinyl upholstery. She wasn't quite sure who had said you could never go home again. She was living proof you could, not that the trip was necessarily a comfortable one.

She passed a broad wooden sign that said, Sandy Be d Welcomes You. The *n* in Bend had first gone missing when Hallie was in sixth grade. After a few years, the Men's Club had given up on replacing it. They'd also given up on removing the magically reappearing red flag that read BANG! from the barrel of the old tank parked in front of the high school.

Hallie supposed she should take comfort from the fact that some things never changed, but that was also why she had stayed away for the past seven years. As much as she wanted to believe she had changed, maybe she hadn't. Coming back to Sandy Bend meant putting herself to the test, finding out whether beneath her glossy new exterior, she was still Horrible Hallie, stuff of Sandy Bend legend.

Horrible Hallie, who caught the village picnic shelter on fire while painting it.

Horrible Hallie, who at least once a summer, managed to sink a sailboard and simultaneously lose her bathing suit top.

Horrible Hallie, semicoordinated tomboy bane of the boys and favored insult target of the girls.

Nothing short of three thick-skulled, closemouthed men could have hauled her back from California to Michigan. Now that she was here, she didn't plan to stay one second longer than she had to.

Sandwiched between Lake Michigan and the broad, slow-moving Crystal River, Sandy Bend couldn't have grown if it wanted to—which it didn't. It appeared to be the same quaint, "no stop light, leave your doors unlocked" town she had fled after graduation. Luckily, it was also packed with its customary mid-June throng of tourists. Hallie pulled into one of the few open spots on Main Street. She pulled a brush from her purse and tamed her hair the best she could. Just to bolster her self-confidence, she applied lipstick and mascara, too. Better. If she wasn't quite Ms. Cosmopolitan, at least she wasn't the humiliated eighteen-year-old who'd hightailed it out of here a lifetime ago.

After detaching herself from her car's upholstery, she tried to camouflage herself by blending into a cluster of passersby. The more time she could buy before someone recognized her, the better.

"You're not the same person," she reassured herself, then headed into town.

As she walked down the block, Hallie noted a trendy clothing boutique where the hardware store used to be, and a coffee house offering iced lattes and Italian sodas in place of the pharmacy. There wasn't a vacant storefront to be found. It looked as though even Sandy Bend wasn't immune to progress.

"Hallie? Hallie Brewer, is that really you, all grown-up?"

So much for camouflage. Hallie focused on the elderly woman closing in on her with amazing speed. Olivia Hawkins had been tiny seven years ago. Now she was working her way down to sparrow-size. Still, Mrs. Hawkins had always ruled Hawkins' Foodland with an iron fist. She was no one to mess with.

Hallie stepped to the curb and pinned on a polite expression. "It's really me, Mrs. Hawkins."

"Well, this ought to put a little kick back in town." She chuckled, then fluffed the pink lace collar to a dress so small it had to have been purchased in the children's department. "I'll never forget that punch you made for the village holiday dance a few years back—"

"Twelve years," Hallie cut in. "A really, really long time ago."

"Substituting ketchup and water for red pop—"

She'd been desperate and not thinking very clearly. Only minutes before they were due at the dance, she'd discovered her brothers had chugged the pop she thought she'd hidden from them.

"Never saw people send punch out their noses before."

It was time to cut the reminiscing. If Mrs. Hawkins decided to dredge up every insane thing Hallie had ever done, they'd be standing there well past sunset. "Well, it was great seeing you, Mrs. Hawkins. You take care of yourself."

"And how about the time you…"

Hallie gave a catch-you-later wave, then slipped back into the stream of tourists and hurried down the sidewalk. At the police station, she broke from the pack and stepped inside.

Really, "station" was too generous a term to describe the little building with its two desks and minuscule lockup. One of the local lawmen was napping in a fifties-style wooden office chair. He looked wonderfully comfortable, with his feet propped up on the desk and an old issue of *Angler's Paradise* magazine draped over his eyes to shield them from that pesky daylight. It seemed almost a shame to disturb him. Except she'd sweated her way across the United States to do just that.

"Explain this," she demanded as she smacked a newspaper clipping onto the desk.

Angler's Paradise took flight and landed next to the clipping. Her brother Mitch scrambled to his feet. "Hallie? Wha—what are you doing here?"

She tapped one manicured nail on the article. "Explain."

Once, twice, Mitch's mouth opened and closed. The part of Hallie's mind that wasn't occupied by being furious with her big brother noted just how much he looked like the largemouth bass gaping up from the neighboring magazine page. Not that it detracted from the good looks all the males of the Brewer clan had.

"Here," she offered ever so sweetly, "let me help you with the tough words. It says 'Chief Brewer on the Mend.'"

"Uh…uh, yeah," he stammered. "It's no big deal. Really."

Wrong answer. "And I suppose it was no big deal that I found out Dad had a heart attack and surgery by way of an anonymous clipping in the mail from the *County Herald?*"

Mitch dragged his hand through his hair—a family gesture equal to an S.O.S. "Dad didn't want to worry you. He figured it would cost too much for you to come

home, and—'' He paused and blinked. ''Have you gotten taller or something?''

Actually, it was the ''or something'' that seemed to
have gained his attention. Mitch had never made it out
to California to visit her, and Hallie had been the classic
late bloomer. The curves she'd always yearned for had
arrived in her sophomore year of college. Better late
than never, she guessed.

''They're called breasts, Mitch.''

Color climbed her brother's face. ''Aw, jeez, Hallie.
You're my sister.''

''Yeah, and as long as we're on the topic of family
relations, Dad's my father. You'd think either Cal or
you could have picked up the phone and said something
like, 'Dad's not feeling too good. Maybe you'd better
come home for a while.' Or when I called last week,
you might have dropped a hint—just a *hint*, mind you—
of what was going on.''

Mitch took a cautious step backward, as if he didn't
have a good six inches and eighty pounds on her. ''It's
not like they cracked open his chest or anything.''

It was Hallie's turn to wince. ''A bit less graphic,
okay?''

''It was just a little heart attack and some angioplasty.
Cousin Althea's been taking care of him—''

Peachy. Althea Brewer Bonkowski was Hallie's
dad's cousin, and one wild number. She was also a
pretty sharp lady. At least now Hallie had a good idea
who'd mailed her that clipping.

''Althea left the commune?''

The corners of Mitch's mouth curved upward. ''Well,
you know what they say…you can take Althea out of
the commune, but you can't take the commune out of
Althea.''

Hallie smiled in spite of herself. ''She's not up to
anything illegal, I hope.''

"More otherworldly. Crystals and aromatherapy and chanting. She's driving Cal and me crazy."

"Not to mention Dad, I'll bet. That's got to be helping his heart a whole lot."

Mitch shrugged. "They're doing okay. Besides, it keeps him feisty, fighting with Althea. And you didn't need to come all the way here to check on him. You could have called and—"

Hallie shook her head. "Talked to the guys who didn't bother to tell me in the first place? I'm not taking your word for it, bro. I want to see Dad with my own two baby blues. I'm not going back to Carmel until I'm sure you guys have things under control."

"You doubt us?" He settled one hand over his heart. "I'm wounded, Hal."

"Don't call me Hal. You know I hate that."

Mitch gave her a crooked smile. "Doesn't fit quite like it used to."

Hallie snorted. "Flatterer." She hitched a thumb at the door. "I'm going to head out to the house now. You'll be home after you get off work, right?"

"Sure," she heard Mitch say as she turned to leave. Before stepping out, she paused to look at a community calendar to the right of the door. Advertisements for local businesses bordered the backing page, and assorted town dignitaries smiled from the space above the calendar sheets.

"You guys sure don't have any lack of ego, do you?" She smiled at photos of her dad—Sandy Bend's Chief of Police—and her brothers, who comprised two of the six town officers. Her gaze wandered past the mayor, then on to the school officials.

When she hit the photo labeled Principal, Sandy Bend High School, Hallie's heart plummeted to her stomach. Impossible. It simply wasn't possible. She tried to shape words, but her mouth was cottony and dry.

Life wasn't kind. Not at all. You'd think the guy could have grown another chin or two, or maybe been whacked with a little premature baldness. But, no, he was as golden and gorgeous as ever.

"You okay, Hal?" her brother asked. She vaguely wondered how long she'd been standing there, gaping.

"H-Hallie," she corrected automatically. Without taking her eyes from that photo, she dragged in a deep breath. "Uh, Mitch, you never mentioned that Steve Whitman was back in town."

That she'd even say this to the brother who considered a heart attack beneath mention proved just how floored she was.

"Didn't think you'd care," Mitch said. "Steve's always been Cal's buddy, not yours."

Hallie tried to shake off the shock. "Right," she murmured. "Of course."

Actually, according to Hallie's Rules of the Universe, *Steve* and *buddy* couldn't be linked in the same thought. *Steve* and *humiliation,* maybe. Or *Steve* and *the start of Hallie's pathetic track record with guys.*

Now that she'd spotted the picture, she had to know more, and it wasn't a good feeling. Asking about Steve was kind of like gawking at an accident on the freeway: Don't want to see, but can't look away.

"So what's he doing here?"

Mitch chuckled. "It says what he's doing right on the calendar. He came back a year or so ago and started teaching. Now he's principal at the high school." Her brother paused before adding, "Are you sure you're not jet-lagged or something?"

Hallie brushed away the damp strands of hair clinging to her forehead. She wished she could go back to being simply sweaty from the heat, instead of sweaty from nerves and a really sick and unacceptable sense of anticipation.

"No, I drove. I was kind of short on cash to fly," she said. "Isn't he young to be principal?"

Steve was the same age as her other brother, Cal— eight years older than Hallie. He was also a member of the trunk-slammer set, wealthy weekenders with expensive vacation homes on Lake Michigan. Just as the arrival of the robin heralded spring, with summer came the sound of slamming trunks as the weekenders unpacked. Heaven forbid they go without any luxury not attainable in Sandy Bend. Brewers, on the other hand, were work-for-a-living townies.

"Yeah, well, after the last principal retired, no one else was crazy enough to apply," Mitch said, coming to stand beside her. "Good thing Steve doesn't need a job to pay the bills. Last year's graduating class had only thirty kids in it. There's been lots of talk about consolidating the high school with Diamond Valley's. It's pretty much a lame-duck gig."

And Hallie was one dead duck. It was one thing to avoid old classmates, for fun and ego preservation. But the game shot to a new level with the knowledge that Steve Whitman was somewhere out there...her own ghost of disasters past.

Mitch settled a hand on her shoulder. "You're looking a little pale under those freckles, Hal. You want me to drive you out to the farm?"

Hallie shook her head. "I'm okay," she lied. "You got any diet pop?" she asked, then mentally added, *Or maybe a good stiff shot.*

"Sorry, nothing here but Cal's deluxe pond scum brew of coffee. You'd better try the Corner Café." He tipped up her chin and looked into her eyes, then gave a concerned shake of his head. "Let me grab my radio and I'll walk you there."

It had been years since she'd let anybody try to take

care of her. Before he could step away, Hallie hugged her brother.

"I've missed you," she said. Comfort seeped into her bones as his arms closed around her. No doubt about it, she had missed the hugs, the teasing and the protection of a big brother. What she hadn't missed—being Horrible Hallie—made this family longing all the more bittersweet.

"I've missed you, too, Hal. Welcome home."

After one last squeeze, she released him. Trying out her best cowboy swagger, she said, "You get your radio, pardner, then I'll get my pop and get outta Dodge."

STEVE WHITMAN knew that anyone who thought small-town life was dull hadn't spent time in Sandy Bend. Take today—this lazy, hot-enough-to-make-a-cold-beer-taste-like-heaven, summer day. It was paradise pretty much anyplace on the Lake Michigan shoreline. But only in Sandy Bend would you find the local cop walking toward you with a leggy brunette on his arm.

In full uniform, yet.

The cop, that is.

Not the leggy brunette. She was wearing a snug little yellow skirt just long enough to be legal and a white T-shirt that shouldn't have been sexy, but somehow was.

In the big city, old Mitch Brewer would have been in a tub of hot water for taking a stroll with his new honey while on the job. Here in Sandy Bend—where admittedly there wasn't a whole lot for the authorities to do—everybody would just look at Mitch and think, *Lucky bugger.* Which, not so coincidentally, were the two words ringing through Steve's brain.

Steve lengthened his stride. He needed to get close and see if this girl was as remarkably pretty as he thought, or if he was totally delusional after a year without a real date. Or even a pretend one.

The brunette was looking up at Mitch as though he could recite the human DNA map while bench-pressing three fifty. And, yeah, she was a knockout with long, wavy hair that seemed to pick up more shades of cinnamon and gold with every step she took. Freckles, too. Steve had always had a soft spot for women with freckles. Mitch Brewer was one Grade A, Certified Lucky Bugger.

"Hey, Mitch!" Steve called, wondering what intelligent chat he could work up to follow the "howdy, neighbor" greeting. All that kept coming to mind was, *Think you could introduce me to your girlfriend, and would you mind very much if I asked her out for a candlelight dinner and some dancing?*

Not that he had to worry about working up small talk or clamping down on idiot offers. For some reason, the brunette had stopped dead in her tracks, leaving Mitch to do a clumsy square dance swing around her. Steve's gaze locked briefly with hers. He was caught between wondering why she looked so damned scared all of a sudden, and if her eyes were really that blue, or if she was wearing some of those eye-color-altering contact lenses. One kid in school had them so that his eyes were silver and the pupils became slits just like a reptile's.

While Steve tried to unscramble his brain, the brunette's expression shifted from fear to anger to something that appeared to be downright dislike. All of it directed at him. Using Mitch like a shield, she backed her way into the narrow alley between Truro's Tavern and the Shady Sands Art Gallery.

Now, Steve knew the alley had been bricked off years before, and was only deep enough for the hot dog vendor to lock his cart behind the alley's iron gate each night. What the leggy honey was thinking, he had no idea.

He should just leave them alone, to whatever it was they were doing. Or more accurately, what she was doing. But he couldn't let the moment pass. He was a little nosy, sure, but that was the joy of living in a small town. Nosiness was written into the Village Charter. Besides, it bugged the stuffing out of him, the way she'd looked at him as if he was every mother's nightmare rolled into one.

The way Steve saw it, his biggest problem was that he'd been trained by his ever-so-socially-correct mother and sisters to be too nice. Too polite. And being both a Whitman and the high school principal meant the eyes of Sandy Bend were upon him. At least those were friendly eyes, though.

He didn't much like being on the receiving end of a squinty-eyed stare from a total stranger. Especially a very, very pretty one. No, he didn't think he could let this opportunity pass him by.

TRAPPED LIKE A RAT. Hallie could relate to the timeworn cliché. Steve Whitman was closing in on her, and there was nothing she could do. She wanted to give herself a swift kick in the rear for the idiotic move of ducking into the alley. And a second one for forgetting this wasn't a real alley.

It had to be something in Sandy Bend's air. She'd survived seven years in California without stepping outside the bounds of run-of-the mill embarrassing behavior—the occasional speck of food between the front teeth, wobbling off heels higher than she was accustomed to, that sort of thing. Less than a half hour back home and already she had ascended to the heights of Horrible Hallie-ness.

She stood surrounded by brick on three sides, and the

unnerving combination of her worst nightmare and favorite fantasy settled into the same tall, tan and muscled body lurked just outside her hiding spot. The mature thing to do would be to step out and offer Steve some witty greeting. But she wasn't feeling mature or especially witty. She was feeling dirty, sticky, tired and too darned stubborn to admit that she'd gotten herself into an impossible situation. She'd just stay right where she was until the cows came home. Or Steve Whitman left.

That was easier said than done, though. Mitch was proving tough to hang on to. Her fingernails were no match for the twill uniform covering his back. What had she been thinking when she coughed up the money for these dragon lady acrylic extensions? Unless she chose to anchor them straight into her brother's skin, all she could do was grab small bits of fabric between her fingers.

"You wanna let go now?" he asked, sounding more bemused than irritated.

"Shh, he's coming," she hissed. "Hide me."

"Hide you? For Pete's sake, Hal."

When he tried to shift away, she went up on tiptoe, wrapped her arms around his neck and muttered, "Oh, no you don't."

"Hey, Mitch, what's new?"

At the sound of Steve's unforgettable voice—deep and just rough enough around the edges to be sinfully sexy—Hallie leaned her head against her brother's broad back. Seven years should have been time enough to get past this silly, schoolgirl skipping of her heart. It wasn't, though.

"Uh, not much, Steve," Mitch mumbled. After that, Hallie counted off seconds of silence until she couldn't take it anymore. She nudged Mitch with her forehead, and he managed to spit out, "So, are you and Cal crew-ing on your dad's boat for the Chicago to Mackinac race this year?''

"Just like we have every year since we were sixteen."

Amusement danced in Steve's voice. Hallie was half tempted to peek out around her brother at him.

"Uh...great. Great. Should be a good time."

She could hear Steve's sneakers scuffing the pavement as he stepped closer. "So who's that hiding behind you?"

"Behind me?"

"Yeah, unless you've taken to wearing women's arms around your neck as some kind of fashion statement."

While Mitch stammered a big, fat mess of nonsense, Hallie closed her eyes and screwed up her courage. She knew that as heavenly as it sounded, she couldn't hide forever. She unwound her arms from Mitch's neck, dragged some air into her panic-constricted lungs, then moved next to him.

It was all she could do not to bolt down the sidewalk as Steve Whitman's admiring gaze traveled from the tips of her toes to her face. Their eyes met. In that instant, the niggling thought that had been forming since she first saw Steve took full shape....

The big lummox had no idea who she was.

2

OKAY, SO IT was irrational to be insulted because the guy she'd humiliated herself over seven years before didn't recognize her. She should be thrilled, doing a double-time happy dance that she was off the hook. Instead, Hallie felt distinctly miffed.

"This is—" Mitch was stammering, when Hallie very coolly cut in.

"Amanda Creswell... *Doctor* Amanda Creswell. I'm an old friend of Mitch's." She wasn't sure what imp had made her add the doctor thing, but it was out and she couldn't take it back.

Steve's mouth quirked into the half smile that had always melted Hallie's adolescent bones. Now she was made of sterner stuff.

She ignored how the stamp of the passing years had made him more appealing. How his eyes were still the most incredible light toffee-brown that grew darker toward the edges. How the new bump on the bridge of his nose—a break that hadn't healed quite right, by the look of things—somehow made him more accessible. She ignored all of that, and was very proud of herself for the effort.

"Well, Doctor Creswell, welcome to Sandy Bend."

Hallie gave a very regal—very doctorly, she thought—nod of the head in response.

Steve was looking at her more closely now. A faint

line appeared between his brows. "You know, you look familiar…"

She shrugged, acting far more casual than she felt. "I've got a familiar kind of face. Really, Mitch and I should be running along."

She tugged at Mitch, but Steve still blocked their way back onto the sidewalk.

"So where are you from, Doc?"

"Arkansas." Hallie winced as the word escaped. Why couldn't she have chosen a state she knew something about?

"Is that so? What kind of medicine do you practice?"

"I'm a neurosurgeon." That, at least, was a safe pick. Good and intimidating. No room for small talk.

"Really?"

His expression was so skeptical that she couldn't let it drop. "What? You don't think there are any neurosurgeons in Arkansas?"

"Oh, I'm sure Arkansas has its share. I was just wondering…"

"What?" The way that word rose in pitch was very uncool. Very uncollected. She subtly elbowed her brother, who sounded suspiciously as if he was choking back laughter.

"Your nails," Steve said.

Hallie glanced at the crimson red daggers attached to the tips of her fingers, then quickly tucked her hands behind her back.

He gave her a slow, arch smile. "Don't those kind of get in the way when you're in surgery? That is, assuming that the 'surgeon' part of neurosurgeon means you actually operate on people."

Hallie scrambled for a plausible answer. "I've, ah, been working on a robotics research project. Vascular microsurgery reconstructing blood vessels in the lower cerebral cortex.''

Not bad. Those hours she'd been spending watching emergency room reality TV were finally paying off. Not only was she less squeamish when she nicked a leg shaving, but she could spin some pretty good ''doctor lines.''

The smile that had been lurking at the corners of Steve's mouth grew into a full-fledged grin. ''Very impressive. And to think Cal told me you'd gotten a degree in Fine Arts. You've been busy, Hallie.'' He brushed the knuckle of his index finger under her chin. ''Good to see you again...Doc.''

He'd chucked her under the chin... as if she was some precocious three-year-old who'd just learned to tie her shoes!

As Steve Whitman strolled away whistling a cheery little tune and her brother let loose with horselaughs that probably carried clear across the lake to Wisconsin, Hallie wished desperately for a pair of ruby red slippers to transport her back to Carmel. Or at least to the other side of that Welcome to Sandy Be d sign.

THE FRECKLES had been the first clue. Hallie Brewer had always had the most outrageous freckles. But not until she'd stuck her hands behind her back had Steve been one-hundred percent certain.

He'd seen that Hallie-gesture too many times before not to be sure. The memories rolled through his mind like a movie montage as he ambled down the sidewalk toward the market. Five-year-old Hallie hiding her hands after flouring the family dog in order to make the poor mutt into a ghost for a ''Halloween in July'' party. Fourteen-year-old Hallie sticking her hands behind her back after shooing a ladybug off his shoulder at the beach, then getting all wide-eyed and blushing Day-Glo crimson. Eighteen-year-old Hallie tucking her hands be-hind her back after baring—

Steve slowed midstep. No, he didn't want to go there. He'd spent a helluva long time repressing that particular memory. Dredging it up now would only complicate matters.

Hallie Brewer was his best buddy's kid sister. He reminded himself that he'd known her since she was in diapers. And even if she had acquired more looks and charm than a woman had a right to, he damned well knew beneath it all, she was still Horrible Hallie. And he was sure that one way or another, she could still make his life hell.

FEELING EVEN STICKIER from the drive into the country, Hallie stepped onto the porch of the oak-shaded farm-house that had been in the Brewer family for over a hundred years. A fat tabby cat lounging on the porch swing gave a whisker-waggling yawn by way of greet-ing.

Hallie smiled. "Hey, Murphy."

While she wasn't quite sure if this was Murphy VII or Murphy VIII, she knew she had the name down pat. In keeping with the Sandy Bend Law of Immutability, the Brewer barn cat's name never varied—no matter whether the particular feline was a boy or girl.

Hallie glanced around for Muldoon, the family dog. Muldoon III, of course. Doonie, however, was nowhere in sight. She couldn't help feeling a little disappointed. At least the dog—unlike Steve Whitman—would have recognized her right away.

Ignoring the internal wince that came with thinking about Steve, she swung open the front door to her child-hood home.

"Dad, I'm—" she began to call, but was cut short.

"Finally here," Cousin Althea finished for her. "I've been waiting."

The jam-packed duffel bag at her cousin's feet was enough to clue Hallie in to that fact.

She skirted the bag and gave Althea a hug. Her father's cousin still smelled of cloves and incense and sounded like a windchime, with her bangle bracelets ringing off one another. As she stepped away, Hallie smiled at the familiarity of it all.

"Funny you've been waiting, since I didn't call anyone to tell them I was coming."

Althea tucked a long strand of salt-and-pepper hair behind her ear. "Some of us are more sensitive than others. I could feel your aura the moment you entered town."

Hallie gave in to that wince she'd been holding in check. "Black with large streaks of crimson embarrassment, right?"

"Oh, I won't deny sensing a few lightning bolts here and there, but I'd call it more zippy than dismal."

A fat lot Althea knew. *She* hadn't been treated like a perennial toddler by a guy she'd spent half her life trying to impress. Or acted like a total loon, either. Still, Hallie kept quiet. Arguing with Althea was like trying to capture the summer breeze with a butterfly net.

"So, what's up with the bag?" she asked instead. "Are you going visiting?"

"I'm going home to the commune in Wisconsin." Althea made the pronouncement with a serenity that Hallie suddenly lacked. "The spirits have decreed—"

Hallie fought the urge to throw herself across her cousin's luggage and refuse to let go. She'd been baited, hooked and reeled in.

"The spirits, huh? So were you reading tea leaves when they made this decree, or auguring with chicken guts?" Hallie raised one hand as though grabbing a brilliant idea from thin air. "No wait—I've got it! It came to you as the spirits were slipping a little newspaper article into the mail, right?"

"It never hurts to nudge the spirits along," Althea said before her mouth curved into a broad, self-satisfied grin. "Or you, either."

Hallie was finding it tough to work up a good and justifiable snit. Still, there was the matter of this Brewer family phone phobia. "And you couldn't have just picked up the phone and called me?"

"I promised your father I wouldn't. Besides, it was simple enough to have a friend send you a hint. That way, technically, at least, I haven't crossed your father, and I've still taken care of business. I've sensed that you've been wanting to come home."

Right. She'd been wanting this about as much as she'd been wanting to get her nose pierced. "I'm not staying."

"Whatever you say," Althea soothed in a humor-the-child tone that set Hallie's teeth on edge. "You'll find your father down by the pond trying to catch the same poor fish he's been harassing all week. Run down and say hello. I should be here a while yet. Thor's not as skilled at picking up signals as I am."

Thor was Althea's husband, and as anchored to earth as Althea was ethereal. "Sure…that, and your microbus isn't equipped with a cell phone," Hallie said over her shoulder as she headed toward the kitchen and the back door. "Promise you'll stay put till I get back."

"If the spirits will it," Althea called after her.

It wasn't much of a promise, but Hallie figured that the spirits—and Cousin Althea—owed her one.

"Hey, Dad," she called as she closed the distance between the back of the house and the pond.

She watched as her father propped his fishing pole into the hole he'd cut years ago into the arm of his

Adirondack chair. Pretty serious about his leisure, good old Dad.

Her father stood and turned to face her.

"How's my favorite artist? About time you got here," he said, then wrapped her into a hug. It was a quick one, because her dad had never been very comfortable with fatherly hugs and kisses. Oh, he always gave it his best shot, but they always came off as a little awkward. A little goofy. Still, she couldn't recall the last time she'd been hugged so many times in one day. It almost made up for the episode with Steve Whitman.

Her father stepped back to survey her, and Hallie did the same to him. What she saw frightened her. In the months since she'd last seen him, her father had aged more than passing time could account for. She'd been without a mother most of her life, but her father, he'd always been there. Even when she'd moved to the other side of the country, he'd called and visited. And had always given her unconditional love.

She tried to keep her smile from wavering. "So you knew I was coming? Did you sense my aura, too?"

Her dad chuckled. "Nah. I can't see an aura any more than Althea can—not that I'd argue the point with her. Mitch called and told us you were on your way. Said something about California scrambling your brains, Steve Whitman and a doctor. Couldn't resist shaking up things right off the bat, could you?"

Since Hallie never meant to "shake up things" and definitely didn't want to discuss Steve Whitman with her father, she veered to another subject. "I saw Murphy on the front porch."

Her father settled into his chair and lifted his fishing pole from its rest. "Murphy? Oh, you mean the Terminator."

She blinked once, twice, trying to identify this impostor who had taken the place of predictable Bud

Brewer. "You named the cat Terminator? What was wrong with another Murphy?"

Her dad shrugged. "Just wanted a change of pace, I guess."

He patted the chair next to him. "Sit down and tell me what's going on, Hallie-girl."

She sat, then worked her yellow skirt back down to a ladylike level. It had been an impulse buy, along with the fake nails. Her dad didn't seem to notice her jazzed-up appearance. Then again, he'd never batted an eyelash when she went through her Smurf-blue hair phase in tenth grade, either.

"First, why don't you tell me what's going on with you?"

"Nothing that out of the ordinary. Too many ice creams and not enough 'heart-healthy foods,' from what the doctors tell me. If they could just make oatmeal and that other stuff taste as good as the ice cream." He sighed and gave a rueful shake of his head. "Anyway, I have to start making some changes."

She knew better than that. "After you've worked through the five gallons of Double Fudge Brownie in the basement freezer, right?"

"More like ten. Folks kept bringing me more when I came home from the hospital. Double Fudge Brownie every last gallon."

He didn't sound exactly pleased, and Hallie suspected his unhappiness had nothing to do with the fat or calorie content.

"You know Sandy Bend and its ice-cream addiction," she replied in a cheery voice. "Gotta keep those doctors in business, right?"

"I'd say in my case, age is doing a good enough job of that. It kinda creeps up on you. One day you're hiking four miles just to get to your favorite fishing spot, and the next it's all you can do to settle your bones into bed.''

Her heart flip-flopped. ''You're still plenty young, Dad.''

''Did you know that I've worked in the same place since I was twenty-one?''

''Uh-huh.'' Hallie had a sinking feeling they had traveled into uncharted territory. After all, her dad had also lived in the same house since he was born, and that had never seemed to bug him.

''And I've never been to Tibet, or seen Mardi Gras, or hiked the Appalachian Trail. And every night for as long as I can remember, I've had the same bowl of Double dang-blasted Fudge Brownie ice cream. Did anyone ever think that once before I die, I might want something different?''

She pinned a nervous smile on her face. ''Are you trying to tell me that you're going back to the commune with Cousin Althea?''

''Nah.'' With angry cranks of the reel, he hauled in his fishing line. ''I don't know what I'm trying to tell you, except— Hell, I don't know what I'm trying to tell you.''

Forget uncharted territory. There was no emotional compass strong enough to point Hallie's way home. The man in front of her was not to-the-point lawman and dad extraordinaire Bud Brewer. This was... This was...

Hallie didn't know who this man was, and she wanted her father back. Immediately. She also wanted to know exactly what had been going on around here. She stood and skewered the house that held Althea the Magic Hippie with a frustrated glare.

''Well, you work on whatever you're trying to tell me, Dad. In the meantime, I'm going to drag my stuff up to my room and settle in.''

Hallie had made it almost to the house when her dad's voice stopped her.

"You sure you don't want to tell me what happened with Steve Whitman? You know I'll hear it from half the town, anyway."

Hallie kept walking.

She had until Saturday evening, when it would be time to climb into her car and sweat her way back to California. Six days to work up a sufficient level of "warm and fuzzies" over her father's health and attitude.

And six days to figure out how to pull off the miracle of the century—to leave Sandy Bend this time with her heart and dignity intact.

3

IT WAS CLOSE TO THE END of that hot summer day by the time Steve wrapped his hand around a cold beer. That, he figured, was like everything else in life. A little waiting was good for the soul. And in this case, good for the taste buds, too.

He took a long swallow of icy cold brew, then leaned back on his ancient redwood lounger with its faded cushion, and did just that—lounged. After the meeting he'd just escaped, he'd earned it.

Trying to save the high school was a losing battle, but he was still going to fight them to the end. And it wasn't simply looming unemployment lighting a fire inside him. It was the knowledge that another piece of what made Sandy Bend more than just a summer vacation spot was disappearing.

He didn't want the town to become a whole bunch of houses holding life only in the warmer months. He wanted it to be one of those year-round places that showed movies in the Village Hall on Friday nights as it had been when he was a weekends-only kid. And the irony of that didn't escape him.

In making Sandy Bend his home, he had moved from the trunk-slammer camp and in with the townies. He'd cast his lot, even if he still wasn't much more than a tenant in his parents' old summer house. Their new one—all modern glass and steel, with more lake frontage than a guy needed to tend—gave him the creeps.

Even as a townie in his heart, Steve understood he couldn't stem the tide of change—or the rise in real estate prices that was forcing the year-round folks out—any more than he could stop the dunes sitting below his house from pushing their way back into Lake Michigan.

He loved it here on his lookout, perched above water so broad and endless he could see the opposite shore only in his imagination. He loved the sound of the wind, the surf and the thunderstorms that broke far offshore and rumbled their way to him long before the first rain-drop hit.

Steve took another slug of beer and gazed at a thin ribbon of gray at the horizon. Something was brewing out there. And something was brewing inside him, too. For the first time in as long as he could recall, he felt lonely. Not the kind of lonely that having a beer and a game of pool with Cal and the gang would fix, either. It might mask the feeling for a while, but it wouldn't make it go away. This was a "something big is miss-ing" lonely, and he didn't like the feeling one bit.

He'd just stop thinking about it. Yeah, that was the ticket. All this introspection was unhealthy for a guy. He'd just stop thinking about how much finer the eve-ning would be if he had someone curled up by him. Someone with freckles and mile-long legs and…

Steve scrambled from the lounger as if it had grown jagged teeth and was ready to chomp down on his sorry butt.

"Black flies biting?" an amused voice called from farther uphill. Steve turned to see Cal Brewer standing on the edge of the empty cedar deck behind the house, a bottle of beer in his hand.

Steve grabbed his own beer, then made the steep climb back through sugary sand.

"I still don't see why you couldn't actually put the deck furniture on the deck. It's not like you don't have enough room," Cal groused once Steve was within speaking distance.

He liked his furniture's out-of-the-way location. "Sometimes it's good to work for things."

Cal grinned. "Says the rich boy."

Steve knew Cal was just kidding, but damn, he hated being called that. He hadn't done anything other than be born rich. And he refused to touch a dime of that Whitman money.

"I'm not so rich that I'm real happy about you snagging my last beer."

"Yeah, well, if you hung out a little closer to your phone, I'd be home drinking one of mine instead of yours." He hesitated, shifting his weight from one foot to the other, then said in a semi-disgusted voice, "Cousin Althea wants you at dinner."

Steve winced. Dining with Horrible Hallie and getting his mind messed some more just wasn't a sane approach to survival. "Say you couldn't find me."

"This is Althea we're talking about—she already knows where you are."

He would never understand how Althea had managed to sucker Cal so thoroughly. "Tell her the storm rolling in must have messed with her radar. You looked everywhere, and—"

"Dad wants to see you, too," Cal cut in.

Horrible Hallie exposure or not, that statement made it a done deal. Bud Brewer had been Dad to half the kids in town each summer, including Steve, whose own father had been too busy with work back in Chicago to do more than occasionally visit. Lately, Steve had been worried about Chief Bud—not just his heart, but the whole guy.

"All right, already. I'll just grab my keys, and—"

Cal took a swig of his beer, swallowed, then said, "No deal."

"What now?"

"Althea doesn't trust you not to run. My orders were to deliver you." He smiled. "Besides, it gives us a chance to get to Truro's for a game of pool. We'll have a quick dinner, and then bolt."

"Now that's a plan," Steve said. Not quite as good as his urge to run like hell and not come back until Hallie Brewer was gone, but he guessed it would fly.

ALTHEA'S SPIRITS definitely possessed minds of their own. Hallie's cousin never made it out of the Brewer front yard, let alone home to Wisconsin. Thor, her husband, had wrenched his back while loading her luggage. Hallie felt sorry for Thor, but was secretly relieved she would still have Thea to lean on.

At the moment, Thea was frowning at the table Hallie thought she'd set to family-style dinner perfection. "We'll need another place."

Hallie recounted to be sure she hadn't lost her math skills along with her sanity, but everything still added up. Only one other diner came to mind. "So Thor's feeling better?"

"No, once his back spasms, he's in bed for days. Lucky for him that Mitch and Cal were here to haul him upstairs."

And one hellacious haul it had been, too. Thor was a retired NFL offensive lineman—retired more in terms of paycheck than tough-guy attitude unfortunately. In all craziness, Hallie had been forced to delay any conversation with Althea until Thor decided whether he wanted to admit he needed help. After that, Dad had come back into the house, and she hadn't been able to get Althea alone for answers.

"Okay, if Thor's not joining us, who is?" Hallie asked as she made sure she'd grabbed an unchipped plate to bring to the table.

"Steve Whitman."

Hallie clenched the thick white crockery between two hands. She was surprised it didn't vaporize with the angry heat that zipped through her. Was there nowhere to hide in Sandy Bend?

"He can have my place," she said before shoving through the swinging door between the dining room and the kitchen.

"So when did you turn into a coward?" Althea called after her.

Hallie pulled up short. Still hanging on to the plate, she turned and walked back into the dining room. "I like to think of it as discretion. Knowing how to choose my moments."

Althea's brows arched. "Discretion, huh?"

"I just need a day or two to get my act together."

"You've had twenty-five years, Hallie, and you look together to me. You support yourself, right?"

"Yes."

Althea shifted a place setting downward to make space for the last guest Hallie wanted to welcome. "You have interests outside of work?"

She had her watercolors, which she hoped one day would be her paycheck instead of a money-eating hobby. "Sure."

"Friends?"

"Of course." And all of them in California. The only three girls she'd been close to in Sandy Bend had also fled after high school. Of them, Emily lived the closest in Grand Rapids, over two hours away. Everybody else around here, Hallie considered more spectators and reporters of her Hallie-disasters than friends.

Her gray eyes calm and knowing, Althea asked, "Then exactly what part of you isn't together?"

The Steve part, Hallie wanted to answer, but didn't.

The admission would make her a candidate to join the chicken currently roasting in its own juices.

She reminded herself that Steve was ancient history. So what if she had filled countless nights with adolescent fantasies about the guy? And then there was that one too real encounter that still made her cringe when she thought of it. Which she hadn't let herself do in years. Okay, months, she revised, trying for personal honesty.

But it was all history. Gone as if it had never happened.

She was Hot Hallie, Happenin' Hallie now. She was learning to walk the walk and talk the talk.

Shoulders back and freckled nose held high, Hallie set Steve's plate on the corner of the long dining table.

"I'm together," she announced. "Totally."

STEVE HADN'T BEEN at the Brewers' very long before he decided he should have taken the run-like-hell option. The clouds gathering outside had nothing on the mood at the dinner table.

Chief Bud loomed at the head, snarling at the steamed vegetables Althea kept heaping onto his plate, and from somewhere upstairs Althea's husband kept bellowing *"Thea-a-a-a"* in a bad Marlon Brando *Streetcar* imitation.

Cal and Mitch were out on official duty—Old Mrs. Hawkins was trying to climb the flagpole at the marina again. Personally, Steve hoped she'd make it to the top one day, and prove whatever she was trying to prove. Just not tonight with lightning jumping around her.

But what really had him ready to tie on the track shoes was the distraction of Hallie sitting across the table. She looked all fresh and pretty, but was glaring at him as if she wanted to challenge him to an arm wrestling match.

The last thing he needed was Hallie Brewer getting the best of him. Or getting to him at all. He gave her his patented squash-the-annoying-little-sister smile. "So, Doc, gonna be here long, or is this just a quick break from all that robotic neurosurgery?"

Hallie's fork clattered against her plate, and Althea made a regretful little clucking sound.

Hallie scowled at him. "I'll be leaving on Saturday, so don't worry about me doing too much damage around here."

He shrugged to mask the havoc her freckles were already creating. Even though he wasn't in the habit of nibbling on his buddies' little sisters, he'd bet she tasted of cinnamon and brown sugar.

"And I might not be a neurosurgeon," she was saying in a don't-mess-with-me voice, "but I do have a job, you know. Two of them, actually." She leaned forward. Steve could almost see her bracing her elbow on the table, waggling her fire-engine-red fingernails and saying, *"So you think you can take me?"*

"I've exhibited my watercolors in juried shows and done pretty well, too," she was actually arguing. "And I'm a house manager for Anna Bethune."

Steve blinked. "Anna Bethune, the actress?"

Hallie rolled her eyes. "No, Anna Bethune the dog-catcher. Of course, the actress."

Anna Bethune and her husband, Matt Colton, were both Hollywood hot stuff. Hallie's job sure beat the tar out of being an almost unemployed high school principal with the old man breathing down his neck for him to quit this nonsense and join the family business. "So you've met Anna Bethune?"

She hesitated before answering. "Not directly."

Ah...some ammo. Steve grinned. "How do you meet someone indirectly?"

Her hot blue gaze narrowed as she answered, "I live

in the gatehouse outside the vacation home she and her husband own in Carmel Highlands. I make sure the place is ready before they stay there.''

Steve knew he should let it drop, but he felt this need to get under her skin. To sit back and watch a few Hallie-type fireworks, just like the good old days when she'd come barreling at him and plant a kick in the middle of his shin.

''So, actually, you work for Anna Bethune's house,'' he said. ''Not Anna.''

''I work for Anna,'' she replied with a deadly calm that he almost bought, except for the way her upper lip was beginning to twitch.

Steve was very close to getting Hallie right back where he wanted her—neatly tucked into the image of a pigtailed, obnoxious kid. He worked up a sigh of mock regret.

''You know, with this new, adult look of yours,'' he said, giving her lethal fingernails a pointed stare, ''I thought maybe you'd outgrown all the storytelling. Remember when you were in fifth grade and told me you'd gotten the Rolling Stones to play at your school picnic?''

''I was trying to get your attention, though for the life of me, I can't remember why,'' she said, sounding absolutely bored. ''I figured even a dinosaur like you might have heard of the Rolling Stones. After all, you and Mick Jagger are around the same age, right?''

Chief Bud slapped his open palm on the table. Both Steve and Hallie jumped. Althea appeared to finally notice Thor's bellows and made good on an escape.

''That's enough,'' Bud barked. ''Mick Jagger's old enough to be Steve's father, as you already know, Hallie. And, Steve, I'm pretty sure you're smart enough to figure out that a house can't sign Hallie's paycheck.

Now if you two are through baiting each other, could you pass me the damned butter?''

"No!" Steve and Hallie answered in alarmed unison.

Bud pushed back his chair, wadded up his napkin, then tossed it in the middle of his broccoli and summer squash. "You're giving me indigestion—not that I want to choke down another plate of rabbit food, anyway. I'm going upstairs and playing some poker with Thor. Maybe even smoke a cigar."

"Dad, you don't smoke cigars."

He stood and skewered Hallie with a steely glare. "Then it's time I start. And before you take your sophisticated new self back west, go on out to the barn and have a look at the Summer Fun float. The parade's this coming Saturday and I don't feel like working on the thing. It's your turn."

Chief Bud stalked off, leaving silence in his wake.

Steve opened his mouth to apologize for screwing things up, for upsetting Bud and for just generally being a jerk, but then Hallie fled, too.

"Great meal," Steve said to the empty table. "Plenty of food to go around." Plenty of guilt, too. He piled more mashed potatoes on his plate and dug in. He'd fill up while Hallie cooled down.

HALLIE ALWAYS THOUGHT of the Brewer barn, with its country perfume of sweet hay, machine oil and dust, as more of a scrapbook than a building. She stepped through the small entry to the left of the huge sliding door and felt herself calm as memories washed over her. Dim, cloud-laden light drifted in from the triple arches of a mullioned window some fanciful Brewer had long ago installed at the peak of the barn. She flipped on the overhead light to brighten things up, and watched Murphy—no, the Terminator—streak across the packed dirt floor.

It had been years since the barn had actually been used for farming. A more modern structure held the equipment the family needed for its annual asparagus crop. Instead, this place held her dad's old Corvette, always tucked under its covers like a baby, except when it took its annual spin in the Summer Fun Parade. Next to the 'Vette was the float that had been the Brewer family project for as long as Hallie could recall.

Summer Fun Days had been started by the town fathers as a way to lure tourists, but now it was like a huge, late-June homecoming. Besides the parade, the week was filled with fishing and baseball tournaments, fireworks and a picnic on the village green hosted by the local politicos and town employees.

Everyone who had moved away came back to visit friends and family during Summer Fun Days. Everyone but Hallie. Living in California had always been a built-in excuse not to return.

Hallie walked to the flatbed trailer that served as the base for the float. Baby-blue plywood waves that reminded her of shark's teeth bordered the outside. On the ground next to it sat an old, flat-bottomed rowboat. She wrinkled her nose. It looked as if her dad had been going for a fishing theme. Again. Though it was a very un-Brewerlike thing to admit, she hated fishing.

Glad she had changed into jeans after her shower earlier this evening, she boosted herself over the shark's-tooth waves and plopped down in the middle of the trailer. She didn't have a problem with working on the float. She'd never been much good at sitting still, and this would give her something fun to do while she got a fix on what was going on with her dad.

As she considered her options, Hallie leaned back on her elbows and gazed at the window on the far wall. She'd make this float into a showstopper, and fish-free, too. Her father had given her a chance to show Sandy

Bend how far she'd come. And while doing it, she'd get a week of solitude. A week of peace—

"Hey, Doc."

Forget the peace and solitude. Hallie didn't return the greeting. She needed to stay mad at Steve. The alternative was unacceptable.

"I'm not disturbing you, am I?" he asked.

Unwillingly, she looked away from the window.

"No," she said, amazed at how easily the lie sprung to her lips. Everything about Steve disturbed her. Always had. Always would.

He gestured at the trailer. "Sorry we don't have more done on this."

Hallie's heart skipped a beat. *"We?"*

He climbed onto the float and sat next to her, his long legs stretched out in front of him. Thunder rumbled nearby.

"I've been trying to help Bud, but things have been a little crazy for me lately. They've been discussing shutting down the school."

"I heard," Hallie said. She didn't want to feel bad for him. In fact, she'd be thrilled if she could figure out how to feel nothing at all—including wiping out the little zing that curled through her at the thought of being close enough to touch him. Just two little fingers tippy-toeing toward him and she could trace the strong line of his thigh.

She scooted away. "Don't worry about the float. I'll take it from here."

He hesitated, then said, "Well, here's the problem. I've been using the float as kind of an excuse to come out and check on Bud. He's not much for being watched over, if you know what I mean."

Hearing that Steve was worried only amped up the zing. She considered climbing off the float altogether.

"It's nice of you to want to check on Dad, but everything's under control," she said firmly.

"Is it?"

He asked the question so gently that she couldn't be annoyed with his meddling. She glanced at his profile and noticed the way his eyelashes curled up at the tips. She'd forgotten about that.

"Let's call a truce, Doc," he said. "For one whole week, let's put the past behind us and get along. Bud's been like a dad to me. Don't let our, ah…problems cut me off from him. Please."

Heavy rain began to bounce off the barn roof. Hallie shivered. If she didn't guard her heart, she was going to fall for the guy all over again.

"If you can behave, I can," she said in a brisk voice that wavered just the smallest bit. "Anyway, it's not like we have to work together. I'll take the day shift and you can take the night. That way we can stay out of each other's way."

His brows drew downward for an instant, but then he gave her a smile. "Whatever you like. I'm busy over at the school most days, anyway."

"Sure," she said, hoping the roll of thunder crossing the fields hid the disappointed note in her voice. She hadn't wanted him to insist that they work together. Not really.

Steve stood and brushed his hands across his thighs. "Good enough." He glanced up at the roof, then at her. "I don't think this is going to end anytime soon."

Hallie stared blankly at him for an instant, wondering how he'd pegged her feelings so well. Then she realized he was talking about the rain. She clambered to her feet.

"We probably should get back to the house," she said.

He made an effortless hop from the float. He held out his hand, as though daring her to take it. Always an easy mark for a challenge, she took hold. Once she was back on solid ground, Steve didn't let go. From a distracted distance, Hallie noticed she wasn't making much effort to pull back, either.

She was feeling a zing. A definite zing.

His eyes glinted with humor as he rubbed his thumb across her fake fingernails. "Since we're putting you to work, I say we go snoop in Bud's tool room. Maybe he has some bolt cutters to get these off you."

Hallie shook off the zing, then tugged her hand free before she was tempted to hold on.

"Race you to the house," she said before flying from the barn.

As she dashed through the rain, her feet hit the ground in cadence to a two-syllable rhythm: *cra-zy, cra-zy, cra-zy*. The past she'd dreaded was nipping at her heels, and all she wanted to do was turn around and run headlong into it.

4

CAL WAS HOME from prying Mrs. Hawkins off the flagpole by the time Steve got back inside.

"Ready for that beer?" Cal asked.

Steve slicked the rain out of his hair and looked around for Hallie. She was nowhere to be seen. Those mile-long legs of hers weren't just for show. "I think I'll pass tonight," he said.

"You feeling okay?"

"Yeah, fine." Actually, he was feeling more than a little uncomfortable, and it all centered around Hallie. He could pinpoint the precise moment almost seven years before that he'd gone from being her favorite hero to an untouchable. Back then, he'd handled matters the best he could. Now, thinking about the whole ugly, awful mess made him squirm. But really, what could he have done differently? *A lot,* his conscience growled.

Cal waved a hand in front of Steve's eyes. "Anybody home?"

"Yeah. Sure." Steve looked up the sturdy oak staircase and wondered if Hallie was in her old room. Then he wondered why he was wondering.

Cal snorted. "If you call this zombie imitation 'fine,' it's a good thing I'm dumping you at home. You'd scare off the women at Truro's."

"Most of the women at Truro's scare me," Steve said.

"Okay, so maybe they get a little carried away with

the makeup, but where else are they going to show off? Unless you have the money to belong to the country club, it's not like there's a whole lot of variety in town." Cal jingled his car keys. "Let's cruise before I get another call. Nobody around here understands the meaning of *off duty*."

Fifteen minutes later, Cal dropped Steve off at the bottom of the two-track lane leading to his house. Twilight cast dusky shadows through the maple and walnut trees stubborn enough to gain a toehold in the sandy soil. The summer storm had passed, and the woods smelled damp and earthy.

Steve drew in a deep breath and marveled at how much more he liked this place than his old digs in downtown Chicago that he'd moved out of two years before. No auto exhaust, no trash skittering in the wind like urban tumbleweeds.

He didn't regret the move he'd made, even if almost everyone thought he was crazy to give up city life. They didn't know that city life—and his father's subtle but constant pressure—had been making him crazy.

When he rounded the last bend in the drive, Steve stopped in his tracks.

"Dammit."

He scowled at the red Miata parked next to his Jeep. It looked like a bit of city life had decided to pay him a visit.

As he climbed the last steps to the large, log lodge that was supposed to be his refuge, he settled on one consoling thought. At least just one sister had arrived to torture him—not all five.

Behind its screen, the front door to his home was wide open. Fat moths had gathered to dance in the light. Steve stepped in, letting the screen door close behind him with a hard smack.

His baby sister Kira didn't even bother to look alarmed.

"You're out of beer," she said from her perch on his well-worn plaid sofa.

"Like you drink it," he scoffed.

She arched one perfectly shaped blond brow. "I knew better than to even look for a good, crisp sauvignon blanc."

"I wouldn't even know how to spell it to buy it." Which was a lie. His French wasn't bad, he just liked beer better. "So what are you doing here?"

Kira took a sip from what Steve recognized as his last bottle of springwater, then said, "I came up for Summer Fun Days, but the painters are working in my room at Mom and Dad's." She wrinkled her nose. "The fumes are awful. I decided that for tonight, you get me."

"And you didn't think to ask first?"

The question was more ceremonial than real. His sisters took shameless advantage of the fact they had him outnumbered.

Want Steve's car for the night? Take it.

Steve's razor to shave your legs? Help yourself.

Short on cash? Forget the bank and raid Steve's wallet. They were lucky that he loved the whole pack of 'em—even slightly snobby, pampered baby Kira.

"Why should I ask? It's not as though you'd have anybody else here," Kira said. "We all know you're the next closest thing to a hermit."

Zombie. Hermit. And deemed untouchable by his former number one fan, Hallie Brewer. Tonight had been hell on his ego.

"The hermit idea's sounding pretty good to me about now," Steve muttered. "Didn't you see the sign on the front door—Cave Occupied?"

Kira breezed right past the little jab. "Where have

you been, anyway? When I saw your car, I figured you were home.''

''I had dinner at the Brewers. Hallie's back in town,'' he added, feeling his mouth shape into a stupid smile he couldn't quite fight down.

Kira rolled her eyes. ''Chapter One in the Book of Who Cares.''

Steve wasn't surprised at his sister's response. Though they'd been really tight when they were little, Kira and Hallie hadn't exactly traveled in the same circles as they grew older. Steve supposed it might have something to do with the time Hallie clipped Kira's hair into a punk cut. He gave it fifty-fifty odds the green highlights had been an accident.

''Well, this is old home week. Susan's in town, too,'' Kira announced. ''She brought her fiancé to show him around.''

The news hit Steve like a well-placed fist to the gut. Susan's family had owned a place in Sandy Bend even longer than the Whitmans. He and Susan had spent plenty of time in sweaty make-out sessions on the old glider behind her folks' guest cottage. Then they'd carried on a long-distance romance through college and beyond. Finally, three years ago they'd gotten engaged after Susan became the youngest partner ever at her law firm. A year later, they had broken up.

He hadn't heard she was engaged again.

This wasn't supposed to hurt, he reminded himself. He was over this. Leaning his hip against the back of an armchair, Steve tried for a casual pose. ''I hope the guy doesn't like Sandy Bend too much. Fat chance she'll come back often.''

''He's a lawyer, too,'' Kira said. ''I doubt either of them will have much time to visit.''

All in all, Steve considered that a piece of good news. He didn't precisely hate Susan for dumping him, but he didn't want to see much of her, either. And he needed time to absorb what her arrival meant to him.

"I think I'll take a walk on the beach," he said to his sister.

Kira nodded. "I need to make a few calls. I forgot my calling card, do you mind?"

Steve shrugged. "No big deal." How much damage could she do with phone calls?

As he neared the door, she asked, "By the way, would you happen to know the country codes for Fiji and Australia?"

Sisters. Can't live with 'em. Can't make 'em camp on the beach.

STEVE WALKED A LINE just above the point where the surf spent itself on the shore. The sky was purple with coming darkness. Down the way he could see the silhouette of a couple strolling hand in hand. Feeling loneliness chasing him, he shoved his own empty hands into his jeans pockets.

He'd always figured by the time he passed thirty, he'd be part of a couple. And he'd always figured that Susan would be the one whose hand he held.

He chuckled as an image of Hallie Brewer's dagger nails suddenly flashed through his mind. Holding her hand would be one wild ride. And probably life-threatening, too. Being with Susan had always been so natural, like taking his next breath or seeing his reflection in the mirror each morning. He'd loved the steadiness of it all. Until he'd strayed further from her goals than she could accept.

Susan had tolerated the fact he'd chosen to be a teacher instead of joining his dad in the family business. Businesses, actually—some manufacturing concerns and a healthy chunk of Chicago Miracle Mile real estate. His father was always coming up with new job offers for him. Steve privately considered them all to be Vice President of Nothing Much. No challenge, no feeling he was having an impact on anything except an already obscenely robust bank balance.

The bottom line for Susan was that the Whitman family still had more money than Fort Knox, and she could tell her friends how wonderful it was he'd "dedicated his life to educating the less fortunate." Which Steve privately thought was a real hoot, since he'd been teaching algebra at a boys' prep school in far-from-impoverished Lake Forest at the time.

Once he'd finished off his master's degree by attending classes at night, he'd carefully raised the idea of moving to Sandy Bend and building a life there. A life that didn't hinge solely on black-tie charity balls and business deals done over golf and rivers of scotch at the country club.

At first, Susan had been gung-ho. She thought a small-town law practice might be fun. Then the reality of icy winters in an empty town settled over her, as did the realization that Steve was serious about not living off the family trust income. When she couldn't talk him out of the move, she broke off the engagement.

Having his plans crumble had hurt a lot more than he'd let on. His family had been shaken but supportive, in their stiff-upper-lip sort of way. He felt as though he'd failed them. If he needed his teaching and a life in Sandy Bend to fulfill his own expectations, the least he could have done was marry a woman with the appropriate social lineage to fulfill theirs.

For months, he'd done little more than function on autopilot. Only lately had Steve begun to feel as if he was really over Susan. That he might be able to be happy.

Of course, it was tough to feel unhappy during a Sandy Bend summer. He could even see the good in having Hallie Brewer land back in his life. Maybe he could finally make things right with her. Or at least not screw them up worse. Pushing back the blues, Steve turned toward home. He needed his rest if he was going to keep up with Horrible Hallie.

HALLIE WOKE LATE the next morning. She gazed at the room that had been hers forever, concluded she still hated pink gingham curtains, then spent fifteen minutes trying to trim her fingernails into submission.

After sending the nail clippers flying, she pondered a variation on Steve's bolt cutter idea, but rejected it. If she slipped she might do something awful like rip a cuticle and bleed, and for all of her former tomboy ways, she remained a complete weenie about blood. Especially her own.

In the end, she leafed through the phone book—possibly the world's smallest—and made an appointment for the following day at the only place in town advertising a manicurist.

Hallie wasn't a snob, but life in California had given her a taste of the finer things. The idea of a salon called The Hair Dungeon made her edgy. She wasn't letting them touch anything but her nails. Even then, she had her concerns about the method the dungeon keeper might use to remove the extensions.

"Five more days, then back to civilization," she reminded herself. She suspected they were going to be the longest five days of her life.

The first problem of the morning addressed, Hallie steeled herself to deal with the rest of them. She met up with Cousin Althea in the hallway.

"We need to talk," she said.

"I'll find you after I give Thor his snack."

Hallie raised her brows at the fruit-laden platter her cousin carried. "Some snack."

"He's eating light until his back mends," Althea replied.

As she made her way downstairs, Hallie wondered whether they'd need a winch to get Thor out of the house once he was feeling better.

Down in the kitchen, her dad sat at the table with a stack of books in front of him. When Hallie said good morning, he just frowned at her. She felt her way around for a neutral topic, settling on, "Did you go to the library this morning?"

"Yes, I went to the library. And I checked on the boys. *And* I had coffee with the Men's Service Club. All while you were closeted away upstairs. You need to get out, get moving and spice things up. Life's short, Hallie-girl."

"And the drive from California was long," she said. "I was just catching up on sleep." And trying to come up with a game plan to survive the next several days.

After pouring herself a mug of coffee, she checked out her father's reading materials. Instead of his usual spy thrillers, he seemed to have wandered over to the non-fiction section. Or more accurately, semi-nonfiction. The books had titles like *Aliens Among Us* and *Understanding Crop Circles*.

"New hobby?" she asked, tapping a fingernail on the crop circle book.

Her father nudged the *Aliens* tome. "Actually, I'm trying to prove that Althea isn't from Earth."

"I heard that," Althea said from the doorway.

"It's nothing I haven't said to your face."

"You're damaging your aura with all that negativity, Bud."

"It's bad enough I have to worry about my cholesterol count. My aura can take care of itself."

Hallie decided it would be wise to separate the sniping cousins. She grabbed an apple from the bowl on the counter, then picked up her coffee.

"Walk me out to the barn," she said to Althea.

Once they were clear of her father's hearing, Hallie asked, "How long has he been like this?"

Althea slowed her pace, making Hallie do the same. "His whole life. And I'm fairly sure he's the alien, not me."

"No, I mean all these weird behaviors—cigar smoking and aliens and not wanting to work on the float."

Her cousin stopped altogether. "Bud's feeling a little lost, you should understand that. It's not easy to be viewed as the same person no matter how much you might have changed on the inside, is it?"

Score two points for the hippie-lady. "So you think he's really okay?"

"The doctors cleared him to go back to work last week, so physically, I'm sure he's fine."

"And otherwise?"

"Your dad has a few things to work through. Be patient, Hallie."

Hallie sighed. Patience was something she'd never gotten the hang of.

"He's seen you through a lot of awkward stages in your life. You can see him through this one," Thea counseled.

As far as Hallie was concerned, her life had been one endless awkward stage. Being the sole female in the Brewer household wasn't quite the same as being raised by wolves, but it often felt that way.

"I just want to be sure Dad's okay before I leave."

Thea's bracelets jangled together as she stretched her arms toward the sky in what looked like a sun-worshipping dance to Hallie.

"Just be sure you're okay, too. You have unfinished business. Steve Whitman—"

Luckily, whatever her cousin had been going to say was cut off by a shout of *"The-a-a-a"* coming from above.

"Deep, cleansing breaths," Althea muttered to herself. "Put yourself in a peaceful place." She gave Hallie a placid smile. "Thor has difficulty relying on others."

Which was about as obvious as Hallie saying she had difficulty dealing with Steve.

"You go on," she said. "I'm going to get some work done on the float."

Once inside the barn, Hallie sat her mug and her apple on the float, then climbed up. As she munched on the tart Granny Smith, she focused on her life in Sandy Bend. Not the time she'd accidentally locked all the police station keys into a cell, or the proms and homecomings she'd never been invited to, but the good times.

For Hallie, days on Lake Michigan had always been the best part of Sandy Bend. When the other girls had been happy flirting with the boys, listening to music and frying to an even brown, Hallie had kept herself company. She had walked and swam and flown kites and sneaked down the beach far enough that she could build towering sandcastles without taking too much teasing.

That was what she wanted this float to be—a private beach paraded down the middle of Main Street.

Hallie envisioned her plans. She'd keep it simple and use some fluttery fabric banners for color. The rest of the decorations should be easy, too. The Brewer house was always packed with beach equipment.

But she still needed sand.

She supposed she could visit the state beach, but she was a little fuzzy on the legalities involved in carting off sand. A new headline for the *County Herald* flashed through her mind: Police Chief's Daughter Arrested for Sand Theft.

She didn't think that was quite what her dad had in mind when he told her to "spice things up."

That left private property, and she had no way of being sure that the people she'd known who had owned cottages seven years before still did now.

Except Steve. When he'd checked in on her late last night, Cal had mentioned that Steve was renting his parents' place from them.

If she wanted to avoid a trespass charge, she probably should ask Steve's permission. Except he said he'd be at the school most days, and she didn't want to bother him at work. It was bad enough being awkward and stupid around him in private.

Besides, she remembered every detail of the Whitmans' cottage. She'd spent enough time as a kid skulking around and trying to get a glimpse of Steve. And then there was the time she'd...

Hallie squeezed her eyes shut and made the unwanted image disappear. After a few of Cousin Thea's "deep, cleansing breaths," she was back on an even keel. Or at least, as close as she'd be getting.

The only way she'd survive a trip to the Whitmans' place was if it was a stealth run. She could get her dad's truck in and out of there—Steve wouldn't even have to know—and she could outrun that awful memory.

An hour later, Hallie pulled her dad's pickup from the dirt track onto the patch of green next to Steve's house. She yanked the truck's parking brake into place, then climbed out.

She loved this house—rambling old dinosaur of a firetrap that it was. When she was younger, she'd play games of make-believe, all centered on when she was married to Steve and was queen of this palace. She'd have sunset cocktail parties on the screened-in porches, and Steve would always be by her side, enraptured by her wit and charm. And she'd never trip over her too-big feet or be clueless when Steve's sister, Kira, made some subtle, gossipy reference to a neighbor who had run off with the penniless Italian count.

Now that she was grown-up, Hallie had met her share of impoverished royalty—Californian dot-com million-aires who'd gone belly-up and needed to work for a living. She could also look at this house and appreciate the cost and effort involved in maintaining eight bed-rooms and antiquated plumbing with no protection from Lake Michigan's brutal winter-winds. No more dreams for her.

No big deal, anyway. The reality of her tidy little Carmel Highlands gatehouse awaited her, just days away. And today was a lovely day for sand theft, sunny and warm. Pushing back thoughts of everything but the here and now, Hallie began to scope out the territory.

The house was set back above a large dune that spilled into the lake. She considered the odds of making it both down and back up the beach slope in a truck close to her own age. Most of the hill had been terraced and reinforced with railroad ties. Each broad step held plantings of ground cover and hardy pines and shrubs. Where the hill had been left in its natural state, the drop was steep, with nothing more than hanks of beach grass and some scrawny scrub oaks holding the sand in place.

"Looks like a no go to me," she muttered.

At the far side of the lot sat a utility shed. If Steve had a wheelbarrow, she still might be able to pull this off. She was pretty sure that opening the shed was breaking and entering, but, hey, no guts...no sand.

The door wasn't locked, which helped her con-science, if not her legal standing. Behind a push mower and a bunch of shovels and rakes that looked as if they could bring in big bucks down at the antique shop, waited a wheelbarrow. Hallie moved the garden tools from in front of it and checked it over. Its tire was a little low on air and the handles were rough and worn. Still, stealers couldn't be choosers.

Leaving her mess to pick up when she was through hauling sand, Hallie stopped at the back of the truck, grabbed the far superior shovel and the work gloves she'd taken from home, then set to work.

As the sun climbed higher in the sky, Hallie's arms began to ache from the unaccustomed physical labor. The sand she'd hauled made a piddling pile in the pickup's bed. Eventually, her legs grew rubbery from impelling the stubborn wheelbarrow uphill, and her eyes stung with sweat.

"Time for a break," she told the shovel.

Hallie peeled off her oversize work gloves and winced at the blisters forming in the vee of each hand between her thumb and index finger.

She gingerly slipped out of her T-shirt and cutoffs, leaving only her tangerine-colored bikini—another one of those comin'-home-and-gotta-look-good impulse buys. If nothing else, she knew she didn't have to be self-conscious about her figure anymore. Though she felt more pride in her development as an artist, she had to admit that no longer being "stick girl" was all right by her, too. Hallie slipped and slid to the base of the dune, then waded into the water. A wave caught her across the front of her thighs.

The cold shock was enough to send the breath from her lungs in a surprised *"Hoo-ah!"* but not enough to make her turn back. Though it was the last place she wanted to call home, she was Sandy Bend born and bred. A current sweeping down from the icy north was a Sandy Bend girl's idea of a spa treatment. Hallie walked past the surf until the water was waist-deep, then dove in and chilled out. She never even noticed when she gained an audience back onshore.

5

THROUGH SOME TRICK OF TIME, Steve's brain had hard-wired into the image of a painting he'd seen in his college mythology class—Venus arising from a clamshell at the edge of a foamy sea. His rational mind told him that freckled and gangly Hallie Brewer was no Venus. But the rest of him—all instinct and unfettered male urge—howled like a hungry hound at the sight of her.

"Look away," he said to himself as she dove sleekly underwater then surfaced farther down the beach. "Just turn around and go back to the house."

Great in concept, but not so easy to do. The best Steve could manage was to retreat from the open sweep of dune to his lounger in its camouflage of beach grass and stubby vegetation.

As he settled in, his gaze still on Hallie's lithe form slipping in and out of the waves, he decided maybe he was more ready to face the permed and perfumed women at Truro's than he'd thought. Nothing else could explain this sudden fixation with Hallie Brewer.

That or maybe he was a sucker for tangerine-colored bikinis.

Back at the end of her senior year in high school, when he'd taken over her calculus class for a teacher on maternity leave, Hallie had been all knees and elbows. He never would have imagined that she could turn out like this.

She'd always been too on edge.

Too anxious to please.

Too overwhelming for him to deal with.

And now...

Despite the way they kept circling each other, preparing for battle, he could see that she had mellowed. Her awkwardness had given way to something smoother, something that made him want to reach out and touch.

Steve clenched his hands into tight fists.

"Get a grip," he muttered, and he didn't mean a grip on Hallie.

She was a walking danger zone. For any number of reasons, it was no more acceptable—or decent, dammit—to be curious about her now than it had been seven years ago. Back when she'd offered herself to him. Of course, she'd been distraught at the time. And naturally he'd given her a clear, firm and nonnegotiable no.

But he'd been curious. Too curious. For weeks afterward, Hallie had kept creeping into his thoughts at the oddest moments. And in the most erotic ways. It had scared him, this bizarre attraction to a girl years younger than he. He'd begun to wonder whether he was some sort of Lolita-chasing pervert.

He'd also been nagged by a sense of disloyalty toward Susan, who, at the time, had been his girlfriend. Susan who was everything Hallie wasn't—not just a baby step away from being jailbait, not uncoordinated, painfully innocent and embarrassing as hell.

Through sheer grit, he'd eventually managed to wipe out any stray imaginings of Hallie. It had been either that or blow big bucks on a shrink's couch.

And now she was all grown-up, beautiful and back in Sandy Bend. Steve stretched out, flipped up his sunglasses, then flung his arm over his eyes to block the sight of her in that jaw-dropper of a bikini. He had known her for too long as his best buddy's kid sister to be having these thoughts. It was definitely time to haul himself down to Truro's for some meaningless fun.

Tonight.

He'd been lying there a while—the human version of an ostrich with his head in the sand—when he heard a slightly breathless, "Hey."

Almost unwillingly, Steve moved his arm. Hallie stood at the foot of the lounger. He didn't allow himself more than a quick glimpse—okay, a really thorough quick glimpse—at her awesome body before swinging his legs around, sitting up and anchoring his gaze on her face.

"Hey, yourself," he said after settling his sunglasses back in place.

"Hope you don't mind that I borrowed your lake."

"My lake, huh?"

"That's what Kira told me when we were little—that you Whitmans owned the lake," she said while slicking her hands through her hair, then squeezing water from the ends.

Steve swallowed hard and focused on what she was saying, instead of that conscienceless hound baying in the back of his mind. *Whoa baby, cover model material right here in your own backyard.*

"Well, Kira's pretty sure she owns all the stores back home on Michigan Avenue, too." He paused, considering the matter. "Actually, I think she has the credit card receipts to prove that one."

Hallie chuckled and then tugged at the bottom of her suit, apparently trying to readjust it for better coverage. Thoughts of the honey-colored skin hiding beneath that skimpy fabric barraged Steve, and with immediate hard and prominent physical effect. He sprung to his feet before it became obvious to Hallie that his mind had moved itself to a new location.

"You're free and clear on using the lake, Doc," he

said, stumbling a little over his words. "But I was kind of wondering about the sand in the back of Chief Bud's truck."

"Oh, that. It's going for a good cause."

He started walking uphill, away from temptation. "Shipping it to the Arctic for a beach party?"

Temptation followed hot on his heels. "Nope, just out to the barn for the float," she said. "Do you mind?"

"If I did, do you think I could get your brothers to haul you off to the slammer?" Putting Hallie behind bars would simplify life.

She laughed. "They'd be happy to lock me up, but I'm pretty sure Dad would spring me."

They were up on the deck by the time she said, "Really, I'm sorry for messing up your day. I didn't think you'd be home. I promise you won't even know I'm here while I finish up."

Fat chance, Steve thought. He seemed to have developed Hallie radar. Even if she were ten miles upshore in Ludington, he suspected he'd know down to the grain of sand where on the beach she stood. And he didn't like the feeling. This kind of awareness was like an echo of those unwelcome feelings from seven years ago.

"Uh, do you want to borrow a shirt or something?"

"No, thanks, my shorts and shirt are by the truck. I'll be fine once I dry off. It's hot enough that it shouldn't take long."

Steve couldn't argue with the "hot" part. "Let me go grab you a towel."

"Really, that's—"

He turned heel. "I'll be right back."

AFTER STEVE retreated into the house, Hallie dragged a white plastic chair from the screened porch to the middle of the deck. The chair was a little grungy, but she really needed to sit. She shivered, and it wasn't just with the chill of wet skin.

Chasing off old ghosts had been easy enough while she was *mano-a-mano* with an impossible mountain of sand. But once Steve had arrived, the past she'd been running from had hooked its nasty claws around her ankles. Judging by the stress ripping though her, she didn't think it would be letting go, either.

Hallie cradled one sore hand in the other, then ran her thumb over her palm. Her blisters were going to sting like the devil once the cooling effect of her swim wore off. But that hurt would be easier to deal with than the current unsettled fluttering of her heart.

Feeling queasy, she leaned back and closed her eyes. The sunny day and the laughter of the gulls wheeling overhead disappeared. All that remained was the memory of a bold and totally reckless striptease that had taken place on this deck. The event was seven long years gone, but obviously never to be forgotten.

She frowned as talk show psychologists' words of self-reliance and tough love and even Cousin Althea's karmas and auras filled her head. The images whirled in a dizzying kaleidoscope of colors and noise that quickly reduced to one thought: She needed to wrestle her past into submission.

There, she'd admitted it. Even putting a mountain range and a desert between herself and her high school years hadn't done the trick.

Hallie sighed as the tension began to seep out of her. She had five days left to do an emotional housecleaning—not just with Steve, but with the entire town. Simply accepting this settled her stomach.

Maybe when she got home to wonderful, heavenly and oh-so-cool Carmel, she'd be able to say yes to the next guy who asked her out, and actually feel some level of enthusiasm. Until now, she'd been too mired in memories of Steve—and her own inadequacies—to move on. The gallery owner where she worked to augment her income as Anna Bethune's house manager had been interested in her since she'd started working there. Before, she'd always felt too unsophisticated—the least au courant woman in the world—to be seen with him. But once she laid to rest the ghosts of Sandy Bend, who knew what might happen?

The sound of the sliding door rattling in its track interrupted Hallie's thoughts. She opened her eyes and sat a little taller as Steve came toward her. It was easier to look at him now, to accept that as much as she'd yearned for him seven years ago, he hadn't wanted her at all. She was sure he'd be as grateful as she would to put it all in the past.

He tossed her a towel. She caught it and gave an involuntary wince when the rough terry abraded her tender palms.

"What's wrong?"

Hallie shook her head. "Nothing, really. My hands are a little sore. I guess it's been a while since I did an honest day's work."

Steve wore the same scowl he'd had since she approached him on the dune. "Somehow I doubt that." He held out his hand. "Let me see what you've done."

Hallie fought the impulse to tuck her hands behind her back. Talk was healthy. Maybe even healing. But touching? No way. She hadn't forgotten last night's zing. It had been totally chemical, not based on emotion, but it was a feeling she didn't care to relive, nonetheless.

"I'll be fine."

"Just do it," he replied in the long-suffering voice she'd heard a lot when she was a kid.

She tried a feeble joke as she gave him her right hand. "Hey, I'm the doctor around h—"

Words gave way to a soft gasp as he brushed against a large blister between her thumb and index finger. It wasn't just his gruff gentleness that undid her; it was that blasted, inexplicable zing. But once she'd reached closure with the guy, she was sure it would give way to a fizzle.

"I suppose you've shown me the good hand, too," he said. "Come on, let's go inside and get you fixed up." Moving his grasp to her fingertips, he helped her up.

Hallie awkwardly wrapped the towel he'd given her around her hips and trailed after him into the house. She sat at the kitchen table like a good little patient while he dabbed antibiotic cream on the worst of her ouchies. And all the while she ignored the zing that wouldn't die.

When he'd finished ministering to her, he washed up, then sat down opposite her.

"I think we should talk about it," she blurted before she could chicken out.

Steve cocked his head. "It?"

She was sorry he'd taken off his sunglasses. His golden-brown eyes were a major distraction. She looked down and rubbed one finger across the table's clear maple grain. "Wh-what happened the night of my senior class party."

"Oh, that 'it,'" he said, sounding as if the executioner's blade was about to drop.

Hallie had to wonder at his attitude. After all, he wasn't the one who'd been humiliated in virtually every way imaginable.

He stood and pushed away from the table. "I'm feeling kind of thirsty. Can I get you anything?"

He didn't wait for her answer before going to the fridge. From her position behind him, Hallie noted that the interior was about as barren as the beach in mid-January.

"Looks like I need to get to the store," he said. He opened the produce drawer and then held up something shriveled and possibly of the citrus family. "A snack, maybe?"

"No, thanks. I'd hate to let hunger get in the way of the world's first petrified lemon."

"It was a grapefruit."

"Better yet."

He tossed his offering back into the drawer.

"Steve, I want to talk," Hallie said. "I want to get this out in the open so I feel like I can draw a breath around you."

Steve shut the refrigerator and turned to face her. "Maybe we should head back outside. I'll finish filling the pickup for you."

She stood. "Really, this is important to me."

"You want to talk," he said, the last word heavy with resignation. He strode out to the living room, and again Hallie followed. "You and every other woman I've ever met want to talk. Did it ever occur to you that there are some deep, dark secrets like cramps and bikini waxing that men don't need to be let in on?"

Back and forth he paced, one hand clamped over the back of his neck as though it was all that kept his skull attached to the rest of him. "And contrary to popular female belief, there are lots of things that can't be fixed or made better by talk. Because if they could, I'm pretty sure I'd still have a job next year. And Susan Miller damn well wouldn't have dumped me."

He took a step backward like a fighter reeling from a punch. Hallie was feeling pretty much the same way herself. Since she'd arrived in Sandy Bend, she'd wondered more than once why Steve wasn't married—and had been too secretly pleased that he wasn't to snoop into the "how comes."

"Where the hell did all that come from?" Steve muttered.

He stalked back into the kitchen and got himself a glass of water. Hallie stood in the doorway and watched him finish the drink in slow, steady gulps. The glass rattled against other dishware when he put it in the sink.

For the brief instant that his back was turned she debated dropping the whole conversation, but that was too much like running off to California, so she stuck to her guns.

"If you're feeling better, I'd really like to—"

His eyes narrowed. "'Feeling better?' I'm feeling great. Top of the world."

"So do you want to—"

He raised one hand in warning, then pushed past her through the narrow doorway. "Don't say it. Just don't say it. Of course I don't want to talk. Pretending your Senior Bonfire never happened was working just fine for me."

Hallie managed not to snort at that whopper of a lie. "When you're at work, is that what you tell the kids who come to see you with their problems? 'Just pretend it never happened, and in ten years—fifteen, tops—you'll feel great.'"

He scowled. "Of course not." He stalked from one end of the broad living room to the other. The man wasn't much for holding still, and she didn't like the way he was eyeing the sliding door. "You're here only a few more days. Why stir things up?"

She was beginning to feel as if she belonged in a nature documentary. She could almost hear the narrator's rowdy Australian accent as he crowed, *"The lioness readies for the kill. She's running her victim to the ground!"*

"Because for me, at least, life has never settled down," she said, hurrying to step into the gap between Steve and the great outdoors. Once he escaped, she'd never catch him. "I'd like to get past this, if you'll let me."

He sized her up. Apparently realizing she wasn't going to give up, he gave a disgusted sigh and flopped onto the couch.

"All right, so talk."

6

WITH COMPETITION like Steve, Oprah didn't have to worry about losing her day job. Still, Hallie wasn't rattled. She'd grown up surrounded by clamp-jawed males. Among the lessons she'd learned was to hammer them with words as quickly as possible.

She tucked her stinging hands behind her back and started talking. "The night of the Senior Bonfire—when you found me on the pier—I wasn't going to jump or anything. Honest. I just needed to get away from everybody."

Especially Mike Henderson, the guy she'd asked to be her date. He'd looked like a younger version of Steve, and Hallie had been trying to transfer her feelings for Steve to a replacement. Luckily she'd failed, since that night Mike had disappeared with another classmate named Dana Devine. Hallie had found them in his car, busy pursuing the making of a Mikey, Jr. Not quite the warm graduation memory she'd been seeking.

Steve's voice brought her back to the present. "Standing at the very end of the pier sure bought you space. But it doesn't explain why you were perched on the edge with your arms stretched out."

"*Titanic* envy—queen of the world and all that?"

He snorted. "No dice. The movie wasn't even out yet."

"Okay, my first beer ever and a lot of stupidity."

"Beer and stupidity, I'll buy."

Actually, she'd dumped most of the beer through the open car window on Mike and Dana. Sheer fantasy was all she'd needed to stand on the pier and imagine taking wing across the lake, then clear to California, where she'd be starting college that fall. Someplace new. Someplace where people wouldn't always expect the worst of her. Or treat her as though she existed only to entertain them.

Steve shifted on the couch as if he was getting ready to bolt. "So we're done? We've wrapped it all up, right?"

"Not even close."

He leaned back against the cushions and muttered something Hallie chose not to hear.

"First, I just needed you to know that things weren't quite as bad that night as you seemed to think they were. And admit that maybe I, um…kind of took advantage of you by coming back here when you offered."

He stood and closed in on her. "You think that the coming back here part was when you took advantage of me? How about when you—"

Even though she backed up a step hastily, Hallie didn't let him finish. "I don't have any excuses for what I did—just an explanation."

"This should be interesting."

What she was about to say made her feel more naked than she had been seven years earlier. "Have you ever wanted something so much, but knew you'd never, ever have it?"

He didn't say anything, and Hallie figured he was just being kind. Steve had always gotten what he wanted. She'd always had to live on dreams.

She drew in a thin breath, then finished. "All I ever wanted was for you to notice me."

Steve eased off, giving her just enough room to relax. And maybe to hide the fact that she was shaking.

"Oh, I noticed you, Hallie. You were kind of tough to miss—especially that night." Without another word, he walked out of the house.

"Nice try, but you're not going to get away that easily," she said to his retreating back.

Hallie joined him by the pickup. He was scowling at her shorts and T-shirt heaped next to the wheelbarrow. He nudged the pile with one bare foot. "Think you could put those on?"

"Sure." She did the best she could, but between sore hands and stupid, chopped fingernails, she had a heck of a time getting the zipper on her worn cutoffs to co-operate. She glanced at Steve to see if he was watching her ridiculous struggle.

"Don't even think of asking for help," he growled, then grabbed the shovel and began heaping a pile of sand still on the ground into the back of the pickup.

"As if I would," she muttered as she coaxed the zipper to close. Properly attired, she stood next to the truck bed and shielded her eyes from the sun with her hand.

"So, turning my magic time machine back to the night of the Senior Bonfire, you think I could have been a little more subtle?"

Steve's shovel hissed as it sunk into the sand. "I don't think you'd know subtle if it came up and bit you."

"Good point." Hallie fell silent and leaned against the sun-warmed side of the truck. Eyes closed, she listened to the smooth, rhythmic sound of his shoveling.

They were both tiptoeing around the particulars of that night. The way she'd loosened her hair from its ponytail and run her fingers through it, just like she thought a temptress might. Or the way she'd untied her bathing suit top and let it slip to the deck.

"I want you," she'd murmured in what she'd hoped was a sultry voice designed to get a man's attention. A real, grown-up, out-of-Hallie's-league man. Then she'd stuck her hands behind her back and locked her fingers together to stop the natural impulse to cover herself.

All the while the last sane shred of her mind had screeched, *Are you crazy? This is supposed to lure him? Your collarbone sticks out farther than anything else!*

Instead of pulling her to him and letting loose pent-up passion, Steve had looked as if he'd been smacked upside the head with a dead trout. He'd yanked off his sweatshirt, chucked it at her, then stalked into the house. After giving her a chance to get dressed, he'd marched back out and delivered a lecture that left her feeling as though she'd had the word *harlot* tattooed across her forehead.

A week later she'd moved to California. Filled with trauma and remorse, she didn't even go on a real date until she was twenty. And now, all these years later, she was finally, thankfully more angry than embarrassed.

"Look, I did a bad, bad thing, stripping for you, but you didn't need to treat me like I had a communicable disease."

He speared the shovel into the ground. "Guess we're not done talking."

"Guess not."

He scowled, but she got the feeling it wasn't directed just at her. "Okay, maybe it wasn't the best move, the way I ripped into you, but you caught me by surprise. You were sixteen—"

"Eighteen."

"Like it matters. I was twenty-five and your teacher."

"Former substitute teacher," she felt compelled to clarify.

"Dammit, what you did was wrong. Your stunt messed me up for a long time. I felt like I'd done something to make you think I was interested, that I'd somehow—" He bit down on whatever he'd been planning to say, then grabbed the shovel and started loading the truck again. Hallie tried not to watch the easy play of his muscles against his white T-shirt as he worked.

She could understand why he'd been so angry seven years ago. She had violated the rules she and Steve had always followed—family friends and nothing more. Today's anger was another matter. Still, she wasn't going to let him off the hook.

"Look, I know the attraction I felt was totally one-sided, but you could have—"

"No, I couldn't! I wasn't thinking, I was going on sheer adrenaline. I was so ticked off—" He shook his head. "No, I'm *still* ticked off, and I won't apologize for not being attracted to a fourteen-year-old stripper in training!"

Interesting, the way he was peeling back the years. Pretty soon he'd have her in diapers. "I was eighteen."

"Could have fooled me by the look of things," he muttered.

In that instant, Hallie felt every bit the awkward, underdeveloped teen she'd once been. She walked to the truck's cab, wrenched open the driver's door and climbed in. She ignored Steve when he slid in the passenger side a few seconds later.

"Hallie..."

She wasn't going to cry. Or at least she'd wait until she got back to her ugly pink-gingham-checked room to sob her heart out. As she had that night, too.

"Get out," she snapped while cranking the key. The

truck coughed and sputtered. "Come on," she urged just under her breath.

Steve gently closed his hand over hers as she turned the key yet again. For the first time she almost resented his touch.

"You're flooding it. Let's just cool down, okay?"

Her sore hands dropped to her lap, and she managed to nod. They were both silent for a few minutes.

"I knew talking wouldn't help," he eventually said in a told-you-so voice that didn't help, either. "Hallie, I'm really sorry for both back then and right now. You have this way of getting under my skin."

She wiped at the tears she'd forbidden to fall. "At least it's out in the open. You think I'm ugly and I think you've got all the subtlety of a skunk."

"Trust me on this, you're definitely not ugly. In fact, you've turned into a knockout." Somehow, he didn't sound very pleased with his assessment.

Hallie knew she was okay looking—maybe not drop-dead gorgeous, but she had all the right parts in their customary places. Still, that eighteen-year-old striptease artist still lurked just beneath the surface. Thanks to Steve's grudging compliment, she could feel the scant beginnings of a smile tickling her lips.

"You're not going to argue the skunk thing?"

He shrugged. "It's hard to fight the truth."

She let the smile escape as her gaze met his. "I'll make you a deal…"

"Yeah?"

"I'll never strip in front of you again if you promise to spend an hour with Cousin Althea undergoing a little sensitivity training."

His brows arched and a sexy twinkle shone in his eyes. "And the upside for me is?"

He was joking, and she was a total zero at sexual banter. Hallie tried for a casual, woman-of-the-world laugh in response, but it came out sounding more like a wheeze. One of those horrible silences settled over them—the kind where both parties want to escape, but neither quite knows how to do it.

"Well, I, uh..." she managed to choke out at the same time that Steve worked up some equally brilliant sentiment. They both gave up. Silence reigned. Silence and something more intense. Hotter, too. It was like some weird gravitational pull, the way they seemed to be leaning toward each other, the way Hallie could feel herself tuning up for something big.

He wants to kiss me. The thought made her feel a little smug. Until the unsettling idea that maybe it was just that she wanted to kiss him popped into her head.

"Isn't this sweet?"

Kira Whitman propped her slender arms on the passenger door and looked through the open window as if she were watching television. While surprised, Hallie felt the oddest leap of pleasure at seeing her. She supposed it was a distant echo of the days when they'd truly been friends. Everybody seemed to believe that their rift had something to do with one of the multitude of Horrible Hallie incidents involving Kira, but it didn't.

The summer they were fourteen, some older guys had invited them to go party. Actually, Kira, who even then had been icy blond and incredibly beautiful, had been the one to draw their attention. Hallie had refused to go, and told Kira she shouldn't, either. Kira had called her "a total baby" and went by herself. Too much beer, a sharp turn in the road...

Hallie and her brother Mitch, whom she'd called in a panic, had been the ones to find Kira after the accident. After making sure the guilty were quietly dealt with, Mr. Whitman had managed to hush up the incident. Not even Steve knew the truth of how his sister got hurt. Hallie never said a word to anyone. Kira was her friend and Hallie had been raised to be loyal.

After Kira's hospital stay, everything changed. She told Hallie that it was her fault she'd been injured because she should have stopped her. After that, she refused to speak to Hallie at all. Hallie's dad, who as police chief, knew what had happened, tried to console her. It was Kira's immaturity talking, he said. She knew she'd been wrong, but refused to take responsibility. One day, she was sure to outgrow it, he promised. Hallie was still waiting.

"Hey, Kira," Hallie offered. "It's great to see you again."

All she got back was a "Hallie" spoken the way one might say "mouse droppings." Then Kira ignored her entirely.

"Steve, I was hoping to find you. Everybody who's anybody is meeting at Truro's tonight. You have to come."

At his sister's words, Steve gave a guy-destined-for-sainthood sigh. "Give me three reasons I'd want to go."

"For one…"

Clearly consigned to the legion of "nobodies" who weren't invited to Truro's, Hallie occupied herself by picking the red polish off her ragged nails. She supposed it was bad form to also whistle tunelessly, but since she was a nobody, who would notice her to complain?

She blocked whatever Steve was saying until she heard Kira whine, "But I promised Susan you'd be there. She wants you to meet her fiancé."

Susan? As in the Susan who dumped Steve? Interesting, though Steve didn't look very intrigued. He was staring out the windshield at some point past the horizon.

"What's everybody going to say if you don't show up?" Kira wheedled. "You don't want them to think you're not over her." Her tone suggested that was exactly what she was thinking.

If Hallie's opinion counted—and she was sure it didn't—she would have offered that if Steve didn't show, everybody would figure he had a firm grip on his mental health.

Just about then he settled an even firmer grip on her knee. She jumped nearly high enough to hit the roof. Steve quickly raised both hands to shoulder height, as though he were waiting for someone to arrest him. He met her suspicious look with an insincere smile.

"Hallie," he said, "I know I promised someplace nicer than Truro's for dinner, but do you think we could stop by?"

"D-dinner?"

If the hand on the knee hadn't been hint enough, his answering glare flashed "Play along with me" in blazing neon. "Sure, a quiet dinner, a little wine...just the two of us. Remember?"

Not hardly.

"C'mon, I know it's an imposition, but we'll just stay for a while." If it weren't for the hint of desperation peeking through all that sweet talk, she would have left him to go down with the ship. But it felt good to be the one doing the bailing out instead of clinging to that last, rickety deck chair. And having Kira look ill at the thought of her big brother hanging out with Horrible Hallie didn't hurt, either.

"I suppose we can stop over at Truro's for a few minutes, if that will make you happy." She batted her eyelashes at him. "Sweetums."

Kira's choking sound and Steve's quiet oath almost masked Hallie's snicker. Having the upper hand against the Whitmans was a mighty fine thing, indeed.

AN HOUR LATER, Steve finally let loose the words that had been grinding at him ever since he'd been cornered into going to Truro's.

"I did, you know."

Hallie looked away from the road just long enough to ask, "Did what?"

She'd taken him up on his offer to unload the truck onto the parade float, but she'd insisted on driving—bandaged hands and all.

"Got over Susan." He had, and far faster than the rest of his family, especially Kira, whose worship of Susan continued to this day. "I'd swear on my Boy Scout manual, if I had one."

She grinned. "I'd find that a little easier to believe if you hadn't coerced me into going to the bar with you."

"There's a difference between getting over someone and being ready to chat it up with your replacement. Especially one you just found out about."

"Do tell?"

Brat. He'd liked her better when she wasn't quite so smug, but she was a helluva lot more interesting now. "You're not going to make this easy on me, are you?"

"Nope."

He had to smile at her glee.

As they pulled down the long drive to the Brewer farmhouse, Steve spotted something odd in the field to his right.

"Pull over."

"Why?"

"No questions, just do it."

Gravel crunched beneath the tires as Hallie dipped off the side of the drive. Steve focused on the motion that had caught his eye. About seventy-five feet off, Chief Bud was spinning in mad circles through the shoulder-high grass. His arms were extended out from his body, and his hands were gripping a piece of rope. A healthy chunk of two-by-four appeared to be tied to the other end of that rope. It sliced through the grass at knee height, creating a tidy circular pattern.

Steve glanced at Hallie. Her shocked gaze was fixed on her father. She muttered some sort of quiet litany. It sounded to Steve like, ''There's no place like home...'' over and over.

''Be right back,'' he said before hopping out of the truck. He watched Bud for a minute before cupping his hands to his mouth. ''Hey, Chief Bud!''

Hallie's dad stopped whatever the heck he'd been doing. After a moment's pause—probably to regain his equilibrium—he wrapped the rope around the wood, then carefully tracked back through the crushed-grass pattern toward Steve.

''So...what's up?''

Bud looked at the tool in his hands. ''Nothing much. I'm making a landing pad.''

''For?''

''Aliens,'' Bud answered in a tone conveying the message that Steve was quite possibly the dumbest person on earth.

A soft gasp from next to Steve was his first hint that other than Bud and the potential aliens, he truly wasn't alone.

''Dad, maybe you need a nap, or—''

Catching Bud's thunderous scowl, Steve wrapped his arm around Hallie's shoulders and brought her against him with enough force to cut off whatever other remedial measures she'd been about to suggest. The lightning strike he'd felt when he'd clamped his hand on her knee back in the truck was small stuff compared to the way his heart jolted this time. Anything for Bud Brewer, he reminded himself—and he felt damned noble for it.

''Aliens, huh?'' he said, giving Hallie another ''keep

quiet" squeeze. He ignored just how very good she felt pressed close to his side. "Like we don't already have enough in the way of local characters?"

Bud gave a pointed look at Steve's hand where it still rested on Hallie's shoulder. "Well, like I was telling my child, here, maybe it's time to spice up life."

Steve put a respectable distance between himself and the "child."

Bud didn't seem to notice. He hitched a thumb toward the truck. "What are you hauling?"

"Sand for the Summer Fun float," Hallie offered in a voice that sounded just about as thin as a little kid's.

Her father snorted. "Half a damn beach. And there you are thinking I'm crazy."

Steve figured there was more than enough crazy to spread around in Sandy Bend. He nudged Hallie back toward the truck. "We don't want to keep you from your work."

Bud grinned. "Or you from yours." To Hallie, he added, "See that you and Althea cook the boy a good meal for all the help he's been giving you."

Before Hallie could lecture her dad for living in the dinosaur age, as Steve could see she was itching to do, he smoothly cut in. "Hallie's taking me out tonight, instead."

Chief Bud began to unreel his landing-pad-maker. "And here I thought the odds were better on enticing a few aliens."

7

THAT EVENING, Hallie pulled her car into the sole open spot in front of Truro's.

"Ready?" she asked Steve, who was sitting in the passenger seat, looking as though he'd rather be in a goat truck traversing the Andes Mountains.

"Give me a second."

Normally, she wouldn't have considered a second a lot to ask. At the moment, though, it was. All this intimacy was becoming too much to handle.

She'd already had to deal with the tempting sound of him singing in the shower after he'd unloaded the sand. Then there'd been his appreciative smile when he'd seen her all done up and ready to face Kira's wealthy crew of trunk-slammers.

She still had to face the night itself, plus the ride home she'd promised him. Her universe—centered around a life without Steve—was reshaping itself into something more complex, more exciting. And more frightening, too. She wasn't sure she could stop it. Or that she wanted to.

Bad thoughts. Very unhealthy. Maybe she was just still freaked out over seeing her father waltzing with a piece of wood in the middle of the field. Or maybe her "past purging" had done nothing at all. Except make the problem worse.

She wriggled a bit in the seat, suddenly wishing her little yellow skirt weren't quite so little, and that it wasn't quite so humid out. She was sweaty enough all on her own.

"Ready yet?" she asked.

"Sure."

He was at her car door and opening it before she'd managed to extract the keys from the ignition.

"Here, let me do that," he said, leaning across her and removing the keys before she could object. Instead, she shivered at his clean, soapy smell.

Steve helped her from the car and closed the door behind her. "Are your hands going to be okay?"

Hallie nodded as she tucked her keys into her purse, then slung it over her shoulder. "I took some aspirin."

"Let me know if you need to leave," he said.

She'd bet her last buck he was thinking more of his own escape than her comfort. "You wish."

He laughed. "Yeah, I do, but I'm not going to back down."

The closer they came to Truro's green door—a door she'd never entered before—the more Hallie slowed.

She froze just inside the entrance. Back in high school, she would have given her right leg for the chance to sneak in and spy on Cal and his buddies—especially Steve. Based on what she was seeing, she was glad she'd hung on to her leg.

A yellowish haze of cigarette smoke filled the air, coated the walls and burnt at Hallie's nose. Horned animal heads sporting glassy-eyed looks of resignation served as décor accents. The ceiling tiles had wadded-up dollar bills clinging to them. She didn't want to think about how they got up there and why they stuck. Music best left in the early '90s blasted from the jukebox.

Then there was the clientele.... Hallie had never spent much time contemplating the social structure of a town where the women were blow-dried and made-up to porcelain perfection, yet most of the guys looked as if they'd just finished changing the oil in their dirt bikes. Maybe now she'd pop back outside and mull the ramifications. Anything other than deal with the pack of semifamiliar faces that seemed to have turned in unison to see who'd come in the door.

Steve settled his hand on her shoulder and nudged her forward. "Let's get this over with. Kira's crowd is probably in the back room."

As Steve guided her through the bar, she returned waves and greetings from people she hadn't seen in years. She couldn't remember them being this friendly the last time she'd seen them, either. It had to be the Steve factor. He was probably still the most popular guy in town.

She glanced at him. He was looking grimmer by the minute. Even though she knew it was a little mean-spirited, she couldn't work up much sympathy. After all, she'd been able to face him after their ugly parting years earlier. Why should he be exempt from a little reunion stress?

They made their way past the crowd and through a door marked Private. Without being told, Hallie knew she'd crossed over from townie-land to the lofty realm of the trunk-slammers. Not that the interior decorator had put much effort into this room, either.

A pool table with two bare bulbs suspended above it was at the center of the room. The walls were covered with mirrors supplied by beer companies—all of them lauding the Red Wings and their Stanley Cups.

Oh, but the crowd was different. The room was filled with walking advertisements for trendy labels that she couldn't begin to afford. She could cover the cost of a year's worth of paint and paper by selling the clothes off these women. Kira, in black from head to toe, was doing her best to pretend she didn't see Hallie. Not that Hallie especially cared.

The guys—even Mitch, who hadn't bothered to mention he'd be here—looked smooth and sophisticated. Steve led her around and introduced her to a good dozen people, but always avoided Susan and the tall guy Hallie assumed was Susan's fiancé. If she left it to Steve, Susan and her significant other would be celebrating their golden anniversary by the time he got there.

Hallie took Steve's hand and hauled him along as she planted herself square in front of Susan Miller, who was every bit as beautiful as Hallie recalled, all smooth ebony hair and creamy white complexion. She mentally grabbed her ebbing self-confidence. This was one time she appreciated that Steve-charged energy zipping from their linked hands.

"Hi there, you probably don't remember me but—"

"Of course I do, Hallie. You're looking…" Her expression melting from cordial to confused, Susan trailed off. Hallie followed Susan's eyes to where her hand was still clasping Steve's.

Feeling a residual guilt she didn't want to think about, Hallie let go and tucked her hands behind her back.

"Lovely," Susan finished off, as though the pause had never occurred.

"Well, 'lovely' might be pushing it, but I clean up pretty well for a Townie."

Susan turned her smile up a notch, but it still didn't quite make her eyes. "Hallie, I'd like you to meet my fiancé, Julio Vargas. Julio's in the international law section at my firm."

Using the unbandaged tips of her fingers, Hallie shook the guy's hand. As they exchanged hellos, she briefly glanced at Steve. He was busy shooting Susan one of those you've-got-to-be-kidding glares, while Susan was firing back a look that spoke too much about lingering feelings, for Hallie's taste, at least.

Poor Julio looked as if he'd just realized he'd slipped into quicksand. She knew it was up to her to be the diplomat, which was a pretty sorry indictment of this party.

While she asked Julio all the standard questions about whether he was enjoying Sandy Bend and how the wedding plans were coming, she kept half her attention focused on Steve. He and Susan were involved in a whispered barb-trading ceremony she figured must be customary among the formerly engaged. Since her chat topics for Julio were tapped out, Hallie had heard enough.

She briefly settled one hand on Steve's arm and smiled at Susan. "I hate to interrupt, but Steve's promised me dinner."

At his blank expression, all she could think was that he'd forgotten about her. Hallie wasn't sure which was worse—the hurt or the embarrassment. She made ready to slink off. Mixing with trunk-slammers had always spelled disaster for her. She had no idea how she could have overlooked that crucial fact.

She scanned the crowd for the fastest escape route. Just then, as if he'd been presented by the gods, an unlikely hero approached. She bestowed a relieved smile on the bulky football-type when he stopped in front of her.

His answering smile was open and sincere. "My name's Travis Owen," he said.

"Hi, Travis. I'm Hallie Brewer."

"How about a game of pool?"

She didn't have a clue how to play, but wasn't about to let that stop her. She'd done her good deed for Steve and gotten a blank look in repayment. She'd find some fun in this disaster.

She was about to answer Travis when Kira sidled up

to him. "Here you are. I thought you were going to tell me how you earned those great big rings."

Hallie winced at Kira's breathy routine, something she wished had gone extinct with the dodo bird. She glanced at her rescuer's hands. "His rings are for the Rose Bowl and the Super Bowl."

"Not bad," Travis said with an appreciative laugh. "How did you know about the rings?"

"Thor Bonkowski's married to my dad's cousin. You can't grow up in a family like that without picking up some football." She didn't bother adding that she'd been the first girl to insist on trying out for placekicker on the Sandy Bend Chargers. Though she was more accurate than the guy the coach had chosen, she hadn't made the team. No male in high school had ever looked at her the same afterward.

"Wow, Thor Bonkowski, the legend himself," Travis said, looking appropriately awed. "What's he up to these days?"

Hallie glossed over the living in a commune part of the tale. "Right now he's laid up with muscle spasms at my dad's house."

Steve nudged Hallie. She jumped, unprepared for him to have emerged from his zombie state.

"Weren't you just saying something about dinner?" he asked.

"Nothing that can't wait." And wait a good, long time as far as she was concerned. She had her dignity. She wouldn't come running simply because Steve beckoned. Travis was equally busy ignoring Kira as she tugged at his arm.

"Thor's here in town?" he asked Hallie.

She nodded.

"Any chance I could meet him?"

"Sure. In fact, I think he's got a poker game going tonight. I can give him a call."

He grinned. "A hall-of-famer and some five card stud. Who could ask for anything more from a small-town, hot summer night?"

Kira practically hissed and stalked off.

Travis shrugged. "I guess she could. Now how about some pool?"

Hallie waved her bandaged hands. "A quick one before I call Thor, but I should warn you, I don't know how to play even when I'm not wrapped up like a mummy."

"I'll teach you."

"It's a deal."

As Travis escorted her to the pool table, Hallie had an inkling of what a Sandy Bend High Homecoming Queen must experience, and the feeling was sweet.

STEVE COULDN'T PEG the moment his night had really begun to stink, but stink it did. Seeing Susan was like stepping back in time, and he wasn't prepared for the trip. Add to that her quiet request that they meet for lunch—just the two of them—while Hallie had been busy charming Susan's Mister Tall, Dark and Perfect, made the evening worse. There was nothing wrong about having a private lunch, but there was nothing exactly right, either, given their track record.

He wanted life to be as it had been just a few days ago, when his troubles had been limited to his job and his father. He didn't need to add a woman—no, *women*—into the mix.

His face hurt from the fake smile he'd been trying to keep in place. The sight of Hallie laughing with a guy who could snap him like a pretzel stick didn't help. Neither did Kira, who was in as snappish a mood as he'd ever seen her, hovering at his elbow.

"She's making a fool of herself," his sister said.

"Who, Susan? The guy's a little polished and smarmy, yeah, but he's not that bad."

"I meant Hallie Brewer. Why did you bring her, anyway?" She sounded indignant. Or maybe disgusted.

"I guess for moral support…or something." To stop sounding like an idiot, he took a swallow of beer. Bottom line was he didn't know what Hallie was to him, and he was in no mood to consider it.

Kira leaned closer and whispered, "Did you notice how Susan keeps staring at you?"

He'd been trying not to notice her at all. "She's probably trying to figure out what she ever saw in me."

"I don't think so. I think you still have a chance to fix things with her. Daddy would be so pleased."

Suffering lay ahead when Kira got that smug tone to her voice. "And I just live to please the old man, don't I?"

"Maybe you should try pleasing him once in a while," Kira said. "He's not getting any younger, you know. If you and Susan just—"

"Look, there is nothing—and I mean nothing—between Susan and me. That happy guy next to her is her fiancé, in case you've forgotten. And if your week is shaping up as a little boring, find yourself a hobby. Knitting, kayaking, bungee jumping, just don't stir up things that should be left alone."

"Whatever. But if I were you—"

"Which you're not." Ignoring the rest of his sister's nudging and nagging, Steve looked through the crowd to the pool table. Travis Owen, who had a summer place up the beach, was putting his arms around Hallie to guide her shot. Funny thing how the football player didn't look as if he was getting the same hot jolt Steve did anytime he so much as brushed Hallie's hand.

Steve tried to look away. High-voltage touches

topped the list of matters best left alone. He had enough to handle right now.

But Kira wasn't the only Whitman turning out to be questionable in the self-restraint department. Giving in to impulse, he thrust his beer bottle at his sister and took off to be the one holding Hallie. Just out of curiosity, of course.

"Mind if I cut in?" he asked when he reached the pool table.

Travis moved aside with a friendly enough nod, but two-hundred-sixty pounds of offensive lineman were the least of Steve's troubles. Hallie was looking downright dangerous.

"You cut in if someone's dancing. If they're playing pool, you—"

"Try to get close enough to apologize for acting like an idiot after we got here?" he suggested in an undertone.

The set of her shoulders eased just enough to let him know he was getting somewhere. He appealed to her competitive nature—the same one that had her bicycling down the sand dunes at full tilt when she was a kid.

"Wanna tag team and beat the big guy?"

It took a second, but eventually a smile tugged at the corner of her mouth. "Only if you play nice the rest of the night."

"It's a deal."

Steve moved behind her. "Line up the shot like this," he said, gently folding his hands over her sore ones and nudging her with his thigh so their hips were aligned.

It was like touching fire. He thought back to the time when he was nine and Chief Bud had given him hell for playing with matches. Hallie would have been all of a year old at the time. But she was no baby now.

"How am I doing?" she asked. He noticed a slight quaver to her voice.

"Good. Very good." Too good.

Her spicy scent—a nip of cinnamon—teased him. He wanted to brush back the tendrils of hair curling over her shoulder and settle his mouth against the tender skin of her neck. Wanted to, but wouldn't. The particular brand of insanity that had prompted him over here in the first place wasn't that strong. He hoped.

"Hey, you two, it's easier to make the shot if you keep your eyes open," their opponent prompted from the other side of the table.

Steve shook off the moment. "Yeah, right." He focused on the game. Hallie drew in a sharp breath as he firmed up his grip. "Sorry, I'll be gentler. Now pull back your arm and…" They sunk the ball with satisfying authority.

She smiled up at him. "I could grow to like this game."

He kept his hands over hers for a tempting instant longer. He could grow to like it too much, and Hallie Brewer was a luxury he couldn't afford.

FOR ALL OF Steve's tutoring, Hallie bombed out big-time when she was on her own. Still, she had such fun playing that she took on all challengers. Pretty soon, almost everyone was standing around the table taking bets on how long it would take her to sink one and making the bulbs above the table rattle with their cheers when she did.

She took occasional sips of the wine cooler someone brought her, almost managing to ignore Kira's snippy comments about her childish taste in drinks, and how she should stick to doing what she could do well—whatever that was.

Between shots she spotted Steve, who looked far

more relaxed, talking to Mitch and Travis. Kira seemed to have given up on flirting with the football player, but Hallie suspected she was just regrouping for a new assault.

On the next shot, Hallie adjusted her grip to relieve the pressure on the worst of her blisters. She drew back her right arm and felt the cue slip from her control, to the extent she'd had control over it to begin with. The cue's backward motion suddenly ended. Jeez Louise, she'd hit something. Or more accurately, someone.

Kira let loose a howl. "My eye! You've—you've wounded my eye!"

Hallie propped the cue against the table, drew in a ragged breath and turned to face her victim. Kira was sitting in a chair pulled a good two feet from any table—well within cue striking range. She had both prettily manicured hands clamped over her face.

The good news was Hallie didn't see anything like blood. The bad news was that Kira was howling so loudly that the Private door had flung open and a crowd had gathered in the entry. It wouldn't be a trip to Sandy Bend without a dose of public humiliation.

Steve knelt in front of his sister and tried to pry her fingers away from her face. "Just let me look at it, Kira."

"It *hurts!*"

Over his shoulder he said to Hallie, "Why don't you go out to the bar and see if you can get some ice?"

"I've got it covered," Mitch said. The crowd parted. In a few long strides, he was gone.

Hallie was beyond mortified. She knelt down next to Steve.

"Kira, I'm sorry. I didn't know you were behind me. Good thing my hands are hurt. At least I couldn't pack much of a punch."

Kira opened her fingers wide enough to give Hallie

a venomous glare out of her good eye. "Just shut up and get me a plastic surgeon."

"Quit being such a baby," Steve ordered. "If anything, you'll have a little shiner."

"A shiner? You mean a black eye?" Kira's voice climbed into operatic upper octaves. "There's no such thing as a little black eye."

Mitch returned and knelt on the other side of Hallie. She felt like one of the three wise men in a church Christmas play.

"It was dumb to pull up a chair where you did," Mitch said to Kira as he handed Steve a plastic bag filled with ice. "Any fool could have seen—"

Kira uncovered her face and shot to her feet, apparently forgetting her "wounded" eye. "*Fool?* Now I'm a fool?"

"All I meant was you could afford to be a little more careful," Mitch said, using a hostage negotiator's level tone.

"I'm not the one who needs to be careful," Kira snapped.

Left with a clear view of Kira's pointy black shoes, Hallie stood and backed away a few healthy steps. She didn't put it beyond Kira to apply a retaliatory kick to the shin. Mitch and Steve stood, too.

"Maybe you better let me handle this," Steve said. "I've got more experience."

Kira closed in until she stood nose-to-nose with Mitch. Actually, more nose-to-chest. "This is your klutz of a sister's fault. She's always out to get me. Do you think I've forgotten the green hair or the time she nearly plucked off my left eyebrow?"

Mitch looked over his shoulder at Hallie. "Her eyebrow?"

She gave a helpless shrug. "We were eleven. I was in my Picasso phase and convinced her she'd look cool.

It could have been worse. The next year I was into Dali—drooped eyeballs and all that jazz.''

Someone in the crowd snickered. Kira shot them a baleful one-eyed glare. ''That's right, laugh, you idiot. But who knows what damage she'll do while she's in town? Hallie Brewer is lethal, I'm telling you!''

Suddenly, the weight of a pool cue settled into Hallie's hand.

''I'll line her up and you take your shot. Just put us out of her misery,'' Travis Owen said in a low voice, but not quite quietly enough.

Kira's gasp was one of real pain.

''Kira—'' Hallie began.

It was too late. Head high, but chin definitely quivering, Kira shoved her way through the crowd and disappeared.

Hallie handed the cue to Travis, who looked as chagrined as she felt. She and Kira were far from friends, but that didn't mean she relished embarrassing her. Figuring she'd done enough damage for one night, Hallie picked up her purse from where she'd set it beneath the pool table.

''I've got to get going,'' she said to Steve and her brother. Without looking back, she left.

''Show's over,'' she could hear Steve announcing as she escaped the back room. By the time she reached the front door, the music had regained its ear-splitting volume. Townies and trunk-slammers were no doubt dividing into their respective groups.

Part of neither group, Hallie stepped onto the sidewalk. She'd forgotten how late the Sandy Bend summer sun visited. It was almost nine at night and the sky was just beginning to wear a twilight-colored cloak. Without any plan other than escape, she crossed the street and walked down the steep slope of the village green.

Glad to be free of the cigarette smoke, the noise and

the sensation that she'd never feel at home anyplace, Hallie sat on a stone bench beneath the sheltering leaves of an enormous maple tree she'd climbed more than once in her life. If it weren't for her blisters and her impractical clothes, she'd be up in that crook about ten feet off the ground right now, figuring out how she'd managed to screw up yet again.

As Hallie sat there, the deceptive simplicity of small-town life crept over her. Couples walked by, hand in hand. A group of people sat on the broad concrete steps leading to the gazebo, laughing and joking. Hallie let the scene with Kira slip away.

She allowed herself to savor the good things—the fresh note of water nearby on the breeze ruffling her hair, the memory of Steve with his arm low about her waist, his hands closed over hers. She could savor it, then on Saturday, leave.

"Hey, taking off without me?"

Steve settled next to her, close enough that Hallie might have rested her head on his shoulder and watched the night unfold.

"I'm sorry," she said, fighting the temptation to seek comfort in the most emotionally dangerous place of all. "With everything that happened, I guess I forgot I was your ride."

"It's okay. I'm sorry about Kira."

She shook her head. "Don't apologize. It's not like you can control her. I'd forgotten how dramatic she can be."

He chuckled and stretched out his long legs before him. "She's been refining her technique. It's pretty much her full-time job."

"She's an actress?"

"Nah, she just cons money out of our dad. She's a pro at it, too."

"Well, everybody's got to find their niche in life."

"That's half the problem," Steve said, shifting a little to face her. "I don't think Kira has ever had to figure out what hers is, and she's a little scared right now. She's done with college, can't hold a job for more than a week and is watching all of her friends move on, just like you've moved on."

Hallie ran her fingertip across the rough top of one chopped-off nail. "I'd call what I did more of a panicked escape."

"Really?" he said, sounding startled. "Your path always looked clear to me."

"Then maybe you should have clued me in. I was getting pretty tired of slipping on all those Sandy Bend banana peels. It's tough being known as the village screwup."

"Is that what you think? To me, you've always been Hallie the Artist—even when you were a kid painting your dog," he added with a grin.

Hallie blinked. While she'd always been serious about her art, she had no idea Steve or anyone else had seen her that way.

"You know," Steve was saying, "it has to rattle Kira to see you again, now that you're so poised and—"

Hallie worked up a scoff. The artist thing she could almost buy, but—

"Poised?"

"Yes, poised. Look how game you were about playing pool, even with hands that must still be stinging."

He cupped her left hand in his palms. It was an act with no overt sexual overtones, yet a shock rocketed through her, and apparently through Steve, too. He pulled back. Even in the dim light, she could read the confusion on his face.

"How do you do that?" he asked.

She drew a shaky breath. To answer was to reveal more about herself than a just-passing-through-town acquaintance should. Still, he'd opened himself to her, which meant she could risk offering him the same in return. "Actually, I've been sure that it's you doing it to me. You feel it, too?"

"Yeah, I feel it. I could be frozen in a block of ice six feet thick and still feel it."

A thought occurred to Hallie. "Maybe the two of us together are like me and cats."

He tilted his head and gave her a warm grin. "You and cats? This ought to be good."

The more she thought about it, the more she warmed to her theory. "I had this instructor in college named Catherine Lassiter. Anyway, we really hit it off, and after I graduated, I continued working with her at her studio. She had this enormous stray cat named Fred she'd taken in. Until I started studying with Catherine, I didn't know I'd grown sensitive to cats.

"Fred could sense that I didn't want to be near him, so being a cat with a full dose of cat attitude, he followed me everywhere. At first I was an allergy poster child, but by the time Catherine moved out of the country last year, Fred could wrap himself around my legs and I wouldn't even sneeze."

"So you think I'm kind of like cat dander to your system?" Steve sounded clearly doubtful.

"Exactly, and if I were around you frequently enough, the zing would be gone."

"You can be tough on a guy's ego, you know that?" He moved closer, and her heart beat a staccato rhythm. "Since you're only here until Saturday, I guess we'll have to test your theory with quality time instead of quantity."

His eyes were lit with a zippy spark she hadn't seen before. His smile was hot and easy. He cupped the back of her head with one broad hand.

"Or we could just leave it as speculation," she offered, even as she tilted her head, seeking that perfect fit of mouth to mouth that she'd yearned forever to experience with Steve.

Her eyes slipped closed as his lips feathered gently against hers, leaving her waiting, wanting, hungry. He brushed his mouth against her jaw, the tender skin of her temple, then took her mouth with true intent.

This was no sweet preteen fantasy of rising violins and lovebirds twittering. Hallie wanted to take him down onto the grass and feel his weight pinning her to the warm earth.

Steve drew back a little. "Come here, let's do this right," he said, his voice low and husky.

As he settled her on his lap with her legs stretched over the smooth stone of the bench, her sole objection was that she couldn't get even closer. Only the snugness of her skirt stopped her from straddling him and finding the fit her body craved.

"Better," he said before again finding her mouth with his.

Hallie concentrated on the details: The silky feel of his thick hair under her sensitive fingertips. The way his heart drummed in time with hers. Just a few minutes longer, and she was sure the memory would be forever imprinted in her "Hallie's Summer Vacation" mental scrapbook.

"Isn't that Steve over there?"

The voice was an intrusion, an annoyance. Hallie tried to ignore it.

Someone else laughed. "Doesn't look like he'll need that ride home."

"Is that really Hallie Brewer with him?" a female voice asked.

Steve drew back and rested his forehead against Hallie's. "Sorry, I forgot where we were."

Hallie's heart lurched as she realized she'd gone from

one public scene to another. In her haste to scramble from Steve's lap—and restore some dignity to her life—she lost her balance. Only Steve's quick grab stopped her from landing on her rump. He hauled her back into his lap.

"Steady there," he said, laughter in his voice.

Hallie braced her hands on his chest and pushed away again, this time making sure her feet were on solid ground.

She glanced from Steve to the cluster of people still standing at the top of the green. Frustration with the spectators, with Steve and most especially with herself kicked her defense mechanism into high gear.

"Bummer. Caught kissing geeky Hallie Brewer on the village green. That's quite a comedown in the world." She picked up her purse from where it had spilled on the ground by the bench. The car keys had sunk to the bottom, of course. "It's pretty late. Let's say we skip dinner."

Steve stood. "Hallie, hang on a second—"

Without waiting to hear what he wanted to say, she headed for the car, avoiding the Steve Whitman Fan Club, of course.

A COMEDOWN? Hallie thought kissing her was a comedown? Life would be one helluva lot more placid if it had been. Kissing Hallie had been a nuclear-powered wake-up call.

Steve knew it wasn't right to get hot and worked up when sitting on a cold granite bench carved in memorial to Luta Mae Wilson, long-dead village librarian. Though he supposed Luta Mae—who was reputed to have been a spicy number in her own right—might appreciate it while looking down from the Hereafter.

One kiss and he'd had to accept that since Hallie's arrival, he'd been steeped in self-delusion. First, he'd tried to pretend she was still a bratty twelve-year-old. When that failed, he'd acted like one himself.

Steve suspected that kiss was going to prove to be either the smartest or the dumbest thing he'd ever do in life. When he'd made his move, he'd convinced himself that it would be a joke-around-with-a-buddy kind of kiss. A prove-to-himself-he-was-over-Susan kiss.

He wasn't sure when his tongue had developed a will of its own and decided to explore the corners of Hallie's mouth. Or to slip inside when she so sweetly opened for him. And she *was* sweet. So sleek and delicious that he'd do it again if she weren't already wheeling down Main Street in her car.

The second he'd felt Hallie warm and willing beneath his mouth, he'd known he kissed her because he wanted to. No, needed to.

But he had to remember who he was. Maintaining a principal's moral high ground after being spotted necking on the village green was one tough proposition. He couldn't afford a public display like that again—especially with his future currently spinning at the end of a financial noose.

He knew all this, but the heat he and Hallie had created had left him hungry and reckless. She was in town only a few more days. What was the harm if they decided to satisfy their mutual curiosity? It wasn't as though they were talking about the traditional Whitman country club wedding with photo spreads in *Vanity Fair* and *Town and Country.*

Steve shook his head as he tried to imagine Hallie hosting cocktail parties with his older sisters, who were smooth and elegant, and definitely incapable of delivering a knockout punch with a pool cue.

He supposed one day he'd have to toe the family line and marry one of those proper women—a woman like

Susan. They could have another generation of proper little Whitman offspring. But not yet.

A slow smile worked its way across Steve's face. For the next few days, he'd do what he'd always liked best. He'd play with fire.

8

AT NINE THE NEXT MORNING, Hallie peered down a narrow stairway on Main Street she'd never given more than passing notice. At the bottom was a door faux-painted to look like a stone wall with a big iron gate closed over it. How inviting. At least the origin of the Hair Dungeon's name was no great mystery.

Figuring her mood couldn't get much bleaker than it already was, she made her way down. A bell chimed when she stepped inside, but no keeper of the dungeon was in sight.

"I'll be right with you," a woman's raspy but faintly familiar voice called from a back room. "Just let me get Mrs. Hawkins settled in the tanning bed...." Whatever else the person was saying got covered by the sound of a radio being switched on. The Barenaked Ladies were contemplating what they'd do with a million dollars.

Hallie had her answer down pat. After last night's disaster, she'd haul her whole family out of Sandy Bend and make them settle in comparatively sane Carmel. But since she was nearly broke, she sat down at the manicure station instead.

"Sorry about that," the same voice said from closer by. "Mrs. Hawkins's back isn't what it used to be. If I don't help her in, she ends up on the ground."

An incredibly tall woman glided into the room carrying something that looked like an egg timer. If her formfitting black catsuit weren't distracting enough, her spiky hair colored white-blond—with some red highlights thrown in for good measure—would have done the job. Hallie squinted. Substitute brown hair, subtract about four inches and you had—

"Dana Devine." This town was too small.

Dana stood taller on her spike-heeled pumps. It hurt just looking at them. "In the flesh."

Hallie tried very, very hard not to recall how much of Dana's flesh she'd seen seven years ago.

"You're looking great, Hallie. Big city all the way. Though you might want to add a few highlights around your face."

"I'll stick with what I've got, thanks," Hallie answered, though she was a little curious about what color highlights Dana would recommend. Purple, maybe.

Dana shrugged. "Just offering some professional advice."

She set down the egg timer, sat at the opposite side of the manicure cart and switched on a small lamp. She gestured for Hallie to hold out her hands. Hallie obeyed more out of shock than any actual desire to cooperate. Dana ran her thumb across the now partially defanged dragon lady nails, then experimentally wiggled one between two fingers.

"You really messed these up. Lucky for you these were put on by someone reputable. At least I won't have to rip them off. Some salons use bad glue, you know."

"Uh, no. I don't make it a habit to wear plastic fingernails."

Dana snorted. "Trying to impress the locals?"

"Trying to scrape up some nerve, mostly." Hallie tugged her hand back when Dana picked up a giant set of clippers.

"I know what I'm doing. Really."

"Just don't hurt me."

"It doesn't look like I could do much worse than you've already done. Burn yourself?"

Hallie gingerly gave over one hand. "Blisters."

"I'll be gentle. Promise." She began clipping, and her words were punctuated by the snap of cracking acrylic. "I know I probably should have told you it was me when you called, but I was afraid you'd cancel the appointment. I just took over the salon from its former owner last month. With the start-up expenses, rent money's looking a little slim. But if you want to go, it's okay. I can give you the name of someone good up in Ludington."

Hallie cocked her head at the two small bowls Dana was filling with some fluid. "No, go ahead, unless that stuff will eat my fingers along with my nails."

"No, it's just acetone, the same chemical as polish remover. Now start soaking. You're going to be here a while."

An egg timer chimed, and Dana stood. "I'll be right back. It's time to flip Mrs. Hawkins."

Hallie closed her eyes as she listened to the muted music from the back room. She swished her fingernails through the bowls of remover in time to the beat. Just as soon as she got these things off, she'd go home and settle in with her sketchbook. Time spent drawing improved even her most miserable days.

The front bell rang. Hallie opened her eyes to see her brother, Cal, walking into the salon. He was dressed for business and acting that way, too. She smiled as he scoped out the room as if he thought there might be nuclear waste hiding in a corner.

"Come for a new do?" she asked.

"Nope, I came looking for you. Thea told me I'd find you here."

Not that he was looking at her. Something on the wall behind her seemed to have captured his attention. Doing her best to keep her hands in their bowls, Hallie peeked over her shoulder.

Cal stared at a large black-and-white, soft-focus photograph. A nude man and woman had their backs to the camera. She was slender and spike-haired. He was broad and muscled. Strips of what looked like black silk bound them together. It was either a bondage scene or art, depending on the viewer's mind-set. Hallie voted for art.

"You were looking for me because...?" she prompted Cal.

He didn't look away from the photo. "Think that's her?" Before it even clicked with Hallie that he meant Dana, he shook his head and gave a muttered, "Never mind."

Hallie watched as he peeled his eyes from the picture, then concentrated on her.

"Dad showed up at the station after the Men's Service Club morning coffee," he said.

At least her father was following one of his usual routines. "So what else is new?"

"You've been enlisted to bring enough homemade potato salad to serve fifty at the village picnic tomorrow. Emphasis on the homemade, too. He said he doesn't want any of that supermarket stuff old enough to be an antique and made out of god knows what."

Make that two routines. Punch for one hundred, a parade float, potato salad for fifty—her dad was infamous for pitching these last-minute assignments at her. "So why isn't Dad home peeling potatoes?"

"He's too busy. He said something about having to drive down to Grand Rapids."

Hallie sighed. "Fine. I'll make the potato salad."

Cal grinned, showing the dimples more than one woman had fallen prey to. "That's my Hal." He turned to leave, then paused and turned back. "I wasn't going to say anything, but I guess I must be getting as gossipy as everyone else around here. What's this about you kissing Steve last night?''

Hallie could see it was going to be a long day. She'd already been grilled for details by Cousin Thea first thing this morning.

"Not to put too fine a point on it, but *he* kissed *me*, not the other way around," she said.

Cal hooked his thumbs into his belt and gave what Hallie privately termed the "Brewer Cop Glare." "It doesn't matter who was kissing who, just that you were kissing. After all these years away, I figured you had to be over that crush you had on him."

"I wouldn't call it a crush at this point."

"Whatever you want to call it. I might love Steve like a brother, but you're my sister, and I want you to be careful. After the mess with Susan, he's a long way off from getting serious about a woman."

"I'm here for a week and you think I'm playing for keeps? What if all I want is—"

He raised a hand to silence her. "Spare me the details. Thinking of you two kissing is weird enough."

Just then, Dana emerged from the back room. "Ready to lose those claws?" she called. Her long strides slowed when she saw Cal.

A wary "Cal" was all she said in greeting.

He nodded. "Dana." He looked back at Hallie. "I have to get going."

But Cal must have decided he couldn't leave without one last look at the photograph. Hallie watched Dana follow his line of vision. For a fleeting instant she looked almost sad, but then her lips curved into a feline smile. She prowled close to Cal and flicked the handcuffs hanging from his belt.

"Great cuffs," she purred. "I love handcuffs. They're so...useful."

Hallie choked back her laughter. "If you ask her nicely, maybe she'll play with you."

He gave them both a look that should have straightened even Hallie's humidity-impaired hair. "Potato salad," he barked as he shot out the door. It probably wasn't the first phrase that had come to her brother's mind, but Hallie was glad it was the last out of his mouth.

After he disappeared, Hallie's and Dana's snickers exploded into full-scale howls. Hallie was sure it was due to nerves and unfamiliarity on both their parts, yet still the day seemed less grim.

"I shouldn't have played with Cal like that," Dana said when they'd both calmed.

"He deserved it."

Dana settled back into the chair opposite Hallie and checked her nails. "So he did."

"For what it's worth," Hallie offered, "I think it's a beautiful photo."

"Thanks. Not everyone around here shares your opinion."

"That's you in the picture, right?"

Dana worked the tip of a manicure tool under one acrylic nail and wiggled it back and forth as she spoke. "I lived in Chicago for a while and did some modeling. But I hit a money crisis, so here I am, back in Sandy Bend, proud new owner of the Hair Dungeon."

"Yeah, but look what you've done with the place," Hallie said with a nod at an uninspired interior of dingy beige walls and a stained white vinyl floor. "It's really got that perky feel."

Dana laughed. "Don't worry, both the name and the décor are changing soon." Her hands stilled. "You know, I'm glad you came in here today. Even though we didn't exactly hang out together back in high school, I always had the feeling I'd like you."

"Why?" Hallie asked out of curiosity, then wanted to yank back the words when she realized how hungry for praise she must sound.

"Why?" Dana echoed, looking startled. "Is this a quiz or something?"

"Just a case of homecoming insecurity, I guess."

"Okay, here's one reason. You never called me Down 'n Dirty Dana."

Hallie grinned. "When you're known as Horrible Hallie, you get pretty sensitive about those name issues."

"Tell me about it." She worked loose the fake nail from one thumb and tossed the scrap of plastic into the trash. "You know, I didn't do the down 'n dirty nearly as often as people liked to believe. And you pouring beer all over me that night in Mike's car didn't make me hurry to do it again."

"So I marked you for life?"

She grinned and sent another nail spiraling to its fate. "A week or two, at least."

"Whatever happened to Mike?"

Dana hesitated before answering. "We got married a couple of years ago."

Hallie offered a polite, "Congratulations."

Her face tightened. She spoke without taking her eyes from her work. "Too late. He left me for Suzanne Costanza. Remember her?"

Hallie nodded. "Detroit family, big mansion on the lake?"

"That's Suzanne. Anyway, Mike and I are divorced."

Hallie decided to speak openly. Dana seemed to be the type who could handle it. "On the basis of my one and only date with him, I can't say I'm too surprised he left you. He hit me as kind of the fickle type."

Dana winced. "I'm sorry about that. I was too

chicken to apologize back then, but I felt really, really bad. I was just so crazy about Mike, and—''

''Don't worry about it. It was a long time ago, and to tell you the truth, I didn't like him all that much. I asked him to the bonfire because he—''

''Reminded you of Steve Whitman?''

''How did you know?''

Dana rolled her eyes. ''It's not like it's a national secret. I mean, look at the mural of the village you painted on the side of the old theater building during tenth grade. Every person in it looks like Steve…the old lady, the girls jumping rope. Even the dog has Steve's eyes.''

She didn't recall painting it that way. Maybe it was time to check the mural out—assuming the Men's Service Club hadn't been merciful enough to paint it over.

''And then there was the way you'd answer every question when he subbed in our math class senior year. Even when he called on someone else, you'd butt right in.''

''I'm over it now.''

''So last night on the village green, that lip lock was just for old times' sake?''

''Word still travels fast around here.''

''Lucky for you, not as fast as Steve's hands on the green last night.''

''Dana!'' Hallie was amused in spite of herself.

''Okay, okay…I'll leave it alone.'' She was silent for all of a tenth of a second. ''I also heard that you've been working for Anna Bethune.''

''I take care of one of her vacation homes.''

''Too bad about her husband. I can't figure out why Matt Colton would be chasing after that wrestler when he's married to someone as hot as Anna.''

''You're losing me here.''

''She caught him in bed with Brandi Flexxum—you

know, the pro wrestler. It's on the front page of yesterday's *Galaxy News*.'' She waved her hand at a stack of tabloids in a basket by the front door.

"Right next to the 'Woman Gives Birth to Three-Headed Calf After Alien Abduction' article, right?''

"Okay, so it's not the most reputable news source. I mean, I just leaf through it when a client leaves it.''

And Hallie enjoyed the guilty pleasure of reading the front page while waiting in line at the supermarket, but that didn't mean she believed any of it.

"When it comes to Hollywood gossip, the *Galaxy* is usually dead on the money,'' Dana said.

"Not this time,'' Hallie replied, sounding much more confident than she felt.

In her three years working for Anna Bethune, she'd never done more than speak to her on the phone. Hallie and Matt, however, had had their share of encounters. Matt, while also an actor, wasn't in the same kind of demand as Anna. He often came to Carmel Highlands when Anna was filming out of the country. The guy was a scary mix of ego and insecurity. Hallie wouldn't put it past him to do something this immoral, arrogant and downright stupid.

She lapsed into silence as she thought about the possibility of losing her job. Sure, she could take a step backward and share a place in Carmel with someone. Or maybe it would be better to find an apartment of her own farther inland where rent was more reasonable. She'd become accustomed to a certain amount of solitude.

Working quickly and quietly, with only one break to retrieve Mrs. Hawkins from the tanning bed, Dana removed the rest of Hallie's nails.

"I didn't mean to upset you with that talk about Brandi Flexxum,'' she said as Hallie was getting ready to leave.

Hallie tucked her change back into her purse, thankful that she could do it with only a few blisters—and no ragged nails—to impair her. "It's okay. I'm better off being prepared in case something does happen."

Dana nodded. "That's the truth. There's nothing worse in life than being caught unaware. Unless it's getting a wake-up call with a beer bath," she added with a grin.

Hallie had to laugh.

"If you get a chance, stop in and see me before you go back to California, okay?"

"I'll absolutely stop by," Hallie said, and meant it. It was an interesting concept, finding a new friend in sort-of-changed Sandy Bend.

A few minutes later, Hallie wheeled a squeaky cart down the narrow aisles of Hawkins' Foodland, intent on gathering potato salad ingredients. She'd just turned the corner from the spices—celery seed was mandatory, as far as her father was concerned—when someone settled their hand on her shoulder. She didn't have to look around to know it was Steve. His touch was enough.

She turned to face him. He didn't look as if he'd gotten much sleep, either. Still, when a guy looked like that, he was sexy and scruffy, while she was puffy and pasty.

"You wouldn't come to the phone last night," he said.

"I was tired."

"And first thing this morning?"

She backed up a step. "Still tired."

"You look awake now. Wouldn't you agree, Mrs. Hawkins?" he added for the benefit of the store owner, who was showing off her golden tan against a display of marshmallows.

"She looks fine enough to me."

A lie if ever Hallie had heard one. She rolled her eyes at Mrs. Hawkins as if to say, "Thanks for the help." The storeowner smirked right back before moving on.

Knowing she was trapped, Hallie parallel parked her cart by the cake mix.

Steve pulled in behind her, then motioned to the items she'd collected. "Potato salad, huh?"

"Yep, enough for fifty people."

"I got the same marching orders from your dad at coffee this morning."

Hallie grinned as she imagined Steve plopped down in the middle of Sandy Bend's daily male gossip session that masqueraded as a community affairs meeting. Her smile faded as she realized that she and Steve now fell squarely under the heading of "community affairs."

Seeking distraction, she looked in his cart. "Last I heard, French bread, champagne and strawberries weren't part of potato salad."

"I turned that assignment over to Kira as a payback for her bad behavior last night."

"Does she have a black eye?"

"Nothing too spectacular has shown up yet. I think I saw a smudge of blue, but she won't take off her sunglasses long enough for me to be sure it's not just makeup."

Hallie felt a tad depressed at the news she hadn't committed grievous bodily harm. She also felt guilty for her lack of moral fiber, but not guilty enough to kill the disappointment.

"So what are the goodies in your cart for?" she asked.

"Getting back in the Sandy Bend swing of things, aren't you?" he teased. "If you have to know, it's for you. I owe you dinner."

It sounded as though he had more in mind than food

if he was planning a dinner involving champagne and strawberries. Hallie panicked. "No, you don't."

"Okay, maybe you owe me dinner after ditching me in town like that, but either way, dinner's happening."

"I really need to work on the parade float."

"The float's as much my responsibility as yours. I've never let down your dad and I don't intend to now. We'll work, then eat."

Hallie scrambled for a way out while simultaneously asking herself if she really *wanted* a way out. "Really, you don't have to help with the float. I told you I can handle it."

He ran one fingertip across her knuckles, then turned her hand over and gently touched the adhesive bandage still covering the worst of her blisters. A shiver chased down her spine.

"Afraid I'm going to disprove your cat dander theory?"

She was. "No way."

"Even after last night?"

Hallie feigned boredom. "You mean that little kiss on the green?"

"It looked pretty big to me," Mrs. Hawkins called from the next aisle over. "In fact, I heard over at the hardware store this morning that—"

"That will be enough, Mrs. Hawkins," Hallie called back. "We're trying to have a private discussion, here."

"Then maybe you'd better pick a more private spot than the middle of my store."

"She's got a point," Steve said. "Dinner tonight, in your barn." He leaned closer and with an intimate smile that curled her toes, whispered, "Be sure you come hungry."

Hallie didn't think she'd have any problem with that.

9

IF WAR WAS HELL, making potato salad for fifty, Hallie-style, ran a close second. Hallie bit back a curse as hot water slopped from the pot she was draining.

"You need to find your center, perhaps take a meditation break," Thea offered from the dining room doorway. After Hallie's earlier mishap with a flying potato, Thea had retreated to safer ground.

"It's going to take something a little more active to fix what's ailing me."

Since leaving Steve at the market, she'd analyzed and reanalyzed every nuance of their conversation. No matter how she looked at it, Hallie remained convinced she was on Steve's menu tonight. When she'd told Thea of her suspicions, her father's cousin had given her standard I-knew-that-before-you-spoke response.

"You really have to stop viewing sexual desire as an ailment," Thea counseled.

"It's definitely an ailment when it has me dropping jars of mayonnaise like fatty hand grenades all over the kitchen." The first one Hallie had put down to clumsiness. The second was proof she'd lost it altogether. She now faced another trip to town for replacement mayo.

"Okay, the veggies are prepped and the last of the potatoes are ready to cool down in the fridge, so I guess it's off to the market for me." As Hallie lifted the potatoes from the old white porcelain farmhouse sink, her mind wandered to what, exactly, Steve might have planned.

And what she planned to do about whatever he had planned.

Did she have it in her to play this game to its inevitable conclusion?

She stopped halfway between the sink and the refrigerator as she considered the issue. If she didn't dwell on the details, yes, she could see herself making love with Steve.

And when she did dwell on the details... Hallie felt warmth climb her cheeks and tingle through her limbs. Her grip on the pot grew lax as she imagined what it would feel like to be able to run her hands over warm flesh and hard muscle.... To live out her fantasies...

"Got it!"

Hallie blinked as she watched Thea finish off a home-base slide at her feet and save the potatoes.

She took the pot from Thea and gave a lame, "Thanks."

Thea stood and reclaimed the potatoes. "I'll take it from here, if you don't mind. And while you're in town picking up the mayonnaise, could you grab some tofu for the men's poker marathon tonight?"

"Tofu?"

Thea looped her hair behind her ears, showing the multiple chains and piercings that reminded Hallie of an Indian princess. "They want potato chips, but Thor needs an early night."

And Hallie needed a late one.

ONE OF THE QUIRKS Steve had forgotten about Susan was how a perfectly reasonable woman could go a little nuts when it came to dining out. If the hostess seated her by the door, she wanted to be by the window. If seated by the window, "toward the middle of the room would be so much better, if you don't mind." Then there was her refusal to eat anything actually on the menu. She'd reduced some of Chicago's finest chefs to whimpering babies.

Today, Steve was relieved to find that Susan was on her best behavior. They'd changed tables only once—so she could enjoy the "quaint" view. Her menu comments had been limited to disappointment over the Corner Café's lack of Boston Bibb for her salad and distress that the fresh mozzarella wasn't of the flown-in-from-Italy variety.

After inspecting her water glass, she took a nervous sip, then said, "I'm so glad you could join me today. I've really needed someone to talk to."

"I've got to say that I'm kind of an odd choice, considering the previous silence on your part."

"You didn't call me, either."

He shrugged. "Didn't see the point."

Her determined smile slipped a notch. "Anyway, Julio was up most of the night working out the kinks of some Australian deal. He'll be dead until evening, which means my plans for tennis this afternoon are shot."

"You're in the same firm. You know what the hours are like."

She nodded, fiddling with her engagement ring. The diamond would have eaten up two years of Steve's salary. "I'm just not sure how we'll fit a marriage into our schedules."

And that was where he differed from Susan. "Maybe you should consider tailoring your schedules to your marriage, instead."

She laughed as if he'd reached the punch line of a real knee-slapper. "That's a good one."

Just then, Kristal, their waitress and also one of Steve's students, arrived with his burger and Susan's salad. After questioning befuddled Kristal on the origins of the balsamic vinegar, Susan turned her attention back to him.

"The wedding is just two weeks away and I feel like I'm suffocating. I'd call the whole thing off if I weren't afraid everyone would start looking at me as the local version of the Runaway Bride. What do you think I should do?"

He'd sooner become her personal chef than answer that loaded question. "I think it's none of my business."

Susan toyed with her lettuce before saying, "Kira says your father has offered you a job."

Steve saw where this was going, and had to wonder at her lack of finesse in directing the conversation. Surely she did better in the courtroom. "He's always offering me a job."

"But she says this time it's different, that you might be fired from your teaching position."

His little sister had obviously settled on the one pastime he'd discouraged: meddling.

"First, I'm a principal now and don't spend much time in the classroom. Second, I'm not about to be fired. There's just some question whether that particular job will exist after this coming school year."

When he'd taken the principal's job, he'd thought he was ready to move on to an administrative role. Now he had his doubts. He missed getting to know a group of kids over a year the way he did when he was in the classroom with them everyday.

"Oh. So even if your job is eliminated, there's no chance you're moving back to Chicago?"

He supposed if Chief Bud succeeded in luring his aliens and they transported Sandy Bend elsewhere, he might. But other than that… "Not a chance."

"I see." And with that she switched topics to gossip about their Chicago friends.

Steve was supremely grateful that he'd managed to kill off the seed of an idea Kira had planted. They finished their lunch without any further discussion of Susan's or his future plans, and he ushered her from the café. When she asked for a farewell kiss, he tried for a dry peck on the cheek like one he'd give his great-aunt Gertrude who smelled of mothballs. Susan had other plans. She latched on to his mouth as if she sought permanent residency. He ended up having to pry her off.

God save him from fickle women.

As Steve turned away, he saw Hallie sitting in her car at the stop sign. The way he figured it, he had two choices: either he could wave or he could pretend he hadn't spotted her. Since Hallie was a reasonable woman, Steve opted for a friendly wave. He didn't receive one in return. Instead, he got a narrow-eyed glare. His hand fell limply to his side.

Steve watched as Hallie's mouth grew into a determined line, her hands shifted to grip the steering wheel as if she were a drag-racer, and she gunned the accelerator. Freckled nose in the air, she pulled away.

Steve shook his head. "Whitman, you are one dead, dead dog."

DEJECTED, Hallie stood before the full-length mirror at the top of the stairs. When she was little, this had been her favorite place to daydream about what she was going to look like when she was all grown up. She was going to be slender and stylish, with hair that cooperated and no freckles. She'd have sandals to match all her summer dresses and she'd never be caught in a pair of blue jeans. In sum, she was going to be Susan Miller.

Well, she was an adult now, and she was no Susan Miller. Seeing Susan and Steve on the sidewalk had made Hallie realize just how far she remained from that childhood ideal. Witnessing their kiss had stung. Only Steve's expression of utter shock had stopped the pain from traveling deeper. Still, the sight had raised a matter she needed to consider.

Steve and Susan came from the same trunk-slammer set. They even looked sort of alike. She supposed if they'd married as planned, they'd be driving his 'n hers BMWs and have a pair of perfectly groomed Golden Retrievers. No children, of course. Not until they'd had time to travel.

Hallie made a face at her paint-spattered white shirt tucked into denim shorts. She was definitely an economy model. She didn't need expensive cars and preferred her travel to be low-key and leisurely. Her needs were simple. She wanted fair treatment and kindness. And to be absolutely positive that when a guy made love to her, he wasn't thinking of someone else.

WHEN STEVE STUCK his head into the Brewer house, Thea issued a Bad Aura Alert on Hallie.

"Disturbing," she said. "Very disturbing."

That almost prepared him for what he found in the barn. The float was done, and Hallie looked done in. She sat in a low-slung folding beach chair in the center of the sandy paradise she'd created. Her long legs were stretched out before her. He supposed her hair had once been in a ponytail, but now it clung to her face and neck in damp strands. Her clothes were paint-covered. A matching smudge of blue decorated one cheek. She looked generally ticked at the world.

Steve approached cautiously, thankful for his buffer of a laundry basket filled with picnic supplies. "Hey there."

Instead of returning his greeting, she said, "What's

up with the polo shirt? You look like you lost your yacht, Skippy.''

He frowned. Hallie seldom had that bite to her tone of voice. "I always wear these."

"With the collar turned up?"

"Oh." Undaunted, he set the basket on the edge of the float. He smoothed the collar to its usual non-pretentious location. "Better?"

"Much."

Steve trolled for a neutral topic. "The float looks great. Did you design the sun characters on the banners?"

"I made those last night when I couldn't sleep. And as you can see, I got the rest of the work finished today while you were off doing...whatever."

So he wasn't going to be allowed to sidestep the topic of Susan. He supposed he could understand why Hallie might be a little disturbed. Heck, he was still a little disturbed.

"Okay, before you have me dragged out of here and summarily executed, I'll confess. I had lunch with Susan today, and she kissed me. You caught that scene on the sidewalk, right?"

"Righto, Skippy."

"Enough of the Skippy stuff. If you want to talk about what you saw, let's talk." He climbed onto the float. "Here's the deal.... Last night, Susan asked me to meet her. I didn't think it was such a hot idea, but couldn't figure out how to say no without sounding like I was hung up on this wedding thing. Anyway, she's suffering from another case of cold feet. It didn't occur to her that I wasn't the best person to share the news with."

Hallie rubbed at a spot of paint on the back of her hand, then said, "Based on that kiss, maybe she figured that was just the news you were waiting for."

"Well, it's not."

"Are you sorry you didn't marry her?"

The truth was, he was feeling more relieved by the minute. The more time he spent with Hallie, the more he accepted that he wasn't cut out for a cool number like Susan. Unlike the rest of the Whitman clan, he seemed to like life with a certain amount of spice.

"Sorry?" he repeated. "No way. It would have never worked. Looking back, I'm not sure what we ever had in common, except the same summer vacation. We don't like or want any of the same things."

She must have seen he was sincere because she smiled. "Not even matching cars?"

"Huh?"

"Never mind." She drew her feet in, braced her hands on her knees, then stood. "Tell you what, I think we're through talking about Susan. I need to go take a shower. You can get dinner set up. There's an old blanket in the wheelbarrow over there."

"I've got it covered."

"Okay." She climbed down from the float. "I'll be back in half an hour."

"Take your time." He had major miracles to accomplish.

BY THE TIME Hallie returned, Steve had champagne chilling, the dark green goosedown quilt from his bed spread over the flattest part of the float, a dozen candles glowing in old Mason jars he'd found on a shelf, and a meal that was the best Sandy Bend had to offer. Diana Krall, his favorite jazz vocalist, sang from his portable CD player.

Hallie hesitated in the doorway. "Wow! You work quickly."

He gave a low whistle at her altered appearance. Her paint-covered clothing had been replaced by a black sleeveless top and white shorts that ended mighty high on those long, long legs. Her hair was clean and dry, and pulled back from her face.

"You're no slouch, either. Come on in and bar that door behind you."

"What, no Do Not Disturb sign to hang out?" She turned and, for an instant, stood with her hands resting against the door latch. Her shoulders rose as though she were drawing a deep breath for courage. Steve held his own breath, waiting to see if she was going to leave the door open as a signal that she wasn't ready for the kind of night he hoped awaited them.

She pulled the door shut and dropped the wooden bar Chief Bud had installed years before to keep Cal and Steve from bugging him while he worked on his 'Vette. The larger, sliding door next to the small entry was already firmly in place. When Hallie turned and gave him a nervous smile, he relaxed. At least sort of relaxed.

"Now come on up here and let me serve you my favorite kind of dinner."

She neared and took his offered hand. "What kind's that?"

He helped her up, then let go before he was tempted to haul her into his arms and forget the food. "The kind where I don't have to do any cooking."

Her answering smile was an addictive sight. Steve ushered her to the quilt. Once they were settled on the edge of it with their feet on the sandy "beach" she'd hauled in the other day, he opened the champagne and poured her a flute.

As she sipped it, he commented, "You know, tonight's the crucial test for your cat dander theory, and I have to tell you I'm not holding out much hope for its validity."

"Really?"

"So here's what I propose. As long as we're on this

float, no matter what we're doing, some part of you has to be touching some part of me. If your theory fails, you won't be able to say it's from lack of effort on my part.''

She frowned, but he wasn't certain whether it was from the champagne bubbles tickling her nose as she drank, or from his proposal.

"Do I get to pick the parts?" she asked.

"Sure, I can be a sport about this."

"Okay, then."

He toed off his worn Top-Siders, too threadbare to be of any use sailing, but still his all-time favorite shoes. "The best thing about the beach is going barefoot, don't you think?"

He reached down and slid off her flip-flops, then tossed them over the side of the float. A little crease appeared between her brows as he began to bury her feet in the sand.

"Now don't move them," he ordered. "I don't want you chickening out and taking off."

"As if I would," she scoffed.

Steve trailed one hand up her leg to the outside of her hip, then over to her elbow as he reached for the strawberries. He hid a smile at the tremor that rippled over her skin.

"Want one?"

At her nodded assent, he popped a small berry into her mouth, then traced one perfect shell of an ear. Hallie glared at him as she chewed and swallowed.

"I thought I got to choose the body parts."

He grinned. "Choose any part of mine you like."

She linked her pinkie with his, then crawled around him to grab the French bread. Once she was settled back in place, she propped her feet across his legs and let go of his hand.

Steve gave a rueful shake of his head as she broke

the heel off the loaf and ate with gusto. "I don't think you're getting the spirit of this."

She grinned. "I'm getting the spirit just fine. Now what else do you have to feed me?"

He rolled onto his side and reached for the asparagus wrapped in prosciutto. As Hallie nibbled, he ran his palms up the silken skin of her shins, which were dusted with the same honey-brown freckles as her nose.

"What's the beach like in Carmel?"

She took a sip of her wine. He noticed her hands were trembling.

"Not very big, but nice," she said. "Still, I don't spend much time there. When I have weekends off, I like to go to Point Lobos, a nature reserve not too far from where I live. If it looks like it's going to be a clear day, I bring my watercolors."

Just to see what she'd do, and because it felt so damn good, he placed his right hand on the back of her knees and began caressing the soft skin. She shivered, but gamely kept on talking.

"Sometimes when it's really quiet, I can hear the sea otters in the bay opening shellfish with their rocks."

With his left hand, he traced the edge of her shorts across the tops of her thighs. She was so apple-pie wholesome he could just about eat her up.

"D-did you know that sea otters carry their favorite rocks with them? There was one off Monterrey that everyone would look for because h-he used a beer bottle instead of a rock."

For the sheer pleasure of watching her, he moved closer and cupped the side of her face with his hand. "Have you ever tried counting your freckles?"

"Mostly I've tried to make them disappear."

"Now why would you want to do that? They're part of what make you...well, *you*." He brushed a kiss against one cheekbone. She scooted back.

"Nuh-uh, no breaking contact," he reminded her.

"You're making me nervous."

"Good nervous or bad nervous?"

"Just nervous."

Good nervous. "So what do you think of your cat dander theory, now?"

"It might need a little reworking."

He grinned at her grudging admission. "It needs to be dumped. But you know, I've been thinking about this problem of ours, too." He stood. "The way I see it, we just need to even the playing field between us."

Hallie's mouth grew dry. He had already knocked her off-kilter with all the touching, but she had a feeling that was small stuff compared to what was to come. "Wh-what do you mean?"

"I mean, this time it's my turn." He tugged off the preppy white polo shirt she'd smirked at earlier and dropped it at his feet. There was nothing to smirk at now. Not that broad, tan chest with just the slightest dusting of golden hair. Definitely not the six-pack abs.

"But you've seen me without my shirt more times than I can count," he said.

She didn't recall him looking this good.

He frowned. "In the interest of fairness, I think we have to carry this a little further, don't you?"

"No, really, I'm sure the playing field's even. Couldn't be any flatter if you steamrollered it." His hand was closing over the copper button at the top of his jeans and she was babbling as though words could hold him back. Her gaze was riveted to the motion of that button coming open, but as his hand moved to the zipper below, she squeezed her eyes tightly shut.

Temptation whispered to her. *So what do you think, is it boxers or briefs? Or maybe nothing at all...*

Deprived of vision, she was hypersensitive to the

slight rustling sounds as he shed his jeans. Still, she kept her eyes closed.

"Now we're a little closer."

Hallie forced herself to open her eyes, but couldn't bring herself to look beyond his face.

"I dare you," he said, laughter and challenge dancing in his dark eyes. "Heck, I double-dog dare you."

Hallie sent her gaze on a journey south.

My, oh my...

Steve was a boxer man.

A midnight-blue silk, trim and sexy, boxer man.

"There's one more thing I have to add before we can call ourselves even," he said.

He sounded so very serious.

"Hallie, I want you."

This was no longer a game. This was real, so real that the rest of her life felt like a warm-up for this moment. He wanted her. Even if he hadn't said it, basic human physiology had already made that impressively apparent.

He wanted her. Whatever choice she made, she'd have to live with it forever. She was on her feet with no idea how she'd gotten there, and no idea whether she intended to fly into his open arms, or flee.

Leaving was the intelligent way to go. Sure, she'd be curious every day for the rest of her life what it might have been like to make love with Steve. But if she gave in to temptation, the loneliness she'd feel once she returned to Carmel would run irreparably soul-deep.

"Hallie?"

She looked back into that face she'd loved—yes, loved—for as long as she could recall. What she saw there erased all her questions. She saw vulnerability. And a genuine care and affection that gave her the courage she thought had deserted her.

She walked a slow circle around him, trailing her

fingertips just above the band at the top of his boxers. His muscles rippled in her wake. She stopped in front of him and dipped one finger to briefly tease his navel.

"Very nice. Quite awesome, actually, but you still haven't shown me anything I haven't seen on the beach before."

"Technically true," he agreed, his voice rough, as though it was a struggle to speak.

She leaned forward and flicked her tongue over his collarbone, then settled her lips on his skin and drew in gently. He was hot and tasted faintly of the tang of salt.

Stepping back, she gave him her best guileless smile. "Still, I wouldn't want you to think that I'm taking advantage of the situation, so here's what I'm going to do."

Hallie's fingers trembled as she slipped each button of her blouse free. She shrugged it off, leaving only a silky little emerald-green scrap of a bra. "Is the playing field even?"

"I'd say we're getting closer." And because he was a man of his word, Steve did just that. Hallie twined her arms around his neck as his mouth closed over hers. She touched her tongue against his lips, asking to be let in. He welcomed her, then explored her, too.

Being skin to skin with Steve was the most incredible sensation she had ever experienced. One broad hand traveled up and down her back, then paused and deftly released the hook on her bra.

Steve broke the kiss long enough to murmur, "Almost there."

Hallie kept kissing him as he slipped his thumbs under her bra straps and drew them off her shoulders.

She stepped away just far enough to let it slide the rest of the way off. He looked down at her. Though she wanted to play it bold, she could feel the crimson heat of a blush staining her skin.

Gently, almost reverently, he ran his knuckles against the sensitive lower curve of one breast. "You are the most perfectly beautiful sight I could ever have imagined."

The start of tears burnt at her eyes. She felt so wholly unprepared, yet unwilling to stop. "I've only done this once before and it was a total disaster."

"And do you think this time will be?"

"Let's just say since I'm involved, the odds aren't good."

He took her hand and settled it over his heart, which pounded a hot and needy beat. With his other hand he cupped her chin, drawing her face upward so she had to meet his eyes. Desire was plain on his face. "Do you really believe that, Hallie?"

"I'm willing to be proved wrong."

The half smile that had always been her undoing played at the corners of his mouth. "Good."

He gently tugged at the broad red ribbon she'd tied her hair back with and freed it. When he burrowed his fingers into her hair at her temples and combed them through to the very ends, she sighed with the pleasure it brought her.

"Silk and cinnamon," he murmured. "I'll never think of you without thinking of silk and cinnamon."

With his fingertips he traced the valley between her breasts, down her sides to her waist, then back up again. He followed the line of her collarbone and stroked the hollow at the base of her throat. He kissed the side of her neck and made slow, lazy patterns with his palms over her hips and bottom.

She clung to him, wriggling closer, mentally willing him to please, *please* touch her breasts.

She wove her fingers through his and brought his hand to her mouth. She wet the tip of his index finger and then guided it to her nipple. Her exhaled sigh of pleasure was matched by his ragged breath.

"I was trying to take this slow and easy for both our sakes, but that's not going to happen, is it?"

Hallie couldn't find her voice, so she shook her head in a slow but emphatic no.

He backed her to the comforter still spread at the far end of the float, and she watched as he dumped the remnants of their meal back into the laundry basket. Standing, he hauled her into his arms and kissed her with a forcefulness she answered in kind. Then she stepped out of his embrace and settled in the middle of the quilt.

Later, when she lifted her hips to permit Steve to slide off her last piece of clothing, the jazz singer on the CD crooned something about peeling a grape. Hallie chuckled at the silly timing.

"Laughter?" Steve commented, then kissed the tip of her nose.

"It was just the song. Honest." She was about to explain when Steve found a new and mind-shattering place to touch her, so she gave up on thought altogether.

Though the air around her was as warm and humid as her damp skin, she shivered when he eventually pulled away long enough to grab a condom from his wallet and ready himself for her. He settled his weight over her again.

She reached up and brushed his hair away from his forehead. He smiled down at her with such tenderness she thought her heart might break.

"Do you still want me, Hallie?"

Always was the answer her heart gave, but she'd never make him feel obligated with those words. Instead, she guided him home and felt him shudder as he entered her.

Much later, when they were both too exhausted to do

much more than lie with their legs tangled together and
share a semichilled bottle of springwater, Steve tugged
her closer and asked, "So was it a total disaster?"

She smiled. "I might be persuaded to try it again."

And Steve Whitman proved to be a very persuasive
man.

BY THE TIME Steve awoke, daylight had worked its way
though the upper windows of the barn and was dancing
over them, the beam thick with dust motes. He yawned
and stretched, smiling a bit as Hallie snuggled closer.

Last night had been stunning, incredible and more
than a little unsettling. He'd always had fairly specific
notions about what he wanted from a woman and what
he was willing to give.

Before he'd thought he wanted a woman close, but
not too close. Not so with Hallie, and it wasn't just
physical, though he'd stay inside her forever, if he
could.

He'd also thought he was a fair sort of guy, one who
was as interested in giving a woman pleasure as in finding his own. Unconsciously, though, he'd always put
himself at the top of the list. Not so when Hallie was
in his arms.

He needed time to figure out why it was so different
with her. Why making love a million times probably
wouldn't be enough to solve this mystery. And why
making love to anyone else suddenly held no appeal.

Hallie stirred. "Hey there," she murmured.

He shifted so he could watch her greet the day. The
more he knew of her, maybe the more he could learn
about himself. "Morning. Did you sleep okay?"

"Well, the bed was a little lumpy, but I'm not complaining." She ran her fingertips along his jaw. "Sand-
papery... I kind of like the feeling."

Not nearly as much as he liked the sensation of her

touch. Still, her words had brought to mind a few realities. He could hardly show up at the school for his morning meeting unshaved and unshowered. And he was equally unwilling to stroll into the Brewer farmhouse and risk running across Hallie's brothers or Chief Bud. He felt uncomfortable enough knowing that all the Brewer men had a good idea of what he and Hallie had been doing last night. What he'd do again right now, if he had the time.

Steve figured he had about half an hour before he should hit the road. To be sure, he checked the watch he'd never quite gotten around to taking off.

Still stretched against his left side, Hallie asked, "What's up?"

"Nothing, really. I just remembered I have a meeting at the high school." He felt her tense, and regretted having to remind her that the world outside this barn awaited them. Before he could say anything more, she cut in.

"I understand," she said while rolling away from him. "You probably need to get going."

The edgy, almost distant tone to her voice set Steve's molars on edge. He refused to be reduced to a night's entertainment. He drew her back into his arms and kissed her until she relaxed.

Smoothing his hand through her hair, he asked, "Is that how you really think this is going to be? One night and we both just walk away?"

She closed her hand over his. "Two days. In two days, we both just walk away," she gently corrected.

It was what he thought he'd wanted. It still remained the only rational route, yet Steve felt as if he'd been sucker-punched. Two days were nowhere near enough.

10

HALLIE HAD NEVER INDULGED in potato salad for breakfast, but today seemed like the perfect day to start. She hadn't eaten much last night and she'd never been one of those half-a-dry-rice-cake-with-celery-sticks women to begin with. Plus, she needed to numb the stress jittering through her.

She'd acted like an idiot with Steve this morning. Hallie had convinced herself she was over their past, but when she'd awakened, her first thought was, *And now he's going to break my heart*. He hadn't, though circumstances might do the job just the same.

After some tiptoeing around each other's feelings, they'd agreed to meet at his place in the afternoon. Hallie planned to pass the morning sorting out what last night meant. And eating potato salad.

The house was blessedly silent. Her brothers were already off to work and her dad and Thea seemed to be steering clear of her. Good thing, since she hadn't scraped together the composure necessary to face them.

Hallie filled her childhood Flintstones cereal bowl to the rim with potato salad, then covered the leftovers and stuck them back in the fridge. Now she had potato salad for forty-nine. Close enough.

She took her bowl and fork and plopped down in front of the television in the den. After spending some time channel surfing through her favorite cartoons, she settled in the more mature realm of entertainment news.

At least, marginally more mature. Some guy with yellow highlights even Dana Devine wouldn't approve of was waving his hands around like helicopter blades as he spoke.

"I saw the dude right in the hotel lobby. He looked way bummed and he had enough stuff with him to be moving in for good, no lie!"

Hallie forked down a chunk of potato salad and prepared to flip back to cartoons when the anchorwoman appeared onscreen.

"Ms. Bethune's publicist confirms that Ms. Bethune and Mr. Colton have separated. The couple asks that their privacy be respected at this most difficult of times."

The potato salad lodged in Hallie's throat like a wad of cotton. She swallowed hard and set down the bowl. With no clear idea of what she was doing, she returned to the kitchen.

Cousin Thea sat at the table, her healing crystals spread out before her. She smiled up at Hallie, but the cheerfulness quickly gave way to a look of concern.

"Another stormy aura," she said as she rolled a piece of amethyst between her fingertips.

"Have you seen my dad?" Hallie hadn't even known she was seeking the comfort of her father until she spoke.

"He's at his weekly meeting with the Ladies' Tea and Blowtorch Society."

Hallie blinked. "The what?"

"The Ladies' Tea and Blowtorch Society," Thea repeated with great care. "Your father joined a few weeks ago. They—"

"Drink tea and weld things?"

"Actually, they drink scotch. And they weld first— at least your dad says that's been the order since they burned down Maddie Vanderjaak's garage."

"Okay, so he's gone until, what, noon?"

"More like suppertime. Is there something you'd like to talk about? This doesn't have to do with Steve, does it?" Thea paused, then quickly added an alarmed, "You did use protection, I hope?"

Hallie suddenly felt a deep and overwhelming need to be away from all blood relatives. "No, no and yes, though I can't believe you'd ask me that." She grabbed her car keys from the hook by the back door. "If Steve calls, tell him I'm at the Hair Dungeon, okay?"

Thea held out a blue-colored rock. "Take this with you. It will calm you. Oh, and some jade, too. We might as well cover our bases."

Hallie slipped the stones into her pocket. They were bound to work better than the potato salad had.

HALLIE FOUND DANA in the depths of the Hair Dungeon dyeing a teenage girl's hair.

"Hope you don't mind that I dropped by," Hallie said.

"Nah, I love the company." Dana painted white gloppy stuff onto a lock of hair she held cupped in foil, then deftly folded it closed. "Today's lucky recipient of my skills is Skye, this year's Summer Fun Princess."

"Congratulations, Skye. I'll be cheering for you in the parade on Saturday."

The girl blushed and mumbled, "Thanks."

Hallie turned her attention to Dana. "You were right about Anna Bethune and Matt Colton."

Their eyes met for a moment in the mirror, but Dana never stopped working. "Wow, I'm sorry about that, but never doubt the *Galaxy News.* What will it mean for your job?"

Hallie shrugged. "Either everything or nothing at all. I guess I'll have to sit tight and wait to hear. At least

I'll still have the part-time hours at the art gallery where I've been working.''

Dana arched a knowing brow. "Which pays?"

"Just about enough to cover my gasoline and a parking permit at the municipal lot."

"Okay, so you need a plan. It just so happens you've come to the right place. I've got a five-year plan, a ten-year plan and even a when-I'm-reincarnated-as-Julia-Roberts plan."

"That one must be good."

Dana grinned. "It's filled a few empty nights." She leaned over Skye. "Picking up any radio signals yet?"

Hallie laughed, but the girl just looked confused.

"You want to stay in California, right?" Dana asked.

"Most of my friends from college are still around Carmel, so yeah, I guess I do."

"Then what can you do to earn a paycheck?"

Which was precisely the same question her father had asked her when she'd graduated from college with that fine arts degree. She didn't like hearing it any better now than she had back then.

"Since Carmel isn't exactly short on artists and I can't live on the three hundred dollars I netted last year, I guess we're down to my other skills." She drew a deep breath and started listing them. "I can coordinate a gardening staff and pool maintenance staff to make sure they're not tripping over each other. I can deal with interior decorators, gate-crashers and snooping paparazzi. I can arrange flowers and sort through a bag of mixed hard candies to make sure only the red ones are served. Oh, and I've gotten to be really, really good at backing out of rooms."

"Handy talents all, especially the last two."

Hallie knew sarcasm when she heard it. "Matt Colton can be a little weird."

"A lot weird, I'd say. But let's get back to those big-ticket skills, such as they were. Maybe you know a re-clusive billionaire in need of a wife?''

"Okay, so my life in California hasn't been very nor-mal. Still, I might be able to get some sort of assistant's job."

"That résumé of yours is going to be a doozy."

"Yeah, and I guess I'd better sit down and start writ-ing it."

Dana folded the last square of foil into the girl's hair. Hallie figured she might have to give her dad a call. With her giant aluminum quills, the Summer Fun Prin-cess looked undeniably alien.

"Hey, are you doing anything for lunch?" Dana asked. "After Skye is finished, I don't have another client scheduled until two. Maybe we could grab some-thing to eat and do a little brainstorming."

Hallie smiled. She wasn't due at Steve's house until one. "I'd love to."

Who'd have ever thought that wild Dana Devine could be more calming than both potato salad and Thea's crystals?

AFTER A LUNCH spent laughing with Dana like a pair of high-schoolers, Hallie arrived at Steve's a few minutes late. She didn't need to worry. The only car parked at the base of the steep stairway to the house was Kira's, an obvious enough deduction considering its Illinois personalized plate read KIRA.

After debating whether she'd be better off waiting for Steve outside, Hallie knocked on the frame of the screen door.

"That you, Susan?" Kira called.

Just dandy. So Susan was going to be showing up. She ranked ahead of even Kira in Hallie's list of Least Likely to be a Good Time.

"No, Kira, it's Hallie Brewer."

"What do you want?" Kira answered with a depth of charm usually reserved for telephone solicitors at suppertime.

"I'd like to come inside and wait for Steve, if it's all the same to you."

"Well, just hang on a minute!"

She would have had time to recite an entire etiquette book by the time Kira appeared at the door. Kira had a Band-Aid plastered under her eye, which in Hallie's opinion looked one heck of a lot dumber than a plain black eye would. She fought to hide her smile.

"I suppose you can come in," Kira said.

"Thanks. I promise not to steal the silver."

As they walked past the kitchen, Hallie noticed a bunch of deli containers of potato salad on the counter, along with canned goods and paper towels. She had to give Kira credit for being smart enough to pick up store-bought salad.

"Want some help putting away the groceries?" she asked, figuring it wouldn't hurt to smooth the path with Kira.

"What groceries? Oh…those. I can take care of it myself."

She shrugged and kept walking as Kira stopped in the kitchen. Once in the family room, she wandered over to the bookshelf to see what was on Steve's reading list. There were lots of biographies and spy thrillers, plus a stack of calculus texts that made Hallie shudder. The only thing she'd ever liked about math was Steve.

Hallie moved on to the mantel, which held family photographs, including one of Kira ages ago—back when she and Hallie had actually gotten along.

"Are you going to snoop through the whole house before my brother gets here?" Kira said from behind her.

The sight of the picture must have triggered a big

wave of nostalgia because Hallie found herself saying, "Look, can we call a truce? I'm only going to be here a few more days and I'd like to have at least one good memory of you."

Kira's eyes—even her bad one—widened for an instant, then her usual cool mask slipped back into place. "A truce? I didn't know we were at war."

Hallie smiled. "Didn't you?" She walked over to a comfy-looking armchair and sat. Kira stood in the middle of the room looking as though she wasn't sure what she was supposed to do next. Finally, she perched on the edge of the couch. They sat in silence, one waiting for the other to make the first move.

Surprisingly enough, Kira caved. "Steve says you're some kind of an artist." ·

Hallie nodded. "Watercolors, mostly, though I'm not to the point that I can give up my day job." Assuming she still had one. "So, what are you up to these days?"

"Nothing much." Hallie was thinking how Kira sounded almost embarrassed, when she followed up with, "Not that I have to do anything as dull as work for a living."

Hallie chuckled. "Lucky you." Then she dealt Kira a home truth. "Actually, I like working. I like the structure and the feeling that I'm productive."

"I've been thinking about going back to school," Kira said in a rush. She tucked a stray strand of blond hair behind her ear. "Or maybe becoming a party planner."

"Both sound like good options."

Kira fidgeted with her earring. "I had a job at a clothing boutique in Chicago, but the hours were horrible. I don't know how people do it. They wanted me to work on weekends and be there by nine-thirty when the shop didn't even open until ten. It simply took up too much of my time."

This conversation was turning out to be more painful for Hallie than continuing the war might have been. "I'm sure if you find something that inspires you, you'll stick with it."

Just then, Hallie heard the screen door rattle in its frame. She smiled her relief—and the love she'd never voice—as Steve walked into the room.

He framed his hands on the armchair, then bent down and kissed her. "Hey, beautiful." Kira made a sound of disgust.

"Sorry I'm late," he said.

"It's okay, I've been doing great," Hallie exaggerated. "Kira and I have been catching up."

Steve's smile was skeptical. He held out his hand. "Come on down to the beach with me."

"I'd love to." She clasped his hand and stood.

They were just stepping off the back deck when Kira came dashing toward them.

"Wait, Steve. I almost forgot. Can I use your house tomorrow for a little bachelorette party I'm planning for Susan?"

He laughed. "You're kidding, right?"

"No, I'm perfectly serious."

"Okay, then I'll give you a serious answer. No way in stinkin' h—"

"Well, you don't need to get nasty about it." Kira turned heel and stalked back into the house.

Steve's sigh was weary. "Let's get moving before she asks me to pop out of a cake."

After leaving their shoes at the top of the dunes, they climbed down the steep hill to the beach below. The breeze off Lake Michigan was cooler than the humid air that had settled onshore. Hallie turned her face into it and gave a deep, appreciative sniff.

"This is paradise," she said.

Steve was silent. She glanced over. His mouth was bracketed by hard lines.

"Want to walk for a while?" she suggested.

"Sure."

They moved down to the hard-packed sand, wet from the waves licking the shore. By silent agreement they headed north, dodging clumps of seaweed and sandcastle-building children. Other than exchanging greetings with people they knew, neither of them spoke until they had turned back and were nearing the patch of beach in front of Steve's house.

Though she still didn't buy into Thea's crystals and auras, Hallie was picking up some pretty uptight brainwaves from Steve.

"Tough day, huh?" she said, hoping to break his emotional logjam.

He gave a dejected kick at the sand. "It stunk." He paused, then his words came out tight and angry. "I don't want to see the high school closed. I don't want kids bused twenty-five minutes each way. And, dammit, I don't want to see Sandy Bend lose its sense of community."

Hallie's job problems suddenly felt insignificant and very selfish. "Is it too late to stop the closing?"

"I don't know. I'm sure as hell trying. It's not that we don't have the tax base to support the schools. Sure, we're down in numbers right now, but the studies show that the school-aged population will be on the upswing in the next few years." He trailed off and rubbed at his forehead. "I'm sorry. Probably the last thing you want to talk about is demographics."

She laid her hand on his arm. "No, really, it's okay. I know this has been bothering you. Sometimes it takes another person's perspective—"

He shook his head. "I don't want to waste your time.

Short of kidnapping kids from Crystal Valley, there's no solution. We can't make it as a school.''

Hallie hesitated, but then plowed ahead. ''At the risk of sounding Thealike, maybe you're being too negative. You might just need to open yourself to other possibilities...to think about the potential gain from this loss.'' Much as she'd been trying to do about so many things, including the sure knowledge that she was going to be walking away from Steve and Sandy Bend.

His laugh was halfhearted at best. ''I'll start meditating at sunrise. A few good chants and no telling what will come to me.''

''It just might help,'' Hallie said, wishing he wouldn't discount her suggestion.

Steve sighed. ''What would really do the job is to sit with you and just forget about this mess for a while.'' He took her by the hand and led her back up the slope. They reached the old lounge chair where she'd found him napping two days ago.

Two days?

The thought startled Hallie, almost frightened her. It seemed so much longer since she'd come home—almost as if she'd never left.

''Hang on a second,'' Steve said as he pulled the cushion from where it had been folded and tucked beneath the chair. He settled it into place, then adjusted the back of the lounge so it was almost upright. He straddled the lounge and patted the open space in front of him. ''Join me.''

Hallie settled in and leaned back against Steve's chest. He wrapped his arms around her and, knees bent, brought his legs close to her sides. The slow rise and fall of his chest lulled her.

He rested his chin on top of her head and they sat that way, simply enjoying each other. Hallie watched a gull circle lazily in the sky and listened to the laughter of the children up the beach. She closed her eyes and imagined life being like this forever.

"I keep trying to find something to say about last night, but everything I think of just sounds shallow," Steve eventually said. "I guess I want you to know that it wasn't all about sex."

She smiled. "Yeah, but that wasn't half-bad, either."

He laughed. "If you only think it was only half-good, I'm going to have to work harder." He bent forward and settled a kiss on her shoulder. "This afternoon, I'm telling Kira that it's time for her to move on. There's no way I'm sleeping anywhere but with you for these next two nights, and there's also no way I'm doing that in your father's house."

The pain of hearing him say how few nights they had left cut through Hallie with razor intensity. Even if she did end up losing her job, resettling in Sandy Bend was a bleak option. She had stepped into Steve's arms willingly, and accepted that no promises were being made. But Hallie had also spent her adolescence trailing after him. Dignity and her tender heart decreed that she must now stand on her own. She was thankful Steve couldn't see her face. She knew he'd spot the sheen of tears in her eyes.

"What, not another float-christening party?" she said, relieved her voice didn't waver.

"A beach—even a pretend one complete with comforter—is a highly overrated location for lovemaking."

Based on the sand in the shower this morning, Hallie had to agree. She guessed she'd always be an old-fashioned girl. The idea of Steve and a big bed was far more tempting.

"So, are you going to be my date for the picnic this evening?" Steve asked.

"A real date? Not one where we show up together, but ignore each other like we did last night?"

He chuckled. "Yeah, a real date. I'll even bring you a corsage like Mr. Hawkins used to do for Mrs. Hawkins."

She smiled as she recalled some of the enormous beribboned creations that weighed down the tiny woman. "They were something, weren't they?"

"Yeah, and she'd wear them for days afterward, until they were shriveled and brown." He hesitated, but then added, "They were what I think marriage should be like. Since he passed away, I've been sending her a corsage anonymously for each village picnic. Kind of goofy of me, huh?"

The love Hallie felt for Steve grew tenfold. She squeezed shut her eyes and fought back unwanted emotion.

"I think it's the sweetest thing I've ever heard." This time, her voice did waver.

"You never answered my question. Will you be my date?" he asked, still sounding embarrassed.

Hallie scooted around and knelt to face him. "You're a tough man to say no to, Steve Whitman."

"Then don't," he said just before she settled her mouth on his. She couldn't have forever and silly corsages, but she could have one perfect afternoon in paradise.

11

MINUTES BEFORE Steve was due to arrive for their date, the call came from Anna's personal assistant. The Carmel Highlands residence was going on the market, and Hallie was officially out of a job. While she was welcome to stay until the house sold, she knew the reprieve would be brief. Anything of Anna Bethune's was a hot item.

As Hallie loaded containers of potato salad into grocery sacks, she told herself not to panic—not now, at least—that it would all work out for the best. Packed and ready, she ran nervous fingers though her hair and patted her pants pocket for Thea's crystals. If the things were working, she hated to think how frantic and frazzled she'd be without them. And if they weren't, she could always take comfort from the fact that she'd bottomed out.

Steve walked in the back door. "Hey, you ready?"

Given her life's state of disarray, she'd thought it was going to be tough to smile this evening. Seeing Steve made it effortless.

"Sure, I'm ready." She gestured at the white florist's box in his hand. "Is that for me, by any chance?"

"Nah, it's for Cal," he joked as he handed it to her. "Hope it's big enough."

Judging by the weight, that wouldn't be a problem.

"Well, come on. I want to know if I measure up to Hawkins's standards. I had it made for your wrist. Since high school, I've dreaded piercing some poor girl's chest.''

She'd never been given a corsage in high school, or any time afterward for that matter. Hallie opened the box, folded back waxy green tissue, and she couldn't hold back her laughter.

This corsage's concept started out sedately enough. A cluster of white and yellow rosebuds were interspersed with greens and baby's breath. It smelled of summertime and all the dances she'd ever missed. From there, though, the flowers took a Sandy Bend twist.

Orange metallic ribbon wandered through the creation in crazy loops. Still, most startling of all were the four chenille bumblebees with bulging goo-goo eyes. Each insect was mounted on a tiny spring to hover over the flowers. She lifted the corsage from the box and slipped it on. When she moved her hand, the bees trembled with anticipation.

''I tried to convince the florist to add a few bells, but he told me bees were where he drew the line.''

Hallie rotated her wrist and grinned. ''Discerning guy, that florist.''

A car horn blared repeatedly in the driveway.

Steve muttered something under his breath that didn't sound especially friendly. To Hallie he said, ''I guess Kira's ready to go.''

Hallie froze. ''Kira's out there?''

Steve grabbed the bags from the counter. ''We're taking her to the picnic, no further.''

''Any reason she can't go on her own?''

''Susan's fiancé had to return to Chicago, so Kira loaned her car to her.''

Hallie settled for a terse, ''Peachy.'' What she really wanted to sat was, *''Well, let me grab my overnight bag and drag it out to the car so your sister will have something else to whisper to her friends about.''*

She knew it was small-town of her to be embarrassed, but small-town she was. Exposing vulnerability to Kira, however, could prove disastrous. Summoning some of that inner peace, Hallie picked up her bag.

Joy and rapture, it was Kira Time.

When they got to Steve's Jeep, he said, "I don't believe it, you moved to the front." He yanked open the passenger door. "Get in the back."

Deciding she'd rather be a little cramped than listen to Kira complain, Hallie cut in. "Really, it's okay. Stay where you are."

She went around to the driver's side. Steve folded the seat forward, then helped her in. The back seat was small enough that her knees and chin risked becoming intimate friends. She angled her legs and buckled herself in. Steve handed her the overnight bag. Kira—in enormous black-eye-hiding sunglasses with some designer's initials emblazoned on them—kept stonily silent until Steve started loading her down with potato salad.

When she opened her mouth to object, she got a "Don't even think of it" from her brother.

Once they hit the road, the Jeep was too noisy for conversation, but Hallie had a rather enjoyable ride to town envisioning Kira strapped to the hood. Steve dropped them at the edge of the village green and helped unload the potato salad.

While he found a parking spot, Hallie and Kira walked down to the huge white tent set up to hold the food. The sides of the tent cut off any breeze. The still air was laden with the mixed scents of barbecue and sweets. Long rows of banquet tables draped with white paper tablecloths marched down either side of the space. Round tables dotted the interior. Enid Talbert, the mayor's wife and control freak extraordinaire, directed women bearing marshmallow delight and cupcakes as if she were readying for war.

Hallie quickly scoped the setup and found the area that appeared to be reserved for salads.

"Follow me," she said to Kira, wondering if she could even see in the shade of the tent with her dark glasses on. "You don't want Mrs. Talbert to get hold of you."

They began to make a space for their offerings between the pickled asparagus and something that looked like aerosol cheese squirted on sliced tomatoes. Hallie nudged the asparagus an inch too far and its serving tongs dropped off the back side of the table, landing between a stake and the side of the tent.

Recalling the village picnic, vintage 1993, when she'd nearly brought down the whole show while trying to rid the tent of a squirrel, she carefully stepped around the back of the table to retrieve the tongs. She'd just bent down to grab them when Mrs. Talbert bellowed from the opposite end of the tent, "Ladies! Yes, I mean you by the salads. After the effort I went through to go to the dollar store and buy matching bowls for everyone, you *will* use them."

"Pssst!"

Hallie stood and frowned. Something seemed to be hissing at her from outside the tent.

"This way." Steve stuck his head between two panels. "If you don't get out now, you're her prisoner for sure."

Hallie shuddered at the thought of an evening spent scooping baked beans.

"Hallie! Hallie Brewer!" Mrs. Talbert was closing in on her. "I want that salad artfully arranged, and I want it done in this bowl." She waved something that looked oddly like Santa's head. There must have been a sale on Christmas items at the dollar store. "And who is that standing with you, that little blond thing? You! You, there!''

Kira whipped her head in one direction, then another, her hair flying, as she sought an escape route.

Steve reached in and closed his hand around Hallie's non-corsage-laden wrist. ''Let's go.''

''But what about me?'' Kira cried as Mrs. Talbert strategically moved between her and the tent's entrance.

Hallie grinned. ''Sorry, but you know what they say about love and war.''

She let Steve guide her to freedom.

THIS PICNIC wasn't turning out at all the way Steve had planned. What was it about Hallie that half the town gravitated to her?

Steve sat alone on the scratchy wool blanket he and Hallie had set up next to the gazebo. All he had were the Tiffanys, a flock of high school girls, most of whom shared the same name, and all of whom were permanently lodged in the whisper-and-giggle phase of adolescence. They kept parading by and serenading him with a singsong, ''Hi, Mr. Whit*m-a-a-n.*'' Between the Tiffanys' too frequent visits, Steve watched Hallie. She laughed and talked with a cluster of people near what was now his favorite stone bench.

Admittedly, he understood Hallie's allure. She was so downright genuine and interested in what you had to say, that you just had to be by her.

He should be pleased she was having fun, but he wasn't. Mostly he was jealous. Jealous of every person who was stealing his time with Hallie. By nightfall the day after tomorrow, she would be gone. The thought made him feel as if he were clawing his way upward in an hourglass.

''You've put me in a bad position.''

Steve cupped his hand over his eyes to shade them

from the orange glow of the setting sun. Cal Brewer loomed over him.

"Yeah, tell me about it," Steve said.

Cal hunkered down on the edge of the blanket and took a swallow from his bottle of water. "You've been my best friend for as long as I can remember. Of all the things I've never wanted to do, pushing my best friend's nose through the back of his face tops the list."

"That's good to hear." He and Cal were about the same height, but Cal worked out with weights while Steve mostly ran. If Cal did decide to come after him, sprinting would be Steve's only prayer. "You know I care about her. A lot."

Cal nodded. "I know." He shifted the water bottle from one hand to the other. "Dad says I'm overreacting, that I should keep out of this. But I want you to remember that Hallie's always been kind of vulnerable where you're concerned."

The flip side of that equation was equally true, but that wasn't the kind of information he wanted to share with Cal. "We've got it under control."

Cal snorted. "That's what Hallie says, too. Not that I've ever seen anything involving my sister 'under control.'" He paused and squinted off into the crowd. "Enough said. Just remember, buddy, when push comes to shove…"

Steve worked up a smile. "Yeah, I know. It's gonna hurt."

Truth was, it had begun to hurt already.

As Cal ambled off, Hallie settled back at Steve's side. She frowned at her brother's retreating figure. "What did Cal want?"

"Just guy talk."

She rolled her eyes. "Sailing or football?"

"Football," Steve answered, figuring at least it was another contact sport.

"It was great catching up with the yearbook gang from high school. You should have joined me."

"I was having too much fun watching you." Another lie, but it was better than admitting how damned greedy he was.

Hallie smiled, and it made him feel a little less stressed, knowing that her pleasure was just for him.

Then she glanced over her shoulder toward the food and beer tents. "Maybe I should go take over for Kira for a while."

He closed his hand over hers and wove their fingers together. "Or maybe you should stay here with me. Kira's long overdue for some of Mrs. Talbert's tough love."

"If you're sure..."

Steve nodded. "Promise." He brought her hand to his mouth for a quick kiss, which proved to be poor timing on his part.

The Tiffanys were still hanging around like the chorus in an old Broadway musical. "Mr. Whitman's in *lo-o-ve*," they chimed, then ran away laughing.

Steve let go of Hallie's hand and made some lame joke about how mouthy the kids got during summer break. He didn't add how damned perceptive they had become, too. The terrifying concept of love lingered in his brain, all the same.

After a brief pause, he picked up the conversation. Hallie and he talked about how she ever started painting in the first place, and who her favorite artists were. He stored away her smiles and laughing comments as though each would buy them more time together.

A while later, Dana Devine—who looked to have some sort of patriotic theme going with red, white and blue hair—waved to Hallie as she walked by. "Been working on that résumé?"

"Mostly just thinking about it," Hallie replied.

Once Dana had passed, Steve asked, "What's this about a résumé?"

"I didn't want to mention it with all the job hassles you're having, but I've lost my job with Anna Bethune. She and her husband are splitting up and she's moving back to England."

Steve guessed he was feeling what the talk-show shrinks called "conflicted." To begin with, he wasn't thrilled that she'd chosen to confide in Dana and not in him, no matter how altruistic her motives. And then there was this bizarre and totally unacceptable feeling of optimism. Maybe he wouldn't have to lift a finger or commit to a thing. Maybe Hallie would end up staying in Sandy Bend all on her own. Then he could figure out whether he was feeling lust, love or just old-fashioned familial rebellion.

"You could have told me you lost your job," he said, pushing aside that power rush of happiness. "That's what friends do, they talk to each other."

Hallie flicked at one of the fake bumblebees on her corsage. They both watched it bounce back and forth. It had nearly settled down when she said, "So that's what we are? We're friends?"

He tipped back his head and looked to the sky for help—or a freak lightning bolt to take him out. "This is one of those questions I'm going get fried for, no matter how I answer it. Yes, we're friends. If you were going to be in Sandy Bend longer, we could, uh…"

He stumbled to a halt. They could *what?*

"Hang out at Truro's together?" Hallie suggested with such sweetness he knew he was a dead man. "I could wear your letter jacket?"

"Uh, no. We could, uh…"

She gave a weary shake of her head. "Steve, you have to know last night wouldn't have happened if I didn't love you."

Steve's first impulse—one he barely managed to quell—was to look around and make sure they hadn't been overheard. He was taking enough guff from the Tiffanys already. And simply put, a public declaration of love wasn't the Whitman way of life. Whitmans loved quietly, with dignity. They didn't spring their love on people without some sort of prior warning—usually a tasteful piece of jewelry. But to be fair to Hallie, this was about seven years too late to be a case of "springing."

"Hallie, I—"

She stopped him from speaking. "I'm not asking for anything from you, okay? No promises you have no intention of keeping, no words you don't mean. But you have to let me keep a grasp on reality. I need to make some personal decisions that have nothing to do with you."

All true, but he was instantaneously ticked off, nonetheless. After all, she'd just said she loved him.

"Nothing to do with me? Well, that sounds real nice and friendly," he heard himself drawling.

"Let's just leave this alone, okay?"

He couldn't. He was too irked, though he knew he had no right to be. "So what are you going to do? You've got no job and no house, correct?"

"Technically."

"Sounds more like really to me."

"I'll be all right."

"It's a lot for you to handle. Maybe it would be best if you moved back home."

Damn, he couldn't believe he'd just said that!

He didn't mean it.

And even if he did, the smarter-than-thou approach was no way to persuade her. Now she'd move to Singapore just to prove him wrong.

Her eyes narrowed. "My moving home would be best for whom?"

"You," he said, though that wasn't the one-syllable, starts-with-an-*m*, ends-with-an-*e* pronoun rocketing through his brain.

Hallie shot to her feet. She pointed her finger at him, and the bumblebees smacked against each other. "Don't you dare feel sorry for me. I spent all my years in Sandy Bend with people feeling sorry for me. And okay, I was a screwup. I admit it!"

She planted her hands on her hips, and the whole corsage jolted with the force of the action. "So maybe I wasn't the most coordinated girl around, or the prettiest. And maybe I did manage to knock over the village Christmas tree two years in a row, but you know what? I got over it!"

She leaned forward and glared at him. "You, Steve Whitman, can save your pity for someone who needs it."

With that, she turned heel and stalked off.

Steve gave a hangdog shake of his head. The best candidate for pity he could think of was him. He'd let his mouth get miles ahead of his brain, and why? Because Hallie Brewer had just given him the most incredible gift he'd ever received—her love. Fool that he was, he didn't know what to do with it.

HALLIE DECIDED the best bet was to walk off her pain. Since the green was a crazy quilt of sheets and blankets with little grass showing between, she picked her way to the perimeter, then permitted her stride to stretch out.

She couldn't believe Steve still saw her as some lost-in-the-forest child. Unemployment was a setback, but nothing she couldn't handle. And if ever—even for a fleeting second—she might have considered returning to Sandy Bend, she wouldn't now.

Dana pulled even with Hallie just as she reached the corner of Main and Sands. "Awesome corsage."

Hallie kept walking. "Thanks."

"So where are we walking to?"

"Just cooling down."

"Then do you think we could walk at a cooler pace?"

Hallie glanced at her new friend's feet. Dana had traded spike heels for red motorcycle mama boots, complete with shiny chrome buckles and enough straps to do any dominatrix proud. Hallie slowed.

"I was up most of last night coming up with a plan to revamp the Hair Dungeon, now known as Devine Secrets Day Spa," Dana said. "Do you have any design suggestions?"

The woman sure knew what to ask to turn an artist's mind from men. "Well, now that you mention it, just because your front entry is located below ground doesn't mean you have to look that way. If you painted the walls of the stairwell a sky blue, then had a grassy pathway with stepping stones painted on the stairs—"

"You're hired. I know it's not your usual line of work, but draw it up for me."

Hallie stopped. "I couldn't take money from you."

Dana looped her hand around Hallie's elbow and turned her back toward the green. "Which is why you netted three hundred bucks last year. I'm paying you." After barely enough pause to draw breath, she said, "So now that we have the chitchat out of the way, do you want to tell me what's bugging you?"

"Nothing much."

"Right. Well, if you don't want to talk about it, let's go eat. The extra pounds on my behind are proof I'm a pro at using food to bury anger. And what better place than the annual village picnic to dig in?"

When they got near the front of the line in the food

tent, Hallie could tell that the Senior Citizens' Gourmet Club had already been through because pretty much everything worth eating was gone. Empty Santa-head bowls and platters with limp leaf lettuce littered the tables. She and Dana decided to make a quick pass of the entrées, then hit the dessert area hard. Chocolate in any form would do.

As they neared the salads, Hallie could hear Kira's dulcet tones—those she used when kissing up—over the other noise in the tent. She motioned for Dana to follow her as she moved to the edge of Kira's circle of admirers.

"I'm so glad you like it," Kira was saying. "The celery seed is an old Whitman family secret. If you sample it against that store-bought salad, you'll see what a difference it makes."

"What gives with the Lady Bountiful routine?" Dana asked Hallie.

"More like Lady Liar. She's taking credit for my potato salad."

"Figures. Should we reinform the crowd?"

"It's not worth the effort."

"Hey, if I were you, I'd be taking the credit due to me."

Hallie shrugged. "I'm a Sandy Bend short-timer, two days left until my escape—not that I'm counting."

Dana sighed. "I'd almost forgotten. Let's do dessert."

Once their plates threatened to buckle, they worked their way through the crowd and out of the tent. Hallie trailed behind a step, watching the double takes at the latest blue additions to Dana's hair. She didn't really notice Dana's chosen course until they were smack in front of Steve, who was talking with Mitch and her dad.

"I, Dana Devine, your devoted servant, bring you food for the stomach and the soul." She thrust her plate at Steve, who managed to accept it without toppling its mountain of brownies. "That's the stomach part, and Hallie here, is the soul." Dana pinned Hallie with a stern frown. "Now play nice. Like you said, you're a short-timer."

She strolled about five feet away, then turned back to look at Hallie's dad and brother. "If you two gentlemen have a couple of free minutes, I'd like to talk to you about Cal. I'm kind of worried about what he's been doing with those handcuffs of his."

Hooked, the men followed. Hallie shook her head in awe. If what she'd seen over the past day was any indication, Dana Devine would one day run this town. And what a town it would be.

STEVE LOOKED at the tribute to chocolate that Dana had foisted on him. The last thing he was in the mood for was food. He wanted privacy, someplace away from the mayor, members of the school board, and most of the senior class of 2004. He needed to set things right with Hallie, and the crowd milling around them wasn't conducive to heartfelt groveling.

"Do you really want to eat that?" he asked Hallie, nodding toward her equally laden plate.

"Not especially."

"Okay." He called over the pack of kids running in circles around the gazebo. "You guys think you can eat all this?"

He took their collective tribal howl as a yes.

"They'll never sleep tonight," Hallie commented as the kids made off with their plunder.

Steve chuckled. "I'm betting they'll run off the sugar buzz." He took her hand. "Come sit with me."

They walked to Luta Mae's stone bench and sat.

"If you hadn't taken off, I would have been able to

tell you I feel a lot of things about you, but pity isn't one of them.''

Hallie's tense expression eased. ''Okay. I'll take just about anything over pity. So what do you feel about me?''

He edited his emotions down to those fit for a public forum. The Tiffanys were still lurking within earshot. ''The shopping list would start with frustration.''

Steve thought he saw the beginnings of humor twinkling in her blue eyes. They might get past his monumental screwup, yet.

''Good frustration or bad frustration?'' she asked in an echo of his question the night before.

Her kindness humbled him. By building a bridge from this moment back to the intimacy of last night, she was showing that she forgave him. Maybe she hadn't been raised with the same advantages as his sisters, who'd grown up elbow-to-elbow with the sons and daughters of society, but Hallie possessed an innate diplomacy they'd never match.

''Good frustration…the best kind,'' he replied in a voice low enough that only she could catch what he'd said.

She moved close and whispered in his ear, ''Want to head on home and see what we can do about that frustration? I promise to play very, very nice, just like Dana ordered.''

Steve sent a brief word of thanks to the heavens for sparing him the lightning bolt he'd been looking for earlier. He was ready to live another day.

THE NEXT MORNING, Steve woke to the sound of his telephone. He groped for his nightstand but got a curvy handful of Hallie, instead. Sometime during their wild night he'd ended up on the other side of the bed. The sheets were tangled at his feet, and Hallie was using the comforter as a pillow.

He leaned across her, thinking just how good it felt to wake to her in his bed, then picked up the cordless phone and gave a bleary, "Hello?"

"Steve, is that you?" bellowed a woman's voice.

"Yes, Mercy, it's me."

Mercy Cooper was president of the school board, and as far from a somber Puritan as a woman could be. "You sound strange. Are you sick?"

As she spoke, Steve moved the phone away from his ear. He suspected if Mercy turned her hearing aid up a notch, she'd shout less. Still, he'd no sooner offer her that advice than he'd point out that her beehive hairdo frightened small children.

"I'm not sick, Mercy, just sleeping."

"Well, glad to hear it. Most everyone's hanging over their toilets this morning. Some ninny served spoiled potato salad at the picnic. Enid Talbert's been in the bathroom so long that Harold has dragged in the TV to keep her company. Now I'm not naming names or anything, but Harold says that Enid keeps muttering about Hallie Brewer."

"Hallie?" Steve croaked.

The woman in question stretched and yawned, then moved to rest her head on Steve's chest. At the same time, Mercy shouted into the phone, "Yes, Hallie Brewer, and if it's true, it's no surprise to me. Remember the punch years ago? Enid's calling her Stomach Pump Hallie."

Hallie sat bolt upright, nearly knocking the phone from Steve's grip. Her howled *"Stomach Pump Hallie?"* was enough to catch even Mercy's limited hearing.

"Steve, is someone there with you?"

"No," he lied, then realized how idiotic that was, so

he said, "I mean yes." He paused, drew in a ragged breath, then said, "Look, Mercy, I'm guessing you called to tell me that my meeting with the board's been cancelled."

Mercy had her own line of questioning to pursue. "Is that Hallie Brewer there with you?"

"A gentleman would never tell." Not that there was any mistaking who was snapping, "Just who's calling me Stomach Pump Hallie and why are they doing it?"

"I'll call you later. Something's just come up." Steve got rid of Mercy just before Hallie wrested the phone from his grip.

When she realized no one was on the other end, she dropped the phone back in its base and glared at Steve. "Do you want to tell me what's going on?"

He knew he was going to have to…eventually. He drew her into his arms and settled her head back on his chest, which was no easy feat since she was holding herself as stiff as a statue. While running his fingers through her hair, he commented, "Anyone ever tell you that stress is unhealthy? I once read this study about—"

"*Now,* Steve!"

He knew he was beat. He'd barely gotten out Mercy's news before Hallie wrenched from his grip, scrambled from the bed and started looking for her clothes.

"Where are you going?" he asked.

"You don't want to know," she said in such a dark tone that a chill chased down his spine.

Discretion being the better part of valor, Steve took Hallie at her word.

12

HALLIE MIGHT NOT have been sick from potato salad, but by the time she arrived at the police station later that morning, she'd had a bellyful of grief.

Mrs. Hawkins had been the first—but not the last—to stop her on the sidewalk and give her the body count. According to the storekeeper, the only people who'd eaten potato salad and weren't ill were those who had stuck with Kira Whitman's wonderful homemade salad and skipped the store-bought.

"That's what comes of driving twenty minutes to a big barn of a supermarket that's pushing all us independents out of business. We're a dying breed," Mrs. Hawkins had chided, apparently forgetting she'd seen Hallie loading her cart with picnic supplies right in her own grocery store.

Mrs. Hawkins had marched back into Foodland, the chenille butterflies on her wilted corsage bouncing in time to her steps. Hallie had walked away, wrongly branded a store-killer. After that, it came as small comfort that everyone else just viewed the picnic incident as Horrible Hallie fodder.

When she'd insisted that she'd actually brought the homemade, all she'd gotten in response were epic retellings of other Hallie disasters and assurances that nobody would hold this newest one against her. She thought that was mighty kind of them since, for once, she'd done nothing wrong.

Hallie wanted her name cleared and the pity ended. As she stood in the middle of the police station giving Cal and Mitch her version of the salad saga, she knew she was coming a little unglued. By the way her brothers were looking at her, they shared that assessment.

"Kira's potato salad was sitting right on the kitchen counter the night before the picnic," she said. "When I offered to help her put it away, it was as if she'd totally forgotten about it. It could have been there overnight for all we know."

Cal frowned as he straightened a pile of papers on the desk in front of him. "Look, I'm as ticked about Kira Whitman being loose with the truth as you are, but I don't think it rises to the level of a criminal investigation."

"So what's the point of having brothers who are cops?"

Mitch shrugged. "All the donuts you can eat?"

"Funny."

Cal rubbed his forehead. "I know they're giving you a hard time. For what it's worth, we got word out early this morning that your potato salad isn't to blame. Both Mitch and I ate some before the picnic and we're not bowed over the porcelain shrine. Problem is, you do have a track record, Hal."

Mitch leaned back in his chair and grinned. "Do you remember the time you made deviled eggs and mistook cayenne pepper for paprika? Or when—"

Hallie left before she was tempted to kick Mitch's chair over. Once she was back outside, she walked with her head down, avoiding the eye contact she knew would just lead to more Horrible Hallie tales.

She had no idea how to fix this mess. First thing this morning, she'd already tried—and failed—to corner Kira. At this point, Hallie supposed the best she could hope for was a dignified exit from town after the parade tomorrow.

Stopping at a bench in front of the green, she sat down. Volunteers were busy taking down the food tent. She was happy to see it go. As she watched them, it occurred to her that she could pack up her things and leave right now, too. With the exception of buying candy to throw to the kids in the crowd, she'd finished the Summer Fun float. While she was worried about her dad's attitude, he seemed in good enough physical shape. At least good enough to create some pretty awesome crop circles.

One person kept her here—Steve. The thought of walking away was tearing her heart and soul to shreds. She had no idea how Steve felt. Oh, she knew he was a tender and attentive lover, but she'd never witnessed him show the same depth of feeling toward her as he did toward this town. And right now, when a good percentage of Sandy Benders were on her Wish I Knew a Little Voodoo list, that really hurt.

The pain of hiding her feelings for him was also becoming a physical thing. Last night, she'd been very careful to hold back any additional words of love, to treat their time together as lightly as he did. Time that was drawing to a close.

Hallie's thoughts were interrupted by a call of, "Hey, look, it's Stomach Pump Hallie!" A cluster of skateboard-toting boys stood laughing and pointing on the other side of the street. "Hey, you gonna catch anything on fire today?" one shouted. "Or plow anything down?" another added.

Great. Her reputation had worked its way down to another generation of Sandy Benders. Leaving definitely wouldn't be all heartache.

With one farewell project in mind, she stood and walked down to Sands Street. Frustrated by her lack of response, the boys shadowed her right to the door of Brogan and Daughters' Bit O' Green Hardware. When Hallie stepped inside, the Brogan daughters were nowhere to be seen. Mr. Brogan stood behind the cash register, looking just as bald and cranky as when she'd last seen him in his prior Main Street location, seven years earlier.

"Hi, Mr. Brogan. I need to buy some paint and supplies."

"With both Emma and Maeve home sick this morning—and you know from what—you'll have to wait until I'm finished ringing up my other customers."

Hallie curbed her temper. "You don't have any customers except me."

"But when I do…"

"Fine."

After a few detours to dust and tidy, he finally moved to the paint area. Twenty torturous minutes later, Hallie scrutinized the paint sample he'd prepared.

"Close," she said, setting the chip back onto the counter in front of the paint-mixing equipment, "but that's not quite it. I'm looking for an early-summer sky. You know, when everything's in bloom and the green of the grass reflects into the sky. Add just the tiniest bit of yellow and let's see what we end up with."

His lower jaw jutted out. "I make what's on the chips and in the paint book. If you're looking for some sort of fancy color, you'll just have to wait for Maeve to come in. That's her department."

"How about if I give it a try?" she negotiated. "You used to let me mix my own paint."

"I dunno," he said, his bushy white brows drawn downward in a dubious slope. "After the potato salad, it might not be safe."

The last of Hallie's patience evaporated. "Are you going to eat the paint? Because if you are, Mr. Brogan,

I can tell you even though it's lead-free, it's not very good for you."

She splayed her hands flat on the counter and leaned closer. "And if you're not going to eat it, let me get this job done so I can get out of this insane asylum of a town."

Mr. Brogan got out of her way.

STEVE FOUND HALLIE painting the Hair Dungeon's stairwell a color he guessed he'd call cerulean blue, if he were feeling creative—which he wasn't. He'd just finished two hours with the non-barfing members of the school board and he'd tapped himself out. The only person he wanted to see or be with was Hallie. The sight of her made him smile, even if it was a tired smile.

"Thank you," he said from the top of the stairs.

Her back was to him, and she didn't turn when she spoke. "You're welcome, but I don't know for what."

He hesitated, wondering at the tight sound of her voice and set of her shoulders under her oversize T-shirt. "For saving my school. I didn't meditate at dawn or lay out a pattern of crystals like Thea did when she got to town, but I did do some serious, positive thinking."

Hallie continued painting in fast, careless sweeps. "And?"

"I'll have to wait until everything can be drawn up and presented to the full board, but I think it's going to fly."

"What's going to fly?" She didn't sound especially enthusiastic, but he was too pumped not to answer.

"My plan. Thanks to your kick in the rear, I focused on what we lack." He began counting down the items. "We have tons of senior citizens and no seniors program. We have young couples who have to work outside the home to afford to live here, but no community-supported day care. We have too much empty space at the high school, but if we fill it with these things, everybody wins. I proposed a program where interested students would be able to intern in day care and help run art and other classes in a senior center. Over the next year, I'm going to focus on finding grant money to help fund this.''

He paused as a new realization dawned. ''I guess this is the first time in my life I can see the bright side of being a Whitman. It's time to break out the tuxedo, throw a few parties and shake the money tree.''

She nodded, and then did something that looked suspiciously like wiping at tears. ''I'm happy for you, Steve. Really, I am.''

He walked down the stairs and turned her to face him. What Steve saw tugged at a heart that was growing dangerously soft. She wouldn't meet his eyes. He took the brush from her and set it on the lid of the paint can.

''Why are you crying?''

''I'm not.''

Using his thumb, he smoothed away a tear and a smudge of blue. Hallie and paint, the two were meant for each other.

''Okay, you're not crying. So what's going on?''

''For starters, your sister has been telling everyone I made the bad potato salad when I didn't.''

He nodded. ''I know what she's up to. I've been doing damage control, and I promise when I get my hands on her, it won't be pretty.''

''Forget it. It doesn't matter.''

He tipped up her chin and looked into eyes that mirrored the hurt she was feeling. ''Obviously, it does.''

She started sobbing in earnest. Knowing his shirt was going to be both blue and wet—and not caring at all—Steve held her close.

''It's not the salad. It's that th-they believe her,'' she

cried as she balled her fists into the formerly white fabric on his chest. "Everyone in this stupid town believes she's the one who peeled and chopped and worked for them. She's Queen Kira and I'm Stomach Pump Hallie. With all the good I've done, all anyone remembers is the bad."

"They know the good. Look at the way everyone flocked to you at the picnic last night."

She pushed away and swiped angrily at her eyes. "And look at the way people turned on me today. All I've heard are Horrible Hallie stories, and most of them aren't even true."

Steve gave humor a shaky try. "So you've attained legend status. That's not so bad."

She glared at him. "I wasn't going to cry over this. It's stupidity. Sandy Bend, never-gonna-change stupidity. They're not worth it. I'm out of here tomorrow night, and I'll never think about this place again."

She couldn't have honed sharper words to cut him. He'd lain awake for hours last night trying to find a good way to broach the subject of Hallie extending her stay. Broach it in a noncommittal, don't risk another Susan-type kick in the teeth way, of course.

"Hallie, don't make too much of this." He'd tried to sound calm and cool—a Whitman all the way—but his desperation was coming through loud and clear. He needed more time with her. He needed her to love Sandy Bend.

"I'm making exactly enough of this," she said. She grabbed her paintbrush and attacked the last patch of gray on the wall. "You know, I really, really hate this place."

Feeling defeated in a way he never had before—not even when Susan dumped him—Steve turned and left.

WRUNG DRY of both hope and tears, Hallie finished painting the base color on Dana's stairwell, then went home to recover. She felt awful about dumping her problems on Steve. It wasn't the sort of stuff a guy who'd signed up for a couple-day fling needed to hear. She wouldn't be surprised if he avoided her for the rest of her time in town. Maybe it was better that way, with no messy goodbyes and no risk of crying all over him again.

As she pulled into the farmyard, she took some comfort at the sight of the Terminator stretched out on the kitchen stoop, napping. She was just stepping out of the car when Mitch jumped out from behind the kitchen door. The Terminator launched himself into the air and took off toward the barn.

Disregarding the fact that he'd just shaved another life off the cat, Mitch said, "Great timing! Anna Bethune's on the phone. Dad's talking to her right now."

Hallie winced at the thought of her father chatting it up with Anna about aliens or what-have-you. "You sure it's Anna?"

"British accent, says her name's Anna, and I'd pay ten years' salary for a night with her on a desert island? Yep, it's Anna."

She dashed to the kitchen and pried her dad from the cordless phone. "Hello, Anna."

"Hallie, I know you received a call from my assistant yesterday."

"Really, it's okay about letting me go," she said as she made shooing motions at her father and brother. "I understand completely."

"Actually, I'm afraid Pamela got ahead of herself. It's quite true I've decided to sell my properties in the States and move back home, but I've also been trying to be certain that Matt's behavior poisons as few lives as possible. I have nothing to offer you in California, but would you consider relocating?''

"R-relocating?''

Her father and brother echoed the word after her, then launched into noisy speculation. Hallie covered her free ear with her hand. When that didn't work, she stepped into the dining room to find some quiet.

"I do have a similar position available in my London home,'' Anna was saying. "I tend to spend the majority of my time at my estate in Cornwall. It would be wonderful to keep the townhouse better staffed for my visits. I'll warn you, it isn't like California. The view's not quite so grand and your quarters wouldn't be separate, of course.''

Hallie tried to absorb everything Anna was saying, but she seemed to be stuck on one word. "London?''

Anna laughed. "Yes, London.''

Hallie's heart began pounding. Catherine Lassiter, her former art instructor, lived in London.

"London sounds wonderful,'' she blurted. Anyplace with a teacher like Catherine sounded wonderful.

"Then you think the position would suit you?''

"I know it would,'' Hallie automatically replied. But then something incredibly strange happened. She heard someone who sounded just like her saying, "But I need a week to think about this.''

Think about what? How an opportunity beyond her wildest fantasies was being handed to her?

"This is so unexpected,'' said the same gremlin that seemed to be shaping her lips and forcing out words she wanted to pull back.

"I suppose it is, at that. A week, then,'' Anna said. "I look forward to hearing from you.''

And Hallie looked forward to regaining control of her own voice. She gave some sort of garbled goodbye, then managed to push the off button on the phone with one trembling finger. She pulled a chair away from the dining room table and worked on some of Thea's cleansing breaths.

"London," she said, testing the word on her tongue. A little frightening, yes, but it tasted sweet, not a bitter drop of Horrible Hallie to it.

"London," she said with more authority as she walked back into the kitchen.

"London, what?" Mitch prompted from his seat across from their dad at the kitchen table.

"Anna Bethune has offered me a job in London."

"All right!" her brother crowed. "That beats unemployment anytime." He came and wrapped her in a hug, then said, "Break time's up. I gotta run. Great news, Hal."

Her dad just drank his coffee and frowned. After Mitch left, he glanced at Hallie. "So, are you taking the job?"

"I told her I needed a week to think about it."

Her father stood and settled his coffee mug into the sink. "Hallie-girl, we need to talk."

"Hallie-girl" usually meant that a delicate conversation awaited. She slipped into defensive mode. "I didn't mess up the potato salad."

"It's not about the potato salad. Come on out to the pond with me."

Her father's words were more a command than a request. From the time she was little, her father would take her to the pond for her "big talks." Nostalgia with a slight tinge of embarrassment rippled through her as she recalled some of them.

"I already know where babies come from, Dad," she said as they made their way out of the house.

He chuckled. "That's one conversation I won't be forgetting anytime soon. There are some discussions a father just isn't ready to have with a daughter, no matter how much he prepares.''

As they walked through the sweet grass, Hallie realized it was a glorious day, something she hadn't even noticed before Anna's call. Red-winged blackbirds' clear warbles danced on the breeze. The cattails on the east edge of the pond whispered and swayed.

Her dad settled into his favorite fishing chair.

Knowing the drill, Hallie sat in the chair next to him.

''I've decided to leave Sandy Bend,'' he said. ''I got a clean bill of health from the doctors in Grand Rapids this week. I also got a list of referrals for every city between here and Sedona.''

''S-Sedona? As in Arizona?'' she managed to squeak.

A satisfied smile spread across his face. ''That's the place.''

She supposed she should be glad he hadn't said Roswell, the mecca of alien-lovers.

''This is just a vacation, right?''

''Nope. I've submitted my resignation to the Village Council. I'm traveling light—a few changes of clothes, a cell phone and a couple of maps in the 'Vette and I'm out of here.''

''Why are you doing this?''

''Because it finally occurred to me that I can. Don't get me wrong, I love Sandy Bend, but it always seemed a little empty to me after your mother died.''

Hallie was floored. ''It's been over twenty years.''

Her father looked off across the pond to the field beyond, burnished gold in the afternoon sun. ''I know how long it's been down to the day. I managed to get you kids raised as decent citizens, did my part for the village as police chief, but now it's time to do something just for me.''

''And Sedona will make you happy?''

"The destination's not all that important. This is about the journey."

She did her best to smile for her father. It was selfish of her to feel like crying, but she did. Even when she was thousands of miles away, she'd always had a sense that all was right with the world because her family was back in Sandy Bend. She didn't necessarily want to be here, but she loved picturing her dad down at the station and her brothers at a pickup basketball game.

"This sounds like a great change of pace for you, Dad."

"Well, you can fill only so much time attracting aliens and welding things. So now that my future's all settled, what's it going to be for you? London? Rome? Sandy Bend?" he teased.

"I'd be crazy not to take the London offer. Remember Catherine Lassiter, the instructor I used to talk about all the time?"

"The one who had her own show at that gallery in Chicago?"

"The same. She married an art dealer and moved to London last year. This could be a once-in-a-lifetime opportunity to study with her again."

"Then what made you ask Anna Bethune for more time to decide?"

Hallie hesitated. "Nothing, really. I'd be crazy to turn down this job, wouldn't I?"

"Only you know the answer to that. What's holding you back, Hallie?"

As she scrambled for an answer that made some sense to her, let alone anyone else, Hallie picked at the loose paint on the arm of her chair. "I guess hearing that you're not going to be in Sandy Bend has me kind of rattled."

"You heard that after the call from Anna," her father reminded her.

She wished he were a little more loosey-goosey with details. "It's just that Sedona is so far away," she tried.

"If you're in London, the difference between Sandy Bend and Sedona is nothing to lose sleep over."

"True, but if I'm not in London..." She shook her head as though she could dislodge the indecision gripping her. "Of course I'll be in London."

He reached forward and plucked a long blade of grass. Twirling it between his fingers he said, "You know, you can always stay here for the same reason I'm leaving."

"What do you mean?"

"Because you can. I think taking off after high school did you a world of good. At least, that's what I would have said right up until this potato salad problem. Now you're letting that old insecurity dog you."

She snorted. "You try living as a walking punch line. I know it shouldn't bug me nearly as much as it does, but it was tough enough growing up the only female Brewer for miles around. Not that you didn't do a great job as both mom and dad."

"I did the best I could." He shifted in his chair and gave her a speculative look. "Have you ever just told people in town that you don't want to hear those stories anymore?"

"No. I guess I've just been conditioned to accept them."

"Then it's time to do a little unconditioning, for both you and them, don't you think?"

"You've got a point."

"Of course I do." He fell silent for a moment. Hallie waited. From the set of his jaw, she knew he was working up another speech.

Finally he said, "As long as I'm making points, here, I might as well go all the way. I've been doing my best not to meddle in whatever you and Steve have cooking, but I can't hold off much longer without failing you as a father.

"He's a good man, Hallie. One I'd be proud to call my son. Maybe sometimes he's a little confused about what it means to be a member of that family of his, but a good, solid man for all of that."

Hallie's smile was the most regret-laden of her life. "You don't need to sell me on him, Dad."

"No, I guess I don't. So here I go into a full-out meddle. Is it Steve holding you back from taking the London job?"

"I suppose, but not because he's trying to." She drew in a breath then let the truth free. "I don't want to be where I'm not wanted. I've always loved him. I know he feels something, but I don't think it's the same for him as it is for me. Besides, I'm not exactly the kind of woman a Whitman marries. He doesn't rub my nose in it, but it's kind of obvious."

"What do you mean, you're not the kind of woman?"

"I'm not the sophisticated type."

"Let me get this straight, you're calm as can be with superstars most people just stammer at, you're an accomplished artist with friends around the world and you don't have the sophistication to deal with the Whitmans?" Laughing, he shook his head. "Honey, I don't think *they* have the sophistication to deal with *you.*"

When her dad put it that way... Dazed, Hallie leaned back in her chair and began to wonder at what else in life she'd missed.

"Now, no matter how positive the doctors are about my health, I don't think this old heart of mine could take knowing the details of what happened between you and Steve when you ran off last time, but I know something did. When you leave this time—if you're set on leaving—you and Steve need to do it right. Tell him how you feel.''

She'd come as close as she dared during the picnic last night. Hallie tipped back her head and closed her eyes. "I can't, not without some sign from Steve. I won't put my feelings on the line again.''

"And that boy's never been the sort to let his feelings out, at least not the ones that really count. That's one tough corner you two have painted yourselves into.''

Hallie looked down at her clasped hands. "I know.''

"So you love him and you're going to walk away?''

She nodded, and a tear landed on her hands.

"I told you this when you came home, and I'm repeating it today. Life's short, Hallie-girl. Don't keep your pride at the expense of your happiness. Before you leave, finish shaking things up around here. You're the woman for the job.''

Hallie stood. "Thanks for the vote of confidence, Dad.''

She just hoped she deserved it.

13

OLD HOUSES CREAKED, but they never giggled. Steve stood outside the closed bedroom door he knew he'd left open, debating what to do next. Either the four-mile, head-clearing beach run he'd just finished hadn't done its job, or someone he'd known for a very long time had been partying hearty this afternoon. And that particular someone had no license to be in his bed.

Steve yanked on the sweaty T-shirt he'd just pulled off in anticipation of a shower. Knowing he was opening one scary Pandora's Box, he slowly turned the knob to his bedroom door. What he saw inside was enough to make him want to slam it and then run another four miles—one way.

Susan lay posed on the covers, wearing an outfit that was best ignored. Except it was mighty hard to ignore a tribute to bad taste constructed entirely of purple mesh and black fringe. He supposed it was one of those teddy things, except that made it sound cute.

Doing his best to avert his eyes, he said, "Ended the bachelorette party early, huh?"

"I was hoping the party was just beginning."

Steve continued to look at the braided rug, the dresser, anywhere but at Susan. "They served martinis, right?" he asked, referring to her traditional drink of choice.

"How did you guess?"

Each syllable was carefully enunciated, a sign she

was trying too hard to sound as if she hadn't been celebrating. He caught a glimpse of one long leg raised and a foot pointed to the ceiling. Red enameled toenails waggled as though waving hello.

"Same way I always did when you and martinis crossed paths," he answered. "Now why don't you just get into whatever you wore here and head on home?"

"No car. Kira is my designated driver, and I gave her the night off."

No two ways about it, between torpedoing Hallie and then this little scheme, Kira was toast. "No problem, I'll drive."

"Don't be such a drag, Steve. How about just one last time, for old times' sake? You can take me home in the morning."

He'd tried to be diplomatic, but he was done. He pulled the comforter from the far side of the bed and folded it over Susan. Now that it was safe to look, he gave her the full force of his anger in one power-packed glare.

"Get up and get dressed. It takes a lot of guts—and stupidity—to think you can use me to back out of your wedding. You don't want to marry the guy, fine, but leave me out of it."

Face, fringe and attitude, Susan crumpled. From what he recalled, she'd always been kind of a delicate, pearly tear and polite sniffle type of woman. Not anymore, apparently. This was a high-volume, openmouthed, from-the-gut howl.

"For the love of Pete," he muttered while grabbing the tissue box and shoving it at her.

She clutched it and wailed some more.

If she weren't uninvited, several martinis past sane and camped in his bed, he might have been a little more sympathetic. As it was, he felt mostly angry. And a little sad.

"This is the *stu-stu-stupidest* thing I've ever done," she wailed.

She'd be getting no argument from him.

"I'm just so *sc-scared.*"

He sat at the foot of the bed. "No one is making you get married. If you're not ready, call Juan, and—"

"His name is *Julio-o-o!*"

"Okay, Julio." He looked around the room for her clothes, but saw nothing. "So where'd you leave your clothes?"

She downgraded from howling to snuffling. "D-downstairs b-by the back door."

"Great." He stood. "Just stay there. Think you can do that?"

"Of course I can." She sniffed.

"I'll be right back."

He was two steps out the bedroom door when another female voice called from below.

"Steve? Are you up there?"

Steve jerked to a halt and debated whether to admit that he was. He figured he was damned if he did and damned if he didn't.

"Steve?"

"I'll be right down, Hallie." He swung back to his bedroom. "Stay and I mean it," he hissed at Susan.

When he got to the top of the steps, Hallie was standing at the bottom. She had a pair of white pants in one hand and a red-and-white top in the other.

"I don't suppose these are yours," she said.

"It's not what it looks like."

"Well, it looks like about two hundred dollars worth of overpriced resort wear." She unfurled the pants. "They're too small for you and too tall for Kira, which leaves—"

"Steve, are you coming back?"

Hallie's eyes narrowed enough to shoot some really evil blue darts his way. "Susan."

"Think you could toss me those?" he asked. He didn't want to risk getting too close.

She hurled them with awesome strength.

"Thanks. If I take these to Susan, do you promise you won't run off?"

"I'm not running anywhere."

Somehow, that didn't sound nearly as promising to Steve as it should.

"Wait for me in the living room," he said.

"My pleasure," she answered, not very pleasantly, before she stalked off.

He was damned either way, all right.

HALLIE PACED the length of the living room, stopping once at the mantel to turn the photo of Kira facedown. She had enough in the way of stress at the moment. Without even realizing what she was doing, she reached into the pocket of her shorts and pulled out the crystals Thea had given her. Any port—even a mystic one—in a storm.

"I'm sorry about this," Steve said as he entered the room.

Hallie turned the blue crystal between her fingers. It was oddly cool to the touch.

He hitched a thumb back toward the stairway. "Nothing happened up there."

"Just like nothing happened the other day on the street corner, right?" Her words were her hurt speaking, not what she felt—no, knew—deep inside. Just as Steve said, nothing had happened up there.

"Look at me, Hallie."

She clenched the crystal tighter, but did as he asked. His eyes were darker than she'd ever recalled seeing them, practically more black than brown.

He moved closer, and she forced herself not to step back, not to run as she had at so many other crucial points in her life.

"Do you honestly think I would sleep with Susan?"

"No," she said, and it was almost as though she could see the tension escape him.

"Kira threw that bachelorette party for her. She was overserved."

At that moment, Hallie found Kira and Susan totally inconsequential. She didn't care if they drank too much, or whether she saw either of them ever again. She cut to the heart of the matter.

"I got an interesting job offer today."

He paused, obviously struggling to keep up with her change of topic. "A job? What kind?"

"Anna Bethune has asked me to join her staff in London. I'll do pretty much the same sort of thing I used to do for her in Carmel."

Steve walked to the couch and sat down hard. "London."

Hallie nodded. Her entire future was on the line, and she wanted to choose each word with supreme care. "What makes this really tempting is that Catherine Lassiter—remember, the instructor with the cat?—moved to London last year. She's giving classes there. This is an incredible opportunity to study with her again."

"That's great."

"Is it?"

"Sure it is."

His enthusiasm sounded a little hollow. Feeling somewhat more encouraged, she asked, "How do you feel about me, Steve? I mean, what have these past few days meant to you?"

"Steve?" Susan stood in the doorway wearing the clothes Hallie had found at the back door. She looked as though she'd had one heck of a crying jag. "I was wondering if I could have a few aspirin?'' Socially correct to the end, she smiled at Hallie. "I'm so sorry to interrupt.''

Steve stood. "Would you mind going outside for a few minutes, Susan?'' He opened the French door from the living room to the deck as a hint that she had no choice. Susan drifted out.

"Sorry,'' Steve said after she was gone, then sat back on the edge of the couch, his elbows braced on his knees and his hands clasped in front of him.

Hallie glanced toward the door with Susan still visible on the other side. She wished for drapes.

"That woman should never drink martinis,'' Steve said. "Now about Catherine Lassiter and London?''

Hallie got the feeling she was losing control of the situation, if she'd ever had it to begin with. She tried to wrest it back. "I need to know how you feel about me, Steve.''

He was staring outside. She followed his line of vision and saw that Susan had decided to take a nap on the deck.

"Steve?''

"Huh? Oh, how I feel about you.'' He rubbed at his forehead, then locked his hands together again. "How long would you be in London?''

"I don't know. A year. Forever. Will you answer my question?''

He looked down at his hands as he spoke. "I think you're one of the most amazing women I'm ever going to meet,'' he said slowly. "The last few days have been like magic, Hallie. I'll never forget them.''

Hallie tried to stop the ragged intake of breath that came just before a tide of tears. It was a tiny sound, but so telling.

"I see,'' she said. Arms wrapped around her midsection to hold in the pain, she turned toward the bookcase.

The letters on the spines of the books wavered in front of her eyes. "I'll never forget them, either." She forced a smile into place, then turned back. "You'll understand if I leave now."

She was almost to the back door when Steve caught up with her. "Hallie, wait. I was thinking maybe I could come over and visit you during Christmas vacation."

Hallie gave him the only answer her pride would permit. "Don't."

HALLIE WAS GONE. Simple as that, she'd left him to figure out what the hell he was going to do with his life. On his run today—before she'd blown his world apart—he'd reached a few conclusions.

First, he'd decided that Hallie was bold, independent and had no interest in snobs. All of which made her entirely unqualified to be a Whitman wife. Of course, the woman with the hideous underwear, who was currently sleeping on his deck was supposed to have been his ideal mate.

That led to his second conclusion. He was entirely unqualified to be a Whitman. He was through feeling guilty because he couldn't bring himself to live the pampered life most of his family members did. And he was equally through feeling guilty because he had some money in the bank. A few days with Hallie, witnessing her head-on approach to life, and he'd changed. He could only imagine what a trip a lifetime with her would be.

Hallie was everything he'd ever wanted. He loved her. Steve didn't know when the love began. It was such a seamless thing, as if it had always been a part of him.

Life was going to be colorless without her, but he wasn't fool enough to think that Sandy Bend could compete with London.

Or that Hallie should have to make that choice. She

needed her chance to seize life and explore her gifts. Sandy Bend was his paradise, but it would stifle her.

Steve wasn't the type to rage or mourn, or to admit anything but the smallest regret. At least, he'd once believed he was that type.

Now all that kept him from letting loose was the knowledge that even though his life was going to be miserable from this day forward, he was a noble man.

Steve Whitman was one fine and noble, lonely man.

14

COUSIN ALTHEA stood in the front hallway with her bags at her feet. "My job is done."

"It was done the day you tried to make me eat tofu lasagna," Hallie's dad said. He picked up one of Thea's duffel bags and slung it over his shoulder. "Is Thor going to be okay getting down on his own?"

Thea's smile was placid. "I hope so, since none of us are large enough to help him."

"Let me get the other bag," Hallie offered. She wondered if she sounded as numb as she felt. She'd slept alone in her old pink gingham room last night. Alone had never felt quite so lonely before.

Thea took Hallie's hand and clasped it between hers. "Everything happens for a reason, Hallie. If Steve isn't ready to open his life, it simply means that…" Frowning, she trailed off. "There's something different here. Your aura—"

"Will do just fine without you, love," a voice boomed from the top of the steps.

"Hey, Cousin Thor, good to see you out of bed," Hallie called up the stairs.

"Not half as good as it is to be out of bed. I've cleaned the town out of poker money and eaten about all of Thea's fruits and vegetables I plan to. It's time to leave." He winced as one size thirteen athletic shoe hit the first step. His enormous hand tightly gripped the oak banister. Everybody on the landing held their breath and moved back.

He grinned. "I haven't crushed anybody in years."

Step by step, he worked his way to the bottom. When he made it, Thea gave his long blond ponytail a playful tug. "You've been milking this back thing, haven't you?"

"Nah, I was just giving you time to feel comfortable about leaving Hallie and Bud."

Thea took Hallie's hand again. Eyes closed, she opined, "Stronger. Much stronger."

"Funny, I don't feel all that strong."

Thea opened her eyes. "Your father says you insist on riding the family float in the parade. That's plenty strong."

Hallie thought about that. "You know, you're right. Considering everything that's happened, I never thought I'd be saying this, but thanks for luring me home. I guess it's been worth it."

Cousin Thea squeezed her hand, then released it. "Now you can look to the future without feeling bound by the past."

Hallie's dad shifted the weight of the duffel bag. "Didn't I hear that on a rerun of that kung fu series?"

Thea remained unruffled. "And you, Bud, are you ready for your new adventure?"

"Well, after I do my stint as Grand Marshal in the parade, I figured I'd just keep driving off into the sunset."

Hallie smiled. "I like that. Maybe we can travel as the Brewer convoy. That is, if I won't be cramping your style."

"If you're set on leaving, we might as well go together," her father said. "Now let's get this show on the road."

Hallie said her goodbyes to Thor and Thea, who were

going to watch the parade, then head back to Wisconsin. After they were settled in their microbus and on their way to town, Hallie hopped into her dad's 'Vette and made ready for her own grand exit.

SOMETIME THE PREVIOUS NIGHT while Hallie lay weeping in bed, Cal had towed the float to the high school parking lot, which also served as the parade staging ground.

Now he stood at Hallie's and Mitch's feet as they dangled their legs over the side of the float. Hallie's dad was busy making sure the Grand Marshal sign wouldn't mar his precious car's paint job. Cal was passing empty minutes by complaining about the indignity of being forced to tow the float with a tractor held together by rust and rubber bands.

"So you're really taking off this evening?" Mitch asked her, ignoring their older brother's ill temper and the high school marching band's out-of-tune tune-up.

Looping a strand of hair behind her ear, she nodded. "I called Emily Matthews first thing this morning. I'm going to spend the night in Grand Rapids and visit with her. We haven't seen each other since high school."

"I wish you weren't leaving, but I guess I can understand why."

"It's for the best." It was also the only alternative her aching heart would allow.

"Maybe if you—" Mitch began.

"Excuse me, everybody," the mayor boomed over the loudspeaker. "I have someone who needs your attention."

The marching band stopped honking and bleating, the Veterans of Foreign Wars stood at attention, and even the animals on the Noah's Ark float seemed to quiet.

Hallie turned and shaded her eyes from the sun. At the front of the parking lot, the mayor handed over his microphone to Kira Whitman, who held it as though she were grasping a rattlesnake. She gingerly closed her other hand over the top of it and whispered furiously at her brother. Even from this distance, Hallie could see the intractable set of Steve's jaw.

And even from this distance, she could feel her tears starting at the sight of him. Heaven help her if she actually had to speak to him.

Kira uncovered the microphone. "Um...I just wanted everybody to know that the little problem with the potato salad the other night was my fault." She covered the microphone again, but not quite well enough. "Is that enough or do I have to make a total fool of myself?" she whined to her brother.

"Do we get a vote?" someone from the "Our Friend the Asparagus" float shouted. Laughter rippled through the crowd.

"Hallie Brewer made the homemade potato salad," Kira forced through her teeth. Working up a perfect smile, she added, "I just kind of took credit for it. I mean, she left me stuck in a tent with that drill sergeant of a woman, and—"

The mayor's chest puffed up like a bantam rooster's and he made a harrumphing noise. This time, Steve covered the microphone with one hand and latched on to his sister's elbow with the other. When he was done talking to her, a pale-faced Kira finished with the most grudging "sorry" Hallie had ever heard, then wriggled free of Steve's grip.

An admission of responsibility was more than Hallie had ever received from Kira before. Of course, an uncoerced admission would have been even nicer, but she knew better than to expect miracles.

"That's it?" she heard Mitch ask in incredulous

tones. Eyes narrowed, he hopped from the float. "Not this time, Princess. You've had it too easy for too long."

"Where are you going?" Cal asked.

"Unfinished business," Mitch called before heading in Kira's direction.

The mayor took control of the microphone. His free hand was clamped over his comb-over hairstyle, anchoring it in the breeze. "Hallie Brewer, I know you're out there, somewhere."

"Stand up," Cal urged.

"Do I have to?" she grumbled, but stood nonetheless. She brushed the sand off the back of her legs, then waved in the mayor's direction.

"On behalf of all potato salad eaters in Sandy Bend, I hereby apologize to you, Hallie," he said in a very official-sounding voice. "The Brewer name is cleared."

Crimson-faced, she called her thanks.

"Yeah, but we haven't forgotten the Christmas trees," someone shouted.

"Or the picnic shelter," added Mrs. Hawkins, who was seated on the Summer Fun Princess's throne. Poor, deposed Skye stood at the storekeeper's side.

"Or—"

The crowd was warming to the topic, but Hallie was getting hot. She cupped her hands to either side of her mouth. "That's enough, people," she shouted. "Maybe it was funny the first ten times you reminded me, but it's no longer open season on Hallie Brewer, got it?"

"You tell 'em, honey," Mrs. Hawkins—obviously an equal-opportunity heckler—shouted.

From his spot next to the mayor, Steve started applauding slowly. Hallie held her head high. She refused to cry.

Float by float, band member by band member, others joined in until the crowd was whistling and cheering. Hallie felt a relieved smile spread across her face. She knew Sandy Benders well enough to realize that the next time she visited, she'd take her share of teasing, but at least she'd made her stand.

"Ready to roll?" Hallie asked Cal.

He scowled at the ancient red tractor. "As ready as I'm going to be."

"Hallie!" Dana Devine was semi-jogging toward them on white, vampy '50s-style high heels. She held a small gift-wrapped box in one hand.

"Even readier to roll now," Cal said, then retreated to the hated tractor.

Dana drew even to the side of the float. "I brought you a going-away present."

Hallie held out her hand. "Come on up. Keep me company during the parade."

"Are you sure? I'm not really dressed for the beach," she said, gesturing at her short, formfitting lace dress that looked like a lingerie fetishist's idea of a bridal gown.

"Positive."

Dana looked around as if she were waiting for the cops to haul her off. Cal, however, was busy ignoring her, and Mitch seemed to have disappeared altogether.

"Well, if you think it's okay…" Dana set the gift in the sand. Hallie helped haul her up with minimal additional skin exposure.

Once she'd kicked off her shoes, Dana picked up the box. "It isn't anything much."

Hallie took it and opened it. Inside was a summertime version of a snow globe. Silver glitter floated in the water. Two small bathing-suited figures played with a brightly colored beach ball. Black print spelled out Sandy Bend on the base of the globe. Hallie shook it and watched the sparkles swirl.

"I thought you could take it to London." Dana paused and cleared her throat as if she were hindered by the same tears as Hallie. "You know, something to remind you of home."

"Thank you," Hallie whispered. "I think I'm actually going to miss this place," she managed to say in a brighter voice.

But she knew she would miss Steve most of all.

Microphone in hand and whistle in mouth, the mayor chose that moment to blow shrilly enough that dogs miles away must have been screaming.

"One o'clock," he bellowed. "Let the parade begin!"

Cal fired up the tractor, which popped and grunted its displeasure. Unable to stop herself, Hallie scanned the crowd for Steve. One last glimpse was all she wanted, but it seemed she couldn't even have that.

Dana laid a comforting hand on her shoulder. "Hallie, he already left. I saw him take off just a minute ago."

Hallie considered pretending she didn't know whom Dana was referring to, but knew she'd always been too transparent on the subject of Steve.

"You guys better sit down," Cal called from the tractor. "It's time to move."

Hallie tucked her gift back into its box, then made sure it was safely out of the way beneath a beach chair. She and Dana each grabbed a pail filled with parade candy and beads, then perched themselves on the end of the float. Mitch vaulted onboard just as they left the high school parking lot.

"Where did you go?" Hallie asked him, seeking something—anything—to turn her mind from Steve.

"Just to fulfill a little fantasy." Her brother wore a self-satisfied smile to match.

"Like what?"

"Not quite as good as the Anna Bethune one," he said, settling on the back of the float next to Dana, "but satisfying in its own way."

"What?" Hallie prodded.

Mitch scooted backward and hauled out a bag he'd stowed under the other beach chair. He tossed Dana a small squirt gun, then handed one to Hallie. He reserved a jumbo, soak-the-town-size unit for himself.

When Dana arched an enquiring brow at him, he answered, "Crowd control."

She laughed.

"Mitch?" Hallie prompted again.

He settled into one of the low-slung chairs. "Let's just say that she who acts like a brat shall be punished like a brat."

"Mitch, what did you do?"

He smiled. "That's between me and Princess Kira."

As he ducked his head into the red plastic tub brimming with surplus candy and beads, Hallie could have sworn she heard him add, "And her highness's royal behind."

She knew she must have been mistaken. But she sure hoped she wasn't.

The float rounded the corner onto Main Street. In front of them, the band played the Cougars' fight song. Behind them, the Ladies' Tea and Blowtorch Society threw teabags to the crowd. Hallie supposed it was safer than chucking scotch bottles.

Dana and Hallie tossed handfuls of candy to shouting

kids lining the curbs. They dove onto loose pieces like beggars out of a Dickens novel. Mitch had passed on the candy duty to exchange squirt gun fire with his buddies.

Dana sighed. "When I saw Steve up by the microphone, I was so sure I was going to witness one of those fairy-tale endings."

"Then you probably should have hitched a ride on the Summer Fun Princess's float," Hallie said as she flung a few strands of bright green beads. "The odds are a little better in that corner of the world."

They were about halfway down the third block of the parade route when the entire show slowed, then halted.

"What's the holdup?" Hallie asked. She was running low on candy and didn't want to be stampeded by a pack of crazed sugar addicts. She stood and turned toward the front of the float.

Dana was already facing that way, her eyes wide. Hallie tried to pick out whatever her friend was looking at in the crowd, but the sun and her lack of sunglasses made it futile. But whatever Dana saw had a grin crossing her face that seemed wide enough to hurt.

"I don't know about that happy ending stuff. The odds are looking pretty good here, too."

"You're just suffering from too much tractor exhaust," Hallie said. "Take a deep breath, then—"

She stumbled to a halt. Steve had climbed onto the tractor and was saying something low and urgent to Cal.

Hallie's old urge to flee took over, except she knew she had no place to run. Thea and Thor had worked their way from the back of the crowd to the street. Her dad, who was in the middle of the parade procession, had abandoned his car and was walking toward her.

"Face your future," Thea called.

"The happy ending odds are improving by the second," Dana said with unholy glee.

Hallie feared more heartbreak. Seeking some sort of defense, she bent down and retrieved her squirt gun. She clenched it tighter as Steve climbed onto the float.

He took a step toward her. Mitch clambered to his feet and moved forward to block his path.

"I know what I'm doing," Steve said to Mitch.

"Hallie?" Mitch said without backing away.

"It's okay," Hallie called to her brother over the ragtime song the marching band had just started.

Steve closed the distance between them.

Hallie aimed her squirt gun at the middle of his chest. "What do you want?"

He looked at the crowd surrounding them. "Some privacy," he muttered as the band wheezed to a stop. When a saxophone player approached, he barked, "Get back with the band, Tiffany."

Hallie waggled the squirt gun to regain his attention. "And we're standing here...why?"

He drew a ragged breath. "I can do this. I know I can."

"Spit it out, son," Hallie's dad advised from his viewing point at the foot of the float.

Steve seemed to shake off whatever was bothering him. "Hallie, last night, when you asked me how I felt about you, I wasn't being honest with myself or you. We need to talk."

"Okay," she said, then waited.

He frowned. "You mean right here?"

She didn't see why not. After all, most of her major life events had happened smack in the middle of Sandy Bend. It was a bit late for reticence on her part.

"It's not like I'm asking you to strip naked and do

the Hokey Pokey,'' she pointed out. Then it occurred to her that she and Steve had already done something darned close to the Hokey Pokey on this float. A giggle escaped.

He must have had the same thought because his answering smile was hot enough to turn the sand at their feet to pure crystal.

He pushed aside the barrel of the squirt gun. ''Hallie, I know I've screwed things up six ways from stupid, and you're only listening to me because you have no choice, but here it is. I love you. And don't bother telling me this is too sudden, because the truth is, I even felt something for you back when you were eighteen. Not love, exactly, but this bizarre curiosity.''

''Bizarre curiosity?'' Hallie repeated at the same time her entire family groaned. ''Steve, where are you going with this?''

''Straight through to the end,'' he said, sounding pretty grim. ''I thought the noble thing to do was to let you move to London. But you know what? I've discovered I'm really bad at being noble. In fact, when it comes to you, I'm downright selfish.''

He went down on one knee, then took her hand in his. ''Hallie, I love you and I'm asking you—no, begging you—to stay in Sandy Bend.''

She tried to speak, but nothing came out. Not that she had to worry with the collective *''Awwwww''* rising from the crowd.

Steve, however, was looking worried. ''I know Sandy Bend isn't exactly your idea of paradise, and the only thing I have to compete with art and culture and movie star bosses is me. My heart. My soul. My body. All of me.''

Hallie knew her answer. She had known it for most of her life. "I—"

"Wait, let me finish," Steve said with an urgency she would have found incredibly endearing if she didn't want to get to the really, really good stuff. "I know it's not exactly a fair deal, so I'll throw in summers in London for you to study with that instructor, if it helps sweeten the pot. Whatever it takes."

She knelt in front of him. "All it would take is this."

If ever, in the history of Sandy Bend, there had been a kiss more telling, more romantic and more enjoyed by a crowd of hundreds, not a single Sandy Bender present that sunny, perfect day could recall it.

Hallie Brewer was home. For good.

* * * * *

*Return to Sandy Bend with Dorien Kelly's
first Harlequin Temptation,*

THE GIRL MOST LIKELY TO...

*Dana Devine wants to be taken seriously...
especially by Sandy Bend's new
police chief, Cal Brewer.
But is he man enough to take on the
town's wild child?
On sale April 2003.*

The Harlequin Reader Service® — Here's how it works:

NO POSTAGE
NECESSARY
IF MAILED
IN THE
UNITED STATES

BUSINESS REPLY MAIL
FIRST-CLASS MAIL   PERMIT NO. 717-003   BUFFALO, NY

POSTAGE WILL BE PAID BY ADDRESSEE

HARLEQUIN READER SERVICE
3010 WALDEN AVE
PO BOX 1867
BUFFALO NY 14240-9952

Get FREE BOOKS and a FREE GIFT when you play the...

LAS VEGAS
GAME

Just scratch off the gold box with a coin. Then check below to see the gifts you get!

YES! I have scratched off the gold Box. Please send me my **2 FREE BOOKS** and **gift for which I qualify**. I understand that I am under no obligation to purchase any books as explained on the back of this card.

311 HDL DRQR   111 HDL DRQ7

FIRST NAME   LAST NAME

ADDRESS

APT.#   CITY

STATE/PROV.   ZIP/POSTAL CODE

(H-D-02/03)

7	7	7	Worth TWO FREE BOOKS plus a BONUS Mystery Gift!
🍒	🍒	🍒	Worth TWO FREE BOOKS!
🔔	🔔	♣	TRY AGAIN!

Visit us online at www.eHarlequin.com

Offer limited to one per household and not valid to current Harlequin Duets™ subscribers. All orders subject to approval.

The Deputy Gets Her Man
Delores Fossen

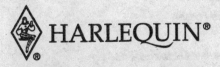

HARLEQUIN®

TORONTO • NEW YORK • LONDON
AMSTERDAM • PARIS • SYDNEY • HAMBURG
STOCKHOLM • ATHENS • TOKYO • MILAN • MADRID
PRAGUE • WARSAW • BUDAPEST • AUCKLAND

Dear Reader,

I met my husband during a simulated war. Yep, you read that right. We were both air force lieutenants stationed in England and met while wearing full chemical suits, including gas masks that made us look like big ugly bugs. We talked for three hours during that staged attack, and by the time peace was declared, he'd asked me out. So what does this have to do with Rios and Rayanne in *The Deputy Gets Her Man*? Meeting my husband in such an oddball way made me see the comedic potential in romance. I love the idea of two people coming together under crazy circumstances and somehow finding their way.

Rios and Rayanne, however, take a little longer than three hours to find their way. It's more like eleven years! And there's nothing simulated or especially peaceful about their approach to romance. When this laid-back cowboy sheriff and his deputy fall, they fall hard, and they have some good laughs while fighting an attraction that can only complicate an already complicated situation.

I'd love to hear what you think of Rios, Rayanne and the other residents of Longhorn, Texas. You can e-mail this Texan at fossent@earthlink.net.

Hope you enjoy,

Delores Fossen

Books by Delores Fossen

HARLEQUIN INTRIGUE
648—HIS CHILD
679—A MAN WORTH REMEMBERING

To my editor, Kathryn Lye.
Thanks so much for everything.

Prologue

"When in doubt, mumble."
—Bumper Ditties by Evie E. Garrett

RAYANNE WATCHED while her almost-lover tried to curse and zip his jeans at the same time. Apparently, the simple tasks were too hard for Rios McKay.

"Why?" Rios demanded. He barely got out that one word before swearing viciously as his zipper nicked his thumb.

Other than wishing his zipper had nicked some other protruding part of his body, Rayanne didn't think there was a lot she could do. She'd just had carnal fulfillment snatched away and had been embarrassed beyond belief. Yet Rios obviously thought *he* was the one who should be upset.

She was clearly missing something here.

"Why?" she mimicked, hoping he would clarify why at the last possible moment he had catapulted himself away from her as if she'd scalded him.

He looked at her as if her ears were on backward. "Why what? Why what! I can't believe you have to ask me that. Why didn't you tell me you've never been with a man?"

"I did." Trying to restore some shred of dignity,

Rayanne got up from the saddle blanket and began to straighten her clothes. No easy feat considering her knit top and skirt were both around her waist. She had no idea where her brand-new midnight-blue lace panties were. The last time she saw them, Rios was twirling them around his finger.

"Yeah, you told me about a second before I almost found out the hard way. Good grief, Rayanne, you should have said something before I got you down on that ground. That's not something you keep from a man."

"I didn't tell you because we've been kissing for the last half hour. Hard to talk with your tongue in my mouth." Giving up on the panties, she wiggled the skinny skirt to its original place and did what she could to cover herself with the stretched-out top. "Besides, why would my, uh, lack of experience make a difference to you? You've been with more women than you can count."

He hitched a thumb against his chest. "I wouldn't have touched you if I'd known." His gaze skated around the woods, looking at everything but her. "I don't mess around with innocent little girls."

Ouch, that stung. Rayanne scowled at him and turned her bra around so her breasts fit in the cups. Not that it made that much of a difference. "I'm not a little girl. I'm eighteen, and I wanted you to be my first."

There. She'd said it. And unfortunately, it was the truth. At least, it was the truth ten minutes ago. She'd longed after Rios for years. He was the bad boy of Longhorn, Texas. And the main character in dreams so steamy they made her blush. Now Rayanne was abundantly sure she wanted to pluck out every strand of his body hair with a pair of bent tweezers.

"Your first?" he repeated. He kicked at some dandelion fluff. Little white umbrellas scattered like snow around them. "Not this man. Not me. I don't want to be anybody's flipping *first,* got that?"

"Yeah, I got that."

Rayanne wanted to deliver a memorable exit line, one that he would remember for the rest of his life. A line like the ones her aunt Evie came up with for her bumper stickers. However, there were a couple of problems. She was so embarrassed she couldn't think of an exit line, and she had no way to exit since Rios was the one who had driven them to Whiskey Creek. Exiting now would mean a ten-mile jaunt on a country road at night.

Still, she considered it.

The distant sound of a howling coyote had her considering it just slightly less.

Mustering what pride she could muster, Rayanne hiked up her chin and looked Rios McKay right in the eye. "Home," she finally managed.

Home? She wanted to bop herself upside the head. She had just experienced the single most embarrassing event of her entire life, and all she could come up with was *home?* Rayanne tried but couldn't think of anything better. Besides, she really did want to get home.

She reasoned the only silver lining to this dreary cloud was that her aunt wouldn't know what a fool she'd made of herself. Rayanne soon learned she was wrong about that. The minute she walked inside the house and greeted Evie with a thin smile, her midnight-blue lace panties untangled themselves from her hair clip and dropped to the living room floor.

Evie arched her daffodil-colored eyebrows. "Something you want to tell me, huh, Rayanne?"

Because Rayanne knew she had to come up with an explanation for the errant panties, she took some advice from one of her aunt's bumper stickers.

She mumbled.

1

"Wherever you came from, you're not there now."

—Bumper Ditties by Evie E. Garrett

New York City
Eleven years later

"YOU HAD NO CHOICE but to apprehend that chicken, Detective Garrett. It was definitely in the line of duty, and that's what I'll tell anyone who asks." The uniformed rookie tried to keep his deadpan expression but was failing miserably. Rayanne could see the corners of his mouth twitching.

"Well, yes," she agreed, hoping that was all he had to say on the subject.

It wasn't.

"I mean, it just kept flying up in your face while you were trying to..." And his serious expression went completely south. "Negotiate with it." He started to snicker as they made their way into the patrol room.

As his superior Rayanne supposed she should correct him, but she couldn't bring herself to do it. She, Detective Rayanne Garrett of the NYPD, had apprehended a chicken during a hostage standoff. Yes, it would be a hard thing to live down. And it had really put a damper on the day, which continued to be damper-riddled. Damper-riddled because Dr. Malcolm Keene, the precinct shrink and her often annoying friend, was waiting for her.

"Are you all right?" Malcolm asked. "Someone said there was a hostage standoff with a radical group."

Rayanne didn't like his edgy tone. The man always seemed to be on the brink of a nervous breakdown. Not a terribly good advertisement for a mental health expert.

"Yes, there was," she said. "But the standoff ended without major incident."

"Well, nothing major except for the chicken." The rookie again. "There was chicken ca-ca all over the back seat of the cruiser."

Rayanne thought he'd already left, and with one hard look, she let him know that's exactly what she expected him to do. He snapped his shoulders straight and walked away.

"A chicken," Malcolm repeated.

"Yes." She considered not adding anything to that sparse response, but then she figured it might sound better coming from her. "Members of an animal rights group locked themselves, some barnyard animals and a deli owner in the back of a semi. When I tried to get them to release the hostage, they let the animals escape. There was this chicken. It kept squawking at me, and it flew in my face. It was in my line of sight of the hostage so I caught the darn thing and put it in the squad car."

"A chicken," he repeated.

"A Rhode Island Red, I think."

"So that's why they're acting like children."

Rayanne was about to ask what he meant by that when the desk clerk handed her three message slips—all telling her that Rios McKay had called.

Definitely more dampers. Big ones. "You're sure about this name?" Rayanne asked.

"Positive." The clerk bobbed her head and cracked a wad of gum. "I even had him spell it."

"Did he say why he was calling?"

"Sure didn't. Said he'd stop by when he got a chance."

"Stop by? Here?"

The woman gave her a blank stare. "That'd be my guess."

Great. That meant Rios was probably in the city on vacation. Why had he picked New York of all places, and why had he felt the urge to drop by to see her? It wasn't as if they'd stayed in touch after the infamous debacle at Whiskey Creek so many years ago. Truth was, she'd just plain avoided him.

Rayanne crumpled the pieces of paper and tossed them into the trash. "If he phones again, tell him I don't want him stopping by and I'll return his call the first chance I get."

Yes, when the equator froze over. That would surely be soon enough. She definitely didn't need a visit from Rios, not after the feathered hostage incident. She needed some time to compose herself and make sure she didn't have any lingering aroma of poultry and poultry by-products on her clothes.

"Will do," the woman assured her after she gave her gum a few more annoying cracks. "Say, I heard about the chicken."

"Already?" Rayanne checked her watch. "It just happened an hour ago."

"News travels fast around here. Makes you wonder why we bother with faxes and stuff."

Rayanne glanced around the squad room. And agreed. News did travel fast, and apparently so did people doing really stupid things. Malcolm's comment suddenly became crystal clear. *So that's why they're acting like children.*

Yes, that about summed it up.

Someone had taped a picture of a strutting chicken cartoon to the outside panel of her cubicle. A ribbon of ratty Christmas tinsel framed it, and underneath were the words Dangerous Fugitive Apprehended at Last.

"See?" Malcolm said, pointing at the picture. "This is exactly what I was talking about the other day. They're making fun of you. This is sexual harassment."

Rayanne rolled her eyes. "It's not sexual harassment." She tore the picture from the padded wall, squashed it into a ball and sent it flying into a nearby trash can. "Poultry harassment, maybe. They're not doing this because I'm a woman. They do this to everybody."

He made a sound to indicate he didn't agree. "You can't tolerate this kind of behavior. It's juvenile—"

Rayanne cut off what he was about to say with a gesture of her hand and looked at the clutter of desks in the squad room. The place buzzed with activity that seemed both routine and chaotic at the same time. Phones rang, people talked, and the smell of bad coffee and stale pastry hovered like smog.

Here, air quality was a contradiction in terms.

She quickly scanned the dozen or so people to locate Detective Steve Beech. The man was a master at pranks, and she could see his handiwork in this one. Besides, he was one of the few people who knew how to use the new copier.

"Beech?" she called, knowing she had to make an obligatory insult to the perpetrator of such a joke. If their situations had been reversed, Beech would have done the same to preserve the camaraderie of the office, and Rayanne would have plastered something equally amusing around the perimeter of his desk. In the grand scheme of things, sulking about it or whining would have been juvenile. A good insult, however, would keep the goodwill flowing.

"What?" Beech answered. He did his part. He at least tried to cover up his grin and look concerned about whatever she was about to dish out.

In turn, Rayanne tried to put some grit in her voice. "Put another picture like this on my wall, and I'll make you a soprano the hard way."

That brought on the expected round of laughter. "Sure. Whatever you say, Rayanne."

"And you think that'll do it?" Malcolm crisply inquired.

She fished through her pocket, located the last of her fruity-flavored antacid tablets and stuck it in her mouth.

"Eventually. They'll get tired of it, trust me. I know you're trying to help, but I don't need a shrink, okay?"

Malcolm nodded, after a long moment where he just stared at her. "All right, we'll try it your way a little longer. Sheez."

Rayanne turned in the direction of his somewhat stupefied gaze and became a little stupefied herself. There wasn't an inch of wall paneling not covered with photocopies of cartoon chickens. Some of them even had little badges doodled onto their feathered chests.

"I'm getting the lieutenant in here right now," Malcolm informed her.

She sighed and caught his arm. "I don't want the lieutenant. Please, Malcolm, just go. I have reports to file. Calls to make. Chicken pictures to remove."

He hesitated, his jaw muscles working. "We'll talk about this tonight at dinner." He did an about-face to plow through the squad room.

"Dinner," Rayanne said under her breath.

Mercy, she'd forgotten all about that. She had agreed to meet with Malcolm to discuss an incident regarding one of the rookies. Rayanne had wanted to have the meeting in Malcolm's office, but he'd somehow managed to talk her into hashing through the details over dinner. She made a mental note—don't do that again. No sense encouraging a relationship with Malcolm that she didn't want encouraged. The man just wasn't her type.

In fact, Rayanne was still sorting out what constituted her type. Her notions were somewhat nebulous in that area, but she definitely didn't want a man like Malcolm who always seemed to be in the middle of a sedative-required moment. Nope. She was looking more for a calming influence in her life. Too bad she hadn't run across even a remote candidate in, oh, at least seven or eight years. If this went on much longer, she might have to lower her standards.

"Say, Rayanne?" Detective Beech called. "Did that guy ever get in touch with you?"

Bracing herself for another joke, Rayanne shrugged. "What guy?"

"He didn't give his name. Tall. Cowboy boots. Said he's been calling but hadn't been able to reach you. He was around here just a minute ago."

"Cowboy boots," Rayanne repeated. She didn't like that little shiver that went down her spine. No, she didn't like it one bit. It was her cop's shiver, the one that had saved her derriere and other body parts on numerous occasions. She cautiously looked in the direction of her desk. The shiver turned into a full quake when she saw the man.

"Rios McKay," she mumbled under her breath.

He sat no more than a few feet away from her. In her chair, no less. Well, perhaps he wasn't actually sitting. He lounged with one long jeans-clad leg stretched out in front of him. His other foot, black snakeskin boot included, was pressed flat against the center drawer on her desk. He looked as if he had spent half his life in that chair. In this office. With his foot on her desk.

The man had the audacity to smile at her.

Rayanne's stomach did a somersault. There was just something about Rios McKay and that cocky smile that made her stomach go into a tailspin. Of course, he did that to most women, she begrudgingly conceded. He oozed sensuality, and to top it all off, he was a cowboy, complete with jeans that were snug in all the right places and a natural ruggedness that only hours in the Texas sun could give.

He was hot stuff.

And he knew it.

Eleven years hadn't changed him much. That dark black hair was still a little too long. It wasn't effeminate, however. Nothing about Rios was effeminate. He could have been a poster model for elevated testosterone levels.

There were tiny lines touching the corners of his eyes. They didn't look like wrinkles, even though he was thirty-three. Character lines, people called them. As if Rios needed any more character on that face.

"What are you doing here?" Rayanne asked when she remembered she had the capacity to speak. She only hoped he didn't notice her voice was a little too breathy. It was definitely not her cop's voice.

"I came to see you."

She would not blush. Would not. Would not. Would not! She was beyond that. She wasn't eighteen now, but a mature woman. She wouldn't give him the satisfaction of thinking he'd embarrassed her all those years ago.

"Well, what can I do for you?" Rayanne gave herself a mental pat on the back when she managed to keep her expression blasé and her tone casual. She didn't feel even a splash of blush creep onto her cheeks.

The corner of his mouth kicked into a wider smile,

causing his dimples to wink at her. "Same old Rayanne. You still do that little thing with your breath."

The mental patting stopped. "What little thing?"

"It's like a little hiccup." Rios imitated it, following it with a husky chuckle. "I'll let you in on a secret. I've always thought it was sexy."

Her blasé expression slipped a notch. She kept her mouth closed so she wouldn't make that sound again. No sense giving him a cheap thrill.

His attention turned to the pictures of the chickens. "A new decorator?"

"No," Rayanne said crisply. "An inside joke." One she had no intention of sharing with him.

"So you like working here?" he asked.

"Yes, as a matter of fact, I do. But, of course, I'm extremely busy, which is why I'm afraid I can't spare you any time." Much, much better. Just like a deodorant commercial. Calm, cool, collected.

Catlike, he came to his feet and stepped toward her. The calm, cool and collected went right out the window. Rayanne forced herself not to take a step back, but it was a battle. She firmly reminded herself she was a cop. A tough hostage negotiator. So why did Rios make her feel like a high school girl with toilet paper in her bra?

It had been years since she had stuffed her bra.

"Please tell me why you've come." There was a smidgen of insistence in her voice. She had no doubt that smidgen would increase significantly if he didn't answer her. It was hard to hold back a blush for very long, especially since the images of that night kept creeping into her mind.

"Your aunt sent me."

Rayanne stiffened. "Is something wrong with Aunt Evie?"

"I guess you could say that. She's in the Longhorn jail."

"In jail?" That wasn't her cop's voice, either. It was something like a squawk. "On what charge?"

"Attempted assault with a deadly weapon."

Rayanne let the wall support her weight. A good thing, too. Between the news, her indigestion and Rios's presence, she thought maybe her legs had turned to banana pudding. "Is this some kind of sick joke?"

"No joke. She took aim at Bennie Quinn."

"Mr. Quinn?" The wealthiest, most powerful man in the county? "Mercy, he wasn't hurt, was he?"

Rios fumbled through a candy dish of M&M's and located a half dozen green ones. Cupping his hand, he funneled them into his mouth. "He's fine. Evie didn't even get a shot off. But Bennie still didn't care much for it. I warn you, Rayanne, he'll try to make sure the charges stick. You know how ornery he can be."

Rayanne pushed her hand over her hair. This had been one long day already, and it didn't seem as if it would end any time soon. "So, the first thing I need to do is post bail for her."

"Nope, she doesn't want bail. Believe me, a dozen people have already tried to do that, including me. Evie says she's not leaving the jail until you come for her."

"Why?"

"Heaven only knows. Remember we're talking about Evie Garrett here. The woman doesn't always operate on logic."

Rayanne didn't reprimand him for the insult. It was true. A logical thought would be very lonely in that woman's head. "Aunt Evie wants me to fly to Longhorn just so I can get her out of jail? She's up to something."

"That was my guess, too."

Her gaze met his. His eyes were the color of iced tea, or so all the girls in Longhorn always said. Rayanne didn't think there was anything icy about them. Slow burn was closer to the truth.

"Any idea why Aunt Evie really wants me to come home?" Rayanne asked, getting her mind on the business at hand. And that business didn't include eye color analysis.

"Nope. I gave up asking when she pulled her I'm-having-a-senior-moment routine. You know, sometimes I find it a little annoying when she does that."

Rayanne agreed, silently. And she knew exactly what Rios meant. Her aunt could stonewall a bulldozer just by pretending to be a sweet little old forgetful lady.

"So, why did Evie send you to tell me all of this?" And while she was at it, Rayanne wanted to ask him what he was doing in Longhorn. The last she'd heard, he was riding the rodeo circuit on the west coast. However, she wouldn't ask him anything about that. It might make him think she was interested in what he had to say. She wasn't.

She really wasn't.

He shrugged. It was lazy, like the rest of his movements. "Evie asked me to come. I came. I'd like to think of it as my good deed for the day." His cocky smile returned. "So, are you coming to Longhorn or what?"

Rayanne shook her head. "No, I'll just call her, and—"

"She won't take your call," Rios interrupted.

"She what? Why?"

He fished through his jeans pocket, pulled out a sheet of paper, unfolded it and began to read. "Don't bother calling me, Rayanne. The only way I intend to speak to you is face-to-face. If you can't get away from your busy job, I'll understand. My lawyer, Clyde Mueller, will do his best to see that justice is served. If he's not successful, then maybe you can visit me at Christmas. Right here. In the Longhorn jail. Love, Aunt Evie."

"Great," Rayanne said at the end of a groan. "She's really up to something." She glanced at Rios again. "How long has she been in jail?"

"Two weeks."

"Two weeks!" Rayanne cursed. It was practically whispered, but as close as Rios was standing, he no doubt heard it. "And no one bothered to get in touch with me before now? I should have been notified immediately. This is my aunt we're talking about."

"You know, Rayanne, you really oughta do something about that cursing. It's not very flattering."

"Really?" Well, now. She hadn't wanted to be petty, but that remark seemed to be a pettiness magnet. "I seem to remember you have a mouth like a sewer."

"Nope. Not anymore. I'm a changed man. Cursing's just not a very creative way to express oneself. Take that often misused word that starts with F, for instance. Somebody says that, and they mean it as an insult. But since when is that an insult? It's something people enjoy—''

"Rios." And she couldn't get out anything else until she put a chokehold on her quickly waning composure. "I don't want to talk about your theories of modern communication."

He shrugged. Rayanne wondered how he managed to express so much with a gesture that didn't even require energy. "So, are you coming to Longhorn?" he repeated.

"Well, of course, I will." Especially since it seemed Evie hadn't given her a choice. "I'll have to make some arrangements, but I think I can get there by tomorrow night."

He slipped the cream-colored Stetson on his head and flashed that knee-withering smile again. "Then I guess I'll see you around."

Only if she was incredibly unlucky. Luck had certainly been with her in the past. In the last eleven years on her dozen or so trips to Longhorn, she hadn't set eyes on Rios. Good thing, too. Seeing him only caused her to relive that night she'd been trying to forget.

He stepped into the squad room. "Know what? Not one of these guys look like the characters on TV."

"No? Well, welcome to reality. We're all just a hard-working bunch of cops."

His gaze came to Rayanne again. "Well, at least you lived up to my expectations. You look great."

It wasn't what she'd expected him to say. And it wasn't something she especially wanted to hear since he added a little surveillance to his observation. He looked her over from her head to her sensible walking shoes, but he paid particular attention to the parts in the middle, including but not limited to her breasts.

Rayanne refused to fold her arms in front of her, but she did consider it. Her chest slowly began to tighten, and she could feel the constricted muscles force her breasts against the flimsy lace of her bra. Rayanne didn't have to look down to know that her nipples were prominently displayed against her top. Rios might as well have touched her with his hand instead of his hot, thorough gaze. Fondling by proxy. It was still just as potent.

Rios touched his fingers to the brim of his hat. "Well, I guess I'd better be heading out now." But he didn't head out. He stood there and smiled at her again. "Rayanne?"

"What?" she murmured, her voice small and wishy-washy. Her whole body suddenly felt like a school cafeteria noodle. Why, why, why did he have this effect on her?

"I should have finished what I started that night by Whiskey Creek."

Oh, no. Not that. Anything but that. She hadn't thought in a million years that he'd bring up *the* embarrassing incident. Rayanne quickly ran through her options about how to answer that, and one by one she discarded each response.

"Uh," she finally said. "Okay."

Wait a blasted minute! *Okay.* That wasn't the best she could do. No way. This moment called for a regular belly-laugh zinger, like those she doled out to her fellow officers. There was a problem with that, however. Just like that night at the creek, she couldn't think of anything. Zip. Nada. Not one remotely insulting, score-settling line came to her.

"I've never given that night a moment's thought," she lied, knowing she had to say something. It barely qualified as *something,* but it sure beat standing there with her mouth gaping open.

"Funny, I think about it all the time." With a flick of his wrist, he reached out and caught a copper curl that had slipped from her hair clip. Skimming the hair and his finger along her cheek, he tucked the tress behind her ear. "I should have done better by you, Rayanne. That means I owe you one. You can collect anytime you want."

She quickly stepped away from him. And swallowed hard. Then it hit her. She'd just been zinged. By Rios. Zinged and reminded of a reminder she didn't want to be reminded of. That got her mouth working again. "You are without a doubt the most arrogant—"

"Yeah, I am."

As fast as lightning and as deadly as rattler venom, he brushed his mouth over her temple. Rayanne managed to get out a protesting gasp before he strolled out of the station house. She was vaguely aware of the catcalls and laughter that rippled through the squad room. But Rayanne just stood there. She could only wonder about the color of the truck that had just smashed into her head-on, but she was certain about the license plate.

Rios McKay's name was definitely on it.

2

"Talk is cheap until you hire a shrink."
—Bumper Ditties by Evie E. Garrett

RIOS WATCHED from beneath the brim of his Stetson. He'd pulled the hat low over his face as if taking a nap, but he didn't think he would get much of a nap in a New York City airport. Too much noise. Too many people. Too many people for him, anyway. And the only person he really wanted to see wouldn't be too happy that he was there.

He spotted Rayanne the moment she walked into the area. She had a sleek black leather bag on one arm and a tall blond-haired man on the other one. Rios remembered Rayanne had called the man Malcolm, and he was a shrink. It was also likely that the guy was Rayanne's, well, boyfriend. It was a term that didn't settle well on his stomach.

Rayanne wore silk. He knew that's what it was by the way it swayed. Moss-green slacks and a top that fluttered and caressed her body every time she moved. It was a far cry from the cutoffs she'd worn as a kid. Yes, a far cry indeed. Rayanne Marie Garrett had grown into one classy woman.

A woman who thought he was one notch below deep-crevice navel lint.

Rios didn't think this trip to Longhorn would improve the situation much. No, not at all.

She had her hair loose, and it fell to her shoulders in a sleek tumble. No fussy curls, nothing overdone, just hair the color of a new penny. It, too, swayed like the silk. Moved with her. And caused heads to turn. But then, Rayanne had always been able to turn heads. Now that she'd filled out, there was just more of her to get those heads turning faster.

"I still don't see why you feel you have to do this," Malcolm said to her as she checked in at the ticket counter. Rios didn't like the sound of his voice. It had a whine to it. "Your aunt's trying to manipulate you."

"Probably," Rayanne answered almost idly. She took her ticket from the attendant and thanked her. She looked around the area, but not in Rios's direction. He slid a little lower in the seat. It wasn't a good idea for her to see him just yet. She might decide to change planes, and for a lot of reasons he didn't want her to do that.

"Then why are you letting her get away with it?"

The whiner again. So, lover boy was trying to talk her out of leaving. Rios didn't think the guy stood a chance. Evie had done her level best to talk Rayanne out of leaving Longhorn eleven years ago, and it hadn't worked. If Evie couldn't talk Rayanne out of doing something, this scrawny fellow didn't have a clue.

Rayanne and the man moved away from the ticket

kiosk but didn't take a seat. Instead, she stared out the window. Rios watched her. And listened.

"I'm going because Evie's the only blood relative I have," Rayanne explained. "She'd do the same for me."

"She wouldn't have to do this for you because you wouldn't pull such a juvenile stunt."

Rayanne's mouth went into a flat line. "Malcolm, I know you mean well, but I'm going to Longhorn. End of conversation."

Rios smiled. *Atta girl, Rayanne. Dish out some of that Garrett hardheadedness.* Malcolm shoved his hands in the pockets of his perfectly creased khakis and stared at her. "Does this have anything to do with that cowboy who visited you yesterday?"

That quickly got Rios's attention. Cowboy? He glanced at his jeans and well-worn boots. Yep, the guy probably meant him. Well, at least he hadn't called him Tex.

Rayanne's gaze whipped to her companion. "No, this has nothing to do with that cowboy." She spoke the last word as harshly as a profanity. "He's just some guy who used to work for my aunt, that's all."

Rios's left eyebrow twitched. He hadn't worked for Evie Garrett in eleven years. Rayanne knew it, too. It sure stung to be dismissed like that, but he'd expected to have to endure a few slings and arrows. After all, he hadn't bought Rayanne's line about not ever thinking about what had happened between them that night at the creek. No, she'd probably spent a long while trying to figure out why he had embarrassed her. Heck, it had taken Rios a while to figure it out himself. Maybe one day he would get the chance to explain it to her.

A slow smile curved Malcolm's mouth. Keeping his gaze on Rayanne, he looped his arm around her waist and hugged her. She ended the embrace soon enough, but it didn't matter. Rios had always known he had a jealous bone when it came to Rayanne, and that did a good job of enlarging it. When he'd seen enough of that little display of affection, he cleared his throat.

As if a current of electricity had passed through her body, her gaze lasered across the room. And lit directly on him. Rios put his thumb to the brim of his Stetson and pushed it back so she could see his face. Not that she needed to. Rayanne obviously knew he was there.

Clutching her bag, she stormed toward him, the green silk streaming around her. "What are you doing here, Rios?"

He slowly got to his feet and tipped his head in greeting, first to Rayanne and then to Malcolm. "That's exactly what you asked me yesterday."

"I don't think I'll like the answer any more today than I did then."

"Probably not. It appears we're booked on the same flight."

Her jaw turned to iron, and her Christmas-tree green eyes narrowed to little bitty slits.

Rios glanced at Malcolm. His jaw and eyes were pretty much the same.

"I don't believe we've met," the man said stiffly to Rios. "I'm Dr. Malcolm Keene."

"Rios McKay."

He offered his hand, and Rios shook it. And just like the hug the guy had given Rayanne, the handshake lingered a little too long for Rios's liking. It was clearly a contest. One he'd win. Even if he broke every bone in his hand. Malcolm's eyes widened with surprise.

"Oh, for heaven's sake," Rayanne complained, apparently noticing what was going on. "Stop this now. I mean it."

She quickly dropped the bag by her feet and latched on to both their hands to pry them apart. Malcolm didn't let go, and neither did Rios. Rayanne pulled harder. Rios lapped his left hand over hers, effectively sandwiching it. Malcolm did the same to her other one.

"Stop this now," Rayanne warned. From the sound of her voice, Rios knew she meant business. She might have on silk and smell like Chanel number whatever, but she could be tough as nails. Still, he didn't move his hands first. He waited until Dr. Whine lowered his.

"I'm sorry about that," Malcolm said to her. He caught her arm but kept his stern gaze on Rios. "Rayanne, I won't let you get on the same plane with this cowboy."

"I don't believe I asked you." Rayanne fired the words back.

She reached out and yanked open Rios's jacket. He held up his hands to let her do whatever she wished. Actually, he liked the bewildered expression on the doc's face. And he also liked Rayanne's wild, out-of-control search-and-seizure methods. It was so much better than that ice-princess act she'd put on the day before. Without consideration to buttons, fabric or even his chest hair, she fished through his shirt pocket until she came up with his ticket, which he had tucked inside. She scanned the information on the boarding pass and lifted her annoyed gaze to his.

Rios shrugged.

"You're in the seat next to me," she said. "But, of course, you knew that."

She didn't give Malcolm or Rios a chance to say anything, she marched to the ticket kiosk and began talking to the clerk. To change her seat, Rios figured. The woman could be predictable when she was riled.

"I want you to leave her alone, Tex," Malcolm said, placing a finger in front of Rios's face.

Rios calmly pushed the man's hand away. "The name's McKay," he enunciated.

"Whatever. Rayanne has been under a lot of stress lately, and I don't want you to add to it."

"It seems the source of her stress is right here. Going home might be good for her." Or not. Rios decided to keep that to himself. It was best not to bring up the negative side when trying to make a point.

"Going home could be a disaster. Rayanne might think the world of her aunt, but anyone can see the woman's manipulating her. God knows what she'll put Rayanne through."

"And this is leading where exactly? It seems Evie Garrett is Rayanne's business, not yours."

"I've made it my business. Because I care about Rayanne."

"Oh, you do, do you?" Rios leaned closer and lowered his voice to a secretive, patronizing level. "Well,

I wouldn't get my hopes up if I were you. You don't appear to be her type. Personally, I'll bet she doesn't give a flying fig about you.'' And it didn't matter that it was a petty thing to say or that it might be a flaming lie, Rios just had to get a jealousy-induced jab in there.

Malcolm had already opened his mouth to say something when Rayanne rejoined them. She picked up her bag, her movements jerky and stiff. ''Goodbye, Malcolm. I'll see you in a couple of days. Oh, and thanks for bringing me to the airport.''

She didn't say anything to Rios. Not that he'd really expected it. But, boy, old Malcolm did.

He aimed a finger in Rios's direction. ''You know what he said? He said you didn't care a flying fig about me.''

Great day in the blooming morning. Rios hadn't counted on Mr. Whine being a tattletale, as well. He sure didn't need a crystal ball to know how Rayanne would react to that. She aimed her narrowed eyes in his direction.

''Why would you tell him something like that?'' she demanded. ''You have absolutely no idea how I feel about him.''

There was an old Texas saying—if you really wanted to get out of a big hole, the first thing you had to do was stop digging. It was real good advice, and usually Rios heeded good advice. Not today, though. There was just something about that wussy look in the doc's eyes and the challenging expression on Rayanne's face that made him want to keep on digging.

''If you cared about him,'' Rios said to her, ''then

that little hug earlier wouldn't have stayed so little. You got away pretty darn fast, if you ask me.'' He added a wink, knowing it would enlarge that hole to the size of the Grand Canyon.

It did.

Rayanne grabbed onto a handful of Malcolm's shirt, licked her lips and pressed them right onto the man's mouth. The kiss was long, slow and slightly brutal. She broke away only when the person on the intercom announced it was time to proceed to the gate.

''Bye, Rayanne,'' Malcolm said somewhat breathlessly. He also had a goofy smile on his face. ''Hurry home.''

''I will.''

Rios got behind her in the line. ''So, I guess you showed me. That's really your boyfriend, huh?''

She didn't even look back. ''If you must know, no. But that is none of your business.''

Too bad it felt like his business. It was also too bad that her boyfriendless status pleased him immensely. ''It's just as well. He seems a little prissy if you ask me.'' Rios stepped forward when she did. The line of people steadily began to move down the corridor through security.

''I didn't ask you.''

He smiled at the sound of her voice. Her normal voice. It reminded him of a rusty gate. Not entirely pleasing, but it brushed against something deep within him. He assured himself it was only because he had gone so long without a woman. A little bit of lust could make even a rusty gate sound arousing.

Yes, indeed. That was all there was to it.

He liked flirting with Rayanne. Loved to tease her. And he cared about her in ways that bothered him at least a dozen times a day. But there was no way he could involve himself with her personally. Not now. There was too much at stake. The woman was definitely hands-off. She could muddy the waters big time.

They boarded, and Rayanne took a seat in first class. His, he knew, was in coach. Way back in coach. So, she'd spent some extra bucks to put some distance between them. She obviously didn't want anything to do with him. Well, he had news for her. If she didn't like being on the same plane with him, she sure wouldn't like what was going to happen when they got to Longhorn.

No, indeed.

RAYANNE LOOKED AT RIOS as if he'd lost his mind—a real possibility considering the source—and she was unerringly certain that she'd misunderstood him. "What did you just say?"

"I said I'm supposed to drive you to Longhorn."

She glanced around the San Antonio airport. It was late, and she was tired. She definitely didn't need offers of rides from ex-boyfriends. She wanted this uncomfortable trip down memory lane to end right here on the swirly patterned carpet in front of gate twelve.

"But I asked Freda to come and get me," Rayanne said. Freda, her aunt's longtime housekeeper and Rayanne's pseudo nanny. Freda had worked for Evie for twenty-five years, and whenever Rayanne made a trip to Longhorn, Freda had been the one who picked her up at the airport. She didn't see any reason for things to change now. Especially when that change involved Rios.

"Evie asked me to do it instead."

Rayanne definitely smelled a rat. A big one. "Why would she ask you to do that?"

"Because Evie didn't want Freda to have to drive at night, especially since we were on the same flight." He motioned toward the exit. "My truck's in the parking lot."

"Great. Just great."

Rayanne stood there for several moments, bag and purse in hand, and rummaged through her options. She could take a taxi, but she had already dropped an extra two hundred and sixty-eight dollars to fly first class so she could avoid sitting near Rios. She was doing okay financially, but that put a dent in her budget, especially since she'd done it to nourish a hissy fit. A rental car was her next choice. Actually, it was her only choice, she decided when she glanced at Rios. That hissy fit feeding apparently wasn't over yet.

"Seems kinda stupid, doesn't it?" he asked.

"What does?"

"You renting a car when it won't cost you a dime to ride with me. NYPD probably pays pretty good, but I doubt if you have money to burn, especially considering that outfit must have cost you a bundle."

It had cost her a bundle. That was also none of his business. Rayanne gave him her cop's stare. All ice. She knew for a fact it was a good one because she'd practiced it enough in the mirror. It didn't, however, seem to have an effect on Rios. Well, no effect except that he grinned at her.

"I'll understand if you decide not to ride with me," he continued. "After all, I know you don't care much for my company."

She laughed, a single harsh burst of air. "Now, that's the understatement to understate all statements."

Rios calmly set down his bag. "Okay, then let's quit understating and stepping around what we've already stepped in. Let's have a real air clearing. Right here, right now. If we don't, you'll end up spending a small fortune and a lot of time just to keep your distance from me."

Rayanne reminded herself not to be petty. Then she looked at Rios. To heck with it. She felt a real bout of pettiness coming on. "There's nothing you can say that I want to hear."

"How about I'm sorry? I *am* sorry, you know. But have you ever considered how you would have felt if I had made love to you that night at Whiskey Creek? How would you have felt if I'd taken your virginity?"

Rayanne glanced at the people who trickled past them. She could tell from their expressions that a few heard what Rios said. She felt herself blush. She wasn't a prude, but she didn't like her past indiscretions, especially embarrassing ones, blurted out for all to hear.

"Like I said back at the station, I haven't thought of you or that night in years." Well, maybe it hadn't been years since she thought of Rios. But definitely weeks. All right. Days.

Rayanne was sure it had been at least a day.

"Well, I have thought about it," Rios said, "and you know what? You would have regretted it. You would have wanted to kick yourself from here to El Paso and back for letting me have you like that. You were looking for a commitment, Rayanne, and that's something I couldn't—"

"How can you presume to know what I thought?" She glanced around her again. They were starting to attract an audience. A rather tired-looking audience of late-night travelers, but still an audience. "This isn't the place to have this conversation."

"All right, if that's the way you want it."

"It is."

"Well?" he said after another long silence. "Do you want a ride, or are you going to let your pride get in the way of saving some money?"

"I want a ride." Rayanne didn't add anything to it. She couldn't. She had bruised her jaw muscles just to say that. She didn't really want a ride, but to refuse would seem, well, abnormally petty. Plain old petty was okay, but she didn't want to move into the abnormal range just yet.

"Then follow me," he said. "I'll have you home in no time."

"I don't want to go straight home. I want to go by the jail when we get to Longhorn."

Rios glanced at his watch. "It'll be well past midnight. Evie will already be asleep."

He was right. There was no reason to wake up her aunt in the middle of the night. However, she did want to see her first thing in the morning, and she wanted to talk to Sheriff Ryland. Rayanne especially wanted to know why the sheriff, who was a longtime friend of the Garrett family, hadn't already convinced Evie to post bond and go home.

They made their way through the parking lot to his truck. Except the vehicle wasn't just a truck. It was a lifestyle statement. Big. Blue. And budget-draining. Whatever Rios was doing these days, he was apparently successful.

"This truck is yours?" she asked.

He nodded and drove toward Highway 281, which led south to Longhorn. "Why'd you ask?"

"No reason." No reason she'd tell him, anyway. Rayanne wasn't about to point out that things in his life seemed to be good. Good in several areas, actually. He was still in good shape. No beer gut. No sagging bottom. No hair growing out of his nose or ears. He looked well-preserved from his high cheekbones all the way to his cowboy-cut jeans—which were too tight, she finally decided.

"When's the last time you were home?" Rios asked her.

She opened her mouth to answer, but he started playing with the ribbed grooves on the steering wheel. Well, just one groove, actually. And he was definitely playing with it. It distracted her for a moment. "Uh, I'm not sure."

But she was sure about that touching thing. She didn't like it. She didn't like the way he used the tip of his middle finger to trace the nipple-like projection. Slowly. Gently. Thoroughly. Over and over again.

"Too long, huh?" Rios asked.

Rayanne heard him. Somewhere in her brain it even registered, but she didn't have a clue what he meant. "Too long huh what?"

He looked at her, but he didn't stop the touching. His finger was barely grazing the small bulge and yet somehow giving it his complete attention. "Too long huh what?" he repeated. "What does that mean?"

"It means what do you mean?"

"It means I was looking for a simple answer to a simple question. All I wanted to know was how long it'd been since you were in Longhorn."

A simple question, yes, and it could have been a simple answer if she hadn't been so distracted. *Mouth, form words,* she ordered.

"New York," she mumbled.

"Huh? Now, what exactly does that mean?"

All right, not the best effort her mouth had ever put forth, but it was a start. She'd requested that it form words, and it had. *Try harder.* "It means Aunt Evie's been coming to New York so there was no reason for me to return home."

"So it's been a while since you were there?"

It sounded almost like a prompt a lawyer would give a confused witness. Rayanne decided it was best if she nodded. She probably was a little confused at the moment.

"Three years," she finally managed to say.

She took a deep breath and tried to steady her heartbeat. It was so stupid, really—her reacting to something so simple as Rios touching his steering wheel. After all, it was just a... Mercy. He stroked it! Not just the little bump, either, but he went after the groove beside it. He slipped his big finger right in there. And rubbed. How dare he rub his steering wheel that way? Rayanne's mouth dropped open. Her breasts tightened. She squirmed on the seat.

"You don't miss it?" he asked.

"What? Miss what?"

"Longhorn."

"Oh." Rayanne heard the desperation in her voice and hoped he hadn't.

He had. Rios looked at her, and he had concern written all over his face. "Are you all right? I mean you're not going to get carsick, are you?"

She wished. She'd rather throw up on him than have his finger drive her crazy. "No, I'm fine."

"You don't look fine. You look like you're going to throw up. Should I pull over on the side of the road?"

"I'm fine!" she snapped. Fortunately, the snapping seemed to realign her hormones, and she knew what she had to do to get this madness to stop. With Rios, the direct approach was always best. "I want you to quit touching your steering wheel like that. It bothers me."

He narrowed one eye as if in deep thought. He looked at her. Then he looked at the steering wheel. "You want me to quit touching my steering wheel," he flatly repeated. "What, people in New York don't touch their steering wheels when they drive?"

"They don't rub them and stroke them. They grip them. Real men grip steering wheels."

She thought he might laugh. She thought she might scream. Well, that was one for the record books. *Real men grip steering wheels.* She only hoped Rios would let it pass without making too much of a big deal about it.

No such luck.

"So, let me get this straight," he said in a tone of deep, mock contemplation. "If I want to be a real New York man, I have to grip the steering wheel. I can't touch it." He paused. "Am I allowed to touch the stick shift or would that qualify me as a genuine wimp?"

Rayanne forced herself to breathe normally. Control was the operative word here. She needed to regain control.

"Conversation," she said. "Normal. Try."

He paused again and looked at her funny. "Will. Do. I'm a little afraid to ask after the discussion we've had for the last few minutes, but what exactly constitutes normal conversing for you these days?"

The list was apparently very short. "Longhorn. Let's talk about Longhorn." It seemed safe, on the surface, anyway. As long as Rios didn't touch anything, she thought she might be okay.

"Sure. Longhorn. Let's see. I've already asked you how long it's been since you've been home. I don't really want to go through that again, so let's try this. Um, do you like living in New York better than you did Texas?" He grinned at her. "How's that for normal?"

"It'll do, and the answer is yes. New York suits me."

"You sure about that?"

Slightly bothered, Rayanne puckered her lips. No, she wasn't sure at all, but she didn't want Rios challenging her when they were finally getting around to having a normal conversation. One normal question, and he was already off track.

"I'm positive it suits me," she lied. "I've made a life for myself there. It's my place in the world, you might say. I would have had a hard time doing that around Longhorn where people still tend to think of me as Evie Garrett's orphaned niece." Or where Rios thought of her as some innocent little kid. "Why do you ask if I'm sure that New York suits me?"

"A couple of reasons. The smell of fruity-flavored antacids on your breath, and you've been acting a little high-strung. Plus your non boyfriend, Dr. Whine, said you were under a lot of stress."

"Malcolm said that?" Rayanne frowned. How dare Malcolm discuss her personal life with anyone, and especially with Rios? Great day, Malcolm was always trying to make something more of their relationship than it was. Of course, that idiotic kiss she'd given him at the airport wouldn't help matters. She would really have to take the time to set him straight, gently, when she returned.

"That riles you a little that Dr. Whine told me that, huh?"

"You're quickly slipping away from the boundaries of a normal conversation, Rios. Let me give it a try. Something normal, I mean." She paused and tried to think of a neutral subject. It wasn't easy. Just talking with Rios was somewhat abnormal. "Okay, I got it. When did you move back to Longhorn?"

"How did you know I'd moved away?"

"Aunt Evie must have mentioned it." Rayanne made it seem as if she didn't know. Actually, she recalled everything her aunt ever mentioned about Rios. For some unexplainable reason those kinds of facts just seemed to stick in her head, no matter how much she tried to unstick them. "She maybe also mentioned something about you being on the rodeo circuit."

"I was. I came back about a year ago."

"Why?"

"Personal reasons."

She hadn't expected a roadblock from Rios, but Rayanne recognized one when she heard it. Well, it didn't matter. She didn't care what personal reasons had brought him back to town. Nope, didn't care one crumb.

Besides, Evie would tell her what she wanted to know.

They rode in silence for a long time, and Rayanne watched the San Antonio city lights give way to the gently sloping countryside. Rios tuned the radio to a country station, and the slow, easy music lulled her into relaxing. Rayanne leaned her head against the seat and nearly fell asleep.

"So, it's really not serious between you and that shrink?" he asked.

Just as quickly her head came off the seat. Apparently, relaxation wasn't in the cards tonight. "I don't want to discuss him with you.'' But no way was it serious. Malcolm was a friend. Period.

"Discussing the shrink isn't in the realm of a normal conversation, either?'' Rios again. But like before, he waited until she'd almost relaxed before he asked it.

"No, it isn't.'' And it didn't hurt matters that Rios seemed a little jealous about Malcolm. Well, at least curious, anyway. Rayanne decided to let him hold on to that curiosity a little longer.

They passed the Longhorn city limits sign, and Rayanne inched closer to the window to get a better look.

"I guess that means you won't be telling me exactly who you're sleeping with these days?'' he asked.

Rayanne was about to glare at him, but she saw something that stopped her attempted glare in mid facial rearrangement. There was a big plastic cow hanging precariously from a cable strung across the main street. On its sagging udders, someone had advertised the dates of the town festival.

"Amazing,'' she mumbled. She shook her head and kept staring at it. "It really is a plastic cow, and it's hanging over Main Street.''

"It's foam rubber, actually. Hal's Hungry Heifer restaurant went out of business over in Floresville, and Evie bought it.''

"Aunt Evie bought Hal's Hungry Heifer restaurant?'' Rayanne asked in disbelief.

"No, she bought the rubber cow that used to be in the party room. You know, the one that kids climbed on all the time? It was there for going on twenty years.

Anyway, Evie decided it was practically a local icon and didn't want to see it thrown away.''

"But why is it hanging over Main Street like that?''

"It wouldn't fit in the barn, so Evie donated it to the town.''

Amazing. Absolutely amazing. "And the town actually accepted it?''

"The town didn't have much of a choice. You know how persuasive Evie can be when she puts her mind to it.''

Rayanne did. In fact, she was living proof of her aunt's persuasiveness. Only Evie could have gotten her to return to Longhorn, and only at Evie's request would she have accepted a ride with Rios. But getting the town to accept a rubber cow? That was quite an accomplishment—even for Evie.

Rayanne kept her attention on the cow as Rios drove beneath it. "That thing won't fall, will it?''

"Already has. A couple of times. Fortunately, it's rubber so it just bounces around until it stops, even though it did mess up Sara Jean Kellerman's new perm. She's thinking about suing.''

The ringing interrupted her from thinking another *amazing*. She automatically reached for the phone that was usually clipped to her belt only to remember it wasn't there. She'd put her phone and pager in her bag.

"I think this one's for me,'' Rios said, answering the phone sandwiched into the console.

Rayanne leaned her head against the window and listened to the sound of his voice. Not exactly comforting, but still so familiar even after all these years.

It was hard to believe she was riding in the same vehicle with Rios. Actually, it was hard to believe she was within twenty miles of him. After that night at Whiskey Creek, she'd sworn she wouldn't give him the time of day. Yet here she was, in his truck, letting the sound of his voice lull her into…not relaxing, exactly.

No, not that at all.

It had lulled her into remembering things that were best forgotten. The lover's things he'd whispered to her that night. The eager caresses, much like the ones he'd given his steering wheel. The kisses. Yes, those hot, wet, brain-numbing kisses. But then he'd blown it, of course, by leaving her high and dry. Despite his apology, she didn't intend to let herself get in that position again. No, sirree. No heated romps on the banks of a creek. Those romping days were over.

"Think we need Doc Keller?" she heard Rios ask. He paused. "Okay, I'll be there in about twenty minutes."

"Trouble?" she asked when he ended the call.

"Just a problem with one of my mares."

"A mare? Are you ranching these days?"

"Some. It's hard not to ranch around Longhorn. Cattle and horses are the lifeblood here."

"You have your own place?"

He nodded and stopped the truck in front of her aunt's house. It looked beautiful in the moonlight. Actually, the moonlight did it a lot of justice. Rayanne knew it was just a two-story house that always needed a coat of paint, the roof fixed or something. Yet she didn't seem to notice those needed repairs when she looked at it. What she saw was home, and as it always did, it made her eyes a little misty.

"Want me to help you with your bag?" Rios asked.

"No, thanks. I can manage."

The front door opened, and Freda came out onto the porch. Cinching her faded chenille robe around her stout waist, she hurriedly made her way across the yard toward the truck.

"Rayanne, honey, it's so good to see you." The woman pulled her into a hard hug and slapped her back. "Always my little ray of sunshine in the middle of a cold spell. Welcome home, honey. Welcome home."

"It's good to see you too, Freda." Rayanne smiled. She always liked the oddball metaphors that Freda came up with. Actually, she liked everything about Freda. Hugging her was like hugging a chocolate-scented teddy bear. "You haven't changed a bit in three years."

"Oh, pshaw, of course I have. I got older, fatter and prettier, in that order. Ain't that right, Rios?"

Still inside the cab of the truck, Rios shook his head. "Nope, only the pretty part's right."

"Oh, pshaw, but so sweet of you to say. Just like hot fudge sauce on homemade ice cream. You've got a real sweet spot in you, Rios."

Rayanne couldn't imagine where he'd been hiding that sweet spot. Even more, she didn't intend to go looking for it. She waved, hoping it would send him on his merry way. "Thanks for the ride. Good night, Rios."

"Same to you, little ray of sunshine in the middle of

a cold spell. Get a good night's sleep. I'll see you around.''

Yes, but not for long. With luck she'd have all of this mess cleared up tomorrow and be on a plane to New York. Without luck, she'd even do it. Putting some distance between her and Rios was a strong motivator to spur her into action.

"Come on in," Freda said, giving her another hug. "We can have a nice cup of cocoa and some homemade snicker doodles. Then you can tell me all about that chicken that attacked you in New York City. Had to arrest it, I heard."

Rayanne turned toward Rios so quickly she heard her neck pop. "You didn't?"

He shrugged. "There are just some things a real man can't keep to himself."

3

"If life's a stage, then I want better lighting."
—Bumper Ditties by Evie E. Garrett

"ARE YOU FINALLY, maybe, almost awake yet?" the small voice asked.

"Huh?" Rayanne grunted and squashed the pillow over her face. Great, now she was hearing voices.

"Are you finally awake yet?" The voice again. "'Cause I've been waiting a long time for you to be awake."

Not just a voice. Not a dream, either. Ugh. Reality. This was probably someone or something she had to deal with if she wanted to get more sleep.

Rayanne pushed the pillow off her face. Her eyelids stirred and finally jarred open. There were streams of piercing bright light coming through the Tinkermouse cartoon curtains on the window. Tinkermouse? Rayanne had been so tired the night before, she hadn't noticed the room, and she hadn't seen those curtains since she was ten. Aunt Evie had obviously decided to try a little retro decor.

The headache-inducing light told Rayanne more than she wanted to know. It was dawn. Or perhaps even later. And she was in her bed. In her room. In Longhorn.

But she wasn't alone.

Her eyes opened wider. Much wider. There, next to her bed, was a child in pink overalls and a ruffled shirt. She wasn't a dream, either. It was a real little girl with brownie-colored curls tumbling around her face. She smiled at Rayanne.

"Are you finally awake yet?" she repeated, the toothy grin nearly as wide as her face. "I mean, I know you're not dressed yet, but it looks like you're awake."

Dressed? No, she wasn't dressed. But just how undressed was she? Rayanne glanced at her silk teddy. Thankfully, the rose-colored swatch covered vital parts of her so she wasn't giving the child an eyeful. There were plenty of times she went to bed wearing only her nail polish.

"You have a little gown, don't you?" the child asked.

Rayanne quickly pulled the sheet over her. "I guess."

"I think it's even littler than mine. Maybe it's even little enough for my doll. But maybe not. I don't have on my gown 'cause I'm already dressed for school, but I have on my Tuesday panties today."

Rayanne had to think—was it Tuesday? And why did it matter if it was? This didn't seem like a conversation she wanted to have right now. Actually, what she wanted to do was sleep just a little bit longer.

"Who are you?" Rayanne asked.

"Mattie. I made you some tea."

"Mattie," she repeated. The name didn't ring a bell, but the prospect of tea was reason to get moving. Rayanne studied the small tray the child had clasped in her equally small hands. Two delicate, miniature china tea-cups, a matching teapot and two Twinkies still in their wrappers. "It looks good." Actually, it looked darn good. It had been years since she'd had a Twinkie. "Mattie, why are you here?"

"To bring you some tea. Aunt Freda said I couldn't come up unless you were awake. You're awake. Finally."

"Well, sort of." Rayanne yawned noisily and scrubbed her hands over her face. She probably wouldn't qualify as awake until she had some caffeine mainlined into her arteries.

"Know what Aunt Freda calls me sometimes? Her little spoonful of sugar in her bowl of granola. What do you think that means, exactly?"

"It means she thinks you're sweet." Rayanne tried to smile. "Actually that's one of Freda's better sayings." At least it was one that made sense. There were plenty that didn't. "Where are your parents?"

Mattie sat on the edge of the bed and started to unwrap the Twinkies. "My mother's away on a trip, and Daddy's working this morning. So when he's working I stay with Miss Evie and catch the school bus over here. Well, except Miss Evie's away on a trip to the jail, so now I'm staying with Aunt Freda." She lowered her voice and cupped a dainty hand around her mouth as if telling a secret. "She smells just like chocolate Easter bunnies. I get hungry when I'm around her."

Rayanne got her mouth to cooperate with a smile. And silently agreed with the child's observation. Ah, so

Mattie was another of Freda's relatives. Now Rayanne understood. For as long as she could remember, Freda's cousins had been coming to Longhorn to stay with Evie. "So, how long will you be here?"

"Don't know. Nobody tells me much. You know how it is."

She did indeed. After all, her aunt had been in jail for two weeks before anyone bothered to let her know.

Mattie put a Twinkie on one of the small plates and handed it to Rayanne. When she poured the tea, however, Rayanne saw that it was only water. Still, a Twinkie and water was more than she usually got for breakfast. In New York, breakfast was a half dozen cups of bad coffee and a couple of strawberry-flavored antacids.

She had just taken a huge bite of the smushy pastry when there was a tap on the door. "Come in, Freda. We're having breakfast."

"Breakfast, huh?"

But it wasn't Freda's voice. It was Rios, and as bold as brass he stepped right into her bedroom.

Remembering Mattie's presence, Rayanne clipped off the snippy protest that nearly slid right out. "What are you doing in here?"

But he didn't have time to answer. The child bolted off the bed and rushed into his open arms. Rayanne had to grab the teapot and cups to keep the water from spilling onto the bed.

"Daddy!" Mattie squealed.

Rayanne's jaw went slack. And then she remembered she had the blunt end of a Twinkie poking out of her mouth. It probably wasn't very attractive. Not that she wanted to be attractive for Rios, but she quickly removed it and stuck it on the plate.

"Daddy?" Rayanne questioned. "Daddy?"

Rios shrugged and planted a noisy kiss on the little girl's cheek. "What are you doing up here, Mattie?"

"Bringing Miss Rayanne some breakfast. It's all right. She's awake, and Aunt Freda said it was okay if she was awake, but it took her a real long time to wake up so I had to wait. She doesn't look anything like Miss Evie, and she wears a teeny weensy gown to bed. I'm talking real teeny."

At that, his eyebrow shot up. And he smiled. Rayanne pulled the covers higher until she was sure every inch below her chin was covered. "This is your daughter?"

"Yep."

Rayanne tried to make her brain process that. It couldn't. "But she said Freda was her aunt."

"She is. Well, sort of. Let me see—Freda's great-aunt is married to my second cousin." He kissed Mattie's cheek again. "Better hurry, sugar. The bus will be here any minute."

"Okay, Daddy." She returned the kiss and slid from his arms. The moment her feet touched the floor, she headed for the door. "Bye, Miss Rayanne. I'll see you when I get back from school."

"Bye, Mattie." The cheery expression stayed on Rayanne's face for a millisecond after the child left. She shifted her position on the bed and gave Rios a look that told him he could leave, as well.

"You probably shouldn't have done that." He

clasped his hands over his eyes in an exaggerated help-me-I'm-blind gesture.

"Shouldn't have done what?"

"Flashed me. I'm a man, after all, and it's a little disconcerting to my male brain to see parts of you that I shouldn't be seeing. Well, unless you're inviting me to see them."

Her mouth dropped open. "Flashed you? What the devil are you talking about? I'm not offering to show you anything and I most certainly didn't flash you."

With one hand covering his eyes, he pointed in the direction of the dresser on the other side of the bed. Rayanne slowly turned so she could see, and there was a lot to see. The whole front of her was covered, but the whole back of her wasn't. From behind, the silk teddy didn't leave much to the imagination, especially since it had ridden up to new fashion heights. She looked like she was wearing a thong.

Ew, and she'd stuck her elbow in Twinkie cream.

Her gaze fired to Rios, and she was prepared to deliver a scathing sermon about him being in her room. But he was gone. Well, almost. Rayanne could hear the sound of his laughter as he made his way down the hall.

So, Rios was a father? A father. Him? As foreign a notion as it sounded, he seemed good at it. He'd been loving, kind and gentle with Mattie. It sure was a different side of a man whose sides she thought she knew all too well.

But if Rios was a father, then there was also a mother. And that meant he was...married?

Married!

She hurdled out of the bed, wiped the sticky white stuff from her elbow and threw on her clothes. Rayanne only hoped Freda was in a talkative mood. If not, she'd find some way to worm it out of her.

Rios, married!

RIOS HEARD the screen door slam, and a moment later he saw Rayanne making her way across the yard toward him. At least he saw the bottom half of her body as he peered from beneath Evie's ancient yellow sedan. Rayanne's skirt wasn't exactly short, but from his angle he had a nice view of her shapely legs. Enough of an angle to wish her skirt were longer so he wouldn't be tempted to wish it were shorter.

''Freda?'' she called.

''She's at the grocery store,'' Rios answered. He checked his watch to time how long it would take her to ask about Mattie. Less than sixty seconds, he figured.

Rayanne leaned down and frowned. She probably would have frowned even more if she'd known he could see right up her slim little skirt. It seemed to be the day for him to get glimpses of her intimate apparel.

''You're flashing me again.'' He let her know. He forced himself to look away.

Rios heard her gasp. Yanking and tugging at her skirt turned out to be futile, but she apparently wasn't ready to give up her attempt to stay put so she could grill him. She got on her knees and looked under the car at him.

''What are you doing under Aunt Evie's car, any-way?'' she asked.

Rios didn't think she'd want to know the truth. It

wouldn't seem right for a grown man to admit he was having fantasies about lacy foundation garments. So he decided to give her the other answer instead. "I'm fixing an oil leak."

"Oh." She took a sip of coffee. Rios could smell it. And her. A mingle of everything that was female. It was a strangely enticing blend, even mixed with the scent of motor oil. "And I suppose you do this often?"

"Sometimes." Of course, it had never been quite this interesting. It gave lubrication tuning a whole new meaning.

Rios pushed himself from beneath the car and got to his feet. He took a rag from his back pocket and used it to mop the sweat off his forehead.

Rayanne stood, too, and leaned against the hood. "Mattie sure seems, um, nice."

He checked his watch. One minute and sixteen seconds. All that skirt tugging had obviously slowed her down a bit. If she'd been wearing jeans, this conversation would have already been on its way. "Let me save you a little trouble here. Her mother is Patricia Quinn."

Rayanne's eyes enlarged to the size of dinner plates. "You married Bennie's daughter?"

"I didn't say I married her." Rios kept his attention on the rag he still had in his hand. "She died about a year ago."

"Died? But Mattie said her mother was away on a trip."

"That's what Bennie tells her. Mattie knows the

truth, but sometimes she likes to pretend Patricia's coming back.''

''Wow.'' And Rayanne said nothing else for a while. ''So, how is it that Bennie didn't force you to marry Patricia?''

''Neither Bennie nor I knew about Mattie. About seven years ago Patricia came out to Denver where I was riding rodeo. We got drunk.'' He shrugged. ''And we slept together. I didn't think much about it until she called last year to ask if I'd raise Mattie.''

Rios made the mistake of looking at Rayanne. They were standing close to each other. Probably too close. And she seemed to be taking in every word. It reminded him of those days when she thought he hung the moon. Now she probably wanted to put him on a one-way space shuttle and send him there.

''So what'll happen?'' Rayanne asked.

''Until Bennie and I can work out some kind of permanent custody arrangement, Evie and Freda help me out sometimes by looking after Mattie. In turn, I fix oil leaks in the car.''

''I see.'' The words were said so softly that Rios looked at her again.

Evidently his eyes didn't intend to behave this morning because they seemed to be taking in everything Rayanne wasn't offering. Those long tanned legs. The curve of her hips. Her breasts. His eyes seemed especially pleased with those and lingered there for a while before moving to her face. That face. God, that face. The woman was hot.

"You've got the greenest eyes in Texas, you know that, Rayanne?"

She blinked. "That sounds like a bad country music song."

It did, but it was better than comparing her eye color to his favorite flavor of suckers.

Rios had a sudden urge to touch her. Well, maybe not just touch. What he had a sudden ache to do really involved clothing removal. He didn't think he should go that far in broad daylight in front of her aunt's house.

But the barn was pretty close.

Her lipstick was smeared, and Rios doubted she knew it. She'd probably set a world record getting dressed so she could find Freda and ask her about Mattie. But since he couldn't haul her off to the barn, it was that smeared lipstick that would give him his cheap thrill for the day.

"Hold still," he instructed. Before she could figure out what he had in mind, he took her coffee and set it on the car.

She opened her mouth, probably to ask what the heck he was doing, but Rios didn't give her a chance. The moment he put his hand around the back of her neck, she went board stiff. That didn't stop him. Touching her mouth, he slowly inched his thumb over her lip, wiping away the stray color. If he had any sense, he would have left it at that, but apparently he didn't have any sense.

Nope. No sense at all.

He grazed the tip of her tongue. It was hard not to think trashy thoughts when he had his thumb in her mouth. Keeping his gaze locked with hers, he brought his hand to his own mouth and licked the lipstick off his thumb. Yep. There was no doubt about it. Rayanne tasted as good as she looked.

She gasped. And stared at him. Then gasped again. ''Why do you always do crazy things like that?''

''Straightening your lipstick is crazy?'' He made sure he sounded like Mr. Innocent. ''It was a thoughtful gesture.'' And a cheap thrill. ''Now, kissing you—that'd be crazy.''

Rios stared at her. And stared. There was a moment, a split second of time, when he thought he'd talked himself out of what he was about to do. He was so wrong.

''Ah, heck,'' he grumbled.

He lowered his head and put his mouth to hers. He wanted to feel the lust, and he did. There was lust galore. But he also felt other things. Things that made the kiss go from just plain wonderful to extraordinary. The softness of her mouth. Her taste. *Her.* Especially her. Rayanne was certainly one of a kind.

A quick slam of desire went straight to the nether region of his body. Not a good direction. Rios knew for a fact that part of him rarely made good decisions. He wasn't counting on it to make a good decision this time, either.

Apparently his mouth was thinking along the same erroneous lines.

''More,'' he heard himself say.

She resisted. But not much. He persisted. A lot. And finally got her mouth open so he could deepen the kiss.

She tasted like coffee and cream and more. It was a taste he'd remembered after eleven long years.

His tongue brushed over hers, sipping again at that sweet taste. If he thought it was hard not to have trashy thoughts with his fingers in her mouth, it was even harder now that they were playing tongue footsies.

Rios waited for her to push him away. Rayanne would lecture him for sure. She would give him a long speech about why he shouldn't have kissed her. Maybe she'd even slap him.

But that didn't happen.

She made a low throaty moan of pleasure and slipped her hand around his neck. Her fingers started to play with his hair. Now that he couldn't handle. There was only so much a man could take, and hair playing was definitely heavy-duty foreplay as far as he was concerned. Foreplay could lead to things that couldn't happen between them. Like making love. Making love really, really couldn't happen. This was one time he would have to veto the whining parts of his body.

Rios stopped the kiss and looked at her.

Her eyelids fluttered open. "Let go of me."

He didn't have any part of her to let go of. As if in surrender, his hands were in the air, and he was leaning back. Rayanne, conversely, had the fingers of her left hand clawed into his chest. Her other hand was wound around his neck, and she was still doing that hair-playing thing.

Looking dazed, she removed her hands from him and stepped back. "Swear to me you'll never do that again."

"Nope."

"Nope?"

"You heard me, and I didn't stutter." But Lord, he should have. Rios quickly pushed that negative notion aside. He felt a roll coming on, and he never liked to pass up a roll even if the premise was just plain stupid. "Remember all the heat that used to snap, crackle and pop between us? Well, it's still there, Rayanne. And don't deny it. Your eyes are glazed, and you're breathing like you're asthmatic."

"What—"

"Don't worry, I've got all the signs, too. I don't want to respond to you any more than you want to respond to me. Wanting you could do nothing but complicate my life right now, and I don't need any more complications."

She took a hard look at his face, apparently trying to figure out if he'd just said what she wanted him to say. "Well, good. At least we agree on something."

"You bet we do. That's why I've thought about us just making love and getting it over with. A good long sweaty bout where we get naked and try to kill each other." He continued before she could make her outraged mouth produce words. "But having carnal knowledge of you won't make anything go away. Well, it might temporarily, but I don't think we're talking more than a half hour or so at the most. So, the way I see it, this is just something we have to learn to deal with."

"Deal with? What the heck does that—"

"I have to go." Rios checked his watch but didn't really want to know the time. He already knew. It was time to get out of there before he forgot everything he'd just said. "Evie should be up by now."

Rayanne's gaze fired to her own watch. "Heavens, you're right." She grabbed her cup of coffee and took a large gulp. "I need to get to the jail." But then she stopped and looked at him. "I trust you won't be here when I get back."

"Never can tell. The world's just full of surprises."

"I've already had my surprise quota for the day. The year," she quickly corrected.

Rios begged to differ. The surprises were just beginning.

4

"Don't play stupid with me. I'm better at it."
—Bumper Ditties by Evie E. Garrett

THERE WERE FOAM rubber cow parts in the middle of Main Street.

Of course, it took Rayanne a couple of minutes to realize exactly what those parts were. The former Hal's Hungry Heifer advertisement icon was toast, or more precisely a mangled heap of manufactured bovine bits.

"Wind," Herman Sheckley, the barber, declared as he walked by Rayanne. "A big gust of wind."

"Wind did that?" she asked skeptically.

He angled his hands apart as if showing the size of his latest catch. "Had to be a big gust of wind."

Maybe, or maybe it was someone with an ax to grind. Those chop marks on the cow's rump looked suspicious. Still, Rayanne wasn't about to suggest a crime had occurred. If someone in Longhorn wanted to chop up that rubber cow, then she didn't want to know anything about it.

"You're here to get Evie out of jail?" Herman asked.

"Yes."

"All the way from New York City?"

Since that seemed to be a question, Rayanne nodded. "How have you been, Mr. Sheckley?"

"Right as rain. Say, Freda mentioned something about you having to arrest a chicken. She said it attacked you."

It was the case that just wouldn't die. Rios told Freda. Freda told Herman. Herman had probably blabbed it over the tristate area.

He chuckled. "Hey, did the chicken squawk when you questioned it? You get it? Chicken, squawk?"

"I get it, but it's not something I like to talk about."

The chuckling continued. In fact, it got so hard, he began to wheeze. "Something you'll tell your grandchildren about, I guess."

No, she wouldn't. No grandchild of hers would ever hear that story. "I'll see you around."

As she stepped around the cow parts and continued down the street, it was easy for her to see that some things never changed. Some things, except for the mutilated cow. The town of Longhorn was pretty much the same as it had always been. Quiet. Laid-back. Even the graffiti on the park bench was spelled correctly and written with good penmanship.

There was Herman Sheckley's barbershop with the poor imitation of a wooden Indian in front of it. A poor imitation because Herman had dressed the statue in his son's old football uniform. Ina Fay's diner still had the Hot Coffee sign in the window. The sign had curled on the edges and offered a steaming cup for a nickel. Or rather an *ickel,* since someone had scratched out the *n.* More often than not, Ina Fay refilled those cups of java for free. It was that kind of hospitality Rayanne missed more than she cared to admit.

She walked down the street until she reached the buttermilk-colored brick building that housed the sheriff's office. It looked exactly as it had for twenty-odd years. There was something comforting about that. Exactly what, she couldn't say.

There was also something else that apparently hadn't changed, and she wasn't the least bit comfortable with it—the way she responded to Rios.

Stupid. Stupid. Stupid.

Stupid.

She'd let him touch her under the guise of repairing her lipstick. That was her first mistake. Then she went from dumb to dumber when she hung around long enough for him to kiss her. Her third mistake, the dumbest, was choosing physical pleasure over common sense.

Kissing Rios had indeed been that—physical pleasure. And maybe it had stirred other areas of her, too. That's why it couldn't happen again. Uh-uh. Thankfully, and miracle of all miracles, he agreed with her. Finally, they were on the same side about something. Now all they had to do was stay away from each other. To make sure that happened, she'd wrap up her business in Longhorn. And wrapping up started with Evie.

Rayanne took a deep breath and went inside the sheriff's office—the place where the buck started.

"Hi, can I help you?" the woman standing behind the desk asked.

Rayanne opened her mouth and closed it just as quickly. The woman was hugely pregnant, her stomach sticking out like a prizewinning watermelon. "Are you—" Rayanne tipped her head to the oversize belly. "All right?"

She smiled and wheezed out a heavy breath. "Not really. I'm due any day now. I wish I could say it looks worse than it feels, but I can't. That's because it feels like I'm carrying a mule." She rubbed her hand over the watermelon. "How are you, Rayanne?"

"Fine." Rayanne studied the woman's face but didn't recognize her. "I'm sorry, but I don't remember your name."

"Arnette Richert. Used to be Arnette Middleton."

"Oh, yes. You were a couple of years behind me in high school."

"Six years, actually," Arnette corrected.

Six years? Something about that didn't set well with Rayanne, and it made her feel more than a little old. Arnette was only twenty-three and already having a baby? Rayanne sincerely hoped it wasn't the ticking of her biological clock that made that information a little hard to swallow.

"I'm the deputy here now," Arnette explained. She waddled to the other side of the room and put a folder in the filing cabinet. That activity apparently exhausted her because she leaned against the wall. "I'm sure it's nothing like what you do. Nothing nearly as important happens around here."

Rayanne wasn't sure of that at all. The kiss Rios had planted on her certainly seemed monumental and illegal. "I'm sure what you do is important to the people of Longhorn." Like cleaning up that rubber cow. The thought of that made Rayanne smile. It might be fun to be a peace officer in a town where the serious crimes roster read like a comedy monologue.

"I suppose you're here to see Evie?" Arnette asked.

"Yes. Is she up?"

"I'm up," her aunt called from the other side of the door. The door marked Sheriff's Office. "Come on in, Rayanne. I've been waiting for you."

Rayanne gave the deputy a questioning glance. "Why is she in there?"

"The jail seemed so dark, and it wasn't big enough for Evie's bed."

"Her bed?"

Arnette nodded. "We couldn't let her sleep on that old cot, so we had somebody bring her bed from home."

Only in a small town could that happen. "Well, thank you." At least they'd tried to make Evie comfortable. That was something, at least.

Rayanne opened the door and peeked inside. She didn't know exactly what she'd expected to see, but this wasn't it. Her aunt was sitting on her giant four-poster bed eating a muffin. A blueberry muffin, to be exact. A cup of steaming coffee was on the bedside table—a table Rayanne recognized as Evie's. Evidently someone had brought that in for her, as well.

There were other little touches that took away any jaillike atmosphere. Fresh flowers next to the coffee. A stack of magazines on the braided country rug. There was even a poster of a winking, grinning, heavily muscled cowboy taped to the wall. He wore boots, his only attire except for a strategically held Stetson.

Evie quickly put her muffin aside and came off the bed. She pulled Rayanne into her arms. "It was so good of you to come."

"As if you gave me much of a choice." Rayanne held the hug a few moments longer, savoring it, then broke away so she could look Evie in the eyes. All in all, her aunt looked healthy. Actually, she looked the picture of health. There were no grayish roots in her sun-gold hair. Her makeup, as usual, was flawless. Even her nails seemed to have enjoyed a recent manicure. In other words, Evie didn't look as if she'd spent the last two weeks in jail.

"I suppose you saw the cow?" Evie asked.

"Cow? Oh, the one on Main Street. Yes, I saw it. Herman Sheckley said the wind blew it down."

"Wind, my fanny. Like Herman Sheckley would know. The man can't see an inch in front of his face. A customer's taking his life into his own hands when he sits down in Herman's barber chair. No, it wasn't the wind that brought down my cow. It was foul play, if you ask me. By the way, speaking of fowl, I heard about the problem you had with that chicken."

"Sheesh. Has Rios told everyone in town?"

"I didn't hear it from Rios. Freda told me when she called this morning. She said it attacked you, huh? Never heard of a chicken doing that, but they can be ornery if you get between them and their chicks."

"Well, it didn't exactly attack me—"

Evie lifted her hands to one of the posters. "What'd you think of him?"

"Of the model?" Rayanne thought she didn't want to talk about him, that's what.

"He's such a hunk. I want to see if I can find some naked pictures of him on the Internet."

Rayanne was about to ask about the shooting, but that stopped her. "You want nude photographs of some model?"

"Oh, but he's more than just a model. He's an actor and he sent me a letter. Well, the president of his fan club did. I'm going to visit him in Hollywood when I'm out of here. Such trying times, these." Evie fanned herself—dramatically so—and walked to the window. "I suppose you're angry because I asked you to come."

"Not angry. Suspicious. And even more suspicious about why you're in jail, uh, or rather why you're in the sheriff's office."

"I'm charged with pulling a gun on Bennie Quinn," Evie said nonchalantly.

"Yes, I heard." Rayanne sat on the edge of the bed. "Tell me exactly what happened."

She dismissed it with a wave of her hand. "I don't want to talk about that now. Tell me about your trip. Did you have a good flight?"

A stall tactic. Evie was awful at disguising them but somehow good at making them work. "The flight was fine. Now—"

"And Rios gave you a ride home from the airport just like I asked him to do. Such a good boy he's turned out to be. Don't you think so?"

"He's not a boy, and I didn't come here to discuss Rios. Or cowboy models. Or the rubber cow or even Herman Sheckley's poor eyesight. I want to discuss your situation, and I'd like to know—"

"Did you meet Mattie?"

Rayanne gritted her teeth. It would be easier to catch a feather in a wind tunnel. "Yes, I met her, and you keep changing the subject."

"I know. It's just the child troubles me so. Such a sad situation. Her mother's dead, you know?"

"Rios told me."

"And Bennie." Evie sighed heavily. "Well, Bennie's being difficult. He's fighting Rios for custody of Mattie."

"No surprise there. I can't imagine he was too happy to learn about Rios and Patricia fooling around. So, did this incident with Bennie have something to do with Rios's custody battle with—"

"I said I didn't want to talk about that."

"Well, I don't see where you have another choice. You're in jail, Aunt Evie, and I want to know what happened."

Evie paused. And fidgeted. And paused again. "Bennie is a cantankerous old fool, and I just wanted him to understand he can't always have what he wants. So, I took your daddy's old beat-up twenty-two rifle and paid Bennie a little visit to try to talk some sense into him."

Heaven help her. "And you thought you could do that by scaring the bejesus out of him?"

"I didn't scare him much," Evie said as if that justified everything. "But the gun was sort of loaded, and even though I aimed it at the knobby hackberry tree near Bennie's barn instead of at Bennie, Rios said that still hadn't been a really good idea on my part.''

It wasn't an easy thing for a cop to hear. And not just her aunt's irrational, nincompoopish ideas of intimidation. Rule one of law enforcement was to substantiate the allegation. Well, Evie had just done that in much clearer terms than Rayanne wanted. A loaded gun, even if it happened to be a bent-barreled, sixty-something-year-old rusty rifle, was still a potentially dangerous weapon in the eyes of the law. The fact that Evie had aimed it could be used against her to prove intent to harm. It likely wouldn't matter that the only thing her aunt planned to harm was a knobby hackberry.

"Will you be able to post bond for me today?" Evie asked.

Rayanne pushed out a breath of frustration. "Of course. That's why I'm here. What I want to know is why the sheriff ever locked you up in the first place. You're not exactly a hardened criminal. He should have forced you to go home by now."

Evie fanned herself again. "He tried."

"Obviously not hard enough. In fact, I intend to speak to him about that as soon as possible." *Speak* wasn't exactly the right word. Rayanne wanted to have it out with Sheriff Ryland.

"How are your headaches?" Evie asked.

"Fine." Now, this was a subject Rayanne didn't want to discuss.

Evie clucked her tongue. "Your stay in Longhorn will be good for you. Next thing you know you'll have ulcers. Or hives maybe. The nerves can only take so much irritating them and they have to flare up. Arnette's grandmother once got hives on her armpits and had to walk around for a week with her hands in the air. I saw her over at the bank and thought there was a hold-up in progress.''

''Aunt—''

''Did you know the sheriff's looking for someone to fill in for Arnette when she has her baby?''

''No, Aunt Evie, don't even think it.'' Rayanne adamantly shook her head. ''I'm not going to work for the Longhorn sheriff's office. I have a job in New York, remember?''

''Well, that place was never the same after Jimmy Smits left.''

''Jimmy Smits played a cop on TV, Aunt Evie. I am one.''

''An unhappy one, from what I can see. Don't twist your face up so. Causes wrinkles.''

Rayanne ignored the wrinkle comment but she did try to relax her face. ''And you think I'd be happier in Longhorn? No, thanks. I have a life in New York. A good life.'' And she didn't intend to continue this conversation. It felt too much like the one she'd avoided with Rios the night before, and it sounded as if she were trying to convince herself. Which she probably was. ''I need to find the sheriff so I can get you out of here.''

''He's usually at the diner this time of morning,'' Evie remarked. ''Bring me back a little box of Cocoa Balls cereal, will you? More coffee, too. And maybe a good magazine. You know which ones I like.''

Rayanne quickly shut the door between her and her aunt before Evie could add more to her requests. She closed her eyes and leaned against the door to catch her breath. What she saw when she opened her eyes did not please her. Arnette was nowhere in sight, but the place sure wasn't empty.

"Rios, what are you doing here?"

He had his feet propped on the desk and his Stetson tipped back on his head. A sucker stem poked out of the corner of his mouth. "Are you going to ask me that every time you see me?"

"Only when you turn up at places you shouldn't be."

"Well, I gotta tell you, this is one place I should turn up." He opened the middle drawer of the desk, and she watched him fish through it, shoving aside paper clips, rubber bands and at least a dozen lime suckers. He took out a shiny silver badge and pinned it to his crisp white shirt. "This is my office now."

No! This could not be happening. This had to be a dream. Or a weird alternate universe. There was no way Rios could be sheriff. "Since when?"

"Since the people of Longhorn voted me in three months ago, right after Sheriff Ryland retired."

"Mercy." Rayanne sank into the first available chair. "You're the one who arrested Aunt Evie?"

"Had to." He pulled the lime green sucker out of his mouth and pointed it at her. "I told you Bennie made sure the charges were filed, so I had no choice but to do what I did. Oath of office and all that stuff."

"And you're the one who didn't call me to let me know you arrested her?"

"Guess I'm guilty of that, too. I wanted to call, but Evie didn't want you to know."

"That is not good enough. I can't believe you did this."

"Just doing my job, Rayanne. And it's not as if I had a choice. Bennie's the one who pressed this issue."

"So you said. But other than his word, what proof do you have that Evie tried to shoot him, huh?"

"Well, I got Evie's full, freely given, signed confession along with Bennie's statement that verifies everything Evie said."

Oh. She hated to admit it, but it sounded as if Rios had done his job and done it well. Heck. Why couldn't he be incompetent in this one area? "What about the statements of witnesses?"

"There weren't any, but I do have a firearm report that says the twenty-two could have been discharged despite the bent trigger and rusty barrel."

"Firearm report," Rayanne repeated flatly.

"Yeah, you know, a scientific process to determine—"

"I know what a firearm report is, Rios. I just didn't know you had evidence like that."

"Well, we're getting quite progressive here in Longhorn. Women can vote now. No telling how that might affect a man's way of thinking. Might just cause all kinds of changes around here. Which brings me to my next point. Arnette doesn't want to come back to work after the baby's born, so I'll need another deputy. Interested?"

It was an easy question to answer, especially with her suddenly rotten mood. "In no way, shape or form."

"That's what I figured you'd say. I just thought maybe you'd like something to do while you're waiting around for Evie's trial. You could fill in until I find someone permanent."

"Her trial?" That brought Rayanne to her feet. "You expect this thing to go to trial?"

"The DA does. Of course, the DA is Ezra Quinn, Bennie's first cousin, so naturally he'll do just about anything that Bennie wants."

She stopped herself short of banging her head against the wall. "When exactly will this trial be?"

"In two weeks. Hopefully."

"Two weeks!" But that wasn't what bothered her most. It was the *hopefully* part. Two weeks in Longhorn. Two weeks around Rios. Two weeks of staying away from him when he seemed to turn up everywhere she went. Two weeks of the tension. The hot kisses.

"Well, if you change your mind about a job," he calmly offered, "you know where to find me."

Change her mind? She was more likely to lose it first. "I want to take a look at these so-called reports you have regarding the alleged crime. And I need to post bail for Aunt Evie. Will you take a check?"

"Sure, as long as it doesn't bounce."

Rayanne ignored the remark and dug through her purse to find her checkbook. "How much?"

"Five thousand dollars."

She dropped into the chair. "Five thousand dollars! You are out of your flipping mind."

"Not me. Judge Ira Quinn set the bond."

"Another of Bennie's cousins," she said under her breath. It wouldn't do any good to find a bail bondsman, either. There was only one in Longhorn—Bennie Quinn.

"You okay?" Rios asked. "You're looking a little pale there."

"I'm fine." And she forced her teeth to unclench while she wrote out the check. "May I use your phone? I need to call my bank and transfer some funds. Don't worry. It's a toll-free number."

He lifted his hand to his phone in a go-ahead gesture. "Need some financing? If so, I can help you out."

"No, thanks," she said crisply. "You've done quite enough already."

Rios shook his head in a mildly frustrated, halfheartedly rankled sort of way. "Guess you'll hold Evie's arrest against me for a decade or so, huh?"

It was a possibility. Well, except he'd obviously gone to furniture-hauling, poster-hanging lengths to make Evie comfortable during her stay. Heck, Rios had even given up his office. That shaved some time off that grudge she'd likely hold because...well, because it seemed too big a grudge to aim it all at Bennie and Evie.

She picked up the phone, not noticing that the line-in-use button was lit. Rayanne was about to hang up, but she heard Evie's voice. And she heard words she didn't especially want to hear.

"Yes, Freda, we're having a party. A big one," Evie

explained. "Tonight. I've already called some people, and they're calling others as we speak."

"Uh, Aunt Evie?" Rayanne interrupted.

"Why, Rayanne, I'm glad you're on the line. You can help. I'm making a list of things that I need you to pick up."

"For the party," Rayanne clarified. "But I don't think a party is a good—"

"Sure it is," Freda and Evie said in unison.

"It's for your homecoming," Evie added.

"But I—"

"It'll be fun," her aunt continued, ignoring what would have been a protest from Rayanne.

"But, Aunt Evie, we have more important things—"

"Pshaw." Freda that time. "Nothing's more important than celebrating your homecoming. And Evie's. It'll be so good to have both pair of my warm fuzzy bear slippers back home again."

She didn't feel like fuzzy bear slippers. Rayanne felt like a blasted Ping-Pong ball. And neither one of them was listening to a word she said. "But we need to get Evie's things moved from the jail—"

"Rios will do that for us," Evie assured her. "Just remember to say pretty please when you ask him. Oh, and invite him to the party while you're at it. Tell him that we won't take no for an answer, that we absolutely insist that he come."

Rayanne huffed. She'd already been roped into doing errands and a request that would guarantee her to spend some time with Rios. And she hadn't yet completed a full sentence. She tried again. "But I need to speak to Bennie Quinn to see if I can get him to drop the—"

Evie took the next round. "Bennie can wait."

As her aunt rattled on about the makings for guacamole dip and her preferred brand of spicy pork rinds, Rayanne's frustrated gaze met Rios's.

"My advice?" He unwrapped a lime sucker and passed it her way. "Surrender. It saves time and breath."

He was right, of course. And there was likely nothing she could do anyway to stop the Texas-size socializing wheels her aunt had already put into motion. Accepting her fate, Rayanne stuck the sucker in her mouth. It appeared she had a party to attend.

5

"Happiness can't buy money."
— Bumper Ditties by Evie E. Garrett

THE PARTY WAS IN FULL SWING by the time Rios finished for the day and made it over to Evie's. He caught a whiff of barbecue and more than a whiff of beer. Some people were trying to reassemble the Hal's Hungry Heifer cow in Evie's front yard. Drunk people, obviously. The result looked like a cloning experiment gone bad.

"What ya think, Rios?" Ned Beekers called.

"You might want to move the hoof off of its ear. Just a suggestion."

In true drunken fashion, Ned stood there and scratched his head. Rios decided to let Ned and his inebriated compadres figure it out for themselves. That probably wouldn't happen for a day or two. While he was at it, he'd collect their keys so none of them would do anything foolish such as trying to drive.

Rios climbed out of his truck and slapped a hand on his jeans to get rid of some of the dust. A party certainly wouldn't have been his first choice for a way to spend the evening, but he thought that after a shave and shower he'd be in the mood for one.

Especially since Rayanne would be there.

He didn't really want to sit around and figure out why that pleased him so. Nothing about his situation had changed. Not really. He still wasn't in any position to start up a full-fledged relationship, even if it would be incredibly satisfying in numerous ways.

Besides, Rayanne would leave town, no doubt soon, and that meant full-fledged would turn into something pathetically temporary. It would be something cheap and tawdry. Cheap and tawdry was all right for some things, but not for a relationship with Rayanne.

"There you are." Evie gave him a beaming smile and held open the front door for him. She had a gallon container of guacamole dip in her hand and an industrial-size bag of corn chips under her arm. "Looks like rain, but I'm hoping the fellas can get the barbecue finished before it starts. Come on in."

"I need to drop by my place and clean up some first. I've been out at the barn with that mare again."

"Oh, is she still not feeling well?"

"She's better, but I wanted to check on her." He stepped onto the porch and gave his jeans another dusting. "Where's Rayanne?"

"I sent her to the store to get a few more things. Don't worry, I made sure the list included some of those green suckers you like so much." She checked her watch and nearly dumped the bowl of guacamole on herself. Rios steadied the dip just in time. "I'm surprised she's not back by now."

He was thankful Rayanne wasn't there yet. He still

had some things to settle with Evie. "Did you tell Rayanne about the land yet?"

"No." Evie gave a weary sigh. "I haven't had a chance. Heck, I've had to send her to the store four times because I keep remembering things we need. And speaking of the party, doesn't the guacamole look good?"

Rios recognized this routine. It was one of Evie's most frequently used stall tactics—changing the subject. "Rayanne has to know," he insisted. "And you can't wait—"

"Mattie just loves Rayanne. That's all the child talked about this afternoon before Freda took her over to Bennie's."

Yep, Rios had learned pretty much the same thing. His daughter was duly impressed with Evie's niece. However, this wasn't at all what he wanted to discuss, and Evie had likely known that when she brought up the subject. "If you don't tell Rayanne about the land—"

"Have you ever thought about asking Rayanne to marry you?" Evie interrupted.

The breath sort of swooshed right out of him. Great day, the woman knew how to take shock and surprise to new heights. Rios put his hands on his hips and stared at her. "No, I haven't."

Well, maybe he'd thought of it a time or two over the years, but that was just some settling-down urges that hit him every now and then. Besides, this was another of Evie's ploys to get him off the subject of the land. He didn't want his brain to have to ponder the notion of marriage.

Well, not at this moment, anyway.

He caught Evie's shoulders, the bulging bowl sandwiched between them. "No more interruptions and no more pretending you can't hold your own in a conversation. Evie Garrett, promise me you'll tell Rayanne tonight."

"Oh, not tonight. Not with the party going on. First thing in the morning." With eyes that seemed to have doubled in size, Evie looked at him pleadingly. "Will you be there with me when I tell her?"

He shook his head as fast and as hard as he could shake it. "Uh-uh. That's not a good idea."

"Of course it is. You have a way with words. Heck, you talked half the young women in this town into going to Whiskey Creek with you, and that was before you owned it. Even Rayanne fell to your charms."

Not exactly, but that was one road he didn't want to go down right now.

"Just help me tell her, please," Evie pleaded. "She'll get upset but then she'll get over it. You'll see. Maybe you can talk her into going up to Whiskey Creek again."

Only if he could convince her it would be a good place to clobber him and hide his body.

He gave Evie's hand a reassuring pat. "This has to come from you. I'll talk to her when you're done, okay?"

She nodded eventually and gave him one of her motherly looks. "For the life of me, I just haven't been able to figure out why you and Rayanne didn't stay together. You seem made for each other.''

"Things just didn't work out." It was Rios's standard answer whenever Evie or Freda asked—which was often.

"But now that you have Mattie, don't you think you need to consider marrying and—"

"No." He waved in a don't-go-there gesture. "I'm not getting married just for the sake of giving Mattie a mother."

"But—"

"No," he interrupted, using one of Evie's ploys. "I gotta go wash up." And to make sure the conversation didn't continue, Rios started to walk away.

"You and Rayanne would be so happy together," Evie called. "Goodness, you're both in law enforcement. Both on the stubborn side. Both single and too old not to be looking harder than you are for something permanent."

"You're talking to the rubber cow." Rios continued to his truck. "Because I'm not listening."

"We'll see about that. I'm wearing you down, Rios McKay. I can see it by the way you slump your shoulders."

He immediately tried to improve his posture but never looked back. The woman could talk Martha Stewart into serving peanut butter and banana sandwiches at a ritzy party, and there was no way he wanted to tangle with Evie tonight.

Too bad she might be right about one thing, though.

Well, a little right, anyway. She *was* wearing him down. Or maybe that was Rayanne's doing.

Before Rayanne returned to Longhorn, before that kiss, he'd been almost certain of the direction the wind was blowing between them. Other than asking Evie for information about him, which Evie readily admitted to him, Rayanne hadn't made any attempt to stay in touch. Neither had he. Well, except for the information about her he'd pried out of Evie. Yet it appeared by the way Rayanne responded to the kiss that she still carried a little place for him in her heart.

So, the question was—just how big was that little place? And did he somehow want to make it a whole lot bigger? It'd be a challenge, all right. Like wrangling a longhorn with a broken shoestring.

He grinned.

Heck, he always did like a challenge.

RAYANNE GROANED. The place was already packed. It was just what she didn't need with a headache coming on. She'd hoped for at least a chance to catch her breath. Apparently, she would have to manage that while she partied with nearly every citizen of Longhorn. Minus the Quinns, of course. None of them would show, even though Evie had no doubt invited them. Evie wouldn't let something like a bitter feud stand in the way of being a good hostess.

She parked her aunt's car in the driveway and with the plastic grocery sack in her hand she started across the yard. A sack that contained lime suckers, one of which she had stuck in her mouth. It was her eleventh one. If she had to face Rios tonight, which she most certainly would, she wanted to do it with a sugar high. It might give her the much-needed edge to resist him.

The rubber cow startled her for a moment. Well, she thought it might be the rubber cow she'd seen hanging over Main Street. The cow, or what was left of it, was near the front steps, like some odd, frightening lawn ornament. It had a hoof glued to its nose and another where its ear should have been. There was some unidentifiable part, perhaps bovine-related, on the tuft of its head. Strange. Very strange.

Rayanne went into the house through the kitchen door. Okay…she managed to get herself *partly* inside the door. The room was jammed with people, all of them sloshing drinks and talking at the same time. Every single one of them welcomed her with a warm hello and some generous hugs. They also gave her some odd looks, but she had no idea what that was about. Maybe her eyes were glazed from the high volume of sugar pumping through her blood.

"Freda?" Rayanne called when she saw her by the sink. She put aside the sucker and grocery bag. "Where's Aunt Evie? I got the rest of her things."

"Rayanne, there you are." Freda pushed her way through the crowd. When she got closer, she gave Rayanne's cheek a jiggling pinch. "My little case of chocolate éclairs with extra sweet filling and green lips."

It took Rayanne a moment to figure out that the last two words weren't part of the metaphor. Sweet heaven. The suckers. "Are my lips really green?"

Freda nodded and carefully studied Rayanne's mouth

as if she were observing some sort of scientific experiment. "Yes, but don't worry about it, they match your eyes."

The greenest eyes in Texas, Rios had said. Well, shoot. She didn't want to walk around all night with color-coordinated facial features.

"What took you so long?" Freda asked.

Rayanne located a napkin and started wiping. So, maybe the attempted sugar high hadn't been such a good idea after all. "I went for a drive."

She looked around but didn't see her aunt or the cause of her drive—Rios. Rayanne could blame the green lips on him, as well, since he was no doubt the reason that particular confection had been on Evie's shopping list in the first place.

Freda gave Rayanne a reassuring pat on the cheek. And pinched it again. "Well, you're here now so why don't you find Rios and talk him into dancing with you? I'm sure he won't mind your green lips at all."

"I don't want to dance with Rios."

"Sure you do. He's a wonderful man—like a big slice of apple pie with ice cream on it—and it doesn't hurt that he puts stars in your eyes, either." And with that absurd but perhaps somewhat truthful observation, Freda winked and headed into the crowd.

Yes, in some ways Rios was wonderful. For example, he could dissolve multiple layers of rust with his kisses. Somehow, Rayanne didn't think Freda meant that as one of Rios's redeeming qualities. The man could certainly fill out a pair of jeans—another noteworthy qual-

ity. And he could make her act like a fool—not so redeeming. But it was certainly a knack of his.

Though all those wonderful, knackful aspects, as lust-
inducing as they were, hadn't caused her to drive
around for the past hour. Nope. It just wasn't easy being
around Rios. She'd spent the first eighteen years of her
life falling in love with him and the next eleven trying
to convince herself that he was toenail fungus.

Great day. Here she was doing it again, whining and
lamenting over a man who seemed to be a constant
source of whining and lamenting. She grabbed a beer
from the fridge and headed straight for the back door.
It probably wasn't a good idea for her to hang around
a party while she felt like the bearer of gloom and
doom. And while she had green lips.

"Don't run into any chickens while you're out
there," Philip Ryland, the banker, called. "Squawk,
squawk. Planning to feather your nest any time soon?"
He cackled with laughter.

Rayanne ignored him and went outside. The first rain-
drop smacked her in the eye before she made it to the
bottom step. More dotted her clothes while she walked
to the stables. The droplets didn't deter her. After the
day she'd had, a storm was indeed a small thing. Even
a belligerent chicken wouldn't have stopped her. Besides, a nice turbulent rainstorm might wash away some
of the green sucker discoloration.

Rayanne stepped into the stables, and the familiar
smell of horses and hay hit her at once. She gave the
roan mare a caress and opened her beer. There were
only two horses stalled here, but when she was a kid,

the place was always filled to the brim. Evie had probably sold them to cut down on her workload. Too bad. Exercising and cleaning up after the horses had never seemed like work to Rayanne, and it would have been a way to occupy her time while she was in Longhorn.

Her eyes slowly adjusted to the darkness. The only lights came from the house, a good twenty yards away. The darkness suited her mood. Man problems, green lips and a headache. It sounded like a warped Dr. Seuss title.

She wasn't sure what alerted her, but Rayanne suddenly knew she wasn't alone. Shifting her gaze from her beer, she looked at the other end of the stables. There was Rios, leaning against a post. He, too, had a beer in his hand and raised it in a pseudo toast.

"Nice night for a party, huh?" he asked.

Rayanne raised her beer in return and slowly walked toward him. It was a nice night for something, she guessed. She was almost afraid to find out what.

6

"Weather forecast for tonight: dark."
— Bumper Ditties by Evie E. Garrett

"WHAT ARE YOU DOING HERE?" she asked Rios. Rayanne knew she'd run into him tonight, but she hadn't expected it to happen so soon.

Rios clucked his tongue. "The same question again."

She took a sip of beer, assumed his pose and leaned against the post across from him. "Do you have a logical answer this time?"

"I wanted to get away from the party and that rubber cow for a couple of minutes. Why are you here?"

"Same reasons," she replied. Rios leaned slightly closer, his pinpointed gaze aimed right at her mouth. "Yes, they're green," Rayanne offered before he could make a joke about it.

"Nice color. They match your eyes."

"So I've been told." She drank more beer, hoping the meager amount of alcohol would dissolve the remnants of her lollipop feast. "Where's Mattie?"

"It's her night with Bennie. She spends three days a week and two nights with him. Of course, he'd like nothing more than to have her there all the time. I guess you've heard he's challenging me for custody?"

"Yes, Aunt Evie told me." And it bothered her. Too much. She'd seen Rios with his daughter and saw the genuine love there. No one, especially Bennie, should be challenging him for custody. "Well, it seems Bennie's trying to cause trouble for both you and Evie. I think I'll drive out there in the morning and see if I can get him to talk to me."

"That's probably not a good idea." He shrugged. "Well, unless you let me deputize you."

"I'd rather eat that foam rubber cow for breakfast," she joked. But his offer did remind her of a childhood dream she'd left behind. "You know, I always thought I'd grow up to be sheriff of Longhorn."

"Really? I didn't know that."

She nodded. "Yep. I used to see Sheriff Ryland with that shiny badge and that authoritative swagger. He always smelled like starch and shoe polish. I wanted to be like that. Not smell like him," she corrected. "I just wanted to walk around town and have people look at me the way they looked at him." *And the way they now look at you.*

"So, why didn't you stay and become sheriff?"

Rayanne opened her mouth to give him an answer and realized she didn't have one. Her usual response was that she wanted to make her own way in the world, but that seemed sort of a dumb reason, especially since Longhorn would always be her home. The truth was she'd left because she didn't want a daily dose of Rios, because she didn't want to have to face him after the embarrassing incident.

Strange, that it had taken her all this time to figure

that out. She'd left the place and family she loved because she was, well, chicken. It was even more ridiculous when she factored in that Rios had left, as well, for years, and she still hadn't bothered to put her pride aside and return home.

Knowing Rios was waiting for an answer, she tried a different approach. "Why are you so anxious to get a badge on me, anyway?"

Rios grinned from ear to ear. "Must be the idea of pinning something to your chest that gets me all excited. That, and I don't like the idea of being without a deputy when Arnette leaves."

"Expecting a crime wave, Sheriff?"

"Well, it's not exactly a high-crime area, but we can have some excitement."

"Oh, yeah? Like what?" she asked.

"The Quik Stop got robbed last month. They got away with a six-pack of nonalcoholic beer and two packages of Ding Dongs. Then someone took an ax to the rubber cow that Evie donated."

"That wasn't exactly a crime," Rayanne retorted. "More like a mercy killing."

"Good point, but Evie wants me to investigate it, so I will. I like being sheriff, but I want to leave some time for Mattie and for my ranch."

Rayanne took another sip of beer. "Exactly where is your ranch anyway?"

"I bought the old Saunders place."

She knew the property well. Too well. It brought back some memories she didn't want to remember. "By Whiskey Creek?"

"Yep, I own it now."

Well, that was appropriate in the cosmic scheme of things. After all, Rios had probably seduced dozens of women at that creek. He could sow oats in the same place he'd sown his oats.

He leaned closer again, his scrutinizing gaze on her lips once more.

"Yes, my tongue is probably green, too," she offered, in case his thoughts were headed in that direction. "And no, I don't need you to verify that for me."

"Well, as interesting as that sort of verification might be to, uh, research, I wasn't thinking about your tongue. You look like you might have a headache."

Great. Now he could read minds, as well. "It's just been a rough day." For a whole host of reasons. Rios was one of those reasons. Actually, he was the main one.

"Anything I can do to help?" he asked.

"Nope." Unless he could somehow change the emotional and hormonal makeup of her body.

"Well, I'm sure you'll work your way through whatever's bothering you. You're one of the smartest people I know."

Confused, she stared at him. "That was, uh, like a compliment. Careful, Rios. You just might make me swoon if you keep that up."

Instead of looking insulted, he smiled. "No swooning allowed tonight. No arguing, either. Let's just stand here and enjoy our beer. And the company."

She didn't frown until he said that last part. Rayanne didn't want to enjoy his company. Well, she did. But she didn't. And it was that *didn't* part that made the *did* part seem all the more interesting. It was no wonder she had a headache.

The rain started in earnest. It tunneled off the stables, making watery curtains in the entryways. Despite the sound of the rain on the tin roof, she could still hear music coming from the house. Patsy Cline was singing about her mental condition. Rayanne could sympathize with her. She had a mental condition big enough for a dozen country music songs.

"Have you thought any more about what I said to you at the airport?" Rios asked.

That entailed a lot of territory, but somehow Rayanne knew exactly what part of their conversation he meant. The part where they discussed *the* incident.

"Let me rephrase that some," Rios continued. "I guess what I'm looking for here is some kind of, well, closure." He shook his head. "Mercy, I hate that word. There's no way for a cowboy to say *closure* and not make him sound wussy. Anyway, wussiness aside, I don't want you going through life thinking I did what I did up there because I didn't want you." He snared her gaze. "Because I did want you. You do know that, don't you?"

Darn it. It was one of those soul-searching questions, and she had to plow through all those years of festering embarrassment so she could make an attempt at being honest with herself.

"I know you wanted me," Rayanne admitted. "I wanted you, too." And she braced herself in case some kind of universal rupture occurred because of what she was about to say. "I should have let you know sooner about my lack of experience."

"And I should have asked."

The fit of orneriness she'd nourished and fed for eleven years landed right on the hay-strewn floor. Confused, stunned, awed, she stood there and stared at him.

He gave a frustrated-sounding sigh. "I just assumed... I mean, you were eighteen. And you were beautiful. *Are* beautiful," he corrected. "Even with those green lips and a headache, you're still beautiful. I just figured your first time had already happened with Trey Jenkins. I mean, not that Trey ever said that you two had, well, you know."

She'd never heard Rios flustered before, and it left her pretty much dumbfounded. That probably wasn't such a bad thing because Rios continued.

"Anyway, I was flattered. More than flattered. I was kind of overwhelmed that you wanted me to be your first." He shook his head. "Sheez, that makes me sound like a wuss, too. Please don't repeat that to anyone. I wouldn't want it to get around that I was ever overwhelmed in a sexual situation. Wouldn't be good for my image."

Her lips twitched, threatening to smile. "Well, I suppose we could strike a bargain here. No more chicken remarks or rehashing chicken stories, and I just might forever put it out of my mind that you were, uh, overwhelmed in a situation where overwhelming would be a definite liability to your stud status."

"That's kind of you." He paused a heartbeat and

fought a grin of his own. "But my guess is you'll tattle first chance you get."

"Absolutely. Just like you'll bring up this green lip thing as often as you can work it into conversation."

His grin verified that. "So, have we officially cleared the air?"

Well, considering they were in the stables with the smell of the horses and horse manure, the air was about as clear as it would get.

"We have," she let him know. "I should have told you sooner. You should have asked. And instead of being grossly embarrassed, we would have ended up a little flustered."

"A lot flustered," he corrected.

He was right. For months leading up to that incident, there'd been a veneer covering the fierce attraction between them. That veneer vanished the moment they started kissing and discarding their clothes. Rios had somehow had the wherewithal to get that veneer and their clothes—minus her midnight-blue panties—back on. No easy feat.

Rios set his beer aside. After doing the same to hers, he caught her hand. "Dance with me."

She was shaking her head as fast as it would shake. "Oh, no. I can't dance."

Rios slipped his arm around her waist and pulled her to him. "Sure you can." He laced their fingers together. "The song's doing all the work for us, and all we have to do is move with the music."

That's what Rayanne was afraid of. All she had to do was move to the music with her body touching

Rios's. And with her face very close to his neck. That kind of stuff would vaporize her quickly waning resistance, and she wasn't ready for the vaporization process yet.

"This goes here," he said, sticking his foot between her feet. It caused his jeans to rub against the inside of her legs. Slowly, he started to sway to the music. "Now, this is the easy part. Just wander with Patsy."

"Wander?"

"Close your eyes and think about what the music's doing. It's just like taking a walk through the pasture on a Sunday morning. Right after it's started to rain. Think about it. About the taste that's on your tongue when you catch the raindrops. About the smell of the fresh grass. Think about the warm breeze on your face."

Rayanne couldn't think of anything else. Rios's voice was as smoky smooth as the tune. She closed her eyes and let him guide her into the rhythm of the dance. For a moment, she'd allow herself to enjoy it.

A moment passed.

All right, she'd give herself two moments.

"Do you remember I taught you how to saddle a horse right here in this very spot?" His breath was warm, and it caressed her face. "You were all of, what, seven years old, and I was eleven."

"Yes, I remember." In fact, she had a lot of memories of Rios. Good memories. Most of those memories involved watching his various muscles flex while he did sweaty, muscle-flexing chores, but there were some non-lust-related ones, too. Like the time she'd helped him deliver the chestnut mare, Penny, that had become the equine love of her life.

Rios started to caress the small of her back with his fingertips. It tickled, but it felt good, too. It made her feel tingly all over. Rayanne quickly choked back what would have no doubt become a giggle and started to move away from him. But Rios obviously had other ideas. His arm tightened around her waist, and he lowered his head so his cheek rested on her temple.

"We can't do this," she said.

He looked at her. "Are you telling me you don't like this?"

She thought about it, even though she already knew the answer. The answer was right in her face, staring at her green lips. "All right, I do like it," she mumbled. "I just don't want it to lead to anything else."

"It's just a dance. That's all. Well, it could be more. Since this feels kind of warm and fuzzy, how about giving me a kiss?"

"No—"

"You're not chicken, are you?"

"Not the best choice of words, but no."

"Well, I know you're not green with envy. Sorry, that one just sort of slipped out." He tapped the corner of his mouth. "So, kiss me right there. Just a little one."

"This is so stupid. We're not in high school anymore."

"I know that as well as you do. We're two grownups with years of mutual attraction between us. That's why I say let's just get it out of our systems."

Kissing him certainly wouldn't do that. Rayanne was

about a million percent sure of it. "And if I don't have anything to get out of my system?"

"Then get it out of mine."

"Hardly. About the only thing a kiss would do is heat us both up." And she was talking a really, really hot kind of heat.

His eyebrow rose. "You're admitting that?"

"No reason not to." But she still couldn't understand why she had. It was like handing over secrets to the enemy. He'd figure out a way to use her admission to put another hole in her resistance.

"Then kiss me so you can torture me. Get me so hot, Rayanne, that I'll get on my knees and beg you. Then you can toss your hair the way you like to do and walk away. That'll show me."

Oh, she liked the sound of that. She smiled. But not for long. Rios touched her. He skimmed his hand down her back and edged her closer to him. Now, that was something she hadn't considered. If she could touch and kiss him in the name of torture, then he could possibly do the same to her. If she let him, that is.

But she wouldn't let him. Uh-uh. She could make herself immune to him. It wouldn't be like that kiss he'd sneaked while straightening her lipstick. No way. She was prepared for this one. She could just turn herself off and—

He touched her again and brushed his body against her. Fully against her. In a place that in no way needed such brushing.

"Just one little kiss," he whispered. He put an exclamation mark on that request by lowering his head and placing his mouth solidly on hers.

But it wasn't a little kiss, nor was it one. Well, maybe it was one, but it was a heck of a long one. Rios nudged her lips apart, though it didn't take much effort. Rayanne soon found herself a willing participant. A hesitant willing participant who no longer had a clue what planet she was on.

Warmth radiated within her when his tongue skimmed over hers. Outside, a rumble of thunder and a vein of lightning announced a full-fledged storm. Rayanne hardly noticed it. She was already at a place where rain or storms didn't exist. And Rios was making her feel like a sizzling griddle.

He deepened the kiss, angling her mouth to his. *Yes,* she thought. *Yes, yes, yes!* It was like kissing the heavyweight champion of kissing. Rios was a real pro at this, and he didn't disappoint her. Her lips were damp, and he used that to move over her without restraint. The torture stuff sort of slipped right out of her mind. Every logical thought, every argument went with it.

Her fingertips began to tremble on his chest. While her fingers were there and moving around, she decided to inch them inside the space between his buttons, then inside his shirt. Chest hair. She liked chest hair. There was something virile about it.

She latched on to the front of his shirt, her grip straining the fabric until a couple of buttons gave way. Better. Now she could feel all the chest hair she wanted. Heck, she could get her whole hand in there, and she did.

Rios must have liked her touching him because he

grunted, and things started to move a little faster. He moved his mouth to her neck, all the while backing her against the post.

"That's right, Rayanne. Purr for me."

"I'm not purring," she complained.

Oh yes, she was. No matter what she said, she was. The muscles in her body had started to quiver. Her breath was rapid and shallow. It was a language she understood all too well. She wanted him. Her sizzling griddle wanted him.

Rayanne moaned when he shifted his weight into her, again pressing her against the post. He nestled himself into the notch of her thighs. It was a very good place to nestle. He found the exact spot that made her squeak and applied just enough pressure to make her sound like a very vocal mouse.

He didn't stop there, either.

Rios kept on kissing. Kept on nestling. And he kept on pushing and rubbing against her. Squeaking, Rayanne decided she'd let him carry on like this for a while longer. Then she could torture him. Somehow. It was so hard to concentrate on torture plans when he was, well, torturing her.

Rios covered her breast with his palm. Her limp blouse and bra weren't really barriers because they were so thin. He gave a throaty growl of approval and feathered his fingers over her nipples, first one and then the other, bringing them to peaks.

"Rios," she whispered when he kissed her breasts through her blouse.

"It's all right." He moved his mouth next to her ear and kissed her there. "I know what you want."

Yes, he did, Rayanne decided. He apparently knew exactly what she wanted. Better yet, he knew how to give it to her. He, well, bumped her in just the right spot.

Rayanne gasped. "Mercy, you blurred my vision."

"That's good. Want me to do it again?"

"Yes. Oh, yes."

Rios did. He bumped her again. And then he kissed her, stroking her with his tongue in rhythm to those magic bumps. He fisted his hands in her hair and forced her head back so he could take her neck.

"Rios," she said again. She returned the favor and kissed his neck and the surrounding areas.

"Yes?"

Without waiting to hear what she had to say, he slid his hands to her waist and pushed up her top. He dragged the cups of her bra down. He covered one nipple and then the other with his mouth, leaving them shiny wet.

He mumbled something, but the drums were pounding in her head so she couldn't hear him. It didn't matter. His face told her everything she needed to know. He would keep right on going unless she stopped him.

She wouldn't stop him just yet.

In another minute.

Rios slid his hand lower, because he obviously knew that's what she wanted. Oh, yes, that's what she wanted. A soft ache spread through her. He touched her, played with her until her nails dug into his back. Until she was driving herself against him, pleading for more. Heavens, yes, it was what she wanted.

''Yoo-hoo,'' someone called.

Yoo-hoo? Rayanne knew she was making odd little squeaky sounds, but she didn't think she had said yoo-hoo. Stunned, confused and incredibly frustrated, she untangled herself from Rios's grip. Looking into the rain, she saw Evie walking toward the stables.

''Oh, shoot,'' Rayanne said. And because she couldn't think of anything better to say, she repeated it.

The torture stuff would have to wait.

RIOS DIDN'T CARE one bit for the yoo-hoo or the person who'd said it. He barely got Rayanne's clothes straightened before Evie came waltzing into the stables.

''What are you doing out here?'' he asked the woman. He didn't say it nicely, either. There was a raw edge to his tone. He couldn't help it. Evie's timing was as awful as her taste in foam rubber cows.

Evie was wet. Soaked. And she stood there grinning, rocking on her heels with her hands behind her back. ''I came to check on you.''

He nearly told her they didn't need checking on, but at the last moment Rios remembered to show some respect. ''As you can see, we're fine.'' He couldn't walk, probably couldn't even move, had possibly permanently harmed his manhood, but he was fine. Now, if only the fabric of his jeans held up. He thought it might rip apart at any moment.

With a sudden look of alarm on her face, Evie leaned

closer and stared at Rayanne. "What happened to your mouth?"

"Uh, I ate some of those green suckers."

Her gaze traveled to Rios. "And you must have been eating them, too," Evie said somewhat smugly. "Because I think I see a tinge of green on your lips, as well."

No doubt. Heck, with all the kissing he'd just done, Rayanne had transferred plenty of color to him.

"You told her, I guess." Evie gave a relieved sigh. "Well, I'm glad you did. Guess those lime-flavored kisses really softened the blow, huh?"

"Softened what blow?" Rayanne asked, sounding as if she'd just woken from a heavy sleep.

"Well, the news about the land, of course."

Rayanne shook her head. "What about the land?"

"Oh, dear. I've said something I shouldn't have." Evie pressed her fingers to her mouth. "I guess he didn't tell you, after all?"

Rios groaned. *Oh, dear,* was right. It was right up there with that blasted yoo-hoo. Rayanne was looking straight at him, and he knew she was about to demand some answers. Worse, he'd have to come up with them.

"What Evie should have told you was—" And here it came. The news that would make Rayanne mad at him for another eleven years. "She sold me some land."

Rayanne stared at him. "What land?"

"Her land. About two hundred acres of it."

Rayanne volleyed glances between her aunt and him, but when she stopped volleying, she narrowed her eyes at him. "She sold you Garrett land? She sold you Garrett land! She sold you—"

"Yes," Rios interrupted.

"She sold you—"

"Yes, she did." He didn't think it was a good idea for Rayanne to keep repeating that thought. She seemed to get madder each time it came out. "But I don't really consider it mine. Evie was just a little short of funds and wouldn't take a loan from me."

Rayanne whirled toward her aunt. "You were short of funds and you went to Rios instead of calling me?"

Evie shrugged. "I didn't want to bother you. It took me a while to get a new bumper sticker contract. Besides, we didn't really need all that land. You're never here, and I got tired of fiddling with it."

"Fiddling with it?" Rayanne repeated. "Aunt Evie, that land has been in our family for over a hundred years."

"Oh, dear. I knew you'd take this hard. Your heart's tied to this place. Well, I'm sorry, but I'm just no good at ranching, Rayanne, and I had a lot more land than I'd ever use. Besides, it's like I said—I needed some cash."

"I could have helped you with the money," Rayanne insisted.

"I didn't want to take your money."

Rayanne hiked her thumb in Rios's direction. "But you'd take his? I cannot believe this. You sold him Garrett land."

Rios stepped toward her, hoping he could soothe her ruffled feathers. Evie looked like she was ready to start bawling, and Rayanne looked ready to implode. He didn't want a bawling implosion happening tonight. Well, unless it involved making love to Rayanne. He was pretty sure that wouldn't happen anytime soon, after what she'd just learned.

"If you have to blame someone, blame me," he told Rayanne.

"Oh, don't worry, I do." She poked him in the chest. "You should have called me the minute Aunt Evie came to you with this stupid idea."

She'd apparently forgotten that she'd ripped his shirt half off him because she looked confused when her poking fingers landed on his chest hair. She looked at the chest hair. Then him. Rayanne made a sound of pure frustration and stormed off.

"You think I should have told her that she's got a pale lime green hickey on the left side of her neck?" Evie asked, her forehead wrinkled in concern.

Rios shook his head. "She'll figure it out soon enough."

Evie shrugged in a suit-yourself gesture. "But maybe you'd like to know that you've got even bigger and darker ones on your..." She leaned closer and had a better look. "Right earlobe. Your collarbone. Your neck, just below your jawline. There's another one on the corner of your mouth. I really hate to be the one to point it out, but I think there's a few in your chest region, as well. It makes you look like you're sort of coming down with some kind of hives."

Well, green spots wouldn't be an easy thing to explain to everyone, especially if Rayanne was sporting them, too. He probably should head home and see if he could scrub them off. If not, then it would add a whole new level of difficulty to the upcoming week. He didn't want that. It appeared the week would be next to impossible as it was.

7

"Behind every argument is someone else's ignorance."

—Bumper Ditties by Evie E. Garrett

THE QUINN RANCH had always reminded Rayanne a little of South Fork from the old television show *Dallas*. There was the perfectly painted white house in the middle of acres of green pastures. Eight hundred and eighty-five acres, to be exact. There were at least that many cows, horses and other farm critters. The place had huge stately oaks, and ponds and barns galore. In the driveway, there was a big white luxury car with longhorns for a hood ornament. Yes, South Fork.

Or something.

Rayanne parked her aunt's car in the driveway and seriously questioned her sanity. Of course, she'd had reason to question her sanity for a while now. Since her return, since the lipstick-fixing session by the car and especially since the wild heated kisses the night before in the stables. It seemed all her sanity questioning had one common denominator. Rios.

What could she possibly have been thinking about when she let him kiss her that way? That was the problem—she hadn't thought. She'd reacted. And, simply put, she had let him kiss her blind. She had a green hickey to prove it, too.

Worse, he'd been kissing her blind all the while knowing he owned a good chunk of her family's land. He also kissed her when he knew he should have told her all about this long before Evie spilled the proverbial beans. He darn sure should have told her before he started putting his hand up her blouse.

And before he started doing that other stuff to her.

Well, one thing was for sure—she needed to get all this cleared up so she could leave Longhorn. She had to get away from Rios before she did something really stupid. Well, more stupid than she'd already done. Of course, it might be hard to top that kiss-and-grind session in the barn.

She'd stayed awake half the night trying to figure out what she was going to do. She finally decided there was nothing she could do about Rios. He seemed to be one of those green-hickey facts of life she couldn't escape. However, there was a possibility she could do something about her aunt. It was obvious that Evie needed some help managing the ranch. Or at least what was left of the ranch.

Of course, she could always move back to Longhorn so she could personally take control of things. But that would be drastic action. Well, sort of drastic. And she'd need a job if she moved back. A job Rios had offered her. A job she really couldn't consider because her mouth just couldn't seem to stay away from his.

Great day in the morning. Why couldn't this be easier?

And even if she moved back and became a deputy, it wouldn't solve all her problems. She also needed to keep Evie out of jail, and the quickest way to assure that was for her to have a little chat with Bennie Quinn. Hence, the visit that she hoped wouldn't be a complete waste of time.

"Mr. Quinn?" she called from the steps of the porch. She waited for a response but heard nothing. "Mr. Quinn, it's Rayanne Garrett. I need to talk to you."

The front door flew open, but he didn't come out. "I got nothing to talk about, and you're trespassing. Your big-city badge don't mean squat around here."

So this was his attitude? She should have expected it from a sourpuss like Bennie. "Mr. Quinn, I think if we could just sit down and talk, then we could clear all of—"

"Did Rios send you?"

"No." If he'd had a say in it, Rios wouldn't have let her come to the Quinn ranch. Fortunately, he didn't know anything about this little visit. "I read the statement you gave about the incident, and I want to discuss what happened between you and my aunt."

He didn't leave the darkened doorway. "She wanted to kill me, that's what. Nothing to discuss. So you can just turn around and leave the way you came."

Rayanne had no intention of giving up that easily. "Please, Mr. Quinn, I just need a moment of your time. This is about Mattie, too. You must know how much she cares for Evie—"

"You leave my granddaughter out of this."

"That's hard to do when it affects her."

A few seconds later Bennie walked onto the porch. Rayanne tried not to stare, but it was hard not to. The years certainly hadn't been kind to him at all. The man's jowls had jowls. His wrinkles had wrinkles. And he had more hair in his eyebrows than he did on his head.

"Mattie told me you'd come back to town." Bennie didn't say anything else for a while. It seemed as if he was sizing her up. "She likes you, you know."

Since that seemed to be a semi-friendly remark, Rayanne offered him a smile. "Well, that's good. I like her, too. She's a sweet child."

And now that Rayanne had gotten a good look at the man challenging Rios for custody, she was more than a little concerned. How could such an old man keep up with an active little girl? It didn't seem right, especially when Mattie had a loving father who seemed more than willing to take care of her.

Rayanne quickly put that observation aside. It wasn't her business. Even though it sort of felt like it was. Rios was a friend, despite all the kissing and embarrassing moments they'd had. And despite that land-buying incident. She certainly didn't want him to lose Mattie. Too bad she didn't know what to do to keep that from happening. Maybe she could somehow work that into her conversation with Bennie, especially since it was the custody battle that had provoked Evie into doing something stupid.

"It doesn't matter how Mattie feels about you," Bennie continued. "I'm not gonna drop those charges against Evie. You don't expect me to forget she tried to kill me, do you?"

"I'm not sure she actually tried to do that. Could we just sit down and talk about this like adults?"

He stared at her hard. And continued to do so for a long time. "Evie wasn't acting like an adult when she came out here that day, now was she? She acted like a dingbat."

Rayanne made a sound of agreement. "But what sense does it make to send Evie to jail? The woman is sixty-one years old."

His response shocked her. He smiled. Bennie parted those wrinkly lips and practically grinned. "From where I'm standing, sending Evie to the pokey makes a whole heck of a lot of sense. That or the nuthouse, which is where she probably belongs. This conversation is over, little lady. It's time for you to leave."

"But Mr. Quinn—"

"I meant what I said." His voice dropped some serious notches. "You are trespassing, and on top of it, you're making things worse for Evie."

That significantly improved her posture. "How?"

"Because you've riled me, that's why. Now, you've got five seconds to get back in that car and get the devil out of here, or I'll call Arnette and have her come out here and arrest you for trespassing."

Great. Just great. Rayanne kicked a rock as she headed to the car. She wanted to kick herself. She'd known Bennie Quinn all her life and knew it would have been easier to bargain with a tree knot than with him. She truly hoped she hadn't made things worse.

She climbed into the car, turned the key in the ignition and heard an odd little clicking sound. That's all. Just that sound.

"You got two seconds left," Bennie called.

Rayanne tried again. More clicks. She stepped out of the car. "It won't start."

"You got one second to get off my land," Bennie offered. And, apparently to prove his point, he pulled a tiny phone from his pocket. "It's sure not gonna look good on your big city police record when you get arrested for trespassing."

Well, this was a fine how do you do. She grabbed her purse and went to take out her own phone so she could call Freda to come and pick her up. There was just one problem—her phone wasn't there. She remembered Evie had borrowed it earlier.

"I don't suppose you'd let me use your phone to call Freda?" she asked.

"Nope." Bennie kept his gaze on her while he punched in some numbers. "You'd best get to walking, little lady, because Arnette's gonna have no choice but to come out here and arrest you. Might go easier on you if you were actually off my property by the time she gets here."

Rayanne stood for a moment to weigh her options. She didn't have any. She didn't know how to fix clicking sounds in a car engine and she didn't have time or the resources to send out smoke signals to Freda.

Rayanne slammed the car door and started walking. Behind her, she heard Bennie continue to make his call. A call that might lead to a potentially embarrassing situation for her.

Rayanne prayed Arnette would come alone. While she was at it, she added something pretty significant to that prayer. Maybe, just maybe, Arnette wouldn't tell her boss. Maybe Rios wouldn't find out anything at all about this.

She was fairly sure she heard the angels in heaven snicker when she added that last part.

RIOS FOUND HER WALKING up the dirt road that led to the highway. Rayanne had covered some distance, about a mile, but she was still a long way from home. She was also a long way from being happy. Her shoulders were hunched. She kicked at rocks. And she was mumbling under her breath. Well, at least this time he wasn't the cause of her unhappiness. Maybe that was progress.

He pulled up beside her and lowered the window of his truck. "Get in. I'll drive you back."

She gave him one of those I'm-having-a-real-bad-day looks. "Are you going to arrest me for trespassing?"

"No, but Bennie will probably file a complaint."

"Great." And she did more of that mumbling under her breath.

"Don't worry. I'll figure out a way to talk him out of it."

"You can't talk that man out of anything." Looking dejected, she climbed inside the truck.

Probably not, but talking him out of it was a figure of speech. Rios would likely pay Rayanne's fine on the sly and never bring up the incident again. It was the least he could do for her after seeing that pale green hickey he'd left on her neck. Fortunately, his had scrubbed off, but apparently he had better suction or more intense color-embedding techniques than she did.

"I can't believe Bennie called you," she commented. "He said he was calling Arnette."

"He did, but she couldn't come. She had the baby this morning. A boy. Eight pounds and a couple of ounces."

"Please tell her I'm happy for her."

But there was nothing congratulatory about her tone. Not that Rios expected there to be. He could guess what had gone on between Bennie and her. She'd tried to fix things, and Bennie hadn't been receptive. Now she felt lower than hoof grit. Well, it was obviously time to try to cheer her up. But how? There weren't a lot of subjects they could discuss that wouldn't lead them right to Evie's dilemma.

Ah, it finally came to him. The perfect subject. "I was lying in bed last night thinking about sex."

She made a face and folded her arms over her chest. "Rios, I don't think I want to hear this. This sounds kind of personal."

"Not that kind of sex. What I had in mind was something more along the lines of making love. To you. I want you, Rayanne. But it's more than just that. I care for you more than I've ever cared for any other woman. I thought it was about time I told you that, and that's why I was thinking about us doing something about it."

She stared as if he'd truly turned to hoof grit right in front of her eyes. "That wouldn't be a smart idea, and that's the mildest way I know how to say it."

True, but this was the really good part Rios thought

she might like to hear. "That's the same conclusion I came to last night. If I started fooling around with you and Bennie found out about it, he'd use that against me in the custody hearing. I've got enough going against me as it is. So, the way I see it, we'll just have to stick with being friends."

Bingo. It was something she wanted to hear. Well, maybe. At first, she looked ready to agree with him. Then her eyebrow slowly came up. "You mean that?" she asked.

"Sure." And he did. But underneath all that logical thought, Rios knew he could never be just plain old friends with Rayanne. Still, he'd keep that to himself. No need to muddy the waters between them when they were just starting to clear up.

"Then…" She paused as if still giving that some thought. "All we have to do is just not kiss or anything."

Yes, that was it. Well, it was except for the *anything* part. That was giving him the most trouble. "That's right. No kissing or anything. I mean, it's for the best and all, since you'll be leaving town as soon as you settle Evie's problems. Uh, you will be leaving, I suppose?"

"Yes. Of course. Except I haven't figured out exactly how to settle Evie's problems yet. One way or another, I need to make Bennie understand how things really are."

"The best way to do that is to let me deputize you." And because he knew she'd put up a fuss, he continued. "Just hear me out. Bennie will have to talk to you if you're wearing a badge. It'll give you a license, a legal one, to get those answers you think you stand a chance of getting from him.''

It seemed she was about to smile or laugh hysterically, but she didn't. There was a split second of satisfaction in her eyes before they narrowed. Obviously, she considered both sides of this coin.

''Sweet heaven.'' She huffed out a breath. ''I can't believe I'm going to agree to this.''

He didn't dare smile. Didn't dare. Didn't dare even let his mouth quiver. But inside he was doing some line dancing. She was going to do it. Rayanne was going to allow him to deputize her. Why that made him so happy, he didn't know. After all, this probably wasn't the best idea he'd ever come up with.

''I'll have to call New York and arrange for a leave of absence,'' she added.

By now the mental line dancing had stopped completely, and Rios was starting to think about the implications of what he'd done. He'd offered Rayanne a job, and she'd accepted. She'd be working for him, no less. In Longhorn.

Now what was wrong with this picture?

Remembering he was in the middle of a conversation, Rios asked, ''Will getting a leave of absence be a problem?''

''No. I'm sure Malcolm can push it through for me.''

So, it seemed Dr. Whine was good for something, after all. ''All right. We can go by the office, pick up your badge, and I can swear you in.''

She held up her hand. "Wait a minute. I have a couple of conditions before I accept this."

Of course. Conditions. Rios hadn't thought she'd give in without some of those. Maybe she would condition herself right out of accepting the job. "What?"

"Well, first of all, you can't boss me around."

"But I'll be your boss," he replied.

"But no bossing, got that?"

Unfortunately, he understood exactly what she meant. "No bossing unless the situation dictates it."

Rayanne didn't answer right away. She gave that some thought. Apparently plenty of thought. She finally nodded. "But even then, you can't gloat."

"Deal. No gloating." He could live with—

"Another condition," she continued. "I notice you don't carry a gun, but I'd want to."

That he could live with, too. "Suit yourself. I don't think you'll find that necessary, though."

"Indulge me. I like the idea of carrying a weapon if I'm also wearing a badge. And that brings me to the third condition—I don't want you to tell anyone about this unless it's absolutely necessary."

"Beg your pardon?"

"I don't want you to tell a lot of people about this like you did about that chicken."

"I only told Freda. She told everyone else."

"Okay, then don't tell Freda. Or Aunt Evie." Rayanne paused. "Or Arnette."

"Then how are you supposed to exert your authority if nobody knows you're my deputy?"

"I'll manage. And another thing—I'm not your deputy. I'll be a temporary law enforcement assistant in the Longhorn Police Department.''

Rios hitched a thumb to his chest. ''A department that I just happen to run because I'm the sheriff.''

She frowned. ''That's awfully close to gloating, and we already agreed you wouldn't do that, right?''

''Right.'' That didn't mean he couldn't gloat later. In private. ''So, let me get this straight. You'll become a deputy, but you don't want anyone to know and you won't take orders from me. Oh, and you want to carry a gun even though I don't.''

''That's right. Do we have a deal then?''

''Not just yet.'' Rios had some conditions of his own. ''I have no doubt that you're a good cop up in New York City, but I don't really want you running this particular investigation. That means I don't want you going off half-cocked the next time you talk to Bennie.''

''I've never gone off half-cocked in my entire life.''

''That's debatable,'' he corrected. ''When you talk to Bennie, you've got to leave the emotional stuff out of it.''

''Emotional stuff?'' She made it sound like some kind of disease. ''I assure you, Rios, I can handle an interrogation.''

''A New York interrogation, yes, but you need a little advice about handling Bennie. It's best to let him think he's in control. If not, he's just going to pull rank and call in one of his cousins. Another thing, when you're interrogating someone in New York, I'm sure it's not personal like it'll be when you talk to Bennie. You have to remember that and stay calm.''

''Thanks for the advice, but I know what I'm doing. Just as soon as you swear me in, I'll go right back out and have a nice long talk with Bennie Quinn.''

Rios tried to keep the groan down to a low volume. ''Then I suppose I'll go with you.''

''Not necessary.''

''Oh, yes it is,'' he assured her.

''That sounds a little like bossing, and we agreed you wouldn't do that.''

''We also agreed I could boss you around if the situation dictates. Believe me, this dictates.''

RAYANNE COULD SEE Bennie's jaw tighten considerably when Rios and she approached him. Rayanne smiled inside. She had a badge pinned to her shirt and was carrying a holstered .38 that she prayed was in working order. She was ready for anything he might try. In fact, she hoped he pulled something, because the idea of arresting him appealed to her.

''That's far enough,'' Bennie yelled from his porch. He tipped his head to Rios, who was standing next to Rayanne. ''What are you doing here?''

''My deputy and I are here to question you about your statement regarding the alleged incident with Evie.''

He made a rough sound of disapproval. ''Your deputy? Since when?''

''Since about an hour ago.''

Another sound, louder and more disapproving than the first. ''Well, well, this is an unholy pact if there ever was one. But don't either one of you come a step farther. Any questions you ask me, you can do it when Buck's around.''

"Buck?" Rayanne softly questioned Rios.

"Buchanan Quinn, his lawyer. And his second cousin. More professional incest.''

Rayanne made a sound of disapproval. "All right, if you insist that your lawyer be present, then I—uh, we expect you at the sheriff's office in one hour. Be prepared for a long interrogation.'' Rayanne paused. "Or you can answer one or two questions now and get it over with. It's up to you.''

She could tell he was thinking about it, and finally he nodded. "Ask your questions and then get off my land.''

Rayanne didn't dare show any signs of relief, but she was very much relieved. Her first challenge, and she'd succeeded. Well, partially. "I'm glad you decided to cooperate. What I want to know is did you provoke Evie in any way before she allegedly aimed a weapon at you?''

"There's nothing alleged about it.''

"Maybe, but did you provoke her?" she repeated.

"No. That crazy woman just drove up, parked her car at the end of the road and aimed a gun at my hackberry tree.''

"At your tree? Then she wasn't aiming at you," Rayanne said.

Bennie screwed up his face. The saggy skin was seemingly twisted around his bulbous red nose. "If she was aiming at my tree, then she was aiming at me. And she wanted to shoot me.''

"Not necessarily. Perhaps she saw some sort of wild animal or something in your yard. Maybe a bear—"

"There weren't any wild animals!" Bennie yelled. "Just one crazy woman with an old bent-up twenty-two aimed at me and my tree."

Rayanne latched on to that. "Bent-up, huh? So, let me get this straight—a sixty-one-year-old woman aims an old bent-up twenty-two, and you automatically assume she wants to shoot you? Mr. Quinn, had Evie ever shown any overt hostility to you before?"

"Overt?" He looked at Rios. "What the heck does that mean?"

"It means obvious. What Rayanne wants to know is did Evie ever threaten you before that day?"

"You know darn well she didn't. I already told you this when you asked me. Now, by my way of figuring it, I've answered enough questions today."

"Not just yet." Rayanne didn't give him time to object. "I want you to go back over what happened that day, and I think you'll see that Evie had no intentions of harming you."

"No intentions? The woman aimed at me."

"Not at you. By your own admission, you said she was aiming at your tree."

Bennie's face twisted up even more, and though Rayanne hadn't thought it possible, his nose got redder. "Now you're turning my words around. I know what happened. That crazy old bat was mad because I wouldn't hand over my granddaughter to Rios, and so she came here and tried to shoot me."

Rayanne put a check on her temper. She didn't like

anyone calling Evie a crazy old bat even if there were times when Evie acted like one. "I'll use your own words again—she was aiming at your hackberry. Therefore, she couldn't have been trying to hurt you. Isn't that right, Mr. Quinn?"

"No. Evie was mad. Now, maybe she didn't actually threaten me in that, uh, overt kind of way you were talking about, but she came here to try to force me into giving up what's mine."

"What's *yours?*" Rios and Rayanne said in unison.

"Are you talking about Mattie?" Rayanne questioned.

"You're darn right I am. She's mine, and I'm not gonna just hand her over to some bar-brawling, skirt-chasing rodeo rider who happened to sweet-talk my daughter into bed."

"So that's what this is really all about?" Rayanne asked, tapping her foot. "It's about custody of Mattie."

"I never said it wasn't." He aimed a finger at them. "I'll even tell you both something else. If Rios will drop his claim on my granddaughter, then I'll drop the charges against Evie."

In Rayanne's opinion, that was the wrong thing to say. Not just the wrong thing, but the most wrong thing that could have ever come out of his wrong-saying mouth. "Why, you old geezer. You miserable, grouchy old geezer."

Rios caught onto her arm. "Rayanne, I think—"

Rayanne quickly shook him off. "How dare you use that sweet child or my aunt to get your way. You're being petty and selfish. Mattie is Rios's daughter, and he has a right to raise her. Patricia wanted that, and you darn well know it. That's what galls you about this. You want something you can't have. And as for Evie, I can see why she took aim at you—your tree.''

''Uh, Rayanne—''

She didn't let Rios finish what he had to say. She was so mad she couldn't see straight, and she aimed that anger at the red-nosed old geezer on the porch. ''Just what makes you think you're good enough to raise Mattie, huh? You're old and you're grouchy. Mattie doesn't need that. She needs a family and she can have that with Rios.''

''And how do you figure that, little lady? Rios is just Rios.''

''Rios is a fine man and a respected peace officer in this town. And he won't have to raise Mattie alone. Evie and Freda will help, and I'll help, too, when I'm here.'' She hadn't intended to say that, but it sort of flew out along with the other things she was yelling. ''What could you possibly offer her except a bunch of ingrate cousins who have their noses stuck so far up your rear end that they can't see their own noses on their own faces?''

She heard Rios groan at that bad analogy. She groaned a little, too. Some people could come up with great lines while under pressure, but Rayanne had to admit she wasn't one of them. Under the circumstances, it was the best she could do.

Bennie's voice rose a considerable notch. ''I've taken all the guff I plan to take from you, little lady. That badge doesn't give you a right to call me names. Now,

get off my land before I phone one of my ingrate cousins. Go home to that crazy old bat of an aunt and tell
her I'll see her in court.'' He turned, went inside and
slammed the door.

Rayanne had to bite her lip to keep from screaming.

''Pardon me if this sounds a little like bossing,'' Rios
said calmly. ''But didn't I tell you not to come in here
half-cocked?''

She made an angry shivering sound. ''He just got me
so mad. He's using Evie to try to get custody of Mattie.
Doesn't that make you furious?''

''Yes, it does, but that's something we'll work out in
court, not here in Bennie's front yard.'' He caught her
arm and started toward the truck. ''Believe me, I'll let
the judge know exactly what Bennie's trying to pull. I
have to believe it'll end up helping my case. In fact, the
judge might dismiss Bennie's petition entirely.''

''But in the meantime, how can you be so calm?''

''What choice do I have? If I get mad and bad-mouth
Bennie, it'll only end up hurting Mattie. He's her grand-
father, and she loves him.''

Lord, Rayanne had forgotten that. She'd apparently
also forgotten everything that centered on logic and
standard police procedures. She'd screamed at the alleged victim of the alleged crime. Worse, she'd majorly
ticked off Bennie, and that couldn't be good for Evie
or for Rios.

''Oh, Rios, I'm so sorry. I probably hurt your chances
with the custody. Bennie will probably call his cousin
Judge Ira—''

''Ira's not deciding this custody case. I had the petition moved to the judge in Floresville. I was about a hundred percent sure I wouldn't get a fair shake with Bennie's cousin.''

''Well, good. That's something, at least. Maybe I didn't mess that up.''

''No, but you do need to work on your interrogation skills.'' He held up his hand. ''I know, that sounds a little like bossing.''

It sounded a lot like it, but he was right. She'd blown it. And it wasn't as if she didn't know how to interrogate someone. She did. She'd let emotion get the better part of her. ''I'm not used to questioning anyone when there's something personal at stake,'' she mumbled.

And in this case there was a lot personal at stake.

However, at the moment Rayanne didn't want to think long and hard about who or what that *personal at stake* involved. It wasn't just Evie or Bennie. Somehow, Mattie had gotten mixed up in this, too. And Rios, of course. But then, he'd been part of the mix for years now. Heck, he was the main reason the mix was confusing.

Rios hooked his arm around her neck. ''Don't worry, little lady,'' he teased, imitating Bennie's croaky voice. ''You'll get the hang of this deputy stuff soon enough.''

Rayanne had to tell him what he could do with that suggestion—that was a given.

But she smiled when she did it.

8

"Time heals, but everybody else wants a fee."
　　　—Bumper Ditties by Evie E. Garrett

"I FIXED YOU some breakfast."

Rayanne forced her eyelids open at the sound of Mattie's voice. It was early. Very early. After working the swing shift for four years, Rayanne didn't think her body could function before ten o'clock. Still, this was Mattie. Even if she couldn't function, she intended to get up, or rather sit up.

"That was nice of you to fix me breakfast." Rayanne looked at the tray, hoping she'd see a Twinkie there. She didn't. There was some very dark crusty toast and a Granny Smith apple. She smiled anyway. This was one of those situations where the company outweighed the menu.

"I wanted you to eat something healthy before you went to work today," Mattie explained.

"Thanks." Rayanne picked up the apple. So, Rios had told Mattie about making her a deputy. Well, of course, he had. There wouldn't have been a way for him to keep it from her.

"Because I wouldn't want you to have to arrest any bad guys or anything if you hadn't had a good breakfast,'' Mattie continued. She sat on the edge of the bed and helped herself to a piece of toast. It crunched like a potato chip when she took a bite. ''Do you get to wear a badge?''

''Yes. Your daddy gave it to me yesterday.''

''And you'll get to work with Daddy?''

''Yes, I'll work with him. Not for him.''

Mattie nodded, apparently grasping that right away. Rayanne only hoped Rios caught on soon enough. ''I have on my Friday panties today. Which day do you have on?''

It took Rayanne a moment to switch subjects. ''Mine don't have days, just colors. I'm wearing—'' She had to look under the covers to make sure. ''My peach ones. They have little polka dots on them.''

''Polka dots are nice. Stripes, too.'' Mattie stood and started to play with the fringe on the bedspread.

Rayanne could tell the child wasn't her bubbly self today. ''Is something wrong, Mattie?''

She shrugged, a gesture that reminded Rayanne so much of Rios. Actually, there was a lot of Rios in Mattie. The dark chocolate hair. Those amber-colored eyes. But Rayanne could see some of Patricia Quinn there, too. The shape of Mattie's face and the graceful ease with which she moved. Rayanne had always thought Patricia moved liked a dancer, and her daughter had definitely inherited that.

''You know, you could tell me if anything was wrong,'' Rayanne added when Mattie stayed silent. ''I'm a good listener.''

Mattie sat on the bed and folded her hands in her lap. "Will you say yes if I ask you to do something?"

"That depends on what it is."

"So you wouldn't say yes without hearing what it is first?"

A little concerned, Rayanne put the apple aside. "I'd have to hear it first, but then I'd try very hard to find a way to say yes. What is it, Mattie?"

She took a deep breath. "Okay, here's the deal. I need a mother day after tomorrow. I was wondering if you could do it because Aunt Evie's real nice, but she's too old and nobody in town would believe she's my mother. Miss Freda's nice, too, but she can't be my mother, either. When I asked her, she said something about me being a bright and shining blessing for her but it wouldn't be a bright shining blessing if she had to pretend it was so when it wasn't." She paused and looked at Rayanne. "What does that mean exactly?"

Rayanne frowned. "I'm not sure." It would have been easy to blame the sleepy fog in her head, but quite often she wasn't able to decipher Freda's analogies.

"Anyway, that's when Freda gave me a glass of chocolate milk and told me to come and talk to you."

"Well, I'm, uh, glad she did." At least Rayanne thought she might be glad. She definitely didn't like the idea of Mattie wandering around with something on her mind. "Why do you need a mother?"

"For Grandpa Bennie. I'm staying with him day after tomorrow, and he's always saying how nice it'd be if I had a mother and how sorry and sad he is that I don't. Well, I figured if I had one then he wouldn't keep wishing that, and then him and Daddy wouldn't get in arguments about me anymore.''

Oh, my. A major problem. Rayanne had hoped it was something simple—like the elastic being shot in her Sunday panties. This didn't sound like a one-minute solution. No wonder Freda had spouted something incomprehensible and told Mattie to talk to someone else.

For better or worse, she was that someone else.

Rayanne put her arm around the child's shoulder. ''I'd love to be your mother, honey, but your grandpa Bennie knows that I'm not.'' Rayanne had to replay what she'd said. Had she really told Mattie she'd love to be her mother? Yep, she had.

Was it true?

Rayanne thought about it.

Yes, it seemed that it was.

But this didn't have anything to do with Rios. No, indeed. This was about Mattie's big brown eyes looking pleadingly at her. Mattie could have been anyone's child, and Rayanne would have felt the same.

She would have.

Honestly.

So, why did she feel an extra little place in her heart when she thought about how happy Mattie seemed to make Rios? And vice versa. And why did that little place feel more right than anything had felt in a long, long time?

''I'll tell you what I can do, though,'' Rayanne continued, forcing herself away from little places and other confusing things. She owed Mattie this much, especially after the way she'd botched things with Bennie.

"Maybe I can figure out a way to talk to your grandpa and your daddy. Maybe I can convince them not to argue about you anymore." And this time she wouldn't go in there half-cocked, either. She'd do it the sensible way.

"You think that'll make it better?" Mattie asked.

"I can certainly try. You know the only reason they argue is because they both love you so much?"

"Yes, I know." The voice of experience. Too much experience for one so young. And there was a twinge of pout added to the tone. "That's what everybody says. I don't think it's all the way true, though."

Rayanne hauled the child into her lap. "You're lucky. I mean, you've got two people who love you—your daddy and your grandpa. Plus, you've got Aunt Evie, Miss Freda and me."

"I like that last part best." As if it were the most natural thing in the world, Mattie slipped her arms around Rayanne's neck and snuggled against her. "I heard Miss Freda say your mother died when you were a little girl."

"Yes, she did. My dad, too. When I was just a couple of years older than you are now."

"So you know what it's like?"

Rayanne nodded, not trusting her voice. She knew exactly what it was like. She'd been fortunate to have Evie. Her aunt had taken her in and raised her, but Rayanne would never get over the ache of losing her parents.

Mattie's voice stayed soft, and she wiggled closer. "And that makes us like friends, then."

"You bet." The knock at the door spared Rayanne's eyes from watering, but it was close. "Come in," she called.

With his hands shoved in his pockets, Rios walked in and eyed them with concern. "Is everything all right in here?"

"Just some girl talk," Rayanne assured him.

Mattie unraveled her arms from Rayanne and looked at Rios. "Did you used to be Miss Rayanne's boyfriend a long time ago? That's what I heard Miss Freda say. Miss Freda said you were like Miss Rayanne's honey-glazed ham and cheese in her mustard and rye sandwich of life."

Rayanne flexed her eyebrows. Freda seemed to be a wellspring of information this morning. First she mentioned Rayanne's mother to Mattie, and now this? She'd have a talk with Freda later. She could certainly do without a wellspring before she'd gotten out of bed.

"Rayanne and I dated," Rios said after a long hesitation. He sat on the bed next to his daughter.

Dated and almost became lovers. Well, that was behind them now. Since he'd deputized her, Rios hadn't made one single sexual comment. And he hadn't given her any of those long, steamy looks, either. So maybe that meant he'd be able to think of her as a friend.

A friend.

That didn't create an oozy feeling in her heart. Instead, much to Rayanne's dismay, it caused a knot in her stomach. Not good. Nope, not good at all. She didn't want knots, and a friendship with Rios was the ideal solution to their occasionally stormy relationship.

Well, maybe not ideal. If it were ideal, she wouldn't be dwelling on it, would she? She wouldn't be wondering what it would be like to try to latch on to what was sitting right in front of her.

A horn blared, and Mattie barreled off the bed. "Gotta go. That's the bus. Daddy, remember to get that saddle for me today. Don't forget." She kissed Rayanne and Rios before she hurried out the door.

Rayanne picked up the apple and took a bite. She was still in such deep thought about Mattie it took her a while to realize she was alone with Rios. And he was on her bed.

He lifted the apple out of her hand and took a big, crunching bite.

"SO, IS THIS WHERE you tell me what a rotten father I am?" Rios passed her the apple and braced himself for the answer. If anyone would give him the truth, it was Rayanne. She wouldn't pull any punches, either. If the truth didn't hurt too much, he thought he might be able to take it.

"You won't hear that from me. From what I can tell, you're not a rotten father at all. You're a good one."

"Really?" That was a surprise. "Then what were you and Mattie talking about?"

"She's just concerned about you and Bennie arguing over her. She wanted me to pretend to be her mother so it'd make Bennie happy. She thought that would solve everything."

Rios shook his head. He should have known Mattie would say something like that. "She's been asking about a mother for days. Well, since you came back to town. I'm sorry she tried to bring you into this."

"Don't worry about it. I like Mattie and I like our morning talks."

Another surprise. He hadn't thought of Rayanne as very motherly. Of course, that probably had something to do with all those steamy fantasies he had about her. Nope. There wasn't a motherly image in that whole repertoire of smutty thoughts.

Still, it pleased him that she'd made this kind of connection with his daughter. There weren't a lot of women in Mattie's life, and with the exception of Rayanne, none under the age of fifty.

That was just one of the problems with the present custody situation. He wasn't sure he was giving Mattie the right role models. Heck, he wasn't even sure he was a good father, despite what Rayanne had said.

His father had left before Rios was born, and he'd never met the man, leaving some serious gaps in his fatherly role models. His mother had passed away the year before Rios learned about Mattie, and that meant he no longer had any family of his own. Well, except for Mattie. And he could lose her in this stupid custody battle with Bennie.

"Don't worry about your daughter, Rios," Rayanne said softly. "She's a well-adjusted kid, and she'll turn out just fine."

Then she did something that surprised him. She leaned closer and kissed him on the cheek. Not a hot, I-want-your-body kind of kiss. A friendly kiss. It was, well, nice. But even *nice* while he was sitting in bed with Rayanne could get him into trouble. Rios had to do something about it before parts of his body starting making foolhardy suggestions that would ruin their renewed friendship.

He caught her hand. "Come on, Deputy Garrett, get dressed. It's time we did patrol together."

Since Rayanne didn't seem to object to that suggestion, Rios left so she could dress. A while later she came downstairs squeezed into a pair of jeans that made him wish he hadn't been so accommodating about the nice part. He'd have liked to have seen exactly how she managed to get herself into those jeans. Margarine was his guess. That and maybe a good shoe horn.

"Patrol duty?" she reminded him.

Rios needed that reminder, too. After all, he'd been standing at the bottom of the stairs looking at her. His mouth was open a bit. But what did she expect when she looked like that? It gave a whole new meaning to the expression armed and dangerous.

"Patrol duty," he repeated, sounding moronic. "We'll take my truck."

"Fine."

"What would you be doing on a typical day at NYPD?" he asked as he drove toward town. Best to keep his mind on things that didn't involve smutty thoughts or her jeans.

"There really isn't a typical day. There's always paperwork, and sometimes I have to testify in court."

"So the chicken thing was a fluke?"

She chuckled. "That was just a little bit of excitement in the middle of a sea of boredom."

"Sea of boredom, huh? Well, I can't promise you much better than…" His words trailed off. "Now, I wonder who did that?"

The rubber cow was back, hanging over Main Street, but it was clear to anyone not legally blind that returning it to that very visible spot was a big mistake.

"Sweet heaven," Rayanne mumbled. "It looks like an ad for *The Texas Chainsaw Massacre*."

On a frustrated sigh, Rios agreed. "Evie must have talked somebody into putting it up there. Well, it can't stay, that's for sure. It'll scare little kids."

She eyed it, then him. "Please don't tell me it's part of my job description to take that thing down?"

Well. For a minute he considered it, but he didn't want Rayanne climbing up a ladder in those tight little jeans. It would probably cause a couple of traffic accidents. It would certainly cause him to trip over his tongue, anyway. "No, I'll take care of it later."

"Did you see the cow?" Herman Sheckley, the barber, asked when Rios parked in front of the sheriff's office.

"Yeah, we saw it, Herman. How did it get up there?"

"Evie talked the boys on the high school basketball team into putting it back up." Herman tattled. "The sign advertising the dates of the festival is missing. You reckon those boys did something with it?"

Rios didn't want to speculate what teenage boys would do with a rubber cow and a sticky vinyl sign, but anything was possible. "I'll look into it."

Herman bobbed his eyebrows. "Or maybe your deputy will look into it?"

Rios saw Rayanne stiffen. "I didn't tell him," he quickly assured her. "I only told Mattie."

"Bennie Quinn told me," Herman proudly volunteered. "He's not real happy about it, but Evie's about to bust a gut she's so proud. She's planning a big party this weekend to celebrate."

Rayanne groaned. "Not another party. We haven't finished cleaning after the last one."

Since Rios didn't think any part of this conversation would please her, he took her by the arm and led her into the office. He fixed them both a cup of coffee and sat down for a much-needed little talk.

"Rayanne, I don't think it's realistic for you to believe people won't find out that you're my deputy. That kind of thing tends to get around."

She nodded. Then shrugged. "You're right, but that's not what's bothering me. It's Evie. I wish I could get her to understand that she can't keep having these parties. I worked up a budget for her, but I know she won't stick to it." Rayanne looked at him again. "I suppose I should thank you for helping her out when she was short of funds."

Rios nearly choked on his coffee. "Beg your pardon? I thought you were madder than a hornet at me for buying Garrett land that's been in your family for over a hundred years."

"I guess I wasn't really mad at you. I was just mad at the situation. I know you were just trying to help out like you always do. Heck, Evie was right. She does own more acreage than she'll ever use. Besides, in a lot of ways, you deserve to own that land. You're the son that Evie never had.''

Like the kiss on his cheek she'd given him earlier, that sounded nice. Nice in a friendly sort of way. That probably meant Rayanne had somehow come to grips with the physical attraction between them. Come to grips with it and squelched it.

Oh.

Rios wasn't sure he liked anything being squelched when it came to her attraction for him. Because in their case, that attraction might be just the…what? The first thought that came to mind was icing on the cake. They had a good friendship. Years of companionship. A whole history together. But mixed with all that history had always been something smoldering. Lust. Well, lust and a few more feelings drizzled in with it. Truth was— and he was finally beginning to see this—just as he was the son Evie never had, Rayanne was the wife he had never had.

Or something like that.

Lordy, it was confusing. Rios was still trying to sort through things when the phone rang. He picked up the extension on the front desk and listened to Jessie Herring tell him what was going on with his neighbors, the Beekers family. The sorting out of his feelings would have to wait. Duty called.

Rios hung up and caught her hand. "This might be right up your alley, Deputy Garrett. It appears we have a hostage situation.''

9

"Lead me not into temptation. I can find it all by myself, thank you."
                        —Bumper Ditties by Evie E. Garrett

THE HOSTAGE WAS A COW.

It was a longhorn, to be specific, and to Rayanne it looked like a bag of bones with antlers. An equally skinny bag-of-bones man was in front of the cow, a baseball bat aimed right between the poor animal's eyes. A rather large woman was standing behind the man, and she had another bat raised high in the air lined up directly with the bald spot on the skinny man's head.

Rios had parked his truck down the road, and they'd walked to the scene, but nowhere along the way had he told her the hostage wouldn't be human. Probably for a good reason. Rayanne wasn't sure she would have come. This looked more like a case for men in white coats than the sheriff's office.

"Don't let them see you," Rios whispered. He caught her hand and pulled her behind a sprawling oak. The limbs grew low and thick, but they could still see the pasture where the situation was going on. Or rather where the situation was stationary. No one was moving. "I don't want anyone to get hurt."

Rayanne hadn't been especially alarmed until Rios made that last remark. "Will they come after us?"

"No, but I don't want to force anyone to play a hand they don't really want to play. They do this about once a month."

This? This happened once a month? Amazing. She hadn't thought a cop would run into a situation like this in an entire career, and here Rios got a monthly dose of it. "So, what exactly is going on, anyway?"

He kept his voice so low Rayanne had to lean closer to hear him. "Well, you probably remember Ned Beekers and his wife, Alice?"

Yes, she remembered them and had seen them at Evie's party. However, Rayanne hadn't heard anything about the persistent problem of taking a longhorn hostage, and Evie had been particularly good at passing on those kinds of juicy tidbits.

"Why is Ned holding a bat on that cow?" Rayanne asked, almost afraid to hear the answer.

"Because it belongs to Alice. She had an affair with a man over in Kerrville about five, maybe six years ago. Anyway, Ned thinks the man gave Alice the cow as a sort of present, something to rub in Ned's face, so to speak. Alice says it wasn't a present at all, that she bought it with her own money because she liked the looks of it. So now, whenever they argue, Ned always seems to bring the cow into it. He threatens to bash it. Then Alice gets mad and threatens to bash him."

"Do they ever bash anything?"

"No," he whispered. He was so close she felt his warm breath on her ear. "But they like to make a big fuss about it. With all that experience you have with chickens, a cow should be a piece of cake.''

"Don't go there, Rios. No chicken remarks.'' But Rayanne smiled. And she shivered because his breath tickled her ear. "So, how do you usually talk Ned and Alice into surrendering their bats?''

"That depends. They both still look pretty mad, so it probably won't do much good to try to talk them into anything right now. Let's give them a couple more minutes and see if they start yelling. Yelling in this case would be a good sign.''

Rayanne figured that yelling, angry people would be the last thing Rios would want on his hands. "And why would that be a good sign?''

"Because it gets them talking to each other again. Then we can sort of turn the tables on them.''

It happened again. His breath brushed her ear. And her cheek. It felt like a caress, and Rayanne didn't like the way it sent her heart racing. She tried to inch away from him so it wouldn't happen again. The problem was, she couldn't inch too far without the Beekers seeing her.

Rios craned his neck so he could look between the tree limbs. The adjustment caused him to shift his posture. So much for her inching away from him. Now his chest was against her back.

Ned Beekers said something to his wife, something Rayanne couldn't hear, but she hoped it was good they were talking. Ending this hostage situation took on a new urgency for her. An urgent urgency. The close contact with Rios was starting to make her a little itchy.

"I'll do it! Don't you think I won't, either," Ned yelled. "I'll bop this miserable excuse for a cow right between the eyes."

"And you'll regret it if you do, you miserable excuse for a buzzard!" Alice shouted. "I'll bash your head in just like an overripe watermelon."

Rayanne grimaced at that gruesome image. She leaned back slightly so she could talk to Rios. "This kind of yelling is good, right?"

He nodded. Rayanne knew immediately that he shouldn't have done that. Of course, she shouldn't have leaned back in the first place. The nod brushed his mouth against her cheek. His lips brushed against her ear. And his middle brushed against the back of her middle. All that brushing had an effect on her.

She stiffened.

So did Rios.

Well, at least Rayanne thought he'd stiffened, but then she realized the stiffening was somewhat localized. Extremely localized. Just below his belt and right in the center of his jeans.

Rios mumbled something indistinguishable under his breath. Rayanne didn't dare ask what. She didn't want to know what. It definitely wasn't a good time for this. That localized stiffening seemed to send a weird primal signal for her body to start softening. This wasn't good. Not good at all.

"Please tell me what's happening here really isn't what I think is happening," Rios mumbled.

"No." Which was a stupid answer, because his question didn't make sense. Well, it wouldn't have made sense to anyone but her. Rios wasn't a fool. He could tell she was breathing hard. Besides, she was probably giving off some primal female scent that his primal male nose picked up right away. "I mean yes, it might be happening, but I don't want to talk about it."

"Well, neither do I, but—"

"No buts, and no talking about it," Rayanne insisted. "Maybe it'll just go away if we don't say anything else."

"Doubtful."

"Shh. I said don't say anything else about it. Besides, it's probably all just some kind of adrenaline reaction to the hostage situation."

Rios glanced at her. "I thought you didn't want to say anything else about it?"

"I don't." Rayanne rubbed her hand over her face. "I was just giving you a reasonable explanation for it, that's all."

"There's a reasonable explanation, all right, and it has nothing to do with an adrenaline reaction. Or cake icing."

Rayanne glanced at him over her shoulder. "Cake icing? What does that have to do with anything?"

"It's a metaphor." Rios leaned into her. Well, he didn't actually lean. He pushed his body against her, and she had no trouble figuring out that the mysterious stiffening wasn't her imagination. Unless Rios had taken to carrying a weapon or a flashlight, she could also guess exactly what it was.

"I can't walk now," he told her. "Satisfied?"

Why would he think something like that would satisfy her? This was exactly what she'd been trying to avoid. Rayanne hadn't done a very good job of avoiding it, but that gave him no reason to think she'd be satisfied that she'd heated him up. Well, maybe she was, a little...

Don't go there.

"You make it sound like it's my fault you can't walk," she complained. "I can't help if you have these stupid reactions to—"

He put his hand over her mouth, but since Rayanne didn't like him doing that she kept right on talking. He kept his hand there until he got an odd look on his face. "Did you tongue my fingers?" he asked.

"Huh?"

"Your tongue. Did you just stick it in between my fingers?"

"Maybe." Except it came out garbled since he was still trying to muzzle her. Maybe she had, but it hadn't been intentional. She'd never intentionally stuck her tongue between anyone's fingers. "Why?" That came out garbled, too.

"Because you can't do it, that's why," Rios insisted in an obstinate whisper. "That spot between my fingers is very sensitive, and it's especially sensitive to a woman's tongue."

"Well, if you would move your hand, my tongue wouldn't get caught between your sensitive little fingers." Her protest sounded like a speech delivered in muffled pig Latin. Rayanne shoved his hand away. "I think it's time to add another rule to our working arrangement—no putting your hand over my mouth."

"I won't put my hand on your mouth if you'll stop breathing hard right in my ear. Deal?"

They stared at each other, both looking pleased that they'd managed to accomplish something. Exactly what, Rayanne didn't know, but she was sure she'd gained something from that tongue-in-finger altercation.

Rios gave her a firm nod. "Let's just get this over with, so we can get out of here. Can you shoot that limb?"

She followed the direction of Rios's gaze and spotted the limb that was hanging directly over Ned's arm. "Sure."

"Then do it."

Rayanne withdrew her .38, slipped off the safety and aimed at the leafy projection. With one shot, she clipped the branch, sending it down on Ned. The man quickly jumped out of the way.

"Drop your bat, Ned," Rios called. "And, Alice, you do the same."

Rayanne wished like the devil that Rios hadn't shouted those demands until he got his mouth away from her ear, but his orders seemed to work. Ned dropped his. Alice dropped hers. And the longhorn stood there chewing its cud as if this were the most boring part of its entire day.

"Well, it seems our hostage situation is over," Rios announced, moving from behind the tree.

It was. It was really over. Rayanne couldn't believe what she'd just experienced. Rios's plan had worked. The laid-back, wait-'em-out, shoot-a-tree-limb approach had worked. The hostage situation seemed to be defused, and no one was threatening each other or the cow.

"But what would you have done if I hadn't had a gun?" Rayanne asked with some smugness. After all, she was the one who had ended the whole thing with her expert marksmanship.

Rios reached down and picked up a small rock. With very accurate aim, he pitched it and hit Ned right on the shoulder.

"Hey!" Ned hollered. "Why'd you do that, Rios? I already put down my bat like you told me to."

"I was just proving a point to Rayanne, that's all, Ned. Nothing personal."

That would have worked, too. Again, Rayanne couldn't believe it. Rios could have solved a hostage situation with a rock and a warning. The man was darn good at his job.

"Now what?" Rayanne asked, trying to keep her mouth from gaping. "Do you arrest them?"

"No sense in it. I'll just talk to them a little bit and try to make them see the error of their ways."

"And you can do that?" It seemed like a tall order, but Rayanne didn't doubt him after what had just happened.

"Yep. I can do that." It seemed to her he had a swagger to his walk when he started across the pasture toward the Beekerses. Or maybe it was just that little stiffening problem he'd made her aware of when he bumped into her.

"Well, you're a regular Sheriff Andy Taylor from Longhorn RFD, aren't you?" Rayanne said mockingly.

The swagger turned into a full strut. "Careful, Rayanne, that would make you Deputy Barney Fife, now, wouldn't it?"

She tried not to. She really did. But she couldn't help it. She laughed at his ridiculous attempt at humor.

She watched him stop in front of the cow and give it an affectionate rub between the eyes. He murmured a few words into the longhorn's ear then turned his attention to the Beekerses. All the while he spoke to them, he continued those gentle strokes on the cow. It was such a simple gesture and not unusual for Rios. He always did have a gentle way with animals. And people.

Especially her.

As she stood there in the warm Texas sun and watched Rios work, she could almost smell the starch on his shirt and the saddle soap he'd used to polish his boots. He was the sheriff, all right. A good one. Along with being a good father. And a good man.

Then it hit her. Rios was more than a soft spot in her heart. Much more than a friend. More than someone to be admired. He was the only man she'd ever loved.

Shoot.

Now that she'd finally worked out that little soul-rocking revelation, it left her with one question. What the devil was she going to do about it?

10

"WHY ARE WE COMING to the Saunders's old barn?" Rayanne asked when Rios stopped the truck in front of the outbuilding.

Rios glanced at her, thankful she'd finally said something. Since they left the Beekerses, she had clammed up. Why, he didn't know, but he figured it had something to do with that little whisper-and-nudge session that had gone on earlier.

"I promised Mattie I'd get a saddle for her," he answered.

"Oh, that's right. This is your barn now." She pointed to the house that was snuggled in the middle of some tall pecan trees. "You gave the place a fresh coat of paint. It looks better than it ever did when the Saunderses owned it."

"Thanks." It was a compliment that pleased him far more than he'd thought it would. For some reason he wanted Rayanne to approve of what he'd accomplished. Odd, he hadn't wanted or needed that approval from anyone else other than Mattie.

Rios glanced around his property, trying to see it through Rayanne's eyes. The place wasn't modern by anyone's standards, but it looked lived-in and cared for. That's because it was. He'd worked plenty of hours clearing away old brush, repairing fences and fixing the house and outbuildings. Now the place was truly his, and he'd done his level best to make it a home for Mattie.

"But isn't Bennie your nearest neighbor?" she asked.

"Yes. A downside to living here, I guess. If we got along better, it'd be good for Mattie, though. All she has to do is walk through that peach grove to get to his house."

Rios pulled open the creaking barn doors and went inside. Tiny threads of sunlight seeped through the gaps in the old wood, but it was still pretty dark. Actually, it was pitch dark. He reached for the flashlight that was usually on a hook by the door, but it wasn't there. Only then did he remember he'd seen Mattie playing with it the night before. She'd probably forgotten to put it back.

"How good can you see in the dark?" he asked Rayanne.

"All right, I guess. Why?"

"The saddle's all the way at the back, and I don't want to trip over anything."

"Here." She picked up an old lantern and shook it. "It still has some kerosene in it. Got a match?"

"In the truck." While she waited, he went to the glove compartment and fished out a box of matches. Once he'd lit the wick, he pocketed the matches and they went inside.

Rayanne fell in step behind him. "Say, this place is huge."

"It is. I use it for storage now, but I'll have to clear it out when I bring in more horses."

"You're planning to do that?"

He nodded. "If I add some more breed stock, I figure I'm only ten years or so away from having one of the biggest operations around Longhorn."

"Really? Bigger than Bennie Quinn's place?"

Another nod.

"You've done well for yourself," she told him.

"That surprises you, huh?" Rios spotted the saddle on a rack on the back wall. He stepped around some bales of hay and made his way toward it.

"Not really. I'd heard you were successful riding rodeo. It figures you could carry that success into ranching."

"Careful with those compliments, Rayanne. They just might go straight to my head." Or his heart. But the caution was too little, too late. It seemed just about everything Rayanne said or did went to his heart. It wasn't easy for him to accept that she had that much power over him.

Rios handed her the lantern and hauled the saddle onto his shoulder. Rayanne walked ahead of him, and when she got closer to the door, she blew out the lantern. Obviously, she blew it out a little too soon. Rios didn't see the last bale of hay, and he tripped over it, sending him and the saddle sprawling. His head collided with the pommel, his shoulder with a post. The rest of him collided with the ground.

"Heavens, are you all right?" Rayanne hurried to him and dropped on her knees beside him.

He rubbed his head, groaned and sat up. "I'm fine, I think. Maybe next time, though, you shouldn't get in such a hurry to blow out that lantern. I wasn't kidding when I said I really can't see much in the dark."

"Sorry. I thought you were right behind me."

"No, I was a couple of steps behind those hay bales."

"Well, don't move until we've made sure nothing is broken." Rayanne retrieved the lamp and used his matches to light it. She set it on a hay bale a few yards away, and the golden light sprayed all around them.

"Okay, where do you hurt?" she asked, kneeling beside him again.

Rios intended to answer her, he really did, but the words didn't make it out of his mouth. That's because he made the mistake of looking at her.

Their gazes locked. His heart slammed against his chest. And it just kept on slamming. Maybe he was still in a lather about that whispering session, and maybe he'd been in a lather since he'd seen Rayanne in New York. Rios suddenly didn't care.

She was here.

He was here.

They were alone.

And he wanted her mouth for supper.

Before he could talk himself out of it, Rios leaned over and put his mouth right next to hers.

"What do you think you're doing?" But she didn't sound puzzled. Or even shocked. There was a lot of breath in her voice, whispery, sexy breath, and she darn sure didn't move away.

"I'm stirring a pot that probably shouldn't be stirred." Rios brushed his lips against her earlobe. "And this time, I won't leave any green hickeys."

Rayanne shivered, and a tiny sound came from deep within her throat. An unconscious invitation for him to give her more. It was the only invitation he needed.

"It doesn't feel like you're stirring a pot," she said. "It feels like you're kissing my ear."

He gave it some thought. "That, too."

She grabbed his shirt with both hands and locked him in a fierce grip. To stop him, was Rios's first thought. But she sure didn't do that. She grabbed him. That was another invitation, as far as he was concerned.

He nuzzled the little area just below her ear, dampening it slightly with the tip of his tongue, then whispered a hot, soft breath over the same spot.

Rayanne whimpered.

The seductive dance with his mouth continued. Rios went from her ear to her cheek, making the journey one long, slow kiss.

"Don't worry," he said, in case she planned to protest. "We'll just play around for a while. No one will ever have to know but us. How long has it been since someone played with you, Rayanne?"

She whimpered again when he kissed her neck. "About three years ago, and I didn't have, uh, much fun."

Three years? And he thought his love life had been

sluggish. Hers had obviously come to a screeching halt. "And you didn't have much fun, you say?"

She shook her head. "A very disappointing encounter."

"Well, heck, I'm surprised you didn't give up on men altogether." He slipped one hand behind her neck and eased her to the ground.

"I have given up on them."

No, she hadn't. She was here with him, and whether she knew it or not, her body was still issuing a lot of invitations. Rios leaned over her and placed a forearm on each side of her head. "Tell you what, Rayanne. Let's see if we can have some fun."

"All right," she said dreamily. "Will you kiss me again?"

His gaze moved to her mouth. And stayed there. With the ease of a man who had all the time in the world, he visually traced her lips. "I was giving that some thought, yes."

"And?"

"And I decided…"

But he paused. Obviously for too long. So Rayanne did something he hadn't counted on. She kissed him. With her hands still filled with his shirt, she wrenched him closer until she forced their mouths to meet. And they met, all right. There were no preliminaries, no yearning looks, no soft caressing breaths, no gentleness. Just them. Two people kissing each other as if they'd never have the chance to, ever again.

"I got tired of waiting for you to decide," she said when they had to break apart to breathe.

"Yeah, I figured that out for myself."

He drew in a gulp of air through his mouth, taking in her taste and scent at once. The sensations raced through him and stirred every drop of his blood.

Rios kissed her again, twisting and knotting his fingers through her hair so he completely controlled the movement of her head. The soft hay shifted, rolling him on top of her. Rayanne didn't resist him. She automatically adjusted her body to accommodate his weight.

The stretchy top didn't give him much resistance when he caught the scooped neck and pulled it down to expose her breasts. He lowered his head and brushed the tip of his tongue over her peaked nipple. She moaned, and her back bowed, thrusting her breasts higher so he could easily take her nipple into his mouth.

When his lips closed around the hard bud and his tongue circled it, drawing it deeply into his mouth, she bucked beneath him. And, Lord, could the woman buck. Rios was suddenly very glad he'd been so good at bronc riding. Of course, that kind of riding had never been quite this exciting.

"I want more," he informed her, fingering the clasp of her bra. He whispered his words directly against her wet skin.

"Yes. Yes. More sounds good."

Very encouraged by her agreement, he decided to give things a little shove. Well, actually a well-placed shove. He shoved his knee between hers, pushing his hard thigh up against a place he thought would please her. It must have because she started making little squeaky noises. Rios kept up that pressure until the squeaky noises turned to moans, and she was bearing down as hard as he was.

Rayanne's breath hitched in her throat. "I'll die if you keep doing that."

It didn't slow him down. This kind of dying was exactly what he wanted her to do. Three years was a long time to go without dying.

He added a new dimension to the torture session. He slid his hand down her stomach and lower, drawing back his leg slightly so he could caress her. Not with fingertips. Not gently, either. He fit his hand to her intimately. As if the fabric of her jeans didn't exist, he touched her.

"Do you like the way I play, Rayanne?"

"Yes," she mindlessly agreed. She ripped open his shirt and ran her hands over his chest. "Play harder."

That wouldn't be a problem. Things were getting pretty hard.

She went after his zipper, shoving it down. "Harder, I said."

Well, now, as if he could turn down a request like that. If the woman wanted harder, that's exactly what she would get. He went after her zipper. Stretching his hand into her jeans, he found a snug little place that made her say things Rios was sure she didn't mean—something about him being a sex god and that she would love and cherish him for the rest of her life.

Well, maybe in her eyes he was a sex god. At the moment, anyway. The woman was certainly entitled to her opinion, even if Rios figured she didn't really have a clue what she was saying.

"More," she demanded.

More was about to mean stripping off her clothes and sinking hard and deep into her. Rios didn't really see a problem with that. Well, it wouldn't have been a problem if he hadn't detected something.

"Do you smell smoke?" he asked.

"Not yet, but keep trying."

That wasn't what he meant, but he liked her attitude. For a moment that attitude distracted him until he caught another whiff of smoke. "Rayanne, I think there's a fire somewhere."

She lifted her head slightly and sniffed. She sniffed again, and Rios saw the alarm come over her face. They both snapped their heads toward the lantern she'd left on the hay bale. It was on its side, and yes, there were flames dancing all around it.

Rios thought they probably broke speed records coming off the floor. Rayanne grabbed a saddle blanket and started slapping at the fire. He peeled off his shirt and began to do the same. Since that didn't seem to be doing a lot of good, he pulled her out of the barn and went for the hose.

"Here!" He handed her the end of the hose while he ran around the side of the barn to turn on the water.

The water pressure seemed to be at a trickle, so Rios decided to try to beat down the flames with the saddle blanket while Rayanne handled the hose. He lost track of how long they worked, but by the time the last ember went cold, they had saved every part of the barn but the door and some hay. He'd even gotten out Mattie's saddle. He was also exhausted. That exhaustion was probably the reason he didn't see the approaching car until it was right in front of the barn.

Rios looked at his visitor and could only shake his head. Mercy, he didn't need this now.

"Yoo-hoo," Evie called. "Is everything all right here?"

Rios looked at Rayanne, at the smeared soot on her face, at her state of undress. With the fire, he'd forgotten that the neckline of her top was below her breasts. He quickly dropped the saddle blanket and tried to fix her clothes. That's when he noticed their jeans were unzipped. He also noticed something else.

Evie wasn't alone.

Dr. Malcolm Keene stepped out of the driver's side of his rental car. Putting his hands on his classically cut khakis, Dr. Whine stood there and looked at them. Evie did the same, except it seemed she was trying to figure out what was going on. Rios supposed Dr. Whine already had a good guess. That in itself would have been uncomfortable enough if a truck hadn't come barreling up the road toward them. A truck Rios unfortunately recognized.

"I saw the smoke," Bennie yelled, throwing open his truck door. "Mattie's not up here, is she?"

"No." And thank heaven, she wasn't. All in all, it was the only redeeming thing Rios could see about this predicament. This was probably what people meant when they said there'd be the devil to pay.

The devil was most certainly demanding payment, and he wondered how much of his butt it was going to cost him.

RAYANNE LOOKED AT the three people who'd arrived at the barn but couldn't decide which of them she dreaded most. It was a toss-up.

There was Aunt Evie, appearing troubled and a little confused. Then Bennie, who was probably ready to explode. His Rudolph nose looked like a sunburned baby's butt. Then there was Malcolm. He looked like all those other things put together—troubled, confused and ready to explode. No sunburned baby-butt nose, but in his case she could add horrified to the things she saw in his expression.

Rayanne hoped Malcolm had brought his anxiety meds. He'd need them for sure, and maybe he'd let her borrow some. She suddenly felt a panic attack coming on.

Since the silence seemed more unbearable than the inevitable, Rayanne fluttered her fingers toward the barn. "Uh, there was a fire," she told everyone. Now, exactly what part of the predicament that would clarify, she didn't know, but it seemed the safest remark she could make. Everything after it would clearly go downhill.

"Is that what happened to your clothes?" Evie asked, wrinkling her nose.

Yes, her clothes. Dreading what she might see, Rayanne finally got enough courage to look down. Nothing exactly vital was showing, but her bra was around her waist, and her jeans were unzipped. It would be hard to explain that. Even harder to explain it in combination with Rios's unzipped jeans and ripped shirt.

"Uh, there was a fire," Rayanne repeated. She hoped they'd think the fire had caused the displaced bra, the unzipped jeans and her somewhat limited vocabulary.

"Did you try to pee on the fire?" Evie asked. "Is that why your jeans are all unzipped?"

Rayanne had to bite her lip to keep from laughing hysterically. She wished she'd come up with that herself. If she agreed now, it would seem too obvious a lie.

"Rayanne." That from Malcolm. But then he just stood there and stared at her. It seemed as if he were trying to figure out what to say, too.

As discreetly as possible, considering three people had their eyes trained on her, Rayanne shoved her bra under her top and zipped up her jeans. "Malcolm, uh, there was a fire."

"Yes, I can see that. Are you all right?"

"Fine." It was a Texas lady's answer to everything. Even if her hair had been in flames, the answer was *fine*. Of course, any moron could see that things were far from fine. "What are you doing here, anyway?"

Malcolm walked closer. "I was worried about you. When you asked for a leave of absence, I thought they were holding you against your will so I decided to fly down and check on you."

She shook her head. Holding her against her will? Rayanne would have told Malcolm just how far off the mark he was if Bennie hadn't interrupted.

"Oh, I get it now. I can see what's going on here."

Rayanne didn't think that took any intelligence on Bennie's part. She didn't dare repeat the line about there being a fire or Evie's suggestion. There were some things that didn't bear repeating.

"I see it all now," Bennie said. "Rios brought you here so it would improve his chances of getting custody of Mattie."

"What?" Rayanne had obviously missed a step in Bennie's reasoning process. Anyone with half a brain could see that Rios and she had been fooling around. And that was fooling around in the most extreme way. "What happened in that barn has nothing to do with the custody disagreement between you and Rios."

"Sure it does." Bennie's ragged voice boomed. "Rios brought you here so you two could get married—"

"Married?" Rayanne howled.

Rios repeated it. Except he howled even louder than she had. "Married? You've lost your mind, Bennie. I didn't—"

"Don't deny it, Rios. It won't do any good. I heard your lawyer tell you the case would go better for you if you got married."

Rayanne looked at Rios for verification. He verified it with a frustrated shrug. She responded with a frown. Why hadn't he mentioned this sooner? She thought they'd discussed every aspect of the custody dispute. Obviously not. Not once had the subject of marriage come up.

"Then you heard me tell my lawyer that I wasn't going to get married any time soon." Rios fired the words at Bennie.

"Yeah, but you musta changed your mind because a

couple weeks later you flew off to New York and brought Rayanne back with you. This is low-down dirty pool, Rios, even for you. Well, I won't let you get away with it. No, I won't.'' He stomped to his truck, got in and drove away.

Rayanne figured that was one down, two to go. Make that three. She didn't like the fact that Rios might have had marriage on his mind when he brought her to Longhorn. She intended to question him about it, and he better have the right answers.

''Well, that didn't go so good,'' Evie said on a huff. ''There's only one thing you can do now, Rayanne. You'll just have to marry Rios.''

''Marry him?'' It had finally happened. Evie had completely exited the real world. ''Aunt Evie, this isn't the Dark Ages. I can darn sure make out with a man in a barn without having to marry him.''

''Oh, it's not about making out.'' Evie paused. ''Was that what you were doing?'' She smiled. Beamed, really.

''Oh, for heaven's sake. What I was doing with Rios is my business. I'm a grown woman—''

Evie latched on to Rayanne's shoulders and used her motherly tone, something Rayanne hadn't heard her use in years. Not since that night Rayanne's midnight-blue lace panties had fallen from her hair clip onto the living-room floor. ''Do you want Rios to lose custody of Mattie to that old man?''

''No, of course not.''

''Then you should be doing something to stop it, that's what. This is all your fault, you know.''

"My fault? How do you figure that?"

Evie's grip tightened. "Because Bennie will go straight to the judge and tell him that you and Rios were fooling around in broad daylight."

"We weren't in broad daylight. We were in a barn." Rayanne was so angry it took her a while to add anything to that. "And even if we weren't, that doesn't mean I've hurt Rios's chances of getting custody of Mattie, and it darn sure doesn't mean I'd marry him. Great day, Aunt Evie, I can't believe you'd suggest such a thing. I wouldn't marry him if—"

Rayanne put the pause button on her hissy fit when she remembered Rios was standing right next to her. Practically arm-to-arm next to her. One glance into his eyes, and she remembered they were indeed the color of iced tea. Heavy emphasis on the iced. She'd obviously hurt his feelings.

"I'm sorry," she said softly. "It's just that I can't marry you to help you with your custody battle."

His voice was low and cold when he spoke. "I don't remember asking you to." He turned, and much like Bennie, he went to his truck, got in and drove away.

Rayanne had only one thought—what the heck had she done?

"Oh, dear." Evie fanned herself. "This didn't turn out at all like I planned. I never thought everyone would get so mad."

In frustration, Rayanne scrubbed her hands over her face. "What does that mean?"

"Well, I have a teeny little confession to make."

Rayanne didn't like the sound of that. There was no

such thing as a teeny confession when it came to Evie.
The woman only made whopper mistakes. "Spill it,
Aunt Evie."

"Well, you see, I sort of came up with this plan to
bring you here. Now, before you get all mad, hear me
out. I knew you'd make a good mother for Mattie, and
it's true you really like her, don't you?"

"I do, but right now I'm far more interested in hearing about this plan of yours." Rayanne hadn't thought
it was possible to produce sound from such a tightly
clenched jaw, but she proved it could be done.

Evie hemmed and hawed a moment. "I took aim at
Bennie's hackberry knowing Rios would have to arrest
me. I knew that would bring you back to Longhorn.
And then, because you wouldn't be able to keep hiding
your feelings, you and Rios, well, I figured you two
would do what comes naturally to two people who are
attracted to each other. I figured nature would take its
course. Then you two would get married, and Bennie
would give up this stupid custody fight. I know in my
heart all he wants is a family for Mattie."

Rayanne squeezed her hands against her head. "I
cannot believe you did something like this."

"I know. Can you forgive me?"

Maybe in a couple of decades, but right then Rayanne
couldn't talk anymore about it. Another word about
marriage, plans and motherhood would send her
screaming through the woods like a crazy woman. She
might do it anyway, even if no one mentioned those
things. She didn't have a lot of options, and going off
the deep end definitely appealed to her.

"Come on, Rayanne." Malcolm hooked his arm through hers. "I'm taking you back to New York."

Finally, a voice of reason. Rayanne took the first step with him before she realized what she was doing. What she was doing was something stupid. This wasn't the voice of reason. It was Malcolm, and he rarely made sense.

Rayanne stopped so quickly he nearly tripped. While he was trying to stop himself from falling face-first into some questionable brown droppings, Rayanne had a revelation. Practically a divine manifestation. She'd come to the proverbial crossroads, and suddenly everything became crystal clear.

"I don't want to go back to New York," she said firmly.

Malcolm shook his head. "You can't mean that."

She did mean that. "I do too mean it."

"But there's no reason for you to stay here."

"Oh, yes, there is. There are more reasons for me to stay than there are for me to go back."

Malcolm obviously didn't agree. He was looking at her as if she'd sprouted feathers and left those questionable droppings. "But what about your job? You're a police officer, not some hayseed hick who belongs here in this cow-patty town."

Okay. She had to give him a little slack here. Malcolm was obviously perturbed and hadn't fully thought out what he'd said, much as she'd done earlier to Rios.

"You're right about the first part—I am a police officer," Rayanne said calmly. "But I don't have to live in New York to be a good cop. And you're wrong about me not being some hayseed hick. That's who I am, that's where I came from, and it'll always be part of me.''

''That's not you.'' He begged to differ. ''That *was* you. But you've shaken all that off and made something of yourself.''

''I was something long before I ever went to New York. I just forgot that for a while. And I'm tired of living someplace I don't want to live simply so I can say I've made my way in the world. Well, I've made my way, and it's brought me right back here, and here is exactly where I want to be.''

Evie started clapping and saying how happy she was. Rayanne tried to concentrate on finishing the conversation with Malcolm.

He didn't seem ready to finish a conversation at all. He looked more confused than ever. ''And what about us?''

Oh, Rayanne didn't like this part. She obviously needed to restate something she'd been telling Malcolm for ages. ''There never was an us, and I think in your heart you know that. We've known each other three years, and the only time we've kissed was that day at the airport. That says it all, doesn't it?''

''I thought you just liked to take things slow.''

Only with him. She hadn't had a problem going full speed ahead with Rios. Now, that said it all. Eleven years the man had been out of her life, and they'd picked up a couple of steps ahead of where they'd left off.

"Go back to New York, Malcolm, and find a woman who'll appreciate you for what you are."

He swallowed hard. "You're going after that cowboy, aren't you?"

She nodded. You bet she was. Rios was the best thing that had ever happened to her, and she was in love with him. The problem was, she didn't know if Rios would even speak to her after the way she'd treated him.

Groveling was a distinct possibility. She only hoped she didn't have to do it in any questionable brown droppings.

IT TOOK THE BETTER PART of the afternoon, but Rayanne finally found Rios. Well, she found his horse first. The roan stallion was grazing in the pasture near Whiskey Creek. Rios was nearby, and she watched as he hauled a calf out of the boggy ground near the water.

Since he didn't notice she was there, Rayanne stood for a while and watched. It gave her some time to try to figure out what she was going to say to him. Or to try to figure out if there was anything she could say that would make him listen. If their positions were reversed, she probably wouldn't listen to him. Heck, it had taken her eleven years to get over him turning her down.

Thankfully, she had finally seen the light.

And speaking of seeing things, she noticed what Rios was wearing. Brown leather chaps over his dusty working jeans. And spurs. When he turned the calf loose, she heard the silver spurs jingle against the thick heels of his boots.

Interesting.

She had seen him as a cop and a daddy, and when he was younger, he'd been into his biker-leather James Dean phase. But this was another side of Rios.

The real cowboy.

Rayanne decided she liked it as much as the other sides of him. Well, maybe more. Maybe even a lot more.

The chaps were a definite plus. They were old and well worn. The leather was pliant. Instead of being shapeless and baggy, Rios had fastened them snugly over his hips and thighs. The opening outlined the front of his jeans. And other things. Manly things.

Rayanne couldn't help thinking of ancient maps she had seen in books where there was a large X placed to denote an area of importance. Or valuable treasure. Yes, the chaps were indeed a definite plus, but they were…cake icing.

She smiled, remembering Rios's odd comment. All the outside of him, as positively tantalizing as it was, was merely icing. The man beneath was far more and far better than the sum total of his looks. She tested one of Freda's metaphors. Rios was her little ray of bright warm sunshine in the middle of a winter storm, and she was disgustingly in love with him.

And finally, she knew exactly what she wanted to do with Rios McKay.

She only hoped he'd cooperate.

11

"Oink, Flap, Oink, Flap…well, I'll be darned."
—Bumper Ditties by Evie E. Garrett

RIOS SAW RAYANNE by the tree and scowled. This was just what he didn't need. Her, anywhere near him. He wasn't in the mood for dealing with anybody right now, but especially her.

"What are you doing here?" he snarled.

"That's my line." She walked closer. Slowly, though, as if she was a little afraid of him. Good! If she had any sense, she'd run in the other direction.

"I came to apologize, Rios. I'm sorry about what I said back there at the barn."

He didn't answer her. Couldn't. He was still steaming over the way she'd spoken about him. How dare she think he'd come up with a plan to trick her into marrying him? And how could she possibly say she wouldn't ever marry him? Just who the heck did she think she was? Huh?

"Aunt Evie confessed to everything," she continued. "She pretended to take aim at Bennie so I'd have to come back to town and get her out of jail. She thought once I was here that nature would take its course. Those are her words, not mine."

He bent and washed the mud off his hands. "So?"

"So, I sent Malcolm back to New York and I told Aunt Evie that I was coming to find you." She stepped even closer. "And it appears I've found you."

"I'm not in the mood for playing games." Rios started toward his stallion, but she caught his arm.

"Well, actually, neither am I." Rayanne looked at his clothes. "You're wearing chaps."

"Yeah, so?"

"Spurs, too."

Was she writing a fashion column or something? "Rayanne, is this conversation actually leading somewhere?"

"Hopefully."

"Then could you speed it up a little bit? I'm in kind of a hurry here."

"Okay." She moistened her lips. "I've decided to stay in Longhorn, and I want to make sure I can keep working for you."

It sounded like a trick question. Or the answer to his prayers. Still, that didn't mean everything was settled between them. She hadn't said a darn thing about staying in Longhorn because of him.

"You can keep your job," he said none too enthusiastically.

"Good. We'll discuss raises and such later on. You don't pay me nearly enough." She shook her head. "But I'm getting off track. I want you to think back to the conversation we had in New York. The one we had about that night at Whiskey Creek. Specifically, the part where you said you owed me one and that I could collect any time.''

''What about it?''

''Well, that's why I'm here—to collect.''

It took him a few seconds to recall the conversation and to realize that Rayanne was talking about making love. With him.

That confused Rios. A lot.

''I...'' Rios couldn't figure out what to say. He was still mad at her, yes. Furious, really. And hurt over her comments. But she was offering something he really wanted—her.

''What's the matter? Is the offer no longer good?''

''It's still good, after we get a few things straight.'' There. Rios had to applaud himself. There probably wasn't a functioning red-blooded male on earth who'd insist on putting off lovemaking just to talk, but this conversation was important. ''I would have never tried to trick you into marrying me.''

She nodded. ''I know.''

That confused him, too. He'd expected a little argument from her. Or at least a little hesitation. But her nod had been a firm nod, and her *I know* had been a genuine *I know*. Okay. The only thing he could do was go on to his next point of contention.

''And I didn't appreciate you getting mad at me before you even asked if I had anything to do with it.''

Rayanne gave another nod. ''I know. I was wrong.''

He squinted one eye and looked at her. ''You mean that?''

''I wouldn't be here if I didn't mean it.''

True. Rayanne wasn't the kind of woman to offer herself to a man she was still at odds with. Well, then. That solved the bulk of his major issues. Later, much later, they'd work out the other things.

He reached out, caught a handful of her hair and roughly pulled her closer. She did some pulling of her own. She grabbed his shirt, knotted it in her hands and dragged him against her. Not that she had to drag much. He'd already started in that direction.

Rios kissed her. Hard. Long. And then kissed her again and caught her shirt. "If you're really taking me up on my offer, then I want this off now." He pulled her to the ground.

She bit his earlobe. "I want yours off, too."

He figured she meant his clothes. Well, maybe not, judging from the way she started kissing his chest. It was entirely possible she was talking about getting something else off. For that to happen, the clothes had to go.

Getting out of chaps, spurs, boots and jeans was no easy feat. It especially wasn't easy with Rayanne's hot little mouth moving all over the place. She had a wild look in her eyes when she wrestled with the chaps. There was definitely something exciting about this sudden urgency she had to strip off his clothes, and he loved it almost as much as he loved her. Rios hurriedly shucked off his leather vest and shirt, slinging them aside.

But he stopped when he realized the notion that had just raced through his mind. *Almost as much as he loved her.* He gave his head a hard shake. No, he didn't mean that, did he? Well, heck, it seemed the answer was—

Rayanne didn't give him time to finish that thought. She caught his ears and pulled him on top of her.

"I wanted you to be my first, but it was that stupid jerk in college," she mumbled through the French kissing.

"I'd rather be your last than your first, anyway."

She went completely still. With a hearty grip on his ears, she looked at him. "Do you mean that?"

Did he mean what? Rios had already forgotten what he'd said. Oh, yeah. He'd said something about wanting to be her last lover, and now she wanted to know if he meant it. Did he? Since the only thing separating his overly aroused body from hers was her pink panties and about a millimeter of his self-control, he was inclined to agree to anything she wanted him to agree to. But he wanted to make sure he was telling her the truth.

"Did you mean it?" she repeated, her voice breathy and hot.

He looked into her eyes, then at her face. Then at her body. Looking at her body distracted him, though. Mercy, but the woman had filled out nicely. He was thinking C-cup here.

"Rios? Did you hear me?"

Yes, he'd heard her all right. Mercy, a C-cup. She had a body better than most pinups he'd seen, and here she was, lying beneath him waiting for him to...answer her.

Again, he nearly forgot the question. Oh, yeah—did he mean the part about wanting to be her last lover?

This time, he didn't let her body distract him. This time, he looked at her and let his heart do his answering for him.

"There's no way I want you to be with another man after this. Just me and you, Rayanne. Got that?"

She smiled, all dreamylike, and sighed. "I think that's the most romantic thing you could have said."

Romantic? He'd actually said something romantic, without rehearsing it or anything. Rios had a hard time concentrating on the conversation but was glad he said the right thing at the right time. The fact that it was true made it a first for him.

Her breasts distracted him again. He used his tongue to wet his fingertips and slipped them over her nipples. First one and then the other. They tightened into rose-colored buds.

Rayanne moaned his name, adding that breathy little hitch to it. "Yes," she said. "Yes."

Since it was obvious that she was enjoying it as much as he was, Rios lingered for a while, making sure her nipples became familiar with his mouth and letting his mouth become familiar with them. He would have lingered even longer if Rayanne hadn't slid her hand between their bodies. She latched on to the only part of him that could get his complete, undivided attention.

His eyes crossed.

"Don't make me wait any longer, Rios."

He completely understood the urgency. He couldn't wait any longer, either, but he didn't want to act like a rute. He ripped off her panties and threw them in the reek. Okay. Since that probably could be construed as rutelike, he slowed down as much as he could.

Capturing her mouth in a deep, wet kiss, he positioned himself, intending to take her slowly. He offered her an inch, but she took a great deal more than that. She took about nine times more than that. All right, only seven times more. Rayanne wrapped her legs around his waist, shoved her body forward and completed the snug, wet, mind-boggling union in one gasp-generating collision.

After the gasp, she gave a moan of relief. After his gasp, Rios grunted. All things considered, he thought he was doing good to get out that grunt. He was deep-seated right in the portal of paradise, and he wouldn't let anything get in the way of making them both crazed thrill seekers.

There was nothing graceful about the rhythm they found. But nothing that happened was ordinary. Rios knew that, and he figured Rayanne knew it, too. That's why he said her name in that last moment, so she would look at him, so he could look into her eyes. Somehow, that was more intimate, more important, more urgent than what they were doing. And he watched her as he pushed her right over the edge.

Yes, indeed. He learned Rayanne could be quite persuasive in those last mindless, thrill-seeking moments. She didn't go through that portal of paradise alone. Oh, no. She latched on to him and took him right along with her.

Rios decided he'd thank her for it later. Right after he let her know that he was head over heels in love with her.

RAYANNE SAW STARS. Big ones. Rios had, too. It was hard for a woman not to be aware of something like that.

At first, she thought she'd killed him. About the same time they had seen those stars together, Rios had gutted out some fairly creative profanity and collapsed in a dead heap on top of her. But he wasn't dead. Every now and then she felt a special kind of stirring—slight, but in the right area to indicate he was not only alive but might be ready for seconds.

"Rios?" she whispered.

He made a groaning sound.

Well, he might not have the breath yet to talk, but she sure did. She wanted to shout it from the treetops that she'd finally made love with the man she loved. What could possibly be better than that? She mentally shrugged. A commitment, maybe. But she wouldn't push things. Not right away, at least.

Rayanne thought the ringing sound was in her head until she heard Rios groan. Not a moaning groan but one of aggravation.

"Phone," he clarified. "Don't you dare go anywhere. I'm not done with you yet." He rolled off her, sat up and began to rake through the heap of clothes they'd discarded.

A phone. Great. They were naked in the middle of nowhere and had been interrupted by a phone call. He finally located the ringing annoyance in his vest pocket, turned it on and pushed it against his ear.

"Sheriff McKay. And it'd better be important."

Rayanne silently agreed. It had better be a matter of life and death. But after seeing the frustrated, aggravated expression on Rios's face, she realized it was probably important on at least a nonpersonal level. That meant they likely had to get dressed and leave. It also meant they might not get to have a second try at finding paradise.

"Now?" Rios asked. He mumbled something under his breath and shoved his hand through his hair. "Give us an hour." His gaze landed on Rayanne. "Make that two hours."

Well, maybe she would get around to those seconds, after all. "Who was that?"

"Evie. She wants us to meet her at my place. She said it's important."

"Is Mattie with her?" Rayanne asked.

"No, she's with Freda. Evie wants to talk to us alone."

"She probably just wants to make sure we're not furious with her. Which we are, aren't we?"

"Well, I'm not happy that she plotted to get us married, but I'm glad she got you back here." Rios grinned, causing his dimples to show. "If she hadn't done that, we wouldn't be where we are right now."

True. So, maybe she wasn't mad at Evie, after all.

He smiled at her and circled her nipple with his finger. "C-cup, right?"

It took her a moment to realize he was talking about

her breasts. She nodded and leaned over so she could kiss him.

"No!" he yelled.

Confused, she stared at him. "No, what?"

"No to the moving part. Not yet, anyway. I want you to stay right there so I can just look at you. If you start touching or kissing me, I won't be able to think, much less appreciate the view. Your kisses turn my brain to stump water."

Rayanne felt a little uncomfortable under his intense scrutiny. After all, she was buck naked and probably had a dozen hickeys. There was probably some mud and grass in places she didn't want to think about.

"You're so beautiful, Rayanne." He gently slid his hands down her back, caressing her along the way. "You're perfect. Your body, your face. *You.* I'm the luckiest man alive."

She smiled. Mercy, but he was romantic. The truth was, they were both lucky. And if she was right about that gleam in Rios's eye, she was about to get lucky in a whole different way.

Rios winked at her. "Now, you can distract me," he said.

Rayanne did her best.

"DO YOU SEE MY underwear around anywhere?" Rios asked when they were getting dressed.

An alarmed expression came over her face. "No. You can't find them? Quick, look in my hair."

"For my Jockey shorts?"

"Just do it."

He looked in her hair. No shorts. But Rios certainly hadn't expected to find them there.

"I just wanted to make sure," she said, as if that clarified everything.

He sifted through his clothes and shook off some dirt and a few roly-polies. "After we talk to Evie, I think you and I need to sit down and discuss some things." Now that she'd agreed to stay in Longhorn, he had to find some way to keep her in his life, as well.

Rayanne grinned at him. And winked. "Maybe you can take me for a, uh, ride somewhere later."

He grinned back. Rios really liked her insatiable appetite, but then he remembered this was serious. They could still do the ride and other things, but he wanted a lot more than that from her. He was looking for some kind of permanent relationship here, and from the romantic look in Rayanne's eyes, she seemed ready to spell out the kind of commitment she wanted. Rios was ready to hear it.

"A penny for your thoughts," he said, kissing her cheek.

"Really?" Her face brightened. "Well, how about you put on those chaps later. No jeans, no shorts. Oh, and maybe the leather vest with your badge on it. Then maybe we could go to the barn and get on one of those bales of hay." She stopped and blushed. "Well, you get the idea."

Yes, and as ideas went, it was a darn good one. Except he wanted Rayanne to wear the vest and badge. Maybe even a pair of cowboy boots, but certainly no underwear, unless they were those little lacy high-cut things. Rios swore and shook his head. If he kept thinking about that, they'd never get out of these woods.

"We'll do that," he finally said. "Later. After we talk to Evie."

And after they talked to Evie, he'd figure out a way to talk Rayanne into giving him a commitment. He hadn't ruled out using sex. And he certainly hadn't ruled out using those chaps. Or begging.

But one thing was for sure—Rayanne Garrett was staying with him.

12

"Oh, what the heck—go ahead and put all your
eggs in one basket."

—Bumper Ditties by Evie E. Garrett

RAYANNE BLINKED to make sure she wasn't seeing
things. No, she wasn't. Evie was sitting in a rocking
chair on Rios's porch. Bennie was in the chair beside
her. And Evie was holding a double-barreled shotgun
on him.

"Well, this should be fun," Rayanne said under her
breath. Together, Rios and she got out of his truck and
walked to the porch steps.

"We've been waiting for you." Evie's voice was
weather-discussion calm.

That calmness scared Rayanne a little. She knew
from experience this was the kind of situation that could
get quickly out of hand.

"Why don't you put down that gun, Evie?" Rios
asked. His voice was calm, too.

"I will in just a minute. Bennie has something to tell
you first."

Bennie's nose was redder than usual, and he was
chewing on the stub of an unlit cigar. "I'm supposed
to say that I won't oppose Rios's custody of Mattie."

Evie gave a satisfied nod. "There, you heard it from the horse's mouth. All your problems are solved."

Rayanne groaned. "Aunt Evie, this won't work."

"Of course, it will. You heard what he said, didn't you?"

"I did, but you can't force Bennie into doing this. He has to feel it's right for Mattie."

Bennie looked at her as if she'd found a cure for every disease known to man. "That's right, little lady. I have to do what I feel is right for my granddaughter. I didn't think you of all people would see my side of it."

"Well, of course, I see your side. You want what's best for Mattie. Rios wants the same thing, and so do I. Aunt Evie does, too, but she just has an odd way of showing it. A *very* odd way."

"But Rios wants to cut me out of Mattie's life," Bennie objected.

"No, I don't," Rios disagreed. "But you have to let me be her father, because that's what I am."

Evie came to her feet. "That's what I've been telling the old geezer—"

Rayanne gave her aunt a look that pleaded with her to keep quiet. Name calling wouldn't get them anywhere. Rayanne knew that firsthand. When she was certain she'd silenced Evie for the moment, Rayanne turned to Bennie.

"I'm sure Mattie has told you how much she loves her father. Mattie and I were talking about this just this morning. She also told me how much she loves you, and she doesn't want you and Rios arguing over her." Rayanne slowly walked up the steps.

"She said that?" There was a softness in Bennie's voice she hadn't heard earlier. Progress, maybe.

"Well, of course, she did, you old geezer." Evie again.

Rayanne had had just about all she could tolerate from her aunt. She snatched the gun from Evie's grip and handed it to Rios. Rayanne tried to remember to speak respectfully to her aunt, but it was rather hard to do. "Aunt Evie, it's a good time for you just to sit back and listen, okay?"

Evie gave an uncertain nod and dropped into the rocker. Bennie, on the other hand, rose from his chair. Rayanne didn't know what he'd do, but she was thankful Rios was with her.

"I talked to Mattie myself, just a little while ago," Bennie continued. "She said she wanted to live with her, uh, father. And that she wanted you to live with him, too."

"Oh," Rayanne muttered somewhat uncomfortably. She glanced at Rios, and he didn't look comfortable with that remark, either. "Well, I suppose that's something we'll have to discuss."

Evie stood again. "Let's just cut to the chase, shall we? You're in love with Rios, aren't you?"

The discomfort went up a notch, not because Rayanne wasn't sure of her answer, but because she hadn't expected to make such a first-time profession in front of anyone but Rios. "Yes, I love him. Very much."

No one said anything for several snail-crawling moments. "Very much?" Rios questioned. "How much is very much?"

She gave a few awkward-looking bobs of her head. "A lot. More than, well, air and other vital necessities."

Traffic-cop style, Evie held up her hand before Rios could speak. "And Rios, don't you love her?"

"Yes, I do. Very much."

Rayanne looked at him. "Very much?"

"Loads. Big giant buckets full."

She caught her bottom lip between her teeth to keep from smiling. It didn't seem a good time for that. Not yet, anyway. She fully intended to do some smiling later.

"Loads," Evie repeated. "Buckets full. And more than air. That sounds like a marriage proposal, if you ask me."

"I don't think they asked you," Bennie grumbled.

"Well, they darn well should have. Mattie can still spend some weekends with you, but she needs a family. A mother and a father. We're not old, Bennie, but we're not young enough to be raising a little girl. That's a father and a mother's job."

Bennie looked at his feet for a while. Then he looked at the trees. Then the yard. Finally, he looked at Rios. "You two would be getting married, you say?"

Rios caught Rayanne's hand and brought it to his mouth to kiss. "If I have anything to say about it, we will."

"You have a lot to say about it," Rayanne assured him.

"Is that a yes then?" Rios asked her.

"It's a yes." She wanted to celebrate. Well, actually, she wanted to haul Rios off to bed, repeat in thorough detail how much she loved him and whisper sweet nothings in his ear. However, they first needed to finish business with Bennie. "Well, Bennie?"

He shrugged. "I guess we can give this arrangement a try."

Rayanne looked hard at him. "No custody battle?"

"No custody battle."

She looked harder still at him. "And what about the charges against Evie?"

Rios stepped slightly closer. "I think he'll drop those, since I won't be charging him with malicious and intentional damage to municipal property."

"Huh?" That from Rayanne.

"He's the one who chopped up Hal's Hungry Heifer," Rios explained. "Since Evie donated it to the city, it's municipal property and protected under the law."

"You chopped up the rubber cow?" Evie gasped. "Of all the sick things you could have come up with."

"Well?" Rios quizzed. "What'll it be, Bennie? If you charge Evie, then I'll have to charge you."

"I'll drop the charges," Bennie said with effort. "If Evie will swear to me she'll give up these stupid plans of hers. The woman's just not very good at this sort of thing."

"I won't ever do anything like this again," Evie declared.

Rayanne didn't believe her, and she was fairly sure Bennie and Rios didn't, either. But since the plan had seemed to, heaven forbid, work, then Rayanne didn't see any reason to criticize her aunt.

Evie latched on to Bennie's arm and quickly hauled him down the steps. ''Well, now that that's settled, we'll just be going so you two can have some privacy. By the way, Rayanne, you got a pair of men's underwear hanging out of the leg of your blue jeans. I don't suppose you want to try to explain that, huh?''

Rayanne looked at the top of her shoe and groaned. Why did she have this penchant for underwear attaching itself to her at the most inopportune time? Rayanne did what had worked for her the last time it happened—she mumbled.

Evie gave a firm nod. ''That's what I figured you'd say. Bennie and I will just be on our way.''

Rayanne had never seen two people move so fast. They looked like cartoon characters hurrying to the car. The aging sedan kicked up gravel as her aunt peeled away.

She looped her arm through Rios's. ''How did you know Bennie had chopped up the rubber cow?''

''Lucky guess.''

''You guessed?'' she asked in disbelief.

''That, and Mattie mentioned there was some sticky paper on Bennie's ax. Paper that advertised the dates of the town festival.''

''Well, that's not much of a guess. That's evidence.''

''I guess.'' Rios slid his arm around her waist. ''So, I figure you must have conditions before you'll marry me, huh?''

''Nope. No conditions. I'm just looking for what

every woman wants. A devoted husband, a tender father, an adventurous lover and joint custody of the remote control. I think you'll do nicely on all accounts.''

His grip tightened around her waist. ''And you said something earlier about loving me?''

''Oh, that. Yep, I'm in love with you all right. Crazy, madly, deeply in love with you. It's the forever-after kind, too. The kind that'll make me act really sappy and totally nuts for years on end. You should have fun with that.''

That earned her a kiss. A long, wet one that had her breathing hard when he pulled away and looked at her. ''You're the only woman I've ever loved, you know that?''

That earned him a kiss. A long, wet one that had him breathing hard when Rayanne pulled away. ''We're going to be good together, Rios. Mattie, you and me.''

He grinned. ''You really do like her, don't you?''

Rayanne shook her head. ''Nope. I love her.'' She shrugged and blinked back some tears of happiness that were trying to sneak into her eyes. ''The way I have it figured, I get to have this wonderful daughter without having to go through all the labor pains and stretch marks. It's a great deal for me. And if we play our cards right, we can eventually give her a brother or a sister.''

A tear escaped, after all, and Rios wiped it away with his thumb. ''It's a great deal for all of us. Come on.'' He caught her hand. ''Before we go to Evie's and tell Mattie, I want you to take a little walk with me to the barn.''

''But the fire—''

"Not that barn. The one in the back of the house."

It wasn't hard to tell what he had on his mind. Funny, she suddenly had the same thing on hers. What better way to celebrate being in love? "Why can't we just go to your bedroom?"

"The barn's more interesting. Hay bales."

"Good point," Rayanne agreed. Really good point. "Oh, yes. I suppose I should let you know I intend to run for sheriff in the next election."

"Oh, will you?" Rios asked calmly.

"Definitely."

"It should be interesting, because I plan to run for reelection."

"Then you're right." Rayanne gave a firm nod. "It should be interesting. Don't worry, if I'm elected, I'll keep you on as my deputy. I'm sure you'd do the same for me."

"Of course. Wait a minute, I forgot something." He led her to the truck and pulled out his chaps and vest from the back. "I'll need these to reenact that little adventure you told me about at the creek."

"Will this adventure involve seeing stars?"

"Absolutely," Rios assured her, adding another of those famous cowboy kisses that made her glad she was on the receiving end of them. "Big ones, darling. Really big ones."

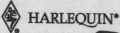

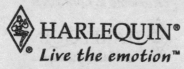

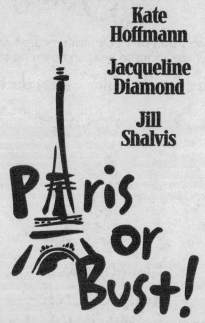

THE BAD GIRLS Club

They're strong, they're sexy, they're not afraid to use the assets Mother Nature gave them....

Venus Messina is...

#916 WICKED & WILLING
by Leslie Kelly
February 2003

Sydney Colburn is...

#920 BRAZEN & BURNING
by Julie Elizabeth Leto
March 2003

Nicole Bennett is...

#924 RED-HOT & RECKLESS
by Tori Carrington
April 2003

The Bad Girls Club...where membership has its privileges!

Available wherever

HARLEQUIN® *Temptation.*

is sold....

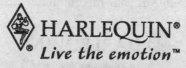

HARLEQUIN®
Live the emotion™

Visit us at www.eHarlequin.com

HTBGIRLS

If you enjoyed what you just read,
then we've got an offer you can't resist!

Take 2 bestselling love stories FREE!
Plus get a FREE surprise gift!